Discovery

Cole opened the worn velvet bag and poured the contents out on his palm. Erin watched as light slid and shimmered over the marble-sized objects as though they were oiled. Most of the stones were colorless. Several were a deep, lovely pink. One was a green so pure it looked like condensed, concentrated light.

Automatically Erin reached for the green stone, then stopped, looking up at Cole's eyes. "These can't be diamonds," she whispered.

"Uncut, unpolished, extraordinary. They're diamonds, Erin. And they're yours for better or worse."

• • •

"*The Diamond Tiger* glitters with a perfect blend of passion and suspense. Ann Maxwell delivers a smoldering mix of sensuality and danger set against the exotic, high stakes world of the international diamond trade. I loved *The Diamond Tiger* and I know Ann's readers will too."
—Amanda Quick

"Only Ann Maxwell could have brought this story to such explosive life. . . . An unforgettable sensory experience, this splendorous tale of adventure is everything a reader could wish and much, much more."
—*Rave Reviews*

Books by Ann Maxwell

The Ruby
The Diamond Tiger
The Secret Sisters

Published by HarperPaperbacks

the Diamond Tiger

Ann Maxwell

HarperPaperbacks
A Division of HarperCollinsPublishers

HarperPaperbacks

A Division of HarperCollinsPublishers
10 East 53rd Street, New York, NY 10022-5299

ISBN 0-06-104079-7

HarperCollins®, 📖®, and HarperPaperbacks™ are
trademarks of HarperCollins Publishers Inc.

Cover design and illustration by Designed To Print

First printing: June 1992

Reissue edition printing: May 1999

Printed in the United States of America

Visit HarperPaperbacks on the World Wide Web at
http://www.harpercollins.com

❖ 10 9 8 7 6 5 4

For Evan,
for all the usual reasons
plus love

Prologue

ABE WINDSOR BETTER BE DEAD OR I'LL BLOODY well kill him myself.

Jason Street's thought was both promise and prayer. He had had plenty of time for both in the ten hours since the call had come in from his spy at Crazy Abe's station in Western Australia. Street had spent every minute of the time since then trying to get to the desolate station and the Sleeping Dog Mines. First there had been the four-hour chartered flight from Perth, then the endless black hours behind the wheel of the battered Toyota Land Cruiser, pushing the vehicle at reckless speeds over dirt tracks, racing toward one of the most isolated areas on the continent.

But it wasn't the brutal drive that fed Street's fury, it was the fear that more than a decade of his patience and cunning had gone up the spout, wiped out by a savage old man's drunken insanity.

Above the land the Southern Cross faded from the sky, slowly overwhelmed by the yellow violence of the rising sun. The daybreak temperature along the southeastern edge of the Kimberley Plateau was 87 degrees Fahrenheit. As the sun rose, so did the temperature. The brutal torrent of light revealed spinifex and stunted gum trees, red dust and occasional out-croppings of stone, and over all was the sun, always the sun, the only true inhabitant of Western Australia.

Stones ricocheted like pistol shots off the under-carriage of the straining vehicle. Lurching, skidding, bucking, the Toyota fought its way over a road that existed more in the driver's mind than on the dry surface of the land itself. But Street had no doubt of his course. He had spent ten years going to and from Crazy Abe's station, trying to tease and wheedle and cozen the old man's secret out of him. After all those years Street was certain of only one thing: If Crazy Abe's secret was still within the reach of pain, Street would have it before the Southern Cross rose above Australia again.

The Toyota shot over the top of a low rise in a shower of dust. Ahead lay Abe's meager station. The old man's possessions were spread out like wreckage across several acres of flat, barren land. There was a ramshackle tin-roof house, a few sun-scoured out-buildings, tractors consumed by rust and misuse, bro-ken mining equipment, discarded four-wheel-drive trucks, and the remains of a World War II RAAF Da-kota that had crashed within sight of the station a few months before V-J Day.

Abruptly a glistening, noisy, and very modern he-licopter leaped into the sky just beyond the house's tin roof. Street stood on the brakes, bringing the Toyota to a shuddering stop. As the helicopter banked and passed overhead with its red belly beacon flashing, Street searched for identifying marks. He expected to see the shield of the Western Australia State Police, the insignia of the Australian Defense Forces, or perhaps the logo of the Flying Doctor Service.

Instead, the sleek sides of the helicopter were blank, as anonymous as an egg. The owners were no more interested in advertising their presence at Abe Windsor's station than was Street himself. Furious and fearful at the same time, he slammed his fist against the steering wheel. Then he rammed the Toyota into gear and drove headlong down the hill.

As the vehicle skidded to a stop in the loose red earth near Abe's shack, Street rolled out and dropped to the dirt, a cocked semiautomatic pistol in his hand. Moving with the precision of a commando, he slid from the cover of the vehicle to the shelter of a rusty stamp mill and from there to the protection of a corner of the house. He risked a quick glimpse through a dirty window.

A single paraffin lamp guttered in the big room of the station house. A barefoot corpse lay beneath a tattered piece of canvas on the long table in the center of the room. The only thing moving was the outback's customary plague of flies.

Cursing through clenched jaws, Street discarded caution and used his heavy boot like a battering ram. The upper hinge of the door popped out of the casement, the latch broke, and the door swung open drunkenly. The smell of old death spilled out into the sultry yard. Street looked at the room over the barrel of his pistol. Nothing looked back. Gagging at the smell, he walked to the table and turned back one corner of the tarp, setting off a cloud of flies.

Abe Windsor had been dead for some time, judging by the condition of his corpse. Even allowing for the heat and humidity of the October buildup toward the "wet," Street guessed the old man had been dead for at least three days, perhaps more. But there was no doubt that it was Abe Windsor who lay beneath the tarp. The heavy ridge of scar on his left wrist had resisted decay better than the softer flesh around it.

With an exclamation of disgust, Street turned and looked around the room itself. He doubted that the occupants of the helicopter had left behind anything but flies. On the other hand, he might have surprised them before they finished searching everything on the station. Grimacing, Street turned back and touched the corpse, pulling the dirty undershirt open and looking for the worn velvet pouch that always hung around Abe's neck. The pouch was gone. Street glanced at the unpainted wooden shelf next to Abe Windsor's rocking chair. The battered tin box was missing too.

"So you went for your last walk in the bush, did you, you old wanker?" Street muttered. "Did you take that bleeding box with you like you always did? Did your secret die out there in the bush with you? And who in hell was watching you besides me?"

There was no answer but that of death's hideous grin. For an instant Street felt as though the old man were still alive, still mocking him.

"You knew what I was after the whole time, didn't you? Christ, but you loved tweaking me! Sod you, old man. You're dead and I'm not."

Tiny sounds came from beyond the kitchen door as decaying floorboards shifted. Someone was headed out of the house.

Street spun and dashed through the doorway into the dark kitchen. He was quick enough to catch a flicker of movement as a dark-clad figure slipped through the back door. Sounds came again, the soft, rapid thud of bare feet fleeing over dusty earth.

Street sprang to the open door and tripped a quick shot. The bullet caught the fleeing man a few feet before he reached the corner of an outbuilding. He sprawled forward in the dirt. Street approached the man cautiously, then checked for weapons. There were none. Street stood and rolled the man over with one booted foot. Chu, Abe's cook, squinted up at Street through eyes that swam with pain. Street pointed the gun at a spot between the cook's eyes.

"Where's the box, you thieving Chink?"

Chu hissed through his teeth, his face contorted with pain, and said nothing.

"Listen up." Street ground down on Chu's wounded shoulder with the flat sole of his boot. "Where's the box and the velvet sack?"

Chu groaned and said something in Chinese, a plea for mercy or perhaps a malediction.

Street bore down harder with his foot. From the corner of his eye he caught a flicker of movement as someone leaped from the cover of the outbuilding. Reflexively his head turned toward the movement.

The instant Street's attention was divided, Chu doubled up and aimed a kick at the Australian's crotch. The two prongs of the attack were so swift and so well-coordinated that Street immediately knew he had fallen into a trap laid by professionals. His own reaction was equally quick and deadly. He fired point blank at Chu and at the same time twisted so the cook's kick was off the mark.

In the split second before the heavy bullet struck, Chu's heel thudded harmlessly into Street's muscular thigh. Street continued the twisting motion, throwing himself off to the side and bringing his gun to bear on the remaining attacker at the same time. He triggered two shots at the second attacker as he hit the ground. Both shots missed, but Street's action avoided a head-high kick that would have smashed his skull.

The attacker flew past Street, who was still in the midst of his defensive roll. When Street reached his belly, he twisted again and calmly shot the attacker twice in the back. Something about the single exclamation of pain and the fall told Street that the attacker was a woman, and that she was now dead. Even as the information registered in his brain, he was rolling again, anticipating another attacker. He came to his feet in a crouch, his back to a wall and his pistol covering the entire station yard.

Fifty meters away a flock of pale cockatoos, startled by the shots, called noisily among the stunted trees. After a few moments the cockatoos settled back onto their perches, leaving the silence of death to spread unbroken over Abe Windsor's station. All that moved were the flies, ubiquitous in the searing October sun.

Quickly Street checked the bodies of the two people he had just killed. No sign of the tin box or the velvet bag. With more patience he went over the bodies again, hoping to discover who had sent them and why. Neither Chu nor the Chinese woman carried anything that might identify them: no papers, no clothing labels, no weapons.

Frowning, Street sat on his haunches and studied the two dead bodies. Chu had been at the station for years now, but Street had never noticed the calluses on the cook's hands and feet. They belonged to a highly trained fighter, not to a simple scutworker. The woman's hands were similarly hardened. And the two Chinese had worked as a team. A team that had been prepared to kill or die.

Now they were dead and Street was no closer to knowing who they worked for than he was to Crazy Abe's diamond mine.

Street spat on the red earth, then turned his back on the bodies. There was little chance that anything of value remained, but after a decade of watching the mousehole, he wouldn't let frustration cause him to overlook any chance at all. It was just possible that the box containing the old man's doggerel and his will were still hidden on the station.

The stench in the house hadn't changed. Street went through the place with the practiced motions of a man who had searched those same rooms many times before. As always, nothing new turned up. Nor did the tin box. Wiping dirt and sweat from his eyes, he went to stand over the corpse of the old man who had evaded him in death as he had in life.

"Ten years of 'Chunder from Down Under,' " Street snarled, his voice low in his throat. "Ten years of your stink and your sly laughter. God rot you, Abe Windsor. And God rot whoever inherits the Sleeping Dog Mines."

1

◆

"TWO PEOPLE DIED GETTING THIS TO ME."

Cole Blackburn looked at the small worn velvet bag. "Was it worth it?"

"You tell me," Chen Wing said.

With a swift motion Wing emptied the contents of the bag onto the ebony surface of his desk. Light rippled and shifted as nine translucent stones tumbled over one another with tiny crystalline sounds. The first impression was of large, very roughly made marbles that had been chipped and pitted by use. Nine of the thirteen stones were colorless. Three were pink. One was the intense green of a deep river pool.

Instantly Cole's hand closed over the green marble, which was as big as the tip of his thumb. The stone was surprisingly heavy for its size. He rubbed it between his fingers. The surface had an almost slippery feel, as though it had been burnished with precious oils. He turned the stone until he found a flat, cleanly chipped face, which he bathed with his breath. No moisture collected on the smooth plane.

Cole felt a sharp stab of excitement. Without a word he walked to a liquor cart that stood against a wall. He picked up a heavy leaded crystal glass and glanced at Wing, who nodded. Cole brought the green stone down the side of the glass in a single swift stroke.

The stone scratched the glass easily and deeply. The stone itself was unmarked. At random Cole picked up other stones from the desk and drew them down the crystal surface. New scratches formed. The stones themselves remained untouched. He pulled a well-worn jeweler's loupe from his pocket, angled the desk light to his satisfaction, picked up the deep green stone, and examined it.

The sensation was like falling into a pool of intense emerald light. Yet this was not an emerald. Even uncut and unpolished, the stone held and dispersed light in a way that only a diamond could. It shimmered between his fingers with each tiny movement of his hand. Light flowed and glanced among the irregularities in the stone's surface and gathered in its luminous depths. There were no fractures and only two very minute flaws, both irrelevant to the diamond's value, for they lay just below the surface, where they would be cut and polished out of existence.

Cole looked at several more stones before he put his loupe back in his pocket and said, "White paper."

Wing opened a desk drawer, extracted a pure white sheet of Pacific Traders Ltd. letterhead, and slid it across the desk. Cole pulled a small chamois bag from his pocket and removed a rough diamond that he knew to be of perfect color.

Though uncut and unpolished, the stone from Cole's pocket had an angular octahedral shape. It

looked almost unnatural next to the worn, irregular
stones from Wing's bag. Cole spaced the diamonds
across the surface of the paper. One of the stones
changed color subtly, becoming more coral than pink.
The other pinks deepened to a lovely clear rose. Most
of the white stones took on a blue sheen that exactly
matched Cole's diamond. One or two showed a very
faint yellow cast to their white, a color shift that only
an expert eye would have detected or cared about.

And the green stone burned more vividly still, an
emerald flame against snow.

Cole lowered the loupe and studied the green diamond with both eyes again. It still glimmered with an
internal fire that was both hot and cold. Years before,
in Tunisia, he had seen a stone that was nearly the
equal of this one. The smuggler who owned the rough
claimed it had come from Venezuela, a claim that Cole
doubted. But before he could raise enough cash to buy
the truth, someone had sealed the smuggler's lips by
cutting his throat.

The smuggler's death hadn't shocked Cole. Random deaths, convenient or capricious, were common
in the diamond fields and gemstone black markets of
the world. When it came to diamonds a man's life was
valuable only to himself, and his death could easily
profit any number of people.

What surprised Cole was that these diamonds
had cost only two lives. He had never seen a handful
of diamonds to equal the ones resting on the white
paper, drawing their color from the peculiar circumstances of their birth rather than from their surroundings.

Cole picked up his own exemplar diamond, put it
away, and examined the dark velvet bag that lay col-

lapsed across the desk's ebony surface. The velvet was
old, so old that the passage of time and the hard surfaces of the diamonds inside had worn the cloth to
near-silk thinness in places. The velvet did not care; it
was dead.

But the stones were not dead, not in the same
way. They shimmered as though gorged with light and
time and man's insatiable hunger for that which is
rare.

"What do you want from me?" Cole asked,
watching the diamonds with brooding gray eyes.

For a moment Wing thought the question was di-
rected at the stones. He had known Cole for many
years, yet the Hong Kong businessman did not claim
to understand or predict the next turning of the American prospector's complex mind.

"Are they diamonds?" Wing asked softly.

"Yes."

"No chance of deception?"

Cole shrugged. The motion made light move over
him. Raw black silk gleamed in his sport coat. His hair
was the exact color and luster of the silk. His skin had
been weathered in the wild places of the world. Fine
lines radiated out from his eyes, legacy of a life spent
of squinting into the light of a desert sun or the flare
of a miner's lamp. Above his left temple a scattering of
silver showed in his thick hair. He looked older than
his thirty-four years. By every measure that mattered,
he was.

"There's always a chance of deception," Cole
said. "But if these were made by a man, he'll be the
ruin of every miner and diamond mine in the world."

Wing smiled.

"If you're worried," Cole suggested, "I can find

someone in Darwin with a thermal inertia tester. Nobody's beat that test, not yet."

This time it was Wing who shrugged. "Unless you brought an instrument with you, there's no time. These stones must be on their way in a few hours."

"Where are they going?"

"America."

"Where did they come from?"

"Kimberley."

Cole was silent. When he spoke, his voice was neutral. "South Africa's deposits are pretty well played out."

"Not Kimberley, Africa," Wing corrected. "The Kimberley Plateau, here in Australia."

Wing smiled as though enjoying the chance to demonstrate that he understood the difference between the two Kimberleys. It was a common enough mistake. Conventional wisdom automatically linked diamonds with Africa, despite the fact that the biggest diamond mine in the world, the Argyle, was in the remote tropical deserts of the state of Western Australia.

Cole smiled in return, but there was little humor in the hard curve of his mouth. "Did the Chen family invest in the Argyle mine on the basis of these stones?"

"I didn't say Argyle, only Kimberley."

Silently Cole thought through the possible implications. If those stones came from the Argyle, the cartel that controlled the world's supply of diamonds had made a major new discovery and had become a little richer in the process. But if the stones were from some new source, the diamond game had a new player and all hell was about to break loose.

Either way, life would become very interesting for the man holding that handful of bright diamond markers in the coming international shoving match.

"Kimberley, Australia," Cole said, pinning Wing with gray eyes that were as clear as glacier ice. "Is that where the stones were found?"

For the first time Wing hesitated. "They came to me from there, but as to where they were originally found . . ." He turned his narrow hands palm up.

"Are there more?" Cole asked, gesturing toward the scattered stones.

"This is all that came to me," Wing said carefully.

Cole walked to the window and looked out over the palms that framed the front lawn of the government casino in Darwin, Northern Territory, Australia, fifteen hundred miles from the Kimberley Plateau. The hard tropical sun and humidity-hazed sky made the Timor Sea look like spun aluminum.

The sun's heat radiated through the double panes of glass in the window close to Cole. In the background came the vague hum of machinery as the casino's air conditioning filtered out tobacco smoke from the gaming rooms below and at the same time cooled the steamy, overbearing heat of tropical October. It was high spring, down under. The buildup had already begun, the season when animals died and men went crazy.

Cole understood why. Tropical Australia in October was one of the few places on earth Cole had found unlivable. For some reason the heat and humidity in the eucalyptus and acacia scrublands affected him more than the same conditions in Venezuela or Brazil.

But inside the Darwin casino, man's machinery kept the tropics at bay, delivering high-tech air that had neither the savor nor the character of any climate or country. Had it not been for the Aboriginal drawings on the wall, the room could have been located anywhere from Hong Kong to Johannesburg, London to Los Angeles, Tel Aviv to Bombay. The furnishings were a synthesis of western woods and eastern artistic traditions. The clothes combined eastern fabrics with Italian design flair.

"Were these diamonds mined in the Kimberley?" Cole asked, being blunt because there was no longer anything to gain from circumspection.

"I hoped you could tell me."

Cole's eyes narrowed beneath black eyebrows. Wing wasn't usually evasive, not when he wanted something. But then Wing didn't usually walk around with a major fortune in uncut diamonds in his pocket. He and his family were too pragmatic to dabble in a mineral commodity whose market price was controlled by a well-entrenched cartel. The Chens usually stuck to mining and refining metallic ores whose names were familiar only to space scientists or weapons makers.

"I can't tell you positively where the diamonds came from," Cole said finally, "but I can tell you they *didn't* come from the Argyle."

"The stones speak to you?" Wing asked skeptically.

Cole waited.

"How can you be so certain?" Wing demanded. "Argyle has pink diamonds, after all."

"The Argyle mine is a bort hole, industrial diamonds almost exclusively. Sure, there are pinks in the place, but these pinks are darker, cleaner, and a hell of a lot bigger than anything the Australians have admitted to finding. It takes the patience of an Indian stone polisher to make jewelry out of Argyle's junk."

Wing stirred the diamonds with his fingertip. Light pooled and gleamed as though the stones were wet. "Are you saying these aren't Australian diamonds?"

"No. Just that they're not from the Argyle itself. Hell, Wing, there are seventy different companies working the Kimberley Plateau. Nobody has found much but industrial-grade goods." Cole paused before adding, "At least that's what ConMin has been putting out."

Wing grunted, his skepticism matching Cole's. ConMin told the world what it wanted the world to hear about diamonds, period. "What else do the stones tell you?"

"They're alluvial."

"Explain, please."

"They've been out of the mother pipe a long, long time, washed out by erosion."

"Is that bad?"

Cole shook his head. "Jesus, you still don't know shit from schist, do you?"

"You didn't disparage my questions when we were partners."

"You didn't bait me with a handful of fantastic rough when we were partners," Cole shot back. "These diamonds are the cream of some old, eroded diamond pipe. The flawed goods and small stuff have been destroyed by time. The stones that survived all had the corners rounded off the natural crystalline shape."

"That's good?" Wing asked dubiously.

"When it comes to cutting time, yes. Stones dug

fresh and sharp from a pipe lose half their weight in cutting and polishing. These alluvial stones will lose no more than twenty percent between the rough state and some spoiled lady's finger."

"Then these stones are at least thirty percent more valuable than nonalluvial rough diamonds of an equal weight?" Wing asked quickly.

Cole smiled. Wing didn't need to know much about diamonds to keep a balance sheet in his head. That was one of the reasons Cole trusted his former partner. He knew what motivated Chen Wing: profit.

"When you take into account color and size as well," Cole said, "you've got at least a million dollars wholesale sitting on your desk, as is. Cut and polished, those stones are worth one hell of a lot more."

"How much more?"

"Depends on how badly someone wants them. The fancies—"

"Fancies?" Wing interrupted.

"Colored diamonds. They're bloody rare, and a true green is the rarest of them all. Wherever that lot came from, it's God's own jewel box."

"Are there mines like that?"

"In Australia? Not that I know of."

"Are there such mines anywhere?" Wing demanded impatiently.

"Ever hear of Namaqualand? Southwest coast of Africa, just below the mouth of the Orange River?" Cole asked.

Wing shook his head.

"About sixty years ago a geologist called Hans Merensky was prospecting on Crown holdings there. He came across some diamonds lying together on top of the ground, neat as eggs in a quail's nest."

Though he said nothing, Wing sat straighter in his chair and leaned closer to Cole.

"Everywhere Merensky looked he found more diamonds," Cole said. "Soon he couldn't hold them all in his hand. Most of them were too big to fit down the neck of his canteen. He had to store them in candy tins."

With a soft grunt Wing looked at the small handful of diamonds on his desk and imagined the sensation of making an even larger find.

"Yeah," Cole said in a low voice. "That's how I felt when I first heard the story. Every diamond hunter lies awake at night and dreams of how it would feel to find a jewel box like that."

"Jewel box. You're serious, then?"

"Jewel box, diamond trap, concentrated gem gravels: call it what you will. It's a place where time and water and gravity have done the heavy work of mining for you. They've worn away the softer rock, carried away the dross, and concentrated the diamonds."

"I don't understand."

Cole curbed his impatience and explained. "Diamonds are heavier and far harder than most minerals, so they sink in quiet parts of river bends, collect behind boulders or in tree roots, or get caught in gravel. Gold does the same thing for the same reason. It's heavy. Most of the big diamond finds started with men looking for placer gold."

"What happened to Merensky?"

"He filled a half-dozen candy tins full of diamonds, diamonds as big as eighty carats. Gem quality, all of them. He sold out his claim for one million pounds, which in those days was a king's ransom."

"To whom did he sell?"

"Come on, Wing, you know as well as I do."

Wing grimaced and hissed a word through his teeth. "Shit."

"That may be your opinion, but stockholders think quite highly of ConMin."

"Do you think these are cartel diamonds?" Wing said, glancing at the stones on the desk.

"No."

"So quick? No doubts?"

"You would have lost more than two people getting the likes of these away from the diamond cartel," Cole said flatly.

"But the cartel would be interested in them?"

Cole laughed derisively. "If those stones are all from the same spot, and that place is a new strike, the cartel would move heaven and earth to grab control of the place. Archimedes said he could move the world with a lever long enough. The mine that yielded those stones is a lever that long."

Wing grunted. "What else can you tell me about these stones? Anything, no matter how small."

"Just that the stones don't 'feel' like African diamonds. The colors are wrong, for one thing. Too much pink. No Cape yellow at all. Several of those whites are twinned crystals, macles. Australia is known for those. The green diamond isn't likely for Africa at all; Brazil, perhaps, but that green is both more intense and yet more fiery than the Dresden diamond, which is the best of the Brazilian greens.

"All in all," Cole continued, "if that's a representative sampling from some prospector's cache, I doubt that it was found in Africa. ConMin's only other significant source of diamonds is the Soviet Union, and the Soviets aren't noted for gem goods, much less for blue-whites. Their goods have a very slight greenish tinge."

"Then this lot could have come from here in Australia?"

"Possibly. The Ellendale find had green gem-quality diamonds. Nothing as big or as deeply colored as that, of course, or presumably the Australian government would have developed Ellendale rather than Argyle."

"What you're saying is that it's possible these stones came from a single strike in Australia?"

A glance at Wing's face told Cole that he could no longer trust Wing, because there was more involved in these diamonds than profit. He had seen Wing in quest of profit before. There was nothing of the cheerful entrepreneur about Wing right now; he was intent, dedicated, and predatory down to the tips of his immaculately manicured nails.

"How badly do you need to know?" Cole asked calmly.

"Not me. Us. You and me."

Cole's expression shifted, becoming subtly harder. "Us? We aren't partners any more. We sold BlackWing Resources Ltd. to your uncle five years ago."

"I think it would be wise for us to become partners again," Wing said, reaching into another drawer and pulling out a sheaf of papers. "This is a partnership agreement very similar to the one we signed when we created BlackWing."

Cole glanced at the papers but made no move to take them. "I read too slowly, Wing," he lied softly.

"So translate the jargon into common English. But don't go all Mandarin and lawyerly on me, or I'll walk right out that door and catch the first plane back to Brazil."

Without hesitation Wing set the papers down on the desk. The fingertips of his right hand moved almost caressingly over the expensive textured sheets. When he spoke, it was slowly, like a man choosing each word with care.

"Ten years ago we formed BlackWing Resources on the basis of your geological brilliance and my financial abilities. It was a good match, a profitable one, because each of us brought different strengths to the deal."

"It also worked because you hired geologists to check my work, just as I hired accountants to check yours," Cole pointed out blandly.

Wing nodded. "There was intelligence in our partnership, at least as much intelligence as trust. The Chen family needs your intelligence again. We need you."

"For what?"

"We believe that you may be a part owner of the deposit in which these stones were found."

The air conditioning made the only sound in the room for several long moments while Cole studied Wing.

"I've bought, sold, and swapped a lot of diamond claims in my life," Cole said finally. "Are you trying to tell me I've overlooked something this good?"

"Sign this partnership agreement and I'll answer your questions. But unless and until you sign, not one more word."

Wing gathered the rough diamonds and began to return them one by one to the worn velvet bag. Cole watched until the green diamond vanished. Then he picked up the papers and began to read.

2

◆

THE POLESTAR SHONE ABOVE TUNDRA, RIVER, AND mountains alike, providing a brilliant center around which the night circled in icy splendor. Moonlight brushed the river with silver. The illumination was ethereal and cold as snow. A black wind from an undiscovered tomorrow rushed down the long valley, whispering of ancient glaciers and a coming midnight that knew no dawn.

That was what Erin Shane Windsor hoped to capture, the delicacy and chill of eternity drawn in moonlight upon a river surface that was slowly turning to ice. Oblivious to the temperature and to her isolation in the vast Alaskan landscape, Erin made a final adjustment on her camera and stepped back from the tripod. She tripped the shutter with fingers that were too cold to feel the texture of the bulb release she squeezed. The shutter opened and closed with tangible reluctance, measuring the length of the exposure she had chosen. As insurance, she exposed several more frames of film. The prolonged silk-on-silk sound of the camera mechanism was loud against the arctic silence.

After the last exposure, Erin immediately went to work on a new combination of settings. When she fumbled the settings a second time, Erin swore softly, her breath becoming a plume of glittering silver moisture. She was impatient; little time remained to capture the shot she wanted. At the moment, the moon was at just the right angle to illuminate three of the river's sinuous curves and to suggest a repetition of those curves in the folds of the mountains themselves.

But the world was turning and the wind was pushing clouds into a single mass. Each instant irrevocably changed the most important element in the entire image—light.

Erin's watch cheeped a warning. She ignored it. That was only the first of several mechanical reminders she had programmed into the timepiece. It was something she often did, for when she was shooting pictures, no other reality existed for her. Her ability to concentrate was a double-edged gift, putting her at odds with a civilization that required time to be divided and subdivided into portions that had no meaning beyond urban landscapes.

"Dammit, hands, settle down," Erin muttered as her cold-numbed fingers made slow work of resetting the camera's finicky time and exposure mechanisms.

The watch cheeped again.

Even as Erin shut out the sound, part of her mind reluctantly acknowledged that there was a world beyond her camera lens, and in that other world she had a plane to catch to civilization, a civilization she had avoided for seven years. Like the geese and shorebirds she had photographed on the tundra, and like the whales she had photographed from skin boats, Erin was southward bound. Unlike the birds and whales, however, she was heading toward days divided into hours divided into minutes divided into seconds, with no time off for good behavior, world without end, amen.

She squeezed the bulb release, advanced the film, then squeezed again, triggering the camera, listening as the shutter delicately framed instants of time that transcended clocks and heartbeats.

Rapt, patient, shivering with a cold she didn't feel, Erin worked over the camera again, compelled by the black and silver starkness of the landscape, photographing her farewell to a land she loved. There was a mythic quality to the arctic that had attracted her on first sight. That quality was reflected in the primitive lives of the Eskimo and Aleut subsistence hunters she had met and lived among.

She had gone with men in skin boats through shifting leads in pack ice, hunting whales. Out in the frail boats she had learned that primitive man feared, loved, and revered his prey. Modern man simply killed with high-tech weapons, risking nothing of himself and therefore learning nothing of himself or his prey, of life or death or transcendence. Erin had known those kinds of men, too, modern men. She preferred the impersonal chill of the arctic.

Her watch's warnings came at shorter intervals until they became constant, reminding Erin of the urgency of the telegram that had been read to her over the shortwave radio that morning: YOU MUST RETURN IMMEDIATELY STOP FAMILY EMERGENCY STOP INSTRUCTIONS TO FOLLOW STOP JAMES ROSEN ESQ.

"Shut up," she muttered. "Just . . . shut . . . up."

She jabbed a numb index finger at the alarm button on her watch, silencing it. But she knew it was too late. Her concentration had been ruined because she couldn't turn off James Rosen Esquire as easily as she had silenced her watch.

YOU MUST RETURN IMMEDIATELY STOP

Erin shoved aside the demand. She had ignored civilization for seven years. She could ignore it for seven more minutes.

She would have ignored the summons forever if she hadn't realized that her own arctic cycle was ending. But it was. She hadn't taken all possible pictures of the arctic, but she had taken all the images that were necessary for her own needs. The imperatives that had driven her into the wilderness seven years ago had faded to a whisper. She was no longer the same person she had been then. The answers she found in Alaska no longer fit the questions she was asking herself.

Jeffrey will be ecstatic, Erin thought, wishing the idea gave her greater comfort. Jeffrey Fisher, her New York editor, didn't understand the part of her life she spent in the wilderness. Nor did he understand the restlessness that sent her out to places where others rarely went. He loved her photographic technique, her artist's eye, but he was forever trying to get her to do "civilized" photography: English farmhouses and French vineyards, ancient Greek statues and modern Mediterranean resorts.

At first Erin had tried to make Fisher understand why she resisted his European assignments. She had tried to explain to him that while civilization removed the abysmal lows of physical deprivation, it leveled off the psychic highs of survival as well. Fisher hadn't understood. Her preferred world of austere Pacific Rim landscapes and remote cultures was simply too distant from Manhattan, and too different in ways both obvious and subtle, for him to grasp. The East Coast looked east, toward Europe and the past. The West Coast looked west, toward the undeveloped Pacific Rim and the future.

Unfortunately Erin had run out of internal and external excuses for not accepting the European assignments, farmhouses and wine cellars and sterling silver by candlelight. She had conscientiously cleared her schedule so that no one would be left hanging if she was gone for several months or even a year. She had done everything but work up enthusiasm for shooting European set pieces when she would rather shoot almost anything else.

She had been to the Continent many times and had been more depressed than impressed. Part of it was simply that her former fiancé had been European, or at least had claimed to be.

FAMILY EMERGENCY STOP

Part of it was that she associated Europe with her father's work, diplomacy and secrets and treachery, the kind of betrayal that scarred its survivors for life. Assuming there were any survivors to scar.

INSTRUCTIONS TO FOLLOW STOP

Instructions, but no truth. Man had invented civilization in order to evade natural truth and had invented time in order to more carefully package human lies.

FAMILY EMERGENCY

Motionless, Erin stood surrounded by brilliant silver light and radiant natural silence, eternity condensed into a shimmering unity that had a sweeping disregard for human concepts such as truth and lies, life and death, fair and unfair.

YOU MUST RETURN

Life wasn't fair or unfair; it was simply unexpected. Sometimes life's surprises were breathtakingly beautiful, like the arctic. Sometimes they were breathtakingly cruel, like Hans. But surprises were always the raw material of life, and she had chosen to live.

Erin silenced her wristwatch alarm for the last time and began packing up her equipment for the long trip to Los Angeles.

3

◆

"How long ago did the two Chinese assassins die?"

The voice, slightly distorted by the satellite link and by the scrambler, had a dry Etonian disdain that dug at Jason Street. Hugo van Luik was a powerfully built Dutchman with a full head of white hair, but he sounded like a whingeing Pom to an Australian ear. Street took a long drink of beer and set the cold over-sized can on his desk before he spoke into the phone.

"Twelve hours, maybe a bit more."

"Why was your report delayed?"

"You want me babbling our business on open phone lines, do you?" Street shot back. "This is bleeding Australia, remember. Anybody with a receiver can listen in on radio phones. I buried the powerpoints, took Abe's place apart, and then got back here to Perth before I called."

Ten thousand miles away, on the fifth floor of the gray, anonymous office building on Pelikanstraat, the main street of Antwerp's diamond trade, Hugo van

Luik closed his eyes against the blinding pain of a growing headache. At the moment he was alone in his office, so he allowed himself the luxury of slumping. He felt as though he were impaled on a giant fishhook. Nausea twisted in his stomach, then subsided. He drew a deep, grateful breath. Van Luik was a powerful man, both physically and in his profession, but he paid the price of power. Lately that price seemed to be more and more steep.

"Very well," van Luik said. "To summarize, the holographic will, the velvet sack, and the tin box were gone by the time you arrived. A decade's work—wasted."

"Too bloody right. You should have let me open Abe Windsor up my own way. He'd have spilled his secret soon enough."

"Perhaps. But more probably a man his age would have died under torture and left the secret to his heir. At the time, the risks seemed too great."

"Not now, mate. Now they look bleeding small."

"Your hindsight is superlative."

Street didn't reply. He loathed the precise Dutchman whose power was hidden behind the bland, meaningless title of Director of Special Operations, Diamond Sales Division. But even while Street loathed van Luik, he feared him.

"Very well," van Luik said. "Now go back over it from the beginning."

It was his favorite tactic with a recalcitrant like Jason Street. Repetition reinforced the subordinate role and at the same time exposed little inconsistencies that suggested information withheld or lies told.

Street knew the drill as well as van Luik did. The Australian took another draft of beer and belched into the telephone. "Not much to tell, really. Abe had been drinking for a few days. Full pissed, he was. Nothing different there. About three days ago he went wonky, grabbed a shovel, and took off into the bush, screaming something about digging his own grave."

"Was that unusual?"

"Hell no, mate. Happens once a month, like a woman bleeding. Only this time Abe was telling the truth. He must have died out there in the bush. His body looked like he'd been slow-roasted on a spit. Dead as tinned fish and three times the smell."

Van Luik felt nausea welling up again, though not because of Street's words. Death and corruption were matters of indifference to the Dutchman. It was the realization of impotence that made him feel sick.

"How did Windsor's body get back to the station?" van Luik asked.

"The powerpoints must have found him."

"Powerpoints?"

"Chinks, wogs, Chinamen," Street said impatiently. Van Luik spoke four languages but couldn't—or wouldn't—remember the Australian slang Street always used. "They trucked him back."

"How do you know that? Did your informant at the station tell you?"

"Sarah? She'd already gone walkabout with her bronze-wing brats. She was drinking with Abe, just like always, and passed out. When she sobered up and he still wasn't back, she called me, then headed for the back of beyond."

"Why?"

"She knew I'd kill her if Abe was dead."

"Then how do you know the Chinese found Windsor?"

"There were no new tracks going into the station. The cook must have called in the chopper when Abe didn't come back. Or else he followed Abe and staked him out in the sun for a chat about missing mines."

Van Luik let his silence reach halfway around the world.

Street kept talking. "The bleeding cook had to be a tout, same as Sarah. Lots of people knew Abe had some nice stones in the sack. Wasn't just us on to him."

Van Luik massaged the bridge of his nose. "Go on."

"It must have been the powerpoints that found Abe out in the bush, brought him back, then ransacked the station, which means Abe didn't talk before he died."

"I profoundly hope so. Unfortunately the 'powerpoints' knew enough to take the tin box as well as the diamonds, didn't they?"

Jason Street took a swig of beer and said nothing. He had been hoping van Luik wouldn't realize the implications of the missing box so quickly.

"Didn't they?" Van Luik's repeated question had an edge to it.

"Yeah, they took the bleeding box."

"So we must assume they are at least as well informed as we are. They must realize that the contents of the bag are worth only a fraction of what the contents of the box may ultimately be worth."

The encrypted satellite channel hummed invitingly, waiting for Street to agree with the obvious.

"I suppose," the Australian said reluctantly.

Van Luik looked out across the wet, gray rooftops that housed the most skillful diamond cutters and the most ruthless gemstone brokers in the world. Sometimes he could relieve the pain by resting his eyes on distant vistas. And sometimes he simply had to endure.

He closed his eyes and endured, trying to think beyond the blinding instants of pain that measured his heartbeats in the blood vessels behind his eyes. Jason Street had come to ConMin with the highest recommendations ten years ago, when Street had been barely thirty. Nothing in the ensuing years had happened to make van Luik doubt Street's abilities or his ultimate loyalties.

Until now. Now something was wrong. Street was temporizing, lying, or withholding some crucial bit of information. Van Luik couldn't tell whether the Australian was dissembling to avoid ConMin's wrath or for some other, less obvious reason.

"Were you able to get any information on the helicopter?" van Luik asked softly.

"I checked every charter operator in Western Australia and the Northern Territory. No luck. No trace of a flight plan in the air traffic control system, either. Must have been privately owned."

"Find that helicopter!" Van Luik almost gagged with the sudden blinding agony his outburst triggered. He breathed shallowly through his mouth for a moment. When he spoke again, his voice was controlled and calm. "We must find out who has the poetry and the stones."

"I'm working on it, mate."

Van Luik shifted the phone to his left hand and massaged his right temple with long well-manicured fingers. Light flashed from the little finger of his right hand, where he wore a five-carat, emerald-cut, D flawless diamond. The stone was pavé set in matte-finish platinum. It was the only jewelry van Luik wore or needed to wear. In Antwerp the stone was a calling card, instantly identifying the wearer as a fellow of the international diamond brotherhood.

"You have, of course, a copy of 'Chunder from Down Under'?" van Luik asked.

"Sarah checked it a week before Abe died. It hadn't been changed since the last time I forwarded a copy to you."

"I don't suppose she was able to copy the will, though?" Van Luik's tone was quiet, almost accusing. When Street didn't answer, the Dutchman added, "Did she even manage to look at it?"

Street drew a deep breath and prepared to tell van Luik what he already knew. "Abe left 'Chunder' on his bedside table, but his will was his own bloody little secret, and he kept it even closer than the stones around his neck."

Van Luik grunted. He opened the file on the desk in front of him and glanced through a sheaf of photographs. They were grainy prints, blown up from the tiny negatives of a Minox camera, page after page of spidery, old-fashioned handwriting on rough, lined tablet paper. Meaningless ramblings or a dead man's cleverly disguised clues to a missing diamond mine. The truth of the poetry was still elusive.

"You have a copy with you," van Luik said.

It was a statement, not a question. Street bit back a savage retort and said only, "Yes."

"Begin."

"Rack off, van Luik. We've been around this course so many times that—"

"Begin," van Luik repeated coldly.

There was a silence, followed by the subtle rustling of paper as Street shuffled through pages of Crazy Abe's oddly lucid handwriting.

"Any particular verse strike your fancy?" Street asked in a goading tone. He knew that "Chunder" offended van Luik in more ways than his inability to pierce its central secret.

"The fourth verse this time, I think."

"Right." Street began reading aloud, his voice uninflected. " 'Find it if you can,/If you dare to go/Where the dark swan floats/Over a dead sea's bones,/Where men are Percys and Lady Janes are stone.' " When he finished reading, Street waited.

So did van Luik.

With a muttered curse, Street began explaining lines he had read and explained so many times he no longer really saw them. "The first line—"

"Is self-explanatory," van Luik cut in. "So is the second. Begin with the third."

"Right. Black swans are all over the outback, like koalas used to be all over the east coast. He could be talking about a strike near a billabong."

"Explain."

"A billabong is a deep river pool that becomes a waterhole in the dry season when the shallow parts of the river dry up," Street said mechanically.

"Go on."

Street's hand tightened on the telephone. Of all van Luik's quirks, the one of making someone repeat the same information over and over again was the most offensive. It was also the most effective in preventing lies, a fact Street understood and had put to use for himself with his own subordinates.

"Abe could have made a strike near a billabong,

except that there aren't any waterholes on his mineral
leases or on his station that are big enough to be called
a billabong," Street said in a monotone. "The only
reliable year-round water is the well at his station
house."

Van Luik made a curt sound that could have
meant anything. Street knew it was a signal to keep
talking.

"That leaves the bleeding 'dead sea's bones,'"
Street continued tonelessly. "Since we don't have a
billabong for the swans to swim in, it's no shocker
that we don't have any waterholes sitting on top of a
marine fossil bed to point the way to the mine."

"Go on."

Street smiled thinly. He suspected that van Luik
found sex distasteful. Abe hadn't. The only time he
wasn't stuck in a woman was when he drank too
much beer and brewer's wilt took him down.

"So Abe tells us to find the mine if we dare to go
'Where men are Percys/And Lady Janes are stone,'"
Street said, drawing it out. "Aussies call their cock
their Percy. Guess what a Lady Jane is?"

Van Luik grunted. He didn't have to guess. He
had heard it all before, many times.

"So Abe is telling us to go where men have a cock
and women have a stone pussy," Street said succinctly. "Welcome to the outback. That narrows the
mine's location down to a few thousand square miles
of uninhabited country."

When van Luik would have spoken, Street talked
right over him.

"In the next verse, an 'amber river' must be beer,
right?" Street said. "You drink enough of it and you'll
'piss a yellow sea.' Then there's—"

"Go to the next verse," van Luik interrupted.

"Right. 'Crawl into my bed and onto my Percy,/ Bridget and Ingrid, Diana and Mercy,/Kewpie and Daisy and Kelly,/Rooting and hooting about love./ Mistresses of lies,/Damn their hot cries.' " Street took a breath and continued sarcastically, "We've already decoded Percy, which leaves us with the other names. They aren't cities, towns, settlements, crossroads, tracks, paths, stations, or any other bleeding thing but Aussie slang for pussy."

Van Luik made a sound of disgust.

"Rooting is screwing," Street continued relentlessly. "Now maybe the old wanker saw mining as a sexual experience or maybe he didn't. Either way, that verse has sweet fuck-all to tell us about where he found his bleeding diamonds."

"Go to the ninth verse," van Luik said.

"You go to it. I've had enough."

"Begin with the fourth line."

Street gripped the phone so hard his hand ached, while he reminded himself that now was not the time to lose his temper. Even though it hadn't been his fault, the secret to the sleeping Dog Mines had slipped through his fingers. If going over "Chunder" one more time was the only punishment he got, he would be lucky.

" 'Stone womb giving me hope,/Secrets blacker than death/And truth it's death to speak.' " Street waited, but van Luik said nothing. " 'Stone womb' is a mine, right? Didn't we decide that—oh, six, seven years ago, when he changed 'woman' to 'womb'?"

Van Luik ignored the sarcasm. "Yes. Go on."

"Wombs, women, and mines are dark places, and

telling where his mine was would have been the death
of Crazy Abe and he bloody well knew it.''

" 'But I will speak to you,/Listen to me, child of
rue.' "

Street said nothing, too surprised by the reversal
of roles, van Luik reading the doggerel they both had
come to loathe.

" 'Let secrets sleep/Waiting for the offspring of
deceit./While 'roos and rutting gins/Leap on the
ground above,/A handful of old candy tins/Rattle
around below.' "

Silence stretched over the communications link
as an unhappy certainty grew in Street. "He's talking
about an heir, isn't he? Not just any poor sod that
happens to be reading 'Chunder,' but his own bleeding heir!"

"I am afraid you are correct. 'Child of rue' can no
longer be understood to be a comment on the general
unhappiness of mankind."

"Bloody hell," Street snarled. "What could his
heir find in that blurter's poetry that we can't?"

The ache between van Luik's eyes grew greater
with each heartbeat. It would have been so much easier if there had been some unmistakable hint of
treachery on Street's part, some tangible proof of un-
reliability from the man on the other end of the line.
But there was not, which meant that some unknown
and therefore utterly unpredictable force was at work
to upset the fragile balance of ConMin's Diamond
Sales Division, a balance Hugo van Luik had spent his
life trying to maintain, a balance that had been
achieved at the cost of so many principles and ideals
and lives.

Van Luik pictured the Australian scene in his

mind, wondering whether Abe Windsor had finally babbled the secrets of his mine to the spinifex as he lay dying. A useless speculation in any case, for the spinifex had neither ears to hear nor mouths to communicate. All van Luik had was the fact that Jason Street had been told about a holographic will and had been shown sheet after sheet of manic poetry; and that, when drunk, Abelard Windsor would talk about diamonds as green as billabongs shaded by gum trees, diamonds as pink as a white girl's nipples, diamonds the color and clarity of distilled water.

Futilely, fiercely, van Luik wished that he had been able to turn Street loose years ago to use his quick, cruel skills. Street would have opened up the old man like a sturgeon, spilling the glistening caviar of truth. Or better yet, if circumstances had permitted a simple, swift death, a death that would have killed the secret of the mine as well. . . .

"No one can prove the mine exists," van Luik said softly, not even aware that he was speaking aloud. "He was, after all, quite mad."

"Dream on, mate," Street retorted. "The mine exists. They called him Crazy Abe and he might have been, but not like that. Diamonds were his children, his women, his country, and his god. I've heard a lot of lies in my day and bloody little truth. Hearing Abe talk about diamonds was like being a priest in the confessional. The truth, no matter how wild. I never got my hands on the stones in the bag, but I'd bet my life they were real."

Silence; then, "The sixteenth verse. Read it."

This time Street made no objection. Before he had only feared that Abe Windsor would leave the secret of the diamond mine to someone other than his friend Jason Street. Now Street was certain. He had sworn the poetry had nothing new to teach him. He had been wrong.

" 'It can be yours, all of it./Say goodbye to mallee root,/Say g'day to my queen,/Go a yard for each year of deceit,/Turn around once—see it?/Stupid merkin./Can't find shit in a loo, can you?' "

Van Luik waited.

"Mallee root is rhyming slang for prostitute," Street said tiredly, finding nothing new in the line. "There's no map or local name like it on any of Abe's properties or claims. As for his 'queen,' it's probably his mine, right?"

Van Luik grunted.

"As for the rest, until you know where to stand and how long Abe was deceived, the words are useless. Same for 'Take a map of Tasmania,/Find the little man in the boat./Go on, row on.' The map of Tasmania is slang for pussy, and the little man in the boat is—"

"Yes, yes, yes," van Luik cut in impatiently. "Knowing that Abe is talking to his heir doesn't suggest any new interpretations to you?"

Street hesitated, then sighed. "Not a hope, mate. Not a bleeding hope. But I doubt the powerpoints will have any better luck making sense out of the poem than we have. They were probably looking for maps or ore samples, anything that would point them in the right direction. It's a big station, and Abe had mineral claims in other places as well."

"But it must mean something to someone! Windsor's heir might be able to decipher it," van Luik said. "That's the possibility we must guard against now."

"Do you know who the heir is?"

"Not yet. We should know soon."

"Find out," Street said. "I'll take care of him. No worries, mate. With the heir dead and the mines abandoned, the government will let the claims lapse. I'll file new ones, you'll underwrite a real search, and the mine will eventually be found and controlled by us. No worries."

"Even with the claims in hand, you'll be no closer to finding the mine than you are right now."

"No worries. I'd find the bleeding thing. All I need is time and money for equipment."

Van Luik smiled weakly. If only it was that easy. But it wasn't. Nothing about the Sleeping Dog Mines had been easy. Nothing at all. The diamonds had been both a siren call and a threat of death since the instant of their discovery.

The siren call had proved to be false. The threat could prove to be all too real.

"We will consider your solution," van Luik said.

"Don't consider too long. This operation is balls-up enough as it is."

The line hummed, telling Street that van Luik had disconnected.

4

◆

DESPITE THE DENSITY OF THE LEGAL LANGUAGE, Cole Blackburn had to read the partnership contract only once. He possessed a nearly perfect memory. It was a quirk of mind that had sometimes helped him and more often brought him pain. Too many things had happened to him that he would rather forget.

The agreement itself was quite clear. The contract allowed Cole to purchase half interest in BlackWing Resources for the sum of one dollar U.S. In return, he would agree to sign over to BlackWing his interests in any Australian mining claims or patents he held. Currently he held no Australian mining claims or patents. BlackWing, on the other hand, had been worth $10 million U.S. five years ago, when Cole had sold his half to the Chen family. Since then, the value of the company had at least doubled.

Beneath all the legal bells and whistles, Cole was being offered $10 million in equity for the investment of a dollar, plus mining claims he didn't hold. The contract itself was fully executed except for the absence of his own signature.

Everything was clear except the reason for the offer. That was why Cole had spent the past nineteen minutes reading between the contract's lines. Granted, circumstances surrounding the dissolution of his partnership with Wing had been unusual. The Chens had paid Cole $5 million partly to indemnify him for the loss of a lover who was their daughter, Wing's sister. But now the clan that controlled a sizeable portion of Hong Kong and Macao seemed willing to compound their mistake.

Cole was no lawyer but he was sophisticated enough to realize there were no loopholes, no tricks built into the partnership agreement, no obvious or subtle way for the Chen family to recoup from him the missing $9,999,999.

Without signing, Cole dropped the document back on the desk. "It's too early for Christmas."

Wing shrugged. "It's not a gift. The incumbent geologists at BlackWing are either too inexperienced or too corrupt to find what we want."

"And what's that?"

"Diamond mines," Wing said succinctly.

"Why do you want them? You've got a half-dozen Pacific Basin holdings that pay better returns than the average diamond mine."

Wing rubbed his palms together thoughtfully, then shook his head. "Have you looked at oil prices lately? At gold? At copper? Iron? Uranium? They are, as you Americans say, in the toilet." He smiled slightly, as though it had been a long time since he had used American slang.

"Diamonds have had their own problems," Cole

countered. "What cost sixty-two thousand dollars American per carat in 1980 costs about twenty thousand at the moment."

"Yes, but take a slightly longer view and you'll remember that in 1974 the same diamond cost only forty-three hundred dollars per carat. Trust me, my friend. I have done my research carefully. Diamonds are the only commodity to have increased in real value over the last fifty years."

"Thanks to the cartel."

Wing sighed. "They're bloody geniuses, aren't they? At meetings of the UN, countries argue and do nothing. At meetings of Consolidated Minerals, Inc., countries agree and make money. ConMin is the only monopoly in history that has channeled rather than released the inherent greediness of man. Prices rise, but slowly. Long-term stability, not short-term profits. ConMin has an almost Chinese appreciation of time."

"And power."

"That too," Wing agreed softly. "That most of all."

"So the Chen family wants a diamond prospector who owes nothing to the diamond cartel."

Wing was momentarily startled. He had seen Cole only infrequently in the five years since his sister Lai had broken her engagement to him. In that time, Wing had forgotten that the American's mind was as quick as his well-conditioned body.

"Yes, that is precisely what we want," Wing admitted.

Cole leaned back in the sleek leather chair and listened to his own instincts. He was used to operating on his instincts at times and in places where more than money was at stake. His instincts had urged him to come to Darwin on the strength of Wing's cryptic phone call.

Instincts . . . or sheer restlessness.

Whichever was speaking, Cole was ready to listen. He still didn't know precisely what Wing wanted. More accurately, Cole didn't know what the Chen family wanted. But Cole did know that touching the luminous green diamond had made him feel more alive than he had felt in years.

Listening carefully to his inner silence, waiting to hear the whisper of instincts telling him to avoid an unseen trap, Cole waited for another minute. He heard nothing but the quickened beating of his own heart. He had found diamonds and diamond mines all over the world. He had made and lost small fortunes, and large ones as well. But he had never found the equal of Wing's green diamond.

And now he was being offered the chance to find a whole mine full of them, God's own jewel box.

Cole pulled a pen from his pocket and signed his name on the contract and its copies with quick, slashing strokes. Saying nothing, he folded one contract and put it in his breast pocket. Then he pulled a dollar bill from his wallet, clipped the bill to the remaining contracts, and flipped the papers back across the ebony desk.

"All right, partner," Cole said. "Tell me about this diamond mine you want me to find."

Wing's smile was amused. "The Chen family didn't hire you merely because you're a brilliant prospector, although you are. We brought you into this because you have a verbal promise from Abelard Windsor of a fifty-percent interest in Sleeping Dog

Mines Ltd. as a full repayment of gambling debts incurred by him during a night of playing Two Up."

For an instant Cole said nothing.

Wing allowed his small smile of triumph to spread into a grin. It was the first time he had ever seen Cole surprised.

"That was twelve years ago," Cole said. "Christ, I didn't even know you then!"

Wing made a dismissing motion with his hand. "Did Mr. Windsor ever pay off that debt?"

Cole made a sound too harsh to be called laughter. "There were times Crazy Abe couldn't remember from one day to the next what happened. He was just too drunk. I was a long way from sober myself. So was everybody else at the station."

"Do you have an IOU?"

"Old Abe wasn't that crazy," Cole said dryly. "Besides, it wasn't serious gambling. We were just killing time in a station shack, waiting out the first storm of the wet."

"This was found at the station," Wing said.

He drew a frayed, worn piece of paper from the center desk drawer. He handled the paper very carefully, holding it by the corner as though to avoid smudging it . . . or leaving fingerprints.

Cole leaned forward and read the faded writing.

I owe Cole Blackburn half of Sleeping Dog Mines Because I lost at 2-up one too many times!

Abe Windsor's signature and the date were written across the bottom of the sheet in a fine, formal Victorian hand.

"The Chen family has taken the liberty of having

two handwriting experts certify this document, so you need not fear embarrassment on that score," Wing said calmly. "Even without the note, it is a legitimate gambling debt. With the note, the debt will be promptly recognized by the Australian government when you press your claim."

"But I won't," Cole said, his voice soft and final. "Crazy Abe is sly and mean as a snake in the blind, but he has never screwed me. He fed me, gave me a place to sleep out of the rain, and as much beer as I could swim in." Cole's voice changed, becoming more matter-of-fact. "I've seen Sleeping Dog One. That hole is never going to produce anything but bort. And if the old man has found a jewel box in one of the other Dogs, he's welcome to it. I sure as hell am not going to try and screw him out of a lifetime strike in the name of a gambling debt I never took seriously."

"Crazy Abe doesn't need his mines anymore. His body was discovered in the bush yesterday."

Cole looked away for a moment. When he looked back, his eyes were the color of winter rain. "God grant a quiet rest to that unhappy old bastard. Going walkabout with him was like stepping back in time, a century at least, sometimes more like ten centuries. He was a real primitive, despite his Continental education."

"So I gather from reading his poetry. There is much of it, all bad."

Wing produced a battered tin box from the belly drawer of his desk. Inside were several documents and a supply of the rough paper on which they had been drafted. He picked up one of the documents and scanned it quickly.

Cole smiled crookedly. "He wrote it by the yard. Which one is that?"

"Something called 'Chunder from Down Under.' I am told that the late Mr. Windsor regarded this particular piece of doggerel as a kind of rhyming treasure map, a guide that would lead his heir to the diamond deposit."

"What?"

"The key to locating the lost mine is hidden somewhere in this swamp of rhyme and memory," Wing said, handing the sheets across the desk.

Cole scanned the closely packed lines. He read at random:

> "'While 'roos and rutting gins
>   Leap on the ground above,
>   A handful of old candy tins
>   Rattle around below.' "

He looked up. "The 'candy tins' is an interesting —er, metaphor, but as a treasure map it leaves a lot to the imagination."

"There's more of it," Wing said, trying and failing to keep the hope from his voice. "But I'm afraid it's all abstruse and arcane."

"Or simply insane. They didn't call him Crazy Abe because they couldn't think of another name. That old man didn't just march to his own drummer— he had his own bloody band."

Wing sighed. "We suspected as much. We were rather hoping the poetry would mean something special to you."

"And if I find this mine, under the contract I just signed, half of my interest is yours, as co-owner of

BlackWing Resources Ltd. In short, the Chen family thinks I'm going to find Crazy Abe's jewel box for you."

Wing nodded once.

"Then you just lost a ten-million-dollar gamble," Cole said calmly. "The jewel box may exist, but it sure as hell wasn't in Sleeping Dog One. It's a pipe mine, not a placer pocket. Dog One's diamonds haven't been washed out of the lamproite. Getting them out is a hammer-and-blast job, and then you have to crush the lot to get to the diamonds. You'll get sharp-edged junk. Ninety-five percent of it is bort."

Wing remained impassive. Cole made an impatient noise. His new partner just didn't understand the difference between the extraordinary, exquisite stones in that worn velvet bag and the largely worthless crap that Crazy Abe had gouged from his Sleeping Dog Mines. Like most people, to Wing diamonds were diamonds—the emperor of gems, the most valuable stone on earth.

"Wing, the biggest diamond Abe ever got out of Dog One was maybe fourteen carats, flawed, fractured, and the color and clarity of bad coffee."

Wing said nothing.

Cole leaned forward. "You aren't listening to me." He pulled the contract out of his breast pocket and tossed the document on the desk. "Rip it up, and while you're at it, burn that forged IOU. I'm not interested in screwing the Chen family out of ten million dollars."

"We consider it an investment."

"In bort?" Cole asked sardonically.

"In the future."

Cole realized that Wing was serious, which meant

that the Chen family was willing to spend millions on a long shot. There could be only one reason for a gamble of that magnitude. Someone was convinced of the existence of the jewel box.

"What makes you think I can find that mine after the Chen family and all its resources have failed?" Cole asked.

"What makes you think we have failed?"

Cole's expression was both cynical and amused. "You wouldn't be calling me in if you had a chance in hell of success on your own. We were partners, but we never were million-dollar buddies. I know you. You know me. Cut the bullshit and tell me what's going on."

"Mr. Windsor's heir is a girl. A woman."

"There's a big difference between a girl and a woman," Cole said dryly.

"Only to an American." Wing shrugged. "To me she is a female manqué."

"Lacking what?"

"A man."

"Haven't you heard? A modern woman needs a man like a snake needs snowshoes."

Wing laughed softly. "She isn't one of those cold females who want only power. She was engaged once. Presumably, her appetites are normal, if rather suppressed at the moment."

"What happened?"

"Officially the man decided he wasn't ready for marriage."

"Unofficially?"

"He was a spy, a Soviet intelligence agent who tried to use the girl to gain access to secret information. Her father and brother are American intelligence agents. All that was almost seven years ago. She was twenty at the time. She has stayed away from men since.''

"Smart woman.''

"There are lessons to be learned from the past.'' Wing hesitated, then added delicately, "This young female may have learned caution too well. The same can probably be said of you.''

Cole's mouth flattened into a thin line. He and Wing both understood that the remark referred to Chen Lai, Wing's sister, a woman of exquisite form and infinite betrayal.

"I learned long ago that diamonds are more enduring than women.''

"And more alluring?'' Wing suggested.

Cole said nothing.

"If a woman was all that stood between you and 'God's own jewel box,' what then?''

For a moment Cole thought about the shimmering green diamond. There was an extraordinary rarity and beauty to the stone that transcended whatever monetary value man might put on it.

Without waiting for an answer, Wing reached into his breast pocket and withdrew a palm-sized picture. He slid the glossy color photo past the diamonds to Cole, who glanced at the picture as a poker player would look at his last card—with a single, comprehensive, expressionless glance.

The woman in the picture had long, lustrous mahogany hair. Where the sun struck it, deep auburn fire burned. Her skin was neither brown nor pale, having instead a golden cast that suggested time spent outdoors in active movement rather than lying oiled and passive on a beach. Her mouth was well defined, full, and smiling. Her eyes were a luminous shade of green that made Cole think of the diamond.

Then he thought of what Wing had said about a girl and a woman manqué.

"Manqué? I don't think so," Cole said. "This is quite a woman. Look at the subtle tension in her expression, a kind of elemental animal wariness watching from the depths of her eyes. There is innocence, too, an untouched quality, a gut honesty left over from a time before language came with its structure of truths . . . and lies."

Wing's eyebrows rose. "It's a good portrait, but not that good."

"I know her," Cole said simply.

"What? How?"

"I've never met her, but I know her work. I recognize her from the jacket photo on her book, *Arctic Odyssey*. On the book, her last name is given as Shane, not Windsor."

"Erin Shane Windsor," Wing said. "She is the great-niece of Abelard Windsor."

For a moment Cole was very still, remembering some of the woman's photos and at the same time hearing in his mind the eerie harmonics of wolves on the frozen tundra. The songs of wolves sang a truth known only to wild animals and restless men. And to a few women. Very few. Erin Shane Windsor was one of them. He had sensed it in her photographs. It had caught him, held him, shaken him.

Discovering *Arctic Odyssey* had been one of the few pleasures in Cole's recent life. Even in memory, the intense sensuality revealed in the photographs remained vivid, textures of ice and sunlight and velvet shades of color that cried out to be touched. He had been struck by something else in the photos, as well. The photographer had an unflinching appreciation of the balance of death and life, darkness and sun, ice and heat. The photographs had been powerful rather than sentimental, intelligent rather than ingratiating. They had spoken to him on a level that bypassed civilization and language and lies.

"Don't bet ten million bucks that I'll be able to seduce Erin Shane Windsor," Cole said. "Her photos suggest that she is neither stupid nor naïve, and a woman this attractive isn't likely to be bored."

"Whether you seduce her or not is your choice. Your job will be to keep her from getting killed while she unravels Crazy Abe's secret or until you find the mine yourself. After that, Miss Windsor no longer matters. Only the mine itself is important. That must be protected at all costs."

"Even at the cost of Erin Windsor's life?"

"Her life. Yours. My own. Next to that mine, nothing else is important. Nothing."

Cole gave Wing a measuring look. Those words sounded less like the owlish graduate of Harvard than like Chen Li-tsao, Wing's uncle. Chen the Elder was a man capable of minimizing the cost of a human life in his power equations. But Wing had not been like that. He had always seemed more gentle, softened by his Western education, as Cole had heard Uncle Li complain more than once.

Apparently Wing had changed in the past five years.

"The Chen family has been working on this a long time, haven't you?" Cole asked slowly.

"Ever since we became certain the Brits were going to abandon Hong Kong to mainland ideologues.

One of my uncles has been living with Abelard Windsor for longer than you have known him.''

Cole rummaged through his visual memories. "The cook. The one Abe always called 'the bloody ugly wog.' The cook was there the night we got drunk. That's how you found out about the gambling debt."

Wing made no response.

Silently Cole let new understanding crystallize around the new facts. The answer was both inevitable and rather breathtaking.

"I'll be damned," he said softly, looking at Wing with new appreciation. "You're going to buck the diamond cartel. I knew the Chen family was ambitious, but I didn't think they were quite ready to take on the world."

"Not the world. Simply Consolidated Minerals, Inc."

"No difference, Wing. A cartel that can hold Uncle Sam and the Soviets by the same short hairs can squeeze the nuts off a Hong Kong clan."

"And the reason the cartel has such power is diamonds," Wing said coolly. "In their implication for the balance of international power, diamonds are as pivotal right now as the atomic device that was exploded at Alamogordo almost a half century ago. But unlike a bomb, diamonds are subtle. Leverage rather than annihilation."

Cole smiled thinly. "The waterhole theory of power. It's not what you own but what you control."

Surprised, Wing said, "Exactly. Diplomacy rather than war. Indirection rather than attack. Diamonds give control without engendering national enmity, for who can hate the emperor that is neither heard nor seen nor named?"

"I can name it. The diamond tiger. Be careful, Wing. You could fall off and get eaten."

"Or I could ride and be ruler," Wing said.

"That's always the lure, isn't it?"

"You should know. You have ridden before."

"Not really," Cole said, shrugging. "Not the way you mean. I don't give a damn for international power games."

"But you have played them in the past, and you have played very, very well."

"Only until I figured out how to get people to leave me alone," Cole said.

Wing smiled faintly. "Only Americans believe they are free. It gives them a certain—ah, piquancy as a race."

Ignoring the other man, Cole looked at the photo of Erin Shane Windsor. Before he had been asked to choose, Cole would have said without hesitation that Crazy Abe's placer diamond mine was worth whatever it took to secure it.

But now Cole was being asked to make the choice, and the answer was as unexpected as the green diamond had been: The life of a woman who was able to create *Arctic Odyssey* was worth a good deal more than Wing thought it was. With that realization came another: If Erin Shane Windsor was to survive being Crazy Abe's heir, she would need all the help she could get.

Cole knew the Chen family. If Cole turned down Uncle Li's offer, the clan would forge a new IOU, using it as bait for the next prospector on their list, a prospector who probably wouldn't appreciate wilderness photographs of the sort that could put a man in touch with his own soul.

Without a word Cole took the IOU and the picture of Erin from the desk. He put the two pieces of paper in his pocket, careful not to look at the photo again. He didn't want to sense the innocence that lay as deeply within Erin Shane Windsor as her wariness. Whether she knew it or not, a place had been reserved for her aboard the diamond tiger, where there was only one rule: Don't fall off, for those who fall get eaten, bones and all.

And the innocent are always the first to fall.

"All right, Wing. Tell Uncle Li he has his man."

5

◆

COLE BLACKBURN'S QANTAS FLIGHT HAD BEEN
forced to land from the west because the Santa Ana
wind was blowing over the Los Angeles basin. Now,
four hours later, the wind had begun to abate. The
San Gabriel mountains at the east edge of the basin
could still be seen clearly, but the smog that had been
pushed out to sea was beginning to filter back into the
high-rise canyons of the city center. Pollution turned
the late-afternoon sky a peculiarly unappealing shade
of orange.

Cole tried to rub the fatigue of two trans-Pacific
airplane flights from his eyes as he studied the central
city from his thirty-eighth-floor window. The queen
city of the Pacific Rim was spread around him like an
architect's rendering. Close by were the international
headquarters of half the money-center banks of the
Southwest, as well buildings wearing the logos of the
most powerful of the Seven Sisters. Unlike the diamond cartel, the rulers of the world oil trade were
welcome to operate in the United States. Cole knew

the two cartels were indistinguishable in operation; the sole difference between them was that oil was an essential and diamonds were a luxury.

Just beyond the tall buildings, in a four-block stretch along Hill Street, was the Jewelry Mart, a mélange of aging business buildings and gleaming new high-rises. The Jewelry Mart was second only to Manhattan in importance to the gold and gemstone trade.

The handful of diamonds in Cole's briefcase would be like a grenade thrown into the midst of those *diamantaires.*

Smiling at that prospect, he closed the long metal window blinds to shut out the distractions of the city, then reached once more for the coffee mug, hoping that caffeine would help him to focus. He felt faintly disoriented, as though he had left part of his mind somewhere over the empty Pacific.

He began rolling up the maps that he had spread on the broad hardwood table and returned them one by one to their tubes in the storage rack. He had spent most of the last two hours studying the best Western Australia maps at BlackWing, looking for some hint of a suggestion, the faintest of clues to help locate the source of Crazy Abe Windsor's diamond mine. The search had been futile. BlackWing's maps were designed to locate metallic ore claims—iron or nickel, uranium or gold. They supplied few of the fine geological details that would help him find diamonds.

Cole looked at his watch, but what caught his eye was the copy of *Arctic Odyssey* that lay open on the desk. He had turned to the book repeatedly in the past twenty-four hours, as though it would somehow help him to understand the woman he was about to meet. The photograph that most haunted him covered two pages. It showed dawn and tundra, ice and nesting geese. "Uncertain Spring" could have been a trite depiction of seasonal regeneration, but it wasn't. Instead, the photo showed an arctic dawn in which life hung on by a bloody fingernail.

Slowly Cole ran his fingertips over the picture, as though he could feel as well as see it. The photo captured a freezing summer dawn. In the background, seen through low streamers of windblown snow, more ghostly shapes than living flesh, adult geese were flattened protectively over nests.

And in the foreground of the picture, beneath a shroud of ice, lay a gosling that would never feel the warmth of the rising sun. The small creature's death was agonizing, as was the beauty of the new day and the determination of the adult geese to save their remaining goslings.

Looking at the picture, Cole knew that Erin Windsor had discovered the fragility, even the absurdity, of life. He only hoped she had learned something about the value of life as well, her own included. If she had, she would be happy to take BlackWing's offer—three million dollars for her interest in an Australian diamond mine that might not even exist.

He wondered if Erin Windsor would recognize the danger of being owner of a unique diamond mine whose output ConMin could neither control nor counter with the contents of their huge London vault. Certainly Matthew Windsor would know the danger to his daughter. Any professional intelligence analyst would be able to calculate such a cost down to the last bit of money, adrenaline, and blood.

Cole hoped that, at twenty-seven, Erin would still listen to her father's advice. If she did, she would be

satisfied with BlackWing's offer. If not, there would
be hell to pay, and Erin would be the one paying it.

He glanced at his Rolex, then at the battered tin
box with its burden of priceless gems and worthless
poetry. He slipped the tin box into a briefcase secured
with a combination lock and fitted with a steel handcuff. With a wry smile he clicked the cuff into place
around his left wrist, knowing that he was more the
briefcase's prisoner than vice versa. Then he left the
office, locking the door behind him.

The thirty-eighth floor of the BlackWing Building
contained the executive offices. The building was expensive and discreet, like BlackWing itself. Cole took
the elevator down to street level and reentered the
push and pull of the everyday world in downtown Los
Angeles. The other offices in the building were dis-
charging their nightly complement of commuters. The
lobby was crowded with clerks and craftsmen and
brokers.

Cole and the chained briefcase attracted no attention. Besides BlackWing, the building housed dozens
of gemstone wholesalers and jewelry dealers. Men of a
dozen nationalities and all races came and went fre-
quently, carrying similar briefcases. It was another
sign of the care with which Chen Li-tsao had been
positioning BlackWing for its assault on the diamond
tiger.

A black Mercedes limousine waited at the curb,
its driver leaning against the gleaming front fender,
waiting with a look of professional indifference on his
face. When Cole emerged from the building, the
driver straightened and moved to open the rear door
of the limo.

"Good afternoon, Mr. Blackburn. Still going to Beverly Hills?"

"Yes."

The driver was young, athletic, Chinese, and had hands calloused by martial arts. He spoke with a relaxed southern California accent. Cole knew without looking at the driver's license that one of man's names would be Chen. A branch of the Chen family had been established in America since 1849.

The driver ignored the Santa Monica Freeway, where afternoon traffic was already beginning to congeal. Keeping to the surface streets, the limousine reached Beverly Hills in twenty minutes. The lights were just starting to come up in the high-rises along Wilshire Boulevard and the boutiques of Rodeo Drive when the limousine pulled under the awning of the Beverly Wilshire Hotel and stopped. A uniformed bellman opened the back door.

"I could be awhile," Cole said to the driver.

"I'm yours for the duration. I'll be here whenever you're ready."

Cole didn't doubt it. The Chens would keep an eye on their ten-million-dollar gamble.

6

◆

ERIN WINDSOR LOUNGED UNHAPPILY IN A BRO-
caded armchair at one corner of the crowded lobby,
watching the jet-setters and the Hollywood groupies
pouring into the stately hotel. She would have preferred some place less grand than the Beverly Wilshire, and some location less ostentatious than Beverly
Hills, but the law firm had booked the suite. Apparently they hoped to impress her. The thought amused
Erin. Even though she had decided to leave the arctic,
she still found civilized ostentation more boring than
amusing and more irritating than either.

To help the time pass, she tried to imagine herself
as the owner of a remote ranch in Australia. Although
she was fascinated by the Pacific Rim, she had never
visited Australia. Now James Rosen, the family lawyer
who owned a lucrative practice in Century City, had
informed her that she was the owner of a "station"
and a set of mineral claims, all of which were the legacy of a man named Abelard Windsor, a great-uncle
she hadn't even known she had. Rosen had been able

to show her the location of the Windsor holdings on maps and had even managed to dredge up some travel-guide photos of the state of Western Australia to show her.

The photos made clear that the Kimberley Plateau was not a hospitable place. It was home to a rack-of-bones breed of beef cattle called Kimberley short-horns, and to exotic fauna that included kangaroos, long-tailed birds of prey called kites, and highly poisonous snakes called mulgas. On the whole, Erin was pleased by the absence of civilization, particularly as she was on the edge of condemning herself to an indeterminate sentence in Europe.

Rosen's information, however, was sketchy. When he tired of her questions, he told her that Cole Blackburn, the courier who was delivering Abelard Windsor's will, would undoubtedly have answers.

Idly Erin scanned the crowd again, wondering what Cole would look like. Rosen had known little about Cole except that he was a geologist who represented the law firm involved in the administration of the Windsor estate, a major firm with offices in Australia and in Hong Kong. When pressed, Rosen admitted that the situation was unusual but hardly a cause for alarm. The other law firm had excellent credentials.

Even so, Erin had purposely chosen a vantage point screened by the crowds in the lobby so that she might be able to pick Cole out before he spotted her. Her decision was not entirely conscious; she always tried to structure encounters with male strangers so that she was not taken unawares. Part of the reason was her natural reserve. Part was a caution learned at great pain.

The lobby was full of travelers with luggage and business people with expensive leather briefcases. Many of the men were tanned and prosperous-looking, but none of them stood around looking from face to passing face like strangers meeting unknown appointments. For a moment Erin thought the casually dressed, long-haired blond man with the oversized leather rucksack might be Cole. The man had the tanned, outdoorsy look that field geologists in Alaska had. He was handsome, with fine features and a gentle smile, the sort of quiet modern male who understates his masculinity. He was the sort of man Erin found herself with much of the time when she was in the world of New York and Europe.

The young man had been standing near the reception desk for a few minutes, scanning the crowd, waiting for someone. Erin was about to leave her blind and introduce herself when a dazzling middle-aged woman in evening clothes threw herself into the young man's arms. Erin saw little television in Alaska but she immediately recognized the woman as the bitch star of an enormously popular weekly series. In person, she looked at least a decade older than her escort.

The couple chatted for a moment, then walked arm in arm toward the lobby bar where a party was already under way. Erin thought the actress clung to the young man in a peculiarly possessive way, displaying him in the manner of a woman leading a small dog in a show. If the young man disliked it, he kept that fact to himself.

But then, lapdogs aren't noted for their teeth.

Erin's wry thought didn't show on her face. As the couple passed, she realized that the young man's tan was salon perfect, not a squint line on his whole smooth face. The leather rucksack was also an affectation. No bulges or scuffs marred its expensive lines. He walked like a man used getting in and out of taxis.

As soon as the couple vanished, Erin's eye was caught by a striking slash of darkness in the midst of all the glitter and gilt—a black-haired man in a black silk jacket and open-collared white shirt. His skin had been changed by sun and weather rather than by carefully applied artificial light. He walked with the unconscious grace of a healthy animal. A black leather case was handcuffed to his wrist.

He was looking right at her.

For an instant Erin's pulse accelerated with a purely female response. Then her elemental awareness gave way to an irritation that was close to anger and even closer to fear. This easy-walking man with his knowing eyes and his powerful body was exactly the sort of man she had learned not to trust. He was a predator. Like her father. Like her brother.

Like Hans.

Erin fought not to show her response to the tall stranger, because she knew she was reacting irrationally. The man was nothing more to her than a business appointment, a courier, an errand boy. He walked to the place where she sat, screened by foliage from the bustle of the lobby. Screened, but obviously not hidden. Not from Cole Blackburn.

There was no hesitation in Cole's stride when Erin came to her feet and stood waiting for him. He had had no trouble picking her out of the crowd. Her natural auburn hair burned like a campfire amid the pale candles of the rinsed, bleached, and dyed jet-set women. She was dressed in a black cotton blouse and slacks that had the relaxed appearance of clothes just taken from a suitcase. The contrast of black cloth with red hair and pale, smooth skin was arresting, but Cole suspected that the clothes had been chosen for their ability to travel rather than for any reason of vanity.

Erin took a step forward, nodding as though to confirm that she was his appointment. As she moved, Cole cursed to himself, feeling as though he had just walked into an ambush.

The static photo of Erin had told only a meager portion of the truth. There was a quality to her movements that put Cole's body on full sexual alert. He had felt nothing like it since Chen Lai with her black eyes and golden skin and hidden laughter. Chen Lai, the honeyed snare from which he had barely escaped intact, because he had given Lai more of himself than he should have, mistaking simple lust for the complex emotion of love. It was a mistake he would never make again.

As they approached each other, Cole studied Erin, looking for some sign that she was conscious of the elemental sexuality in her movements. If she was, she gave no indication of it. There were no sidelong looks to determine if the men around her were reacting to her presence. There was no careful gilding of the female surface—no artful makeup, no gleaming-red nails, no tousled hair or undone buttons. Lai's sexuality had been calculated to the last fraction. Erin's wasn't, which only increased its allure.

And her eyes were the same incredible green of the diamond that men had died for in the past and would doubtless die for in the future.

The thought made Cole smile crookedly. He had seen men die for much less tangible, much less beautiful things than a diamond that was the color of every summer God ever made. Ideology, theology, philosophy . . . none of them could be cut and polished and set to shimmering and dreaming in shades of green on a man's palm.

"Erin Windsor? I'm Cole Blackburn."

Erin's eyes widened as he stopped in front of her and she realized how big he was. Cole was accustomed to the reaction. He kept his hand extended until she recovered enough to take it.

"Mr. Blackburn," Erin said, releasing his hand immediately. "I was expecting someone—er, different. Mr. Rosen, my lawyer, called you a courier."

"I've been called worse. Is there a place where we can talk privately?"

"Is that necessary?"

He shrugged. "Not to me. I just thought you'd like to be alone when I hand more than a million dollars in rough diamonds to you."

"You're joking," Erin said, startled.

"Do I look like a stand-up comic?" Cole lifted the hand that held the briefcase, showing her the chain and handcuff that leashed it to him. "You can see the diamonds right here if you prefer, but I'd advise privacy."

Erin made her decision quickly, on the basis of survival instincts she had developed in the arctic. Considering who and what Cole Blackburn was, the risk involved in having him in her hotel room was less than the risk of taking possession of a fortune in rough diamonds in a very public lobby.

"My room is on the ninth floor," she said, turning and walking toward the elevators.

Cole followed, telling himself he was past the age

to get aroused by something as trivial as the arc of a woman's hips. His body silently, emphatically, disagreed. The elevator doors thumped softly closed, shutting out the hushed seething of the lobby. Erin gave the machine a destination. Instantly it began to rise.

"What did your lawyer tell you?" Cole asked.

"That he had been contacted by a highly reputable international law firm, which informed him that I was the sole heir of a great-uncle whose name I had never heard. I was told that a Mr. Cole Blackburn would arrive at five P.M. in the lobby of the Beverly Wilshire. He would deliver the will and answer all my questions."

"Your lawyer was half right."

"Which half?"

"I'll give you the will. But you'll have more questions than I'll have answers."

"How can you be sure?" Erin asked.

"Any woman who can take a picture like 'Uncertain Spring' asks the kind of questions that have no answers."

Surprise showed clearly in her green eyes. "You called me Windsor. How did you know I'm Erin Shane?"

"The photo on the jacket of *Arctic Odyssey.*"

The elevator stopped and the doors whisked aside. Erin looked warily at Cole, as though changing her mind about taking him to her room.

"Your first instinct was correct," Cole said matter-of-factly. "I'm not going to touch you unless you extend a platinum invitation." The elevator door started to close automatically. Cole caught it with his big hand and held it open, looking directly at Erin as he added, "And you're not in the business of extending invitations, are you?"

"No," she said evenly. "Are you always this blunt?"

"It saves time. You have about four more seconds before the elevator door starts buzzing. Your room, my limousine, or some neutral third choice?"

Erin looked at the man whose gray eyes were as clear as ice and infinitely more alive. She had the sense of being pressed to make a decision whose ramifications were totally unknown. A few years ago she would have refused all choices and gone back to the known dangers of the arctic, but a few years ago she hadn't been restless, feeling as though something vital was missing from her life, from herself. A year ago she would have been frightened by a man like Cole. Now she wasn't, not entirely. The realization gave Erin a heady sensation of being freed from a cage of her own making. It was a feeling similar to watching dawn after a long arctic night.

"My room," Erin said, walking past Cole.

When they were inside she closed the door, tossed her purse on a nearby chair, and turned toward Cole. He looked at her for a long moment, then bent and worked over the combination lock on the briefcase until it opened. Using a key that had been left inside the briefcase, he unlocked the cuff. A moment later he pulled out a tin box, removed a worn velvet bag, and handed the box over to Erin.

"Abe's will was holographic," Cole said. "It's on top but it's pretty simple. It leaves everything he owned to you. Most of the rest of the papers are covered with doggerel."

Erin blinked. "Poetry?"

"Not as far as I'm concerned."

Cole's tone drew a smile from Erin. "Not much good, huh?"

"I don't want to prejudice you. You might like it. After all, some people like goanna charred whole in a campfire."

"Goanna?"

"Lizard."

Erin smiled wryly, remembering some of the things she had eaten in the arctic. She took the will and began to read it, frowning over the spidery, faded writing.

I, Abelard Jackson Windsor, being of sound mind and body, do hereby bequeath all my worldly possessions and mining claims to Erin Shane Windsor, who is the daughter of Matthew McQueen Windsor, who is the legal son of my brother, Nathan Joseph Windsor.

With the exception of thirteen rough diamonds and the papers in this box, all my possessions and claims are to be held in trust for Erin Shane Windsor until (1) she has been physically present on the Windsor station for a minimum of eleven months of every year for five years or (2) until she finds the mine these diamonds came from, whichever occurs sooner.

In the event that neither (1) nor (2) occurs, my possessions are to be given to charity (with the exception of the thirteen diamonds, which in any case belong to Erin Shane Windsor), and my mining claims are to be forfeited.

Signed Abelard Jackson Windsor
Witnessed by Father Michael Conroy

Erin: Trust no man who deals with ConMin,
He'll sell your soul for a handful of tin.

Your heritage is a jewel box
Kept beneath stone locks.
Poetry will show the ties.
Goodbye, my Queen of Lies.

And I am the King.

Erin read the document again, then gave Cole an odd look.

"Questions?" he asked.

"ConMin? Is that what I think it is?"

"Consolidated Minerals, Inc."

"Diamonds," she said succinctly. Her gaze went to Cole's briefcase for a moment.

"That's the most famous aspect of ConMin's holdings," he agreed. "But diamonds are only part of it. ConMin also deals in everything from iron ore to rare earth elements. Their speciality is strategic minerals. ConMin is the most powerful, most lucrative, and most discreet cartel on the planet."

Erin flipped through the poetry quickly, then returned to the will and read aloud, " 'Trust no man who deals with ConMin,/He'll sell your soul for a handful of tin.' "

Cole didn't react.

"Are you employed by ConMin?" Erin asked.

"No. I don't like working for anyone."

Erin digested that for a few seconds, then smiled slightly. It was a point of view she shared. "Is that why Abe sent you?"

"Your great-uncle didn't send me. I haven't seen him in years."

There was silence, then the sound of papers being shifted while Erin scanned the sheets of doggerel again.

"Are you a lawyer?" she asked, without glancing up from the papers.

"I'm a diamond prospector. Do you know anything about diamonds, Ms. Windsor?"

"They're hard, they're expensive, and they're rare."

"And some of them are extraordinary," Cole said softly. "Some of them are well worth killing for."

Erin measured him for a long moment of silence. "Are my great-uncle's diamonds extraordinary?"

"All the stones I saw of his were bort, which is the lowest grade of industrial diamond, which is the lowest grade of diamond, period."

"Worthless?"

"Not quite. But nothing to make my pulse leap, either."

Wryly, Erin wondered just what it would take to disturb this very controlled stranger. "Then my great-uncle's diamonds aren't extraordinary at all, are they?"

"Hold out your hand."

"What?"

"Hold out your hand."

"Why?"

"Just do it, Ms. Windsor."

"Go to hell, Mr. Blackburn."

His expression didn't change.

Erin had the feeling she had been tested in some way she didn't understand. She had no sense of whether she had passed or failed or would be tested again.

Moving with a deftness surprising in such a big man, Cole opened the worn velvet bag and poured the contents out on his own palm. Erin watched as light slid and shimmered over the marble-size objects as though they were wet or oiled. Most of the stones were colorless. Several were a deep, lovely pink. One was a green so pure it looked like condensed, concentrated light.

Automatically Erin reached for the green stone, then stopped, looking up at Cole's eyes. For the first time she realized that his eyes weren't a colorless gray. Tiny shards of pale blue and green and silver radiated out from the pupils in a subtle display of color that was mesmerizing.

"Hold out your hand," he said softly.

This time she didn't hesitate.

Cupping Erin's smaller hand in his own, Cole poured the stones into her waiting palm. There were muted crystal sounds when the stones moved against one another.

"These can't be diamonds," she whispered.

"Uncut, unpolished, extraordinary. They're diamonds, Erin. And they're yours, for better or for worse."

Silently she picked up diamonds at random as though to assure herself of their reality. She held first one, then another, up against the overhead light. The stones were transparent. They drew light the way a magnet draws iron.

"They're vsi or vvsi, or flawless," Cole said.

"What?"

"Very small imperfection or very, very small imperfection."

"I wasn't looking for flaws. It's just . . . the colors," she said, awed. "My God, I didn't know that colors like this existed short of rainbows and lasers. So pure. So damned *pure.*"

"You should look in your mirror more often."

"Why?"

"The green is a dead match for your eyes."

Erin's head came up at the personal comment. Abruptly she realized she was standing very close to a man she didn't know, his hand was cupped beneath hers, and his breath was mixing with hers in an intimacy that should have frightened her. For the space of one shared breath, two, three, she waited for fear to spread through her body, a fear that had been brutally beaten into her seven years ago.

All that happened was an increase in Erin's pulse rate that came not from fear but from an equally elemental response to being close to a man she found attractive. The realization that she was once again capable of physical response went through Erin's mind like sunrise through night, changing everything it touched.

"Which of Abe's mines did those diamonds come from?" she asked, her voice low, almost husky.

"I don't know."

"Are there more like these?"

"I don't know."

"Does anyone?"

"I don't know."

Erin looked at the powerful, impassive stranger who was still standing close to her. "What *do* you know, Mr. Blackburn?"

"That I prefer to be called Cole."

She retreated across the room, opened the curtains, and looked out over the glittering city that was condensing from the darkened sky.

"What do you know about the source of these diamonds, Cole Blackburn?"

"They are probably Australian, but not from any known mine. They have been out of the mother pipe a long, long time. The green diamond is unique. The pinks are superb. All but one of the whites is of highest quality." He paused, then added calmly, "I also know that if you keep your inheritance, you'll have to give up standing in front of windows."

Swiftly Erin turned around to face him. "What does that mean?"

"Ask your father."

"My father is a difficult man to reach. You're right here. I'm asking you."

"If I tell you," Cole said, "you'll have a thousand doubts and questions to match. If your father tells you, you'll believe him. That will save time."

"It will be even quicker if you tell me right now."

"Whoever owns the Sleeping Dog Mines is a moving target," Cole said flatly. "That means you."

"Why?"

"The colored diamonds are unique. ConMin has nothing like them in its vaults."

"So?"

"If there is a mine full of stones like yours, ConMin must control that mine's output or lose its monopoly. Monopoly is power. Right now ConMin has enough power to cut deals with First World nations, to control Second World nations as often as not, and to buy Third World nations outright. The Sleeping Dog Mines threaten ConMin's power," Cole said calmly, "and, in doing so, threaten the entrenched interests of various nations who have a stake in the diamond tiger. When you ride that tiger, the only rule is survival. ConMin has ridden for more than a century."

Erin looked at the gleaming, shimmering stones. "You make my legacy sound more like a curse than a gift."

"It is." Cole looked at his watch. "Call your father. The first thing he'll want to do is have the diamonds appraised. Make very certain that the appraiser does *not* have ConMin connections, or the appraisal will be worse than useless. I would give you the name of a reliable appraiser, but then your father would assume collusion."

"You must know my father quite well."

"I've never met him, but I've dealt with men like him. I'm one myself."

"CIA?" she asked coolly.

"No. Survivor."

When Cole looked up from his watch, Erin froze. His intensity was almost tangible. He was wholly focused on her in the same way that she focused upon her photography when she worked. At that instant she was the only thing in the world that existed for Cole Blackburn. To be the focus of such scrutiny was both unnerving and exhilarating.

"You don't like taking orders," Cole said in a soft voice, "and I don't like giving them. But I know what the stakes are. You don't. At least two people died getting those stones into your hands. I'm betting that you're intelligent enough not to defy me for no better reason than pique. If I'm wrong, I'll survive. You won't. You have a choice. Trust your father, trust me, or trust God that the next stranger through that door doesn't have a gun in one hand and a revised version of Crazy Abe's will in the other."

"I'll think about it."

"You do that, Erin Shane Windsor. Think very hard. And while you're at it, think about 'Uncertain Spring' and the baby geese that froze to death in an unexpected blizzard."

For a slashing instant Erin remembered the cruel, beautiful dawn when she had discovered the goslings lying rigid beneath their glittering shrouds. She had wept at seeing the tiny bodies encased in ice. Yet before the tears had frozen on her cheeks, she had taken out her camera to catch the brutal perfection of a time and a place and a dawn that owed nothing to man.

"Life has always defined death, and death, life," Cole said, watching Erin intently. "Anyone who understands that as clearly as you do should be able to decide how much a diamond mine that might not exist is worth—but whether or not the mine exists, owning it could cost your life. When you understand that, you'll sell your inheritance to someone who knows the territory."

"Someone like you?"

"Yes."

"What would you pay me for a mine that might not exist?"

"More than you need. Less than your life is worth." Cole turned away and walked to the door. "I'll call you at the end of the week," he said, opening the door. "If you want to reach me before then, call BlackWing. The number is in the tin box with the rest of your legacy."

The door closed, leaving Erin alone with a handful of extraordinary diamonds.

For a long time she stood motionless, staring at the rough diamonds in her palm, watching light shift and shimmer through their enigmatic crystal cores, absorbing a reality unlike any she had ever seen before.

Curious, she touched the tip of her tongue to the green stone. It was cool, clean, faintly salty. She tasted her own skin for comparison. Less salt. She tasted one of the colorless diamonds. No taste at all.

Suddenly Erin was certain that Cole Blackburn had handled the green stone more than once, had held it in his hand, smoothed his thumb over it, watched the heart of summer shimmer and glow on his palm. A strange frisson of awareness shot through the pit of her stomach when she realized that the vague saline flavor of the green diamond had come from Cole's skin. What disturbed her even more was the temptation to taste the stone again. To taste him.

With abrupt motions Erin put the stones back into the worn velvet bag. She picked up the first sheet of poetry and began to look for clues. She scanned the sheets quickly, then more slowly, frowning. When she was finished, she read the sheets again, shaking her head. None of it made sense. Although diamonds were mentioned several times, drinking, pissing, and screwing were mentioned much more often. There was no mention of a mine at all.

Muttering about crazy old men, Erin stuffed the pages back into the tin box and picked up the will again. When she finished reading it, and its warning, she felt no more at ease. Nor did remembering her conversation with Cole Blackburn comfort her.

Whoever owns the Sleeping Dog Mines is a moving target.

You make my legacy sound more like a curse than a gift.

It is. Trust your father, trust me, or trust God that the next stranger through that door doesn't have a gun in one hand and a revised version of Crazy Abe's will in the other.

Cole's words and her own echoed uneasily in Erin's mind as she stood in the silent room. Mysteries were her father's meat and wine. He lived in a world where every act was examined, cut into thin sections, put under an electron-scanning microscope, and the results argued at the highest levels of government. It was a world where every man had more than one shadow, where names changed more often than Paris fashions, where betrayal was the only reality that could be trusted. Her father's world. Her brother Phil's world. Her ex-fiancé's world.

Erin's head moved in an abrupt, negative gesture that sent streamers of her hair sliding across her cheek. Automatically she brushed the hair aside. Just as automatically she brushed aside memories that had nothing new to teach her. Treachery existed. Betrayal existed. She accepted that. But she no longer existed for them.

Seven years ago she had been a victim in an undeclared war. She was a victim no longer. She had learned to defend her body with techniques both ancient and modern. She had learned to defend her mind by discovering other worlds, incredible worlds, places where ice was alive and mountains radiated light, places where people laughed and shared their last bite of food with a hungry stranger, places where death existed, yes, but as a natural extension of life processes rather than as a premeditated act of perversion and political power.

Perhaps there was even a place out there in which the incredible green stone was real, a place where the restlessness in her body would be stilled, a place where she could trust men again.

And if not all men, than at least one.

"That's the question, isn't it?" Erin asked herself softly. "You can't answer that question alone. What's important is the future, not the past."

The phone felt cool in Erin's hand, smooth, an impossibly perfect surface against her sensitive skin. It was the thing she found most arresting about civilization, all rough surfaces smoothed into a beguiling perfection. A false perfection, because beneath the surface terrible worlds seethed, waiting for a crack through which to explode into being. The primitive world was the opposite, its rough surfaces concealing a serenity of emotion that was beguiling . . . and also, in its own beautiful way, false. Primitive and civilized shared one central truth: Death always waited for the unwary, the unlucky, or the unwise.

But life also waited, a fire burning beneath ice.

Erin punched in the telephone number that remained the same no matter where her father happened to be stationed at any given time. When the phone was answered, she spoke quietly, clearly, and hung up.

Then she sat on the bed, stared at the handful of stones that could be diamonds or glass, and waited for Matthew Windsor to be summoned by his beeper to return his daughter's call.

7

"PEOPLE DON'T WALK UP TO YOU AND HAND YOU A million bucks in a tin box. Not in the real world. Not even in the Beverly Wilshire Hotel. It's just flashy glass, baby. Next time this Blackburn guy calls he'll be selling you a map to the mine."

Erin stared at the phone she had just hung up, listening to Matthew Windsor's cool voice echo in her ears. Her father's words irritated Erin. Part of her agreed with Windsor. Another part of her believed that the stones were real, because Cole Blackburn was real.

All too real.

With a muttered curse, Erin turned away from the phone. After a few more verbal pats on the head, Windsor had agreed to make "discreet inquiries around D.C." for Erin. When—and if—he had anything interesting, he would call. She hadn't argued; as a senior officer of the Central Intelligence Agency, her father had access to every data base in the government, from the FBI to the U.S. Geological Survey.

Twenty minutes later the phone rang. The instant Erin picked up the receiver, Windsor began speaking in a clipped voice.

"Describe Cole Blackburn."

"Big," Erin said, running through a kaleidoscope of impressions in her mind. "Even bigger than Phil. Not fat, though. Hard. Caucasian. American accent. Intelligent. Confident. Moves well. Black hair. Gray eyes. Well-defined mouth, off-center smile. Faint scar along left jawline. Random scars on his hands. Big hands, by the way. Long fingers. No rings. Expensive clothes but not fancy. There's nothing fancy about the man. In all, I suspect he would make a bad enemy."

Windsor grunted. "You've got a good eye. That's Blackburn to a T."

"I'm a photographer, remember? I make my living looking at things." Erin waited. Only silence came over the line. "What's going on, Dad? Is Cole Blackburn a con man?"

"I can't go into it on the phone, baby."

Erin felt a flash of anger. Part of it sprang from her uneasiness with the world she had tried to avoid for seven years, but most of it rose from even older memories, memories of being shut out of the enigmatic world of spy and counterspy that occupied so much of her father's life.

"Did Blackburn show you any identification?" Windsor continued.

"Just himself. To a T, I believe you said. Should I believe what he told me?"

"Baby, I can't—"

"Yes or no," Erin interrupted. "One word."

"It's not that easy. I'll be in LA tomorrow. We can talk about it then."

Erin looked at the phone as though it had just grown fur. "You're coming to LA?"

"Don't sound so shocked. I haven't seen you for almost a year." His voice changed, becoming harder. "Just to make sure I don't miss you, stay put in the hotel room. Have room service take care of the food. Rest up. Do you hear me, baby?"

"Yes," she said, understanding that Windsor didn't want her to leave the room. "But I don't like it."

"I'm not wild about it myself," he said flatly.

There was a three-beat pause before Erin said, "All right. I'll be here when you get here."

"In your room."

"In my room," she said between clenched teeth.

There was the sound of air rushing, as though Windor had let out a relieved sigh. "Thanks. It means a lot to me. I love you, baby."

Before Erin could answer, the connection was broken. Windsor had told her many times that he loved her, but for the past seven years he hadn't waited to find out if she loved him in return.

Slowly Erin hung up the phone and wandered restlessly around the room, turning on lights against the darkness beyond the closed drapes, wondering why her father had insisted she stay in the room. Perhaps he would tell her tomorrow. Perhaps not. He had spent his entire life in the forest of mirrors that nation-states construct to mislead one another. Circumspection had become second nature to him. Most of his life had been conducted in places he couldn't admit to having been, not to his wife or his daughter, perhaps not even to the son who had also become an officer of the CIA.

Erin understood the necessities of her father's work, but she resented his job deeply, not only because of what it had done to her but also because of what it had done to the intelligent, thoughtful, human man she knew her father to be. Secret wars meant secret lives, and secret lives made human trust impossible. Erin wanted to trust her father, just as she wanted to trust the rest of the world.

But trusting everyone wasn't a very bright way to live and could be a very painful way to die. She had been lucky once. Next time she might not live to learn.

8
◆

LATE-AFTERNOON LIGHT BURNED THROUGH THE west-facing windows of the hotel suite. As the shafts of sunlight flowed across the rosewood tabletop, thirteen rough crystals shimmered to life. Erin Windsor stood very near the table, bent over her camera equipment, totally focused on the stones. She was consumed by the pure colors, entranced in a dazzling new world seen through the extreme close-up lens of her camera. She had spent the past day totally focused on the enigmatic, obdurate lumps of crystal.

More than once she had despaired of capturing the subtle play of light and the violently pure colors, the flashing glitter and fathomless shadows, the tiny rainbows chained among the curved hollows that high magnification revealed on the surface of the stones. When she turned them just so, light fragmented across the table. When she turned them another way, light pooled and shimmered as though the crystals were alive, breathing. When she turned the stones yet another way, light glowed from within like flame burning within ice.

"Are you really diamonds?" Erin asked, in a combination of exasperation and curiosity.

As she stood there, the afternoon light changed, deepened, becoming a golden torrent. The crystals burst into fire. For an instant Erin froze over her camera, transfixed by the changed stones. They were a song sung in silence, inhuman in their beauty, the translucent tears of a rainbow god.

Suddenly Erin didn't care if the crystals were diamond or YAG, zircon or quartz. She worked like a woman possessed, triggering the camera, shifting stones, composing shots, reloading film, driven by the stones' savage beauty and her own equally savage need to capture the instant when crystal and light became lovers, transforming each other.

Not until the light was spent within the crystals and the stones slept once more did Erin straighten and move away from the camera. Unconsciously she put her hands in the small of her back and stretched, relieving the tension of hours bent over the arrangement of lens and bellows and tripod. She felt exhausted and exhilarated at once, an explorer returning from an undiscovered land, her mind replete with new visions and yet hungry for more.

Reluctantly she turned away from the stones and looked at her watch, wondering if she should set up some fixed-light shots or if her father would arrive soon, bringing with him unanswered questions from a past she didn't want to discuss. Perhaps he would have answers for her future instead, answers she could listen to without feeling angry and betrayed.

There was a brief knocking at the door. "Baby? It's me. Open up."

At first the security locks and latches defeated Erin. Then she got the sequence correct and opened the door. Her father stood in the hallway, as tall and handsome as ever, dressed in the charcoal business suit, white shirt, and silk tie that was the male uniform in the world of business and diplomacy.

"I wouldn't mind a hug if you wouldn't," Windsor said, his mouth smiling and his eyes very serious.

There was no hesitation before Erin stepped forward and wrapped her arms around her father. He closed his eyes and hugged her in return, lifting her off her feet with the embrace.

"Hugs don't bother you anymore, do they?" he asked very softly.

For an instant, Erin looked surprised. Then she realized it was true. She no longer was fearful of being held by a powerful man.

"I hadn't thought about it, but you're right," she said, pleasure in her voice.

"That's why you're leaving the Arctic, isn't it? You're finally over that *schleimscheiber* Hans. Thank God, baby."

Before Erin could say anything, Windsor released her and stepped back. A woman stepped from the shadows where she had been waiting patiently.

"Hello, Erin Shane Windsor. I'm Nan Faulkner."

Startled, Erin took the blunt, broad hand that was being held out to her. The fingers were as firm as they were dark. Like the woman herself, the handshake was no-nonsense, controlled, and short. The business suit she wore had a narrow skirt and was a darker shade of gray than Windsor's, and she wore no tie. She was a solid presence, buxom and broad without being fat. A thin black cigarillo smoked in her left hand. The same hand held a black box with a single gauge on the surface and a wand plugged into the side.

Windsor was the last one through the door. He secured the various locks without a fumble. Faulkner took one look at the stones shimmering on the table and swore.

"Holy Christ!"

In a controlled rush, she went to the table. She threw her smoking cigarillo in Erin's half-empty coffee cup, swept open the curtains to take advantage of the falling light, and switched on the black box. In rapid succession she touched the tip of the wand to stone after stone, beginning with the smallest stone and working her way up to the biggest.

"Jesus," she muttered as stone after stone registered in the diamond range of thermal resistance. Then she touched the green stone. It, too, registered in the diamond range. "Sweet . . . Jesus . . . Christ."

After she touched every stone, Faulkner shut off the machine and pulled a loupe from her coat pocket. She scanned each stone before she turned to Windsor.

"All but one of the white ones are of the first water, D, O+, River, Finest White, Blanc Exceptionnel, call it what you will," she said. "They are the most pluperfect bastards I've ever had the privilege of seeing."

"Shit," muttered Windsor.

"The colors might be irradiated," Faulkner continued, "but I doubt it. Radiation is too easy to pick up on. It's used to cover flaws or off-colors, but these babies don't have any problems worth mentioning, much less trying to hide. I'm a betting woman, and I'm betting these are high-ticket fancies."

Windsor said something beneath his breath. Then, "How bad is it?"

"Couldn't be worse. Next to these colored stones, hen's teeth are as common as sand in the Sahara."

"I don't understand," said Erin.

Faulkner set aside all the diamonds except the green one. "Take an average diamond mine. Only twenty percent of what's found is gem-quality goods. Less than one percent of the gem-quality stones will be over one carat after they've been cut and polished. In other words, less than two tenths of one percent of a diamond mine's entire output ends up bigger than a carat of gem goods. Of those, only a goddam small percentage is D flawless."

Erin blinked and looked at the diamonds. They were a lot bigger than a carat.

"I'm too old to be a top color sorter any more," Faulkner continued, "but I'd bet my firstborn that all but one of those whites is a D. D or not, the bastards are flawless. Rare diamonds. Very, very goddam rare."

Windsor grunted.

"Yeah," Faulkner said. "But that's not the worst of it. When it comes to fancies, you have to invent another word for rare. That's what makes this pile of stones so dangerous. If they were just big and flawless, ConMin would still be able to beat you into line with Namibia's stones. But Namibia has nothing like these. Nobody does. That green is absolutely unique."

After a moment of silence, Faulkner turned away from the beautiful, dangerous stones and looked at Windsor. "We should have brought a couple of marines. This is worse than anybody thought. And"—she smiled coldly—"better, too. I've waited a long, long time to get van Luik where the hair is short."

"Are you the agency's resident diamond expert?" Erin asked.

Faulkner hesitated, then shrugged. "Matt says you can be trusted. I hope he's right. At the moment I'm a government consultant to the largest American jewelry trade association. The job requires that I work with a company that can't operate directly in America because monopolies are illegal here."

Erin felt the floor shift beneath her feet as she was drawn back into the forest of mirrors that was international power politics. Her father's world. The world that had nearly destroyed her.

"Have you had them certified?" Faulkner asked, gesturing to the diamonds.

Erin shook her head.

"Good," Faulkner said. "The diamond world is wired together like a power grid. You walk into the GIA out in Santa Monica or into some little appraiser's office down on Hill Street with these stones and you'd generate a surge that would register in London and Antwerp in a matter of hours. ConMin uses computers to keep track of every important piece of rough in the world, even the ones they don't own themselves. And believe me, these are important pieces of rough."

"Why does the agency care?" Erin asked bluntly.

"Diamonds are a big cash item in the economies of a dozen nations around the world. You'd be surprised what countries will do for American dollars or Japanese yen, especially countries whose ideologies are based on Karl Marx rather than Adam Smith. When my predecessor left, he told me the world revolves on a diamond pivot," Faulkner said. "It's not always true, but it's true often enough to put the fear of God into a heathen like me."

"That's why I want you to let me handle it for you, baby," Windsor said. "I don't want you hurt again."

Erin looked at her father. For the first time she noticed the lines in his face, the heavy splash of silver in his formerly dark hair, and the circles beneath his eyes. He also looked tired and uncomfortable, as though caught between his impulses as a father and his duty as a sworn officer of an intelligence service.

"Did the diamonds come with a note or a map," Windsor asked, "or a claim register or a bill of sale, anything to indicate their origin?"

"Everything came in an old tin box that had no markings."

"Delivered by this Blackburn?"

She nodded. "He told me to have the diamonds appraised by someone not connected to ConMin." Erin glanced at Nan Faulkner. "I'm not sure you meet those requirements exactly, but at least I know your first allegiance isn't to the diamond cartel."

"Did Blackburn tell you anything else about the diamonds?"

"Only that they had belonged to Abe and that two people had died to see that I got my legacy. He told me that I would die, too, if I weren't careful. Then he told me to call you."

"I owe him a favor. So do you. He probably saved your life. Let me handle your legacy for you, Erin."

"I couldn't, even if I wanted to, which I don't. The terms of the will require that I live on the station for five years to gain final title, or until the mine is found."

"No amount of money is worth getting killed for."

"It isn't the money," Erin said quietly. "In fact, there's no guarantee I'll find a single diamond. Apparently Abe was the only one who knew where the diamond mine was, and he didn't talk before he died. He didn't leave a map, either."

Windsor refused to be deflected from his main point. "If you're not after money, why are you going to Australia?"

"It's a whole new continent. A whole new world. I want to smell it, taste it, see it, photograph it, live it."

"That's the point, baby. You could die there instead of living."

"I was told the same thing about the arctic." Erin tried to avoid a confrontation by changing the subject. "Do you know much about Abelard Windsor?"

Her father shook his head. "Dad never mentioned him."

"His own brother?"

"Things happen, Erin. Things that tear families apart."

Things like Hans Schmidt, foreign agent.

But neither father nor daughter spoke the thought aloud.

Erin got up, took the tin box from her oversize purse, and pulled out the sheaf of papers.

"Until I knew the stones were real," Erin said, "I didn't know if the whole inheritance was an elaborate hoax. Frankly, after reading 'Chunder from Down Under,' I thought Great-uncle Abe might have concocted the whole thing in some Australian rubber room. Here. Read this. Clues to finding the mine are supposed to be in it."

For several minutes the only sound in the room was that of dried, rough paper rustling as Windsor scanned a sheet rapidly, then passed it to Faulkner. He glanced up after the fifth sheet.

"Is it all the same?" he asked Erin.

"Different words, but the same."

He grunted, shuffled through the remaining pages, then took the first page from Faulkner again.

"It doesn't improve with rereading," Erin said. "I've read it and read it and read it, using all the tricks and tools I learned as an English major at the university."

"And?" Windsor asked.

"I didn't find any meanings but the obvious one. The hero eats raw croc liver, drinks, talks about black swans, drinks, pees, drinks, apparently screws everything that moves and some things that don't, eats more raw croc, pees. And he drinks. Did I mention that?"

"It could be a code or cipher of some type," Faulkner suggested. "Would you mind if we copied it and sent it to Washington for analysis?"

"I suspect an Australian might be more helpful than a code expert," Erin said. "Do you know what 'chunder' is? Poetic thunder, maybe?"

"Never heard of it," Windsor said. "My parents might have been Australian, but they never talked about their life before America."

"That's kind of odd, isn't it?"

Windsor shrugged. "Runs in the family, like chasing after a diamond mine that might not exist but could kill you anyway."

Erin's shrug was an exact match of her father's.

"Shit, baby. Why are you really doing this? What does Australia have that you don't have here? A crazy old man's mythical diamond mine? Is that what you want from life?"

"It's not a bad start," she retorted. Then she sighed and tried to put into words something she had sensed about herself but never pinned down. "After *Arctic Odyssey,* there just hasn't been another project I wanted to do. I found some peace in the arctic, but I no longer believe it's my future. Maybe Australia is. Maybe it isn't. I won't know until I go there."

"What about here in America?"

"I don't think I'd see you any less if I live in Australia than I've seen you while I was living off and on in the arctic."

"Baby—"

"That's just it," Erin interrupted calmly. "I'm not a baby. I've been making my own decisions for seven years."

Windsor closed his eyes for an instant, then opened them again, focusing on his daughter, the image of the woman he had loved and lost when a drunk driver failed to hold his lane at ninety miles an hour.

"It's all yours, Nan," Windsor said finally. "I told you she wouldn't turn it over to me."

Windsor went to stand by the window, his back to the room, clearly separating himself from whatever happened next.

"I have a child myself," Faulkner said, lighting up a thin cigarillo. "If he were in this kind of fix, I'd be standing by the window and letting your father explain the facts of life. A good man, your father. But he's personally involved, so he's not calling the shots for the agency on this one. I am."

Motionless, Erin waited while Faulkner drew on her cigarillo and blew out a streamer of smoke.

"Let's build a couple of scenarios," Faulkner said. "If we assume Abe was simply crazy and had nothing more on his station than cattle and flies, there's no problem. You'll go to Australia, and then you'll stay there or come home. No big deal. Right?"

Erin nodded.

"A pretty scenario," Faulkner said, staring out the window. "It would be nice if it were true. But I've got a gut certainty it isn't."

"Why? Just because you and my father have chosen to live in a world of conspiracies and betrayals and lies doesn't mean that my world has to be that way."

"Until you became Abe's heir, you had the choice. Now you don't. Consider this scenario. Maybe the diamonds are real but not from Australia. Maybe they were stolen from Namibia by dissidents who used them to purchase arms."

"Then how did Abe get them?"

"Does it matter? The normal route for submarine goods—smuggled diamonds—is to European or American cutting centers via Egypt. Maybe some of Abe's old prospector cronies were smugglers. Maybe they preyed on the smugglers or knew those who did. Maybe Abe was a smuggler himself. What do you think, Matt?"

"I hope to hell he was, because it would mean there was little danger for Erin in Australia. Smugglers certainly wouldn't approach her to buy or sell or hold their goods. Smuggled goods would also answer the question of why Erin was warned of ConMin. Con-Min, after all, would be the legal owners of those diamonds."

Erin didn't like what she was hearing, but there was a logic to it that she was too intelligent to dismiss.

"But that scenario still leaves open the question of Abe's 'jewel box,'" Windsor continued. "Was it simply a cache for stolen Namibian gems? If so, then Erin is in some danger if she goes to Australia, because other people—smugglers—will know about the cache."

"Your father's right," Faulkner said, turning back to Erin. "The danger to you could be finessed if Abe were just a smuggler, a conduit. You could go to Australia with a cadre of accomplished bodyguards and stage a determined, very public search of the station premises. You would find nothing. You would leave to take photographs of the outback and then fade from the picture. Nobody would ever bother you again."

A long plume of smoke rose from Faulkner's full lips.

"Here's another scenario. Assume Abe was crazy like a fox. Assume he really had God's own diamond mine hidden somewhere on his station. A mine that could yield tens or even hundreds of *pounds* of diamonds such as that handful you were given."

Faulkner watched Erin's instant disbelief followed by speculation and then by unhappy realization.

"That's right," Faulkner said, nodding. "You're talking about the kind of money that goes beyond wealth to become power. Raw political power. The kind of power that people, corporations, and nations kill for."

"I don't want that," Erin said.

"What you want and what you get aren't the same thing," Faulkner said, continuing relentlessly. "Scenario number four. Do you have any idea how many new gem-quality diamond mines have come into production in the past fifty years?"

"No."

"I do," Faulkner said. "I did a survey that's locked in a vault in Virginia right now. New mines have entered production in the Soviet Union, in Australia, and in a few African republics that can be brought to heel by the cartel. The Soviets had to invent some polite ideological fictions, but they fell right into bed with ConMin because ConMin controlled the world outlet for their stones. Australia did the same. Only a handful of mines have been discovered, though, maybe a new one every decade."

"Not surprising. Diamonds are rare."

"That's what ConMin tells us every chance it gets," Faulkner retorted. "The diamond cartel has hundreds of geologists exploring all over the world. They're the cream of the diamond geologists, the expert elite. They have never—repeat, *never*—found a diamond mine. Not once. The only new mines in the last fifty years were found by prospectors who didn't work for ConMin, prospectors working over ground that ConMin geologists had thoroughly explored. Does that suggest anything to you?"

"Either ConMin's geologists are very bad, ConMin's luck is incredibly bad, or ConMin doesn't want to find new mines," Erin told her.

"Fast, brief, and right on target. Too bad you hate your daddy's profession. I could use you—but only if you use your damned brain. Think about anonymous diamonds and warnings, ConMin, and Crazy Abe's jewel box. The diamond cartel has its hand in every new mine, anywhere in the world, that's capable of producing significant amounts of gem-quality rough diamonds. That monopoly has political as well as economic ramifications."

"The diamond pivot again?" Erin said, not wanting to believe, but finding less and less justification for doubt.

"You got it," Faulkner said. "The balance of power is just that—a balancing act. When something is that delicately poised, it doesn't take much to rock the boat. There's nothing the U.S. would like better at the moment than to get control of a diamond mine that would give us more leverage within the cartel. So would a great many other nations."

"Do you understand now?" Windsor asked quietly. "If Crazy Abe had a diamond mine, whoever owns it will find himself a moving target. I don't think you have the skill to duck quick enough, long enough. I do. Let me handle your inheritance, baby."

Silently Erin went to the window. Without consciously remembering Cole's warning, she stood to one side, able to see out without being seen. The lights of the city were like a lake lapping against the base of black mountains.

"You'd both like Cole Blackburn," Erin said finally. "He wants me out of the game too. I'm supposed to see him tomorrow, to give him my answer to his offer to buy out my inheritance."

"How much is he offering?"

"Three million dollars."

"That plus those thirteen diamonds would make you rich," Windsor said quickly. "You'd never have to do a thing you didn't want to do. How much money do you need, anyway?"

"If it's more than three million," Faulkner put in smoothly, "I know investors who would top Blackburn's offer. We'd all be a lot more comfortable with American investors than with a loose cannon like him."

The room was quiet for a moment. Erin looked at the stones on the table. Even in the dim room, fugitive light shimmered through them like whispered secrets, vanishing as she looked, reappearing along unexpected curves, then vanishing once more. The crystals fascinated her as nothing ever had, not even arctic ice.

"Thank you, but no," Erin said softly. "I'm keeping my inheritance. Every last undiscovered bit of it."

9

◆

COLE BLACKBURN SAT WITH HIS FEET ON THE MAP table, staring out over the city of Los Angeles to the darkness that was the Pacific Ocean twelve miles beyond. He was trying to interest himself in the task of plotting a new run of computer data onto the LandSat maps of Western Australia that were spread on the flat table. But he had been unable to get rid of the idea that the exercise was useless. Crazy Abe had been a dinosaur. He hadn't belonged to the twentieth century, so his secrets weren't likely to yield to twentieth-century methods.

On the other hand, there was little else Cole could do but look at satellite maps until Erin allowed herself to be bought out. *If* she allowed herself to be bought out. If not, he might have to resort to the IOU Wing had thoughtfully provided. Cole didn't like that solution, for it would keep Erin in the game. Better to buy her out and be done with it.

A glance at his watch told Cole that he had an hour to kill before Erin and her father came to

BlackWing for a meeting. Matthew Windsor's appearance wasn't surprising, but it was a complicating factor. Cole hoped that Windsor would tell his daughter to sell out rather than buck the diamond tiger.

At the same time, Cole knew that Windsor was CIA, and the CIA had a vital interest in the diamond cartel. Corporations, clans, and government institutions were all alike in one way—each required complete loyalty, the sacrifice of children, wives, and private lives to the greater glory of the collective. As a matter of principle, independent men or women had to be seduced, intimidated, bought, or removed. Independence was anathema to Consolidated Minerals, to the Central Intelligence Agency, and to the Chen family.

If Matthew Windsor was a devoted CIA officer, he would think nothing of using his daughter's inheritance as a stalking horse for American interests. If he was a truly amoral player, he would use his daughter without telling her.

Darkness was turning the windows on the thirty-eighth floor into partial mirrors. The city beyond was still there, but reflections from the room flickered across the face of the glass each time Cole moved.

And even when he didn't.

Cole's conscious mind was still registering that fact as he spun away from the desk and came to his feet in a single motion. A knife blade gleamed in his hand as he went swiftly, silently to the door joining the two rooms of the office suite.

"Impressive," a voice said from the next room, "but a pistol has more range. I'm Matthew Windsor, by the way. I can prove it if you don't mind letting me reach into my pocket."

Cole looked at the tall, solidly built man in a dark suit who was waiting in the doorway that led to the hall. The man wore an expression of well-chilled competence. He also had eyes the same shape and color as his daughter's.

"You're early," Cole said, returning the knife to its wrist sheath with an easy movement.

"Nobody knows I'm here. I'd like to keep it that way."

A tongue of adrenaline licked through Cole, quickening his whole body. "What did you do with the guard?"

"Don't worry. I didn't stuff anybody in a closet. The floor guard at the elevator was very polite. He's getting a cold glass of water so I can take my heart medicine."

"I'll see to it he's retrained. Maybe we can find a job for him in the infirmary." Cole gestured toward the hall door. "After you."

"Cautious man."

"I want to live long enough to take heart medicine."

Windsor laughed softly and went back out into the hall. Cole locked the door and jerked his thumb to the right.

"That way. Conference room is the fifth one on the left."

Windsor glanced around as they moved past suite after suite of offices. He stopped in front of the fifth door on the left, tried the handle, and stepped back. "It's locked."

"That didn't bother you before," Cole said, unlocking the door.

When Cole flipped on the lights, jarrah wood

paneling from Australia glowed in shades of cream and rust.

Windsor turned to Cole and said without preamble, "If I knew who owned you, I'd know whether to ignore you or take you out of the game."

Cole didn't comfort himself by thinking that Windsor was bluffing. Beneath that graying hair was a hard body and a mind that had twenty more years of nasty tricks to draw on than Cole Blackburn did.

"Nobody owns me," Cole said flatly. "I like it that way. That's the way it's going to stay."

"No one is that independent."

"Who's talking, Windsor? The spook or Erin's father?"

"Let's start with the spook," Windsor said. "The spook sees all kinds of red flags in the files marked Cole Blackburn. You're a killer, for one thing. You have anything to say about that?"

"Which incident bothers you?" Cole asked.

"Start with the eighteen-year-old killer, the one who went into the marines instead of going to jail for murdering a man."

Cole walked to a leather chair at one end of the conference table and sat down, wondering why Windsor was trying to get under his skin—and why it was working.

"It was manslaughter, not murder," Cole said. "A bar fight that went sour."

"Dead is dead."

"As for the marines, it used to be a fairly common sentence, where I came from."

"So you went into the marines, forward recon," Windsor said coldly. "Good outfit for killers."

"Cut the crap. You're not the one to ride me over

spilled blood. You've sent plenty of men over the fence."

"Some men like to spill blood. Some men are indifferent to it. Which are you?"

"Neither," Cole said.

After a moment Windsor nodded, as though satisfied with the answer. "Let's fill in some gaps in your file. How did you make the jump from recon marine to geologist without going to college in between?"

There was silence while Cole decided whether to answer the question. In the end he shrugged and answered because it didn't matter. "My gunnery sergeant served in a dozen countries. He learned all he could about gems and geology in every place he was. He talked about it to anyone who would listen. I was the only one. He bought me my first Brunton compass and nursed me through basic geology texts. He was a hell of a man."

Windsor nodded again. "Marcel Arthur Knudsen, right?"

For the first time, Cole looked surprised. "So that's what the M stood for. He never told me."

"He never tells anyone, if he can help it."

"How well do you know him?"

"I know people who know him," Windsor said. "There are still people in the Pentagon who think he was God's topkick. But you've done a lot of traveling since the sarge knew you. For instance, Zaire."

"Yeah, I was there." Cole smiled thinly. "How much did it cost you boys to bail Thompson out of that jail in Kinshasa?"

"The Agency wasn't as amused as you are. If the political police had found out who Thompson really was, he'd have been executed. Your little stunt nearly killed him."

Cole's smile changed, becoming as cold as his eyes. "You're breaking my heart. Thompson tried to get me killed. Damn near managed it. If he tries it again, I'll put him in the ground any way I can."

Windsor grunted. "You're even-handed, I will say. You gave the same treatment to the KGB agent in Cairo in . . . 1982, was it?"

"Was Schmelling really KGB? I thought maybe he was just a particularly filthy dealer in submarine goods."

"Full colonel in the Overseas Directorate," Windsor said.

"If I'd known that, he would have ended up another one of those bodies you seem so worried about."

"That would have been unfortunate. He was doubled, working for us at the same time. Hell, Schmelling was more valuable than Thompson ever thought of being."

"Not to me. He was about as much use as my Brazilian partner."

"The one you killed?"

"The one who stuck a knife in my back, missed anything vital, and lived to regret it."

"But not for long," Windsor said dryly.

"Two months. Long enough."

"Think you're hell on wheels, don't you?"

Slowly Cole shook his head. "I'm just a man who likes to be left alone. That annoys some people. It annoys them a lot. They start crowding, and I don't like being crowded, and things go from sugar to shit real fast. So why are you crowding me, Windsor?

Does the CIA want me to get out of its picture? Has the agency decided to preempt Erin's inheritance?"

"I don't know. All I know is that I don't like a lot of what I saw in your file. You're lethal and you're unreliable. Nobody has ever figured out how to control you, except maybe that sour old gunnery sergeant in the marine corps. I'd just as soon you didn't come anywhere near my daughter."

"I'm not lining up to be your son-in-law. I'm just trying to buy Crazy Abe's mineral claims."

Windsor hesitated, drew a deep breath, and let it out. "That's the problem, Blackburn. I don't think Erin is going to sell. She won't take help or direction from me, and she won't divest herself in favor of investors put forth by the agency. She's got the bit in her teeth and there's damn-all I can do about it."

For an instant Cole wasn't sure whether to swear or cheer. He had guessed that Erin was a woman who answered to herself and for herself, a person who chose her restraints as carefully as he did himself. But even while the maverick in Cole cheered a kindred spirit, the pragmatist in him swore quiet, unhappy oaths. Erin's love of freedom could cost her life.

Not to mention Cole Blackburn's.

"Shit," he said, his eyes narrowed against a combination of anger and admiration that surprised him.

"Yeah," agreed Windsor. "Shit. My daughter is lovely, talented, and bright, but she knows zip about bucking nations and corporations. As a matter of fact, up to now she has structured her life with total privacy in mind."

"Do you blame her?"

"No. There are times I'd like to retire from the world myself. But I didn't just inherit the Sleeping

Dog Mines. Erin did. If she won't sell her inheritance, she'll have to live with the real world.''

"Or die with it."

"I'd like to avoid that. What about you?"

"I think the woman who created *Arctic Odyssey* is worth more than her weight in fancy diamonds."

There was a moment of startled silence before Windsor laughed. "They were right. You're a real loose cannon."

"Who is 'they'?" Cole asked dryly. "The spooks you work for?"

"Among others." Windsor hesitated before continuing. "I've been with the CIA for thirty-two years. I've had to do some hard things in that time, but I'm proud of my agency, of my record, and of my country."

Cole made a neutral sound.

"This is the first time in my entire career that I've put my own interests and those of my family ahead of the agency's," Windsor said simply.

Cole suspected the other man was telling the truth. But Cole also understood that Windsor was a trained, experienced, and skillful operator of covert schemes.

"That's very uplifting," Cole said blandly. "But you're forgetting I know what you do for a living."

The other man smiled grimly. "I spent a long night last night, reading and rereading your file. In some ways, the important ones, we're a lot alike. You've never betrayed a friend or forgotten an enemy. I want Erin to be your friend. I want you to help her even if she won't sell you Abe's claims. In return I'll do everything I can to help you. I won't betray the agency, but I'll cut every corner I can as long as I can

—information, logistical support, whatever you want. When the time comes that Erin is ready to move on to something else, I'll guarantee you the inside track on the sale of her claims. Just keep her alive."

"I'll do what I can."

For an instant Windsor was furious. Then he looked at Cole's pale crystalline eyes and realized he meant every word. He would do what he could.

"All right," Windsor said softly. "But there are a few things I still don't understand about you."

"Do they matter?"

"They might. How did you get hold of Abe's will?"

Cole shook his head.

"That's what I thought," Windsor said coldly. "So maybe you can tell me this: How can a man who prizes his independence so goddam much belong to one of the most ruthless tongs in Asia?"

"Easy. I don't belong to the family of Chen."

"Do they know that?"

"Not my problem."

"It will be if you make the mistake of thinking Erin's interests in this are identical to the Chen family's."

"I don't give a damn about Uncle Li's interests," Cole said matter-of-factly.

After a moment Windsor nodded curtly. "Good. That saves me the trouble of taking you out of the game and finding someone else to look for Erin's diamonds, someone I'd control. There are a half-dozen good geologists in the agency."

"Baker is the only one who could find shit on a tablecloth," Cole said, "and he's on loan from Con-

Min. If the CIA ever really wants to find a diamond mine, give me a call."

Windsor smiled and said softly, "I just did, didn't I?"

The door opened and closed and Cole was alone in the conference room. He took a long breath, let it out soundlessly, and wondered how a much younger Erin had found the guts to go against her old man.

10

◆

ERIN WAS ON HER WAY OUT OF THE HOTEL ROOM
when the phone rang. She answered, expecting either
her father or Nan Faulkner, who had quietly insisted
on coming to the meeting with Cole Blackburn. The
faintly hollow sound of the connection told Erin the
call was long distance even before she heard the voice
of Jeffrey Fisher, her New York editor. He was her age
and one of the hottest young stars in the field of art
publishing. He was also so excited he could hardly
speak.

"How do you do it?" Fisher demanded. "You're a
witch, aren't you? You cast spells on people from your
den up there beyond the Arctic Circle. That's it.
You're a sorceress. I used to think I was the only one
haunted by your aloofness, but I can see you own the
whole world. They're dying to beat a path to your
door and cover you with wealth and glory."

"Jeff, what in the name of God are you babbling
about? Slow down."

"Slow down? No way, can't do it, no reason to do

it, and you'll be as wild as I am when you hear what just happened. It's the chance of a lifetime. It's a book that will make you the most famous photographer in the world. It's fantastic, it's incredible. It's . . ." His voice died as he searched for the word he wanted.

"Spit it out, Jeff. It's . . . ?"

"Diamonds," he said in a hushed voice.

A chill moved over Erin. "What?"

"Diamonds. You've just been invited to do a definitive—no, make that *the* definitive—book about the most glamorous thing on the face of the earth."

"Invited?" She cleared her throat. "Really? By whom? When?"

"The people who own all the diamonds in the world, that's who. Consolidated Minerals, the company that controls the output of every diamond mine worth mentioning. ConMin has decided to cooperate in the most extensive and expensive photographic study of their product ever undertaken. They want one and only one photographer to do it. Erin Shane. Apparently somebody saw your work in *Arctic Odyssey* and said, If she can do that for ice, think what she can do for the real thing."

Erin closed her eyes and thought about coincidences.

After a moment Fisher realized that Erin wasn't nearly as excited as he was. "Hey, kid, listen up," he said. "You've been out in the cold too long. It's frozen your brain. Harry Conner went nuts for the idea, especially because ConMin would be underwriting the project. He's talking a solid advance—middle six figures at least, maybe more. If you play your cards right, your agent might be able to get it to seven figures, all to the left of the zero. That would be for world rights, of course."

Erin made a sound that could have meant anything from joy to despair. "Jeff?"

"Yeah, I know, it's just too—"

"When did they call?" she asked, interrupting ruthlessly.

"Who?"

"ConMin."

"I got the first call about an hour ago, some guy with a Dutch name, Hugh van Louk or something like that. He and Harry are thrashing out the details now."

"I see."

"No, you don't, or you'd be over the moon the same way I am," Fisher retorted. "Remember that book you wanted to do years ago? Well, this is it. *Diamonds, Grit to Glitz.* This time ConMin will let you into a London sight. This time anything you want from them is yours, and they'll pay you a queen's ransom in the bargain. The timing is perfect for you. It will mean delaying your European book, but I didn't get the feeling you were exactly tearing down doors in your eagerness to do that one."

Erin listened for a few minutes longer, asked a few more questions, and hung up. She wanted to believe in coincidences but she couldn't. All she could do was wonder how ConMin had found out about her so quickly.

Maybe her father would know. Or Cole. Neither thought was comforting.

Erin arrived at the BlackWing Building ready to push as hard as she had to in order to get answers. Cole met her as she got off the elevator. As she looked at him, she realized they both were wearing the same clothes they had worn yesterday. Both shirts showed signs of having been put through a hotel's laundry-room wringer, telling Erin that she and Cole traveled the same way—light. The thought was oddly reassuring.

"Is my father here yet?" she asked.

"The guard hasn't called up for him," Cole said, neither lying nor telling the whole truth. His eyes narrowed as he noted the stark lines of tension around her eyes and mouth. "What's wrong?"

"I don't know. I won't know until I get a few answers."

Before Cole could reply, the phone rang. He picked it up, listened, and hung up. "Your father is on his way up now. There's a woman with him."

"Nan Faulkner. She has something to do with diamonds."

A few minutes later the guard returned with Matthew Windsor and Nan Faulkner in tow. Impassively the men introduced themselves and shook hands before taking seats in the conference room. Faulkner sat. Erin didn't. She turned and looked at the three other people.

"Which one of the players benefits if the fact that I'm Abe's heir gets out?" Erin asked.

"What do you mean?" Faulkner asked.

"Just what I said. Who benefits? The agency? ConMin? Cole? Me?"

"ConMin," Cole said.

Faulkner and Windsor looked at each other. "ConMin," Faulkner agreed.

Erin turned to Cole. "They're offering me a million. How much did they pay you?"

"Not a cent."

"Erin, what the hell is this about?" Windsor demanded.

She answered without looking away from Cole. "ConMin called my publisher and offered me the kind of access that most photographers would kill for. Just because I'm brilliant, they said, just because I'm the only button pusher in the universe capable of producing images for a definitive—no, *the* definitive—book on diamonds. ConMin is so thrilled with the idea that they're hinting they would underwrite a million bucks in advance."

"Jesus," Windsor muttered.

"I doubt that he had anything to do with it," Cole said. "Who called you?"

"Jeff Fisher, my editor. Harry Conner, the publisher, is hammering out the details right now. Old Harry is over the moon, and Jeff thinks he's finally going to make publishing history."

"What do you think?" Cole asked.

Erin made a dismissing gesture. "The idea's a good one. I tried to interest Jeff in doing a grit-to-glitz book on diamonds five years ago. He couldn't get me in the door at ConMin. Nothing personal. They had turned down every other photographer and publisher in New York. Company policy." She took a deep breath. "So why did they change their minds?"

"Easy," Cole said. "They must know you're Abe's heir."

"Brilliant, Mr. Watson," Erin retorted. "Of the four of us in the know, who the hell tipped ConMin?"

Nan Faulkner's chuckle was soft, almost inaudible. Erin glanced at her sharply.

"Matt, you worry too much about your little girl," Faulkner said. "She's smart enough to come in out of the rain. The good news is that the leak didn't come from the agency. Matt and I are the only ones who know, and we aren't talking."

"It didn't come from me, either," Cole said.

"Prove it," shot back Faulkner.

He shrugged. "I knew where Erin was. ConMin had to waste at least two days trying to contact Erin through her publisher, which means ConMin didn't know where she was. If they did, they would have skipped the middleman and made their offer in person. In addition, I want to buy the mineral rights Erin inherited. So does ConMin. I wouldn't give them a handful of spit."

Erin thought it over for a moment, then nodded. "All right. Then who did?"

"I don't know." Cole looked at Faulkner, then looked back at Erin. "Who made the approach?"

"A man named Hugh van Louk, or something like that."

Faulkner's breath hissed out. "That's Hugo van Luik, ConMin's number-one badass. Director of special operations for DSD—that's Diamond Sales Division—and a half-dozen ambiguous titles, all of which boil down to one job—troubleshooter. When the cartel has trouble, he shoots it dead."

"You know him?" Erin asked curiously.

"I butt heads with him every fifth Monday, all year round. As a matter of fact, I'm flying to London from here."

Cole looked at Windsor. "How long has Ms. Faulkner worked for ConMin?"

"Never, babe," Faulkner shot back. "I represent the U.S. diamond industry's interests at the advisory level, not ConMin's. There are a shitload of people in the business who'd like to have ConMin's seat on the diamond tiger. We just haven't quite figured out how to pull it off."

"Every fifth Monday," Erin said, remembering her research for the diamond book her editor hadn't been able to sell to Harry Conner five years ago. "The sights, right?"

Faulkner's sharply penciled eyebrows rose. "Right." She struck a match and held it to the tip of a narrow cigarillo. "Ten times a year, always on Mondays, the world diamond industry assembles in London and receives its marching orders from DSD in the form of allotments of rough." She blew out a pungent stream of smoke. "At my end, on the advisory level, the producer countries are informed of DSD's needs, how much rough they will buy. At the other end, the cutters and brokers—there used to be three hundred; now there are only a hundred and fifty—are shown the goods and quoted a price."

"Tell her about the negotiations," Cole said ironically.

"What negotiations?"

"That's what I mean." Cole looked at Erin. "There aren't any negotiations. It's all take it or leave it, on both sides. The diamond producers are told what ConMin's Diamond Sales Division will buy and how much they'll pay, and the cutters and brokers are told how much rough they'll buy and at what price. If they agree, they pay cash. If they decline more than once, they're never invited to a sight again, which is about the same as being cut out of the diamond business in its entirety."

"ConMin wants me to take pictures of that?" Erin asked. "If that's how they do business, they'd be smart to keep it a secret instead of inviting me to do a book about them."

Faulkner dismissed the suggestion with a wave of her hand. "They're so powerful they don't have to apologize or hide. As long as they stay outside the United States, beyond the reach of the Sherman Antitrust Act, ConMin can do business any way it wants."

"Sounds like OPEC," Erin said.

"Close," Faulkner said, nodding. "ConMin is just as high-handed as OPEC ever thought of being. The difference is that the world can get by without diamonds a hell of a lot longer than it can get by without oil. We had no choice but to break OPEC. The diamond cartel is a different matter. Diamonds are a luxury, not a necessity, or we'd have busted ConMin as fast we cracked Sheikh Yamani's brainchild. There would have been no other choice."

"If ConMin is that powerful, why are they bothering with this charade about the book?"

"Deniability," Faulkner said promptly. "The folks who run ConMin are powerful, not stupid. If you were Tiffany Anyone instead of Matt's daughter, I suspect you would have died before you got a chance to count old Abe's diamonds. But you're Matt's daughter, so ConMin has to use titty-fingers. They aren't preventing discovery of a new diamond deposit, they're sponsoring an art project. They aren't threatening your little ass, they're offering to put it in mink-lined luxury."

She sucked hard on the dark cigarillo.

"Hell, babe, by the time they're done wining and dining and waving money, you'll hand over the mineral rights and kiss their corporate cheeks in thanks for the chance. You don't *know* there's a mine out there, right?"

Erin nodded.

"And even if there is, there's no guarantee you'll find it. So ConMin has entered the game with a sure million and a career-making book versus whatever Blackburn is offering."

"Three million," he said.

"Presuming you're good for it," Faulkner said scornfully. "I'd get a Dun and Bradstreet, a Standard and Poor's and every other kind of check on this character, if I were you. He looks like trouble to me, even if his suitcoat is silk and fits like a lover. Let ConMin romance you around a little. What can it hurt? It will give your daddy and me time to get a team into Crazy Abe's station and vet the place for you." She pinned Erin with a black glance. "What about it? It makes everybody happy, except maybe Blackburn."

The silence in the room was so complete that Erin could hear the distant sound of a jet plane lifting from LAX. She looked at her father and then at Nan Faulkner. Their motives were clear and understandable, even if she didn't entirely share them. She looked at Cole, who was as enigmatic as the diamonds he had brought to her. Then she looked at her father.

"Is Cole ConMin's man?"

"I can't be certain," Windsor hedged.

"Best estimate," Erin said coolly, using language her father couldn't fail to understand.

"He's not ConMin's."

"Is Cole a diamond prospector?"

"Yes."

"A good one?"

Windsor nodded.

For a moment there was silence while Erin reviewed the options that had been outlined by her father. She still didn't care for any of them.

So she chose none of them.

Erin reached into her purse, pulled out the worn bag, opened it gently, and shook out the stones onto her palm. She admired their shifting, mysterious light for a moment, then returned all but the deep green stone to the velvet prison. Silently she looked from the diamond to the man who had handled the stone long enough to leave his taste on its time-polished surface.

"I won't sell you the mineral rights," she said to Cole, "but I'll give you one half the output of any diamond mine that you—"

"Erin, for the love of—" began Windsor.

"—help me discover on my claims," she continued relentlessly, ignoring her father's interruption. "Nobody will make you a better offer, because nobody will be willing to give up half the mine and the power it represents. To seal the bargain, I'll give you this."

She held out the green diamond, letting it shimmer and glisten on her palm. Cole whistled softly through his teeth. His eyes focused on Erin with an intensity that was almost tangible.

" 'Help you discover,' " Cole repeated. "That's means you're coming with me."

Erin nodded. "The will requires it."

"How good are you at taking orders?"

Windsor's hard laughter was all the answer anyone needed.

"Yeah, that's what I figured," Cole said. "That's not good enough, Erin. There will be times and places where I'll give orders and I'll give them once because there won't be time for explanations."

"I can live with that."

Cole smiled slightly. "Then pack for London."

"Why?"

"It will make ConMin feel better." Cole didn't say that it would make Faulkner and the agency feel better, too. "If they think they're going to co-opt you, they won't be as eager to reach for more drastic measures."

Erin didn't like it, and it showed, but she said, "All right."

"Second order. We're roommates from now until the mine is discovered or you sell out your interest, whichever comes first."

There was a time of electric silence while Erin measured the big man who was watching her.

"Do it," Windsor said flatly to his daughter. "If you're going to be so stupid as to go through with this, you'll need someone like Blackburn around."

"Suite-mates," Erin corrected, her voice clipped.

"Only if the connecting door stays open," Cole countered. "All the time, Erin. Every damned minute."

She nodded curtly, then flipped Cole the stone without warning. He caught it, his hand moving so quickly it was a blur.

"Done," Cole said.

Faulkner slanted Cole a bleak, furious look. *"Mazel und broche,* babe. I hope you step on your cock."

11

◆

Erin sat in the window seat of the new hotel room, watching darkness descend on the Los Angeles basin. She sensed the crowded streets and sidewalks around her like a heavy weight. The hotel suite with its two bedrooms and comfortable sitting area was spacious, but she still felt confined. She wasn't used to sharing her living space with another human being, especially one as large and flatly masculine as Cole Blackburn. His presence in the other half of the suite was both a lure and an irritant.

Abruptly Erin stood up, giving in to her restlessness. She paced the room, not even seeing the luxurious fabrics with their Jacobean design or the indigo richness of the carpet. Pacing wasn't enough. She felt as though she had been caged inside buildings forever. What she wanted was the vast, isolated sweep of the arctic. She would settle for the solace of the Pacific Ocean's far horizon.

When Erin appeared in the open door of Cole's bedroom, he looked up from the desk where he had

been working over the maps he had brought from
BlackWing.

"Could we . . . ?" Erin began, only to have her
voice fade.

The husky contralto of her voice made Cole's
body quicken. She sounded like a woman with a little
loving on her mind, yet she was standing in the doorway as though poised to flee at the first sign of interest
on his part. It had been that way from the beginning,
conflicting signals that kept him aware of her all the
time.

Not that he needed any help keeping her on his
own internal scope. His body had decided after one
look that it wanted to get as close as it could to Erin
Shane Windsor. He would have made steps in that
direction, if it hadn't been for her obvious unease at
sharing a suite with him. She wasn't acting like a
woman who wanted a man.

Yet she was looking at him as though she wanted
him.

"Could we . . . ?" Cole asked encouragingly.

"I need to get out. To walk. On the beach. I know
it's dark, I know you'll tell me it's not safe, but I have
to get out and I'm going to. With or without you."

There was no mistaking the staccato urgency in
Erin's voice. For a moment Cole considered his alter-
natives. If he had been certain that danger was immi-
nent, he would have tied Erin to her bed. But he
wasn't certain. ConMin was a business, not a government or a criminal clan. ConMin would try to co-opt
Erin before they tried to kill her.

And he had to admit that her presence was having an unsettling effect on him. If he stayed in the
hotel room with Erin while she was putting out all

those restless signals, he would almost certainly have a hell of a time keeping his hands in his pockets. Making a pass at her wouldn't be smart. If she wanted him, she would have to hand out a clear invitation.

She hadn't come close to that yet.

"I could use some fresh air myself," Cole said.

"Three minutes," Erin said instantly and turned back into her room, moving fast.

A bit less than three minutes later, she reappeared just as Cole was grabbing a black windbreaker from the closet. Without waiting for him, she headed toward the hallway door.

"Erin—"

She didn't even pause in her eagerness to get out. Cole crossed the room in a silent rush. Just as she opened the door a few inches, his hands shot over her shoulders and pinned the door. She made a startled sound. His powerful arms were braced on either side of her. He was all around her, surrounding her, trapping her.

Erin froze, remembering another time, another door, another big man trapping her. Memories welled up in a choking black tide, threatening her control.

"What the hell are you thinking of?" Cole demanded. "You don't just open a door and walk through like a—"

With an incoherent cry Erin turned and attacked him. The side of her palm slashed toward his throat. He barely blocked the blow in time. He deflected her knee with his thigh even as her head slammed into his jaw. Off balance, reluctant to hurt her, he went in low, scissoring her feet out from under her, pulling her down until she was flat on the rug beneath him.

Silently, fiercely, Erin struggled, using everything

she had learned in the past seven years. It was futile. Cole countered the blows with his greater strength and skill, keeping her from hurting either one of them. Quickly she realized she was wasting her strength. She went completely still and waited for him to mistake her submission for defeat.

Cole looked at the green eyes so close to his and felt a chill move over his skin.

"Erin, listen to me, I'm not going to hurt you, but I can't let you walk blithely into a hallway until I check it out. I'm not going to hurt you, honey. I'm on your side."

He repeated the words again and again while Erin watched him with feral eyes. Gradually what he was saying sank through fear to the intelligence beneath.

"I understand," Erin whispered. "You can let go of me now."

"Not a chance," Cole said instantly, his voice no longer soothing. "Not until you tell me why you were doing your best to kill me a minute ago."

"I'm sorry. I . . . panicked."

"I noticed. Why?"

Erin's voice died as she realized that Cole was holding her helpless, his body heavy over hers. She should be terrified, but she wasn't. More than his soothing words, more than anything he could have said, his restraint calmed her. She had attacked him; he had done nothing more than defend himself. Even now, despite the blood oozing from a cut on his lip and the bruise on his chin where she had butted him, he was being careful of her.

"You didn't hurt me," she whispered. "You aren't hurting me now."

The wonder in Erin's voice startled Cole, but before he could ask what she meant, she was trying to explain.

"When you slammed the door it was like Hans all over again, going to the door and he caught me and then he let go and I ran and he caught me and it happened over and over. . . ."

"Hans?" Cole asked softly, but there was nothing soft about his eyes.

For a moment she said nothing.

"Talk to me, Erin. We're going to be living in each other's pockets. I don't want to step on a land mine again."

She closed her eyes. Cole was right.

"Hans was my fiancé seven years ago. He was as big as you. As strong. Oh, God, he was so strong." Erin shuddered, then went on in an odd, flat voice. "I found him going through my father's wall safe, photographing every bit of paper. I turned around to run, but it was too late. He was so quick. Like you."

Cole waited, his pupils dilated almost as much as hers.

"When I tried to scream, Hans hit me in the throat," Erin whispered. "Then he hit my shoulders. I couldn't scream, I could barely breathe, my arms were numb, my fingers wouldn't work. Then he let me run to the door again but I couldn't open it, couldn't move my arms, couldn't make my fingers close. When he got tired of my kicking he dislocated my knees.

"Then I couldn't move, I could only feel and see, and whenever I closed my eyes he hurt me."

Erin's voice dried up and then resumed again, terrible in its lack of emotion. Cole listened despite the nearly overwhelming urge to make her stop talking.

He didn't want to hear her low voice describing just how much of a blood sport sex had been to her fiancé.

Even as Cole locked his jaw against the bile rising in his throat, he wondered at his own primitive response. He had heard worse, seen worse, the kind of savagery that is labeled inhuman because sane people don't want to believe the depths to which humanity can sink. Cole knew he shouldn't be surprised, shouldn't be appalled, and he certainly shouldn't be enraged at what had been done to Erin.

But he was.

As he listened he clenched his teeth against the turmoil of emotions ripping through him, a combination of despair and killing rage the likes of which he hadn't felt since Lai had casually aborted his child and married another man on the command of her family.

Slowly Erin's words faded into silence. She realized that Cole had long since rolled onto his side, removing his weight from her, touching her only in the slow sweep of his hand over her hair while she talked. She looked at his eyes and saw both rage and a sadness that made tears burn against her eyelids. Without stopping to think, she curled against him, needing the reassurance of his warmth, wondering if he ever needed reassurance in the same way.

"Are you all right?" Cole asked finally.

Erin nodded. "I thought I had forgotten. But I hadn't. Not really. I feel better now. Lighter. Kind of floating." She rubbed her cheek against his chest and let out a long sigh. "Thank you for being . . . gentle."

"You're the first one who ever accused me of that," Cole said, smiling oddly.

After a moment Erin looked up and saw a drop of

blood slowly welling from Cole's lower lip. She touched the small cut with her fingertips. "I'm sorry."

"No problem."

Her fingertips slid down beneath his chin, sensing the slight raised area where her head had bruised him.

"Here too," she said. "I hurt you."

Cole tried to subdue his elemental response to Erin's touch. She frowned as she looked at the bruise. She touched him even more gently, almost caressingly. He closed his eyes and told himself she didn't know what she was doing.

"I'm sorry, I wasn't thinking," she said, lifting her fingertips as the tension in his body communicated itself to her. "It must hurt to have me touch it."

He made a sound that could have been a throttled laugh or an equally throttled curse.

"It doesn't hurt. It feels good. Too damn good," Cole said bluntly.

"What?"

"Your fingers. My skin. I like the combination. What about you?"

Erin's hand hesitated, then resumed touching Cole. Silently she acknowledged that she was caressing him rather than looking for signs of injury. Very slowly he turned onto his side and resumed stroking her hair. After a time his fingertips traced the shadows beneath her cheekbones and the outline of her mouth. She made an odd sound and looked up at him. His eyes were closed and his expression was intent, focused on the sensations coming from his fingertips as he traced again the curve of her lips.

"You're smiling," he said without opening his eyes.

"It tickles."

"Does it?" Cole asked, running his fingertip across Erin's full lower lip again. "Is that why you're holding your breath?" He felt her body tighten as he bent down to her. "Don't panic, honey," he breathed against her mouth. "This won't hurt, I promise. I won't even hold you. I just want to know if you taste half as good as you fight. Okay?"

Surprised, caught off balance by the combination of humor and hunger in Cole's voice, Erin waited for fear to claim her. Nothing happened except a delicate, intriguing brush of warmth against her lips when Cole exhaled. A spear of sensation went from her breastbone to her knees, making her shiver.

"Frightened?" he whispered.

"I . . ."

He waited.

"After Hans . . ." she said, then took a deep breath. "Afterward, the psychiatrists told me that virgins who had been brutalized the way I was nearly always became whores or nuns. I haven't let a man get close to me in seven years. I don't know if I can even now. I might panic again."

"I'll risk it if you will," Cole said.

"Will you . . . be gentle?"

"What do you think?"

Erin looked into the gray eyes that were only inches away and wondered how she had ever thought they were cold.

"Yes," she whispered.

The tip of Cole's tongue slowly traced the sensitive skin at the edge of Erin's upper lip. At the first touch, she made a small sound. The gliding caress was unexpected, exquisite, unlike anything she had ever known from a man. Slowly her body relaxed and softened, lifting subtly toward him, wanting more of his warmth. He repeated the gentle touch, tracing her whole mouth, enjoying the chaste caress with an intensity that surprised him.

When Erin felt the tip of his tongue along her lower lip, she shivered and instinctively closed her eyes, wanting to focus only on the sensations radiating through her from his touch. As Cole slowly outlined her lips again and yet again, lingering to probe the sensitive corners of her smile, everything shifted around her, fear vanishing, nothing existing but the warm caress. Even when Erin felt the resilent heat of his biceps beneath her palms, she didn't realize that she had reached out and was holding on to him.

"Cole . . ."

"Yes, like that," Cole said, his tongue sliding between Erin's open lips, touching the tip of her tongue with his own. "Let me taste you. Just a taste, honey. That's all. I won't hurt you. You know that, don't you?"

As Cole spoke he caressed Erin's mouth again and again, not holding her, not forcing her, touching her with nothing but the tip of his tongue and the warmth of his breath.

And because it was the only way in which Cole permitted himself to touch her, his senses narrowed down to the tip of his tongue. He felt the heat and textures of her mouth with a sensual intensity that was as new to him as it was to her. The vividness of the experience intrigued him. He traced her tongue again, dipping into the heat and softness underneath, tasting her as he had never tasted a woman in his life, savoring and caressing until he felt as though every nerve ending in his body was concentrated in the tip of his tongue.

Finally Cole forced himself to stop. He eased away and came to his feet in a lithe motion, not trusting himself to stay close to Erin any longer without trying to mold her to the hungry length of his body. He wasn't used to kissing a woman and not having her. The experience was as new to him as discovering the astonishing sensitivity of his own tongue.

Erin's eyes opened slowly. Her palms felt cool without the warmth of Cole touching her. So did her lips, her mouth, her tongue.

"Cole?" she asked huskily.

"Time for that walk, honey."

She looked at the big hand he was holding out to her. When she took it, he pulled her to her feet and slowly, deeply, interlaced their fingers. His palm was warm and hard. The inner surfaces of his fingers were smooth and hot. She caught her breath at the sensations shivering up her arm when he flexed his hand. When he would have let go of her, she protested.

"Wait."

Cole froze.

Erin touched the cut on his lip with a fingertip that trembled very slightly. When she traced the edge of his mouth, the rasp of his stubble was pronounced, underlining the surprising smoothness of his lips. While the silence lengthened she traced his black eyebrows, his cheekbones, his chin, and then his lips again. He closed his eyes, permitting the gentle, exploratory torture for as long as he could trust himself.

"No more," Cole said finally.

Erin saw the pale blaze of his eyes as they opened

and automatically stepped back. He didn't release her hand.

"I'm sorry," she said quickly. "I thought you liked it."

"That's the problem. I like it way too much." He looked at her, making no effort to disguise the elemental hunger he felt. "I wanted you the first time I saw you. Nothing that's happened since has changed my mind. But I've never kissed a woman without having her, even when I was fourteen, and—"

"Fourteen?" Erin interrupted. Then, as realization hit, "Never?"

"She was nineteen and she knew exactly what she was doing. So did I, after she was through." Cole smiled and put his finger under Erin's chin, closing her parted lips. "Don't look so shocked, honey. Where I came from, I was a slow starter, but I caught on real quick. I didn't want to marry so I didn't go looking for the kind of girl who kissed and said no. The girls I went out with didn't know the word. Dinner, a movie, and the back seat of a car."

"The movie, no doubt, was optional?"

Cole smiled crookedly and flexed his hand again, rubbing his palm over Erin's, drawing her closer to him without meaning to. "So was the dinner, most of the time," he admitted.

"Are you bragging or complaining?"

"Neither," he said, bringing Erin's hand up to his lips once more. Very gently he caught her index finger between his teeth, tasted her, and released her quickly. "I'm trying to explain that in some ways I'm as new to this kind of playing as you are. Or did you see a lot of bad drive-in movies through steamy windows when you were a teenager?"

Erin tried to laugh, but her breath was too thick in her throat. "No. I was thirteen until I turned nineteen. Gawky and shy and plain. Phil, my brother, didn't help. I had a terrible crush on a boy who was three years older, a senior. When he asked me out, Phil called the guy and told him that if he so much as kissed me he'd be history. Saturday came and the guy didn't show up. I found out later that he had a thing for virgins. Kept a regular scorecard."

"Funny how different men are. I never was interested in a virgin until you."

Erin closed her eyes. "Not so funny after all. I'm not a virgin."

"You've never given yourself to a man," Cole said matter-of-factly. "That makes you a virgin in my book." He released Erin's hand. "Stay put while I check the hall."

The hall was deserted. So was the lobby of the hotel. A valet brought Cole's rental car. They drove west on Wilshire, headed for the beach. Cole drove erratically, first slowly, then quickly, studying the traffic in his rearview mirror for cars that matched his speed. When they reached the Pacific Coast Highway, he cruised several empty parking lots, still looking for followers, before he stopped and parked at Will Rogers State Beach.

Erin reached for the car door, then looked over at Cole. He was studying the rear and side-view mirrors. Despite her impatience to be out on the sand with nothing in front of her but seven thousand miles of water, she didn't open the door.

"You're a fast learner," Cole said approvingly.

"Pain is a great teacher."

"I'm sorry. I tried not to hurt you."

"You didn't hurt me," she said quickly. "That was why I stopped fighting. I expected to be hurt and I wasn't. You're damned heavy, though."

Cole smiled slightly. "Next time I'll let you be on top."

Erin gave him a startled sideways look and then the kind of almost-shy smile that told him the thought intrigued her.

"Two choices, honey," he said. "Go for a walk or take a remedial course in window steaming."

She smiled sadly. "Don't tempt me."

"Why not?"

For a moment the car was silent. Erin turned around to face the man who had taught her more about sensual pleasure in a few minutes than she had learned in her entire life. More importantly, he had taught her the nature of the restlessness that had driven her from the arctic. The discovery of her own sensuality was as unexpected as Cole's gentleness had been.

"I'm interested in what you're offering," she said, "but I don't know how much and I won't until it happens. Or doesn't happen. That's not fair to you."

"Honey, if life was fair, someone would have gutted Hans before he had his first wet dream."

Erin stared. Though Cole's tone was casual, his eyes were like hammered silver.

"But life isn't fair," he continued. "Only damned unexpected. Back in that hotel room you taught me something new about pleasure, and I would have sworn that was impossible. We could die before we take our next breath, or we could live to teach each other something else new about ourselves. So I'll take what comes and not worry too much about what doesn't. How about you?"

"I—I don't know."

"Think about it. And while you do, think about this. A man who can't control himself belongs to anyone who can. I don't belong to anyone but myself. We could be dead naked and you could be all over me like a hot rain, but if you changed your mind I'd get up and get dressed and that would be the end of it." Cole's ice-pale glance went from mirror to mirror as he spoke. "While you think about that, let's walk. We've both been caged up more than we're used to."

Erin waited until Cole came around and opened her car door. Prudence rather than etiquette guided their actions. When he laced his fingers through hers once more, she found herself smiling. He saw the pale gleam of her teeth in the moonlight and smiled in return.

"You really like being outside, don't you?" he said.

"Yes, but that's not why I'm smiling. I feel about sixteen again, holding hands beneath the cool moonlight." She gave him a sideways look. "I suppose you were about six when you started walking out with girls."

He laughed softly. "Enjoy it. When we get to Australia, you won't even want to stand close to another person, moon or no moon."

"Why?"

"Too bloody hot. The Kimberley is in the upper part of the continent. The tropical part."

"Tropical? The pictures I've seen of the Kimberley look more like desert."

"Oh, it's dry all right. Most of the year. Then the

buildup begins, and great rivers of clouds pour in from the Indian Ocean. You sweat and the sweat just stays on your skin, making you hotter than ever, because sweat can't evaporate into air that's already saturated. The body can't cool itself, and the sunlight is a razor slicing into your skin. The temperature goes way over a hundred, and the humidity gets right up to the point of rain and then it sticks there and sticks there until men literally crack up and go berserk."

Erin made a sound of disbelief.

"It's true, honey. The Aussies even have a name for that kind of madness. They call it going troppo. I've come close a few times myself. It taught me something. I avoid the buildup now."

"You make it sound irresistible."

"Oh, that's not the worst of it," Cole said, taking a breath of the cool brine-scented air. "When the wet finally comes, the country is impassable. For months at a time you can't travel except by plane."

"What about four-wheel-drive?"

"Not unless it floats."

"No bridges?"

"Only on the one major highway," Cole said. "When the wet is really on, those bridges are under water a lot of the time. You see, they're built low and with removable railings so that trash doesn't get caught and create a dam. Even so, they wash out a lot." He looked over at Erin. "That's what ConMin is trying to do by offering to fly you all over the world to photograph diamond mines. ConMin knows that if you don't get into Crazy Abe's claim in the next few weeks, you'll have a hell of a time getting in at all until summer dries things out. I should be in the Kimberley right now, prospecting before the temperature goes to a hundred and twenty and the air is too wet to breathe.''

"Then we shouldn't go to London at all."

"It will keep Faulkner and van Luik off our backs while Wing sets up things on the other end."

"Wing?"

"My partner."

"Oh. That's right. Black*Wing.* Dad said something about that."

"Yeah, I'll just bet he did." Cole looked down at Erin. "Don't worry, honey. If your mine can be found, I'll find it for you."

"Yes. Dad said that too."

Cole walked in silence for a time before he stopped and very gently pulled Erin toward him. When there was no resistance on her part, he bent and brushed his lips over hers.

"Don't go to Australia. You'll be safer with your father. He may have gray hair, but he's one tough bastard."

Erin started to object, only to be distracted by the gliding caress of Cole's tongue over her lips and the warmth of his breath as he spoke urgently.

"The climate and the land have killed men who were much stronger and more experienced than you are. The Kimberley Plateau is no place for a white woman."

"People told me the same thing about the arctic," Erin said absently. Curious, she tasted his chin as she had once tasted the green diamond. "Salty. Masculine. Warm. You taste good, Cole."

His breath came in with a ripping sound. Suddenly he caged Erin's face between his hands. "Woman, you do love to take risks, don't you?"

"Risks?" She looked up at him with eyes made dark and mysterious by moonlight. "How so?"

"I could make you stay home. I could crowd you sexually until you turned and ran for cover."

Erin went very still, searching the hot silver gleam of Cole's eyes. Then she sighed and smiled almost sadly. "Yesterday you could have, when I didn't know you. But not today. Today I found out that you're a hard man but not a cruel one. You're not at all like Hans."

"There's a world full of people who would disagree with you," Cole said flatly.

"I'm not one of them. I'm the woman you had laid out like a lamb for slaughter, but all you did was stroke my hair while I cried, and then you kissed me so gently I felt like crying all over again. I would have sworn I would never trust a man after Hans. I was wrong." She touched his mouth with her fingertips. "It's too late to make me afraid of you, Cole. I'm going to Australia, and I'm going to be with you every step of the way."

Cole told himself that he was sorry he couldn't intimidate Erin, sorry that she stood so trustingly in his arms, leaning against him, her breath a warmth rushing over his skin. He told himself, but he didn't believe any of it.

For a long time Cole simply held Erin, listening to the surf and wishing he had exaggerated the difficulty of living and working in the Kimberley. But he hadn't. The buildup was a corrosive time, fraying men's tempers to the point of violence and beyond. The wet wasn't much better. When the wet arrived, it would wash the land right back into the Stone Age, where the most simple things were difficult, even survival.

Especially survival.

12

◆

"I've been attending funerals." Chen Wing's voice was made empty by more than the satellite relay joining him to Cole. "They have an unsettling effect."

Cole smiled grimly. "You didn't expect to make war on ConMin without suffering a few casualties, did you?"

Wing didn't reply for a moment. Then he changed the subject. "Have you made any progress?"

"Directly, none."

Wing muttered a quiet curse in Cantonese.

"Relax," Cole said. "At this stage, that's the best news you could hope for. I've spent most of the last three days examining maps from the BlackWing files."

"And?"

"Nothing. That's good news. If I could find Windsor's jewel box in a few hours using existing maps, so could any other geologist, including the ones on your staff. You told me they reported finding nothing, correct?"

"Yes."

"Now I can reassure you they probably weren't lying. The maps told them nothing. The other possibility is that the maps told the story but your geologists withheld it to sell it to someone else. If so, I didn't find what they were selling."

"If you haven't found it, they didn't. You're the best. You always have been. Lucky in mines, unlucky in love."

"Number one, that isn't how the saying goes," Cole said. "Number two, my love life is none of your damned business."

There was a brief silence, followed by a sigh. "I'm sorry," Wing said, his tone soft, almost whispering. "Funerals have an unfortunate effect on my common sense. One of those funerals was that of my second cousin and brother-in-law, Chen Zeong-Li."

Images flooded through Cole's memory, images of the passionate black-eyed woman who was Wing's sister, the woman who in the end had loved her family and power more than she had loved any man, including Cole Blackburn.

"Zeong was a decent man," Cole said finally. "I'm sorry to hear he's dead."

"Are you? There was a time when you would have killed Zeong and danced on his grave."

Cole said nothing.

"If you choose to resume the relationship with Chen Lai," Wing continued, "this time the Chen family would not intervene."

This time.

The words echoed in Cole's mind, reminding him of things he would rather have forgotten. Shortly after he had signed the original BlackWing agreement, Lai had dumped him because the family of Chen disapproved of a non-Chinese husband. A secret lover was tolerated while Cole was needed to advance the Chen family's mineral business, but when it came to marriage and children it was more important to consolidate blood and business ties in Kowloon.

Now Zeong-Li was dead, Lai was widowed, and the family of Chen was offering Cole the very woman whom they once had forbidden to him.

"No, thanks," Cole said calmly. "A smart man only wipes his ass with poison ivy once."

From the other end of the line came a charged silence, followed by the sound of harsh, humorless laughter. "You haven't changed."

"Hard to harder, half smart to smarter. That's a change, Wing. It's the only change that matters. I've survived."

"What will you need at Abe's station?"

Cole accepted the change of subject without a pause. "I'll need a helicopter to do photo, radar, magnetic, and scintillometric studies of Abe's claims. Ideally the information from the last two should be recorded on separate transparencies, laid over the first two, and then integrated with information that I'm putting on the topo and geological maps, but I won't have time to handle all the integration and programming myself."

"We have a mainframe here," Wing said.

"I don't like that. It increases the chances of a leak."

Wing said nothing.

Cole shrugged and conceded. "Can you set up a ground station at Windsor's place—modem, satellite link, and printers to handle the output from your end?"

There was a pause. "I'll need several days."

"You'll get it. What about the inputting on your end?"

"I'll do it myself."

"Then I'll transmit data as fast as I can accumulate it. Set up a secure file in BlackWing's main computer, code access 'chunder.' "

"Chunder," Wing repeated. "Within an hour you can have a printout under that name from any Chen business computer anywhere in the world."

"Good," Cole said. "What about the rest of the transparencies I'll need? Who will do them?"

"My people."

"Be damn sure you trust them."

"They are of the family of Chen, and they won't know where the scraps of land they're working on exist in reality. They will have only a grid to work from. I am only one who knows the latitudes and longitudes."

Cole laughed quietly. He understood Wing's kind of trust, the kind that was weighed and measured. "That leaves us with just one problem—the helicopter. I put the names of nearby mining exploration outfits through the computer."

"I saw the printout."

"Then you know all of them are tied to ConMin in one way or another. The only way we'll have a chance against the cartel is if we keep them off balance, wondering what's going to happen next. That means working fast and as quietly as possible. If we have to go to New South Wales or the Nullarbor for the chopper, the logistics of fuel supply will be impossible. If we get one closer to home, ConMin will have a direct pipeline into our operation. Take your pick, Wing."

"I did. I reran data and selected the five companies that are least indebted to ConMin. Several of them are also indebted to Pacific Enterprises, Inc., Pan-Asian Resources Ltd., or Pacific Rim Development and Resources Ltd."

Cole recognized all three firms. They were powerful forces in trade among the countries that circle the Pacific Ocean. Apparently all were under control of the Chen family to a greater or lesser degree.

"What's your best pick? Pan-Asian Resources?" he said.

"We have enjoyed amicable relations with them for years, yes," Wing admitted.

"Which of the Australian firms do they control?"

"Control? None. We are simply in an advisory capacity."

"Yeah. ConMin does a lot of that too."

Wing ignored him. "Metalworks and Mines Ltd. is my first choice for a helicopter, with Western Australia Iron and Gold Surveyors second. I will make inquiries immediately."

"What if neither one comes through for you?"

"I can say with great certainty that Metalworks will have a helicopter available for short-term lease. I will see to it personally. Do you need a pilot?"

"I'll fly it myself. What about that list of survey equipment I faxed you?"

"It will be at the station when you get there," Wing said.

"Someone to set it up and guard it would be nice.

I'm a miner, not an electronics expert, and I'll be away from the buildings most of the time."

"Noted. Anything else?"

"Maybe some of the amenities of life. Abe's idea of furniture was a dirt floor."

"Noted. Will you require a single bed or a double?"

Cole broke the link without answering. Immediately he put in Matthew Windsor's number.

It was time to find out what Erin's father was willing to do for his daughter.

13

◆

"FOR THIS I PACKED MY CAMERAS AND CLOTHES and sent them to London without me?" Erin asked, disgusted.

"No," Cole said, without looking up from his maps. "You did that to make ConMin think they had you coming to heel nicely. Confuse, mislead, and misdirect. It's the only way to survive."

"One more run through 'Chunder' and I won't care if I survive," she retorted.

Erin tossed aside the sheets of Abe's doggerel. She had been sitting in the window seat of a Darwin hotel, studying the poem and looking out at the lush tropical landscaping, but neither could hold her attention any longer.

Cole glanced up from the desk in the living area of the suite. Transparent topographic and geological maps of Australia were spread across the hotel desk in front of him, as were maps showing the distribution of active and reserve mineral claims in Western Australia and the Northern Territory. On top of those maps were transparencies of the Kimberley Plateau and of Western Australia. A compass, ruler, and pencil were close at hand, as was a lined note pad.

He didn't really expect to find the answer to the Sleeping Dog Mines in the maps, but they gave him something to think about besides Erin's warm tongue and husky voice approving of his taste.

"Not surprising," Cole said. "Chunder is Aussie slang for vomit."

"Lovely," she muttered. "Old Great-uncle Abe was a real literary light, wasn't he?"

A slight smile was Cole's only response. Chunder was the most elegant of the slang contained in Abe's doggerel. If Erin had any idea of the meaning of the words she had been reading aloud, Cole suspected she would have blushed to the soles of her feet. Abe had been a randy bastard right up to the day he died.

"What time is it?" she asked.

"Too soon to go to bed."

"Damn."

Yawning, Erin abandoned the idea of sitting in one of the lush upholstered chairs. Instead she went and stood next to Cole, looking over his shoulder at the maps.

"Then how about explaining some more of these maps to me?" She braced herself with a hand on his shoulder as she leaned closer. "This time I'll try not to yawn in your ear."

"Sit down before you fall down," Cole said, gently pulling Erin onto his lap.

Instantly Erin tensed. Calmly Cole began pointing out features on the nearest map. As he talked, she gradually began to relax, trusting her weight to the muscular support of his thighs and chest, feeling the heat of his body sink into hers. Though Cole savored each small softening of her body against his, all he spoke about was the maps.

"I understand topographic maps," Erin said, "but what is this one?"

Erin shifted in Cole's lap as she leaned forward. The pressure of her hips against his groin made his breathing thicken. With a silent curse at his unruly body, he concentrated on the transparency she was pointing to. The clear plastic was four feet by four feet, exactly the scale of the topographic map and covered by seemingly random patterns of rainbow colors.

Deliberately Cole reached around Erin with both arms and slid the transparency over the topographic map. The motion also brushed his biceps against her breasts. The contact made her gasp. Her breath unraveled suddenly, but she didn't withdraw. His arms moved again, caressing and freeing Erin in the same motion. While he spoke, he traced lines with a calloused fingertip.

"The blue lines are sandstone. There's a lot of it in the Kimberley. The brown crosshatches are limestone. The yellow diagonals are volcanic rocks. The pink dots are water deposits. The white dots are wind deposits. It makes a difference to us, because usually only water deposits contain diamonds."

As Erin grew accustomed to looking both at and through the transparency, she could see how the water deposits almost always coincided with rivers or beaches or low spots on the topographic map. But there were a few places where pink dots appeared without any sign of rivers or lakes or ocean.

"Is this a water deposit?" she asked. "There's no sign of water anywhere close."

Cole looked at the slender finger with its clean, unpolished nail. When he saw where Erin was pointing, he gave her full marks for quickness.

"That's what geologists call a paleo-floodplain, a place where a flooding river used to overflow and leave silt and stones behind. The river is long since gone, but the characteristic deposits of a floodplain are still there."

"Does that mean diamonds could be there?"

"If the ancient river flowed through diamond-bearing rock, yes."

"Did it?"

"Probably not. It didn't flow through any volcanic rocks."

Erin frowned. "I didn't know the Kimberley Plateau had volcanoes."

"The Kimberley's volcanoes are ancient. They've been eroded flat and sometimes even down beyond that, to the magma chamber itself. Nothing is left but the barest bones of what once was an awesome piece of living nature. When you're digging for diamonds, honey, you're digging up a grave."

"Lovely thought," Erin muttered.

Cole reached for another transparency and drew it onto the top of the stacked maps. This time Erin didn't flinch when his arms brushed the sides of her breasts.

"Since nothing volcanic shows on the surface," he continued, keeping his arms around her, "we have to look down below."

"How?"

"This map outlines stations, mining claims, and mineral reserves in the Kimberley: stations in green, active claims and reserves in red, lapsed claims and reserves in blue."

Erin made a sound of dismay as she saw the network of overlapping lines. "There's nothing left of the Kimberley. Somebody's been over every inch of it already!"

"They've staked out claims and then abandoned them. That's a big difference." Cole's arms tightened, shifting Erin subtly on his lap, allowing himself to brush his lips against her soft hair. "I don't need virgin land to find pay dirt, because most men are no damn good at what they do."

The warmth of Cole's breath against her neck made Erin shiver. It was pleasure rather than fear that rippled over her skin, pleasure making her lean more fully against him. Cole smiled, caressed her again, and went on speaking in a deep, slow voice, as though he had nothing more on his mind than maps.

"Most of Abe's claims were worked over in the 1920s by men looking for gold. When nothing worthwhile was found, the claims were abandoned. Since then no one has been there except an occasional jackeroo or a walkabout Aborigine."

Erin stared at the piled maps, seeing lines and designs and colors and more lines and designs, and no answers at all.

"The problem isn't that the plateau is too well known," Cole said, pulling another transparency out and lining it up with the underlying maps, caressing Erin with every motion, every breath. "The problem is that we don't know nearly enough."

Erin tried to speak, but couldn't. Cole's strength, his heat, his very breath surrounded her.

Yet all she could think about was getting closer.

"This transparency shows what kind of plants grow," he said, allowing his lips to linger against Erin's neck. "Plants change with elevation, rainfall, and soil. They can tell you whether limestone or sandstone or volcanic rock is underneath the soil."

Cole moved another transparency onto the pile. He took a lot of time stacking it, for every motion of his arms revealed another soft curve of Erin's body.

"This shows roads, trails, dams, airstrips, towns, houses, windmills, microwave relays, and whatever else man has added to the landscape. Look at it, honey. Look at it real carefully."

As he spoke, Cole released Erin from his touch. She stared at the final transparency, trying to gather thoughts scattered by the unexpected splinters of pleasure that had pierced her with every brush of body against hers. Gradually she realized that the final map had the least marks of any map on the pile.

Man had touched Western Australia only lightly, and the Kimberley barely at all.

"In that pile is all we know about the Kimberley," Cole said. "Put your hand over a part of the map. Any part."

Puzzled, Erin did as he asked.

"You have a few thousand square miles under your hand. Lift it and tell me what we know about that piece of land."

She moved her hand aside, looking at the transparency and then at the key that ran down the side.

"No paved roads," Erin said. "One graded road, and a few station roads that are little better than wild-animal trails. Five station houses." She leaned closer. "Three of them are abandoned. A handful of windmills." She leaned forward even farther, looking through the top map to the one just beneath. Again she looked at the color key on the map's margin. "Lowland grasses, spinifex, scrub gum."

Cole lifted the top two transparencies, which allowed Erin to see the ones underneath easily.

"Parts of three stations," she continued. "About seven mineral claims sort of in a line." She bent lower. "The claims run along a river," she said, reading through to the topographic map. "Well, some of the year it's a river. The rest of the time it's dry. Dashed lines, right?"

"Right. Go on."

Frowning, Erin went on to the next map. "The land is nearly flat. Sand and sandstone. No permanent water."

"What else?"

There was a long silence while Erin sifted through the maps again. Finally she looked up at Cole. "That's it."

"Think about it, Erin. Thousands of square miles, and you've summed up man's knowledge of it in less than three minutes."

Erin made a startled sound.

"You could call the station owners pioneers and you wouldn't be wrong," Cole said. "The twentieth century is only a rumor out in the Kimberley. Western Australia is a different place, a different land, a different time. Civilization is whatever you can carry in on your back."

After a moment Erin asked, "How old was Abe?"

"Had to be eighty, at least, when he died."

"What was his health like?"

"He could walk most men into the ground," Cole

said. "He could drink the rest right under, including me."

She frowned. "Then there's no place on Abe's cattle station or on his claims that he was too old to prospect?"

"Doubt it. Not when I knew him, anyway. And he discovered his jewel box before I knew him."

"All right, what about Sleeping Dog One, Sleeping Dog Two, and all the rest?" Erin asked. "What makes you so certain those mines are worthless?"

"I've been in Dog One. It's a pipe mine, pure and simple, and not much of one at that; bort was the rule. The diamonds in that tin box came from a placer mine with a high percentage of gem-quality stones."

"What's bort?"

"Industrial diamonds," Cole explained, "useful only for abrasives or drill bits."

"No gemstones?"

"Nothing like your diamonds. His were all sharp edges, flaws, and yellow to brown."

"Are all Abe's mines like that?"

Cole smiled at the disappointment in Erin's voice. "I'm afraid so. Not one of them is located on or near a modern river course, either, which means the Dog mines just aren't a likely source of placer diamonds."

Gloomily Erin looked at the maps. "What did you mean, 'modern' rivers? What other kind of river is there?"

Absently Cole's fingertips smoothed over the paper as he thought about the passage of time over the face of the land, time transforming everything it touched, wearing down old mountains and building new ones.

"Paleo-rivers," he said finally. "Old as the hills. Older."

"I don't understand."

"The Kimberley Plateau has spent a billion and a half years above sea level. That makes it the oldest land surface on earth. The rest of the Australian continent—and all the other continents as well—have been recycled top to bottom in one way or another in that time. Not the Kimberley."

Cole leaned away from Erin for a moment, pulled a big opaque map of Australia from the bottom of the pile, and spread it out on top.

"Look," he said. "Australia is the flattest inhabited continent on earth. The driest, too. The Kimberley Plateau is about the only thing west of Ayers Rock that's high enough to make a decent hill anywhere else in the world."

Erin made a startled sound and looked at the map again.

"In the center of Australia," said Cole, "the land is so flat that rain collects in circles like dew on a gigantic picnic table."

His long index finger traced the shallow rise of the Kimberley Plateau. "This area stayed high and dry, but the rest of Australia, the flat center and even flatter southwest, have been underwater more than above. There are huge limestone and sandstone beds covering them to prove it."

When Cole glanced up he found Erin was focused on the map with an intensity that was almost tangible.

"At the edge of the Kimberley the land rumples a bit. The locals call them mountains. Anyone else would call them hills. They're what's left of a limestone reef that was buried and then resurrected by erosion."

" 'A dead sea's bones,' " Erin quoted softly, remembering a phrase from Abe's poetry.

Cole's eyes narrowed. He pushed the continental map aside and pulled out the map of the Kimberley Plateau. He traced the line of the Napier Range and the other limestone ranges that ring the Kimberley today as the living reefs once ringed the Kimberley long ago. Seven of Crazy Abe's claims straddled limestone outcroppings. Three of them were within the boundaries of the station itself. None of them was near a Dog mine.

"Cole?"

Instead of answering, he grabbed another map, this one showing major modern watercourses. There were no year-round rivers, but in the wet more rain came down than even the parched, porous land could absorb. The result was a series of on-again, off-again "rivers" that were little more than flood channels several miles wide.

Erin watched while Cole's intent, nearly silver eyes measured distances and catalogued possibilities. The speed and decisiveness of his work suggested an intelligence that was as formidable as his body.

As Erin watched Cole, her restlessness increased, forcing her to admit just how drawn to him she was— and never more so than now, when the intelligence and discipline in him were almost tangible. She knew it was dangerous even to think about becoming his lover, because she wasn't the kind of person who did anything by halves. If she gave herself to him physically, it would be impossible not to give the rest of herself as well. There was no guarantee Cole wanted anything more than her body, and she knew it. Yet the lure of him was sinking into her more deeply with each minute she spent in his company.

Without warning, Cole looked up and caught Erin's luminous green eyes admiring him. When she realized it, she looked away hastily.

"Well?" Erin asked, gesturing to the map.

He shrugged. "About two thirds of Australia can lay claim to being the burial ground of a dead sea's bones."

"Oh," she said, disappointed.

"On the other hand, when it comes to checking existing claims, I'll concentrate on the areas with limestone outcroppings first."

A smile transformed Erin's face. "Then I helped?"

Cole smiled. "I hope so. We've got a hell of a lot of land to cover any way you look at it."

"Is there a river?"

"Not the way you mean it. There were paleo-rivers, though. They drained into the shallow sea where reefs were formed. There were beaches, too, maybe like Namibia's beaches, where every time you dig down to the oyster line you come up with diamonds running out of both hands."

"Where are the old rivers on Abe's claims?"

"I never saw any sign of them," Cole said, "but they're there. They have to be."

"Because of the diamonds?"

"No. Because the Kimberley Plateau has always been there, and a sea was usually there, and water always runs down to the sea."

Unconsciously, Erin worried her lower lip with her teeth, something she often did when nervous or thinking hard. "What about your maps? Do they show old rivers?"

"No," Cole said. "The only maps I can get my hands on are of the tectonic sort. They're useless if you're looking for something that's smaller than a hundred square miles."

"How big are diamond pipes?"

"Most of them are only a few hundred acres square on the surface. A lot of them are smaller. Some are huge."

"Talk about a needle in a haystack . . ."

"I'd settle for that," Cole said sardonically. "If it was a needle, I'd whistle up an industrial-strength magnet and suck that bit of steel out in nothing flat."

His eyes went back to the maps. Instantly he was absorbed, pursuing some line of thought Erin could only guess at. She watched him openly, wishing her cameras were lying on the table instead of on the chair next to her bed. Though she rarely did portraits, preferring the timeless beauty of wilderness to the transient faces of humanity, she wanted to photograph Cole. Like the land, there was more to him than his harsh exterior.

Erin was still thinking about that when she fell asleep in Cole's lap, her fingers curled around an imaginary camera and her face tucked against his neck.

14

◆

HUGO VAN LUIK PASSED DOWN THE LONG HALL-way as silently as a ghost. The luxuriant green wool carpeting, the tapestries, and the heavy curtains soaked up any sound he made. A closed-circuit television camera mounted on the wood-paneled wall tracked his progress. Depending on the time of month, this office was the repository for anywhere between two and three billion dollars in rough diamonds.

When he reached the heavy, hand-carved wooden door at the far end of the hall, he stopped and tapped a four-digit code into the security key pad. The lock retracted, allowing him to push the door open and pass into the next long hallway to the next electronic locks, until finally he was inside the conference room.

Although meetings of the "steering committee" of the Diamond Sales Division of Consolidated Minerals were "unofficial," "advisory," and never publicized, such gatherings were crucial to the economic expectations and requirements of the nations that attended. Individual diamond sight-holders always made their needs known to the DSD through formal channels, but what happened in this room today would determine how—or whether—those needs would be met. To an extent startling to outsiders, DSD enhanced or diminished the economic health of nations.

Van Luik checked his own watch. Given a choice he would have put this meeting off for five weeks, until the next sight. By then the monsoon season would have started in Western Australia and the matter of Abelard Windsor's dangerous bequest would be moot for another six months. But putting off the meeting wasn't possible.

Abruptly he turned to the majordomo who was hovering by the half-open door.

"Send them in."

The representative from Israel strode in first. Moshe Aram was lean, wiry, and fit. He was a member of the Israeli secret service, Mossad. The diamond trade was too crucial to Israel's economy to be left in the hands of *diamantaires* or politicians. That was how the troubles had begun back in the 1970s.

The United States representative, Nan Faulkner, followed on Aram's heels. Faulkner sat down, poured herself a glass of ice water, drank it, and poured another. Then she lit a cigarillo and balanced it on the lip of a heavy crystal ashtray.

Van Luik nodded at the woman but said nothing. Although Faulkner was an old hand at DSD meetings, van Luik had always maintained his distance from her, believing her to be a political token rather than a real player in the game of international power.

Van Luik went to his own chair at the head of the

table and watched calmly as the others took their places. There was little polite talk. Each person was there to ensure that his country's interests in the diamond trade were known to the diamond cartel.

The Soviet representative, Boris Yarakov, looked unusually surly. Attar Singh, India's representative to the cartel, was as politic as Yarakov was boorish. Singh had no choice but to be accommodating. India no longer produced diamonds, so it no longer commanded the attention it once had. What India brought to ConMin and DSD in the late twentieth century was a bottomless well of cheap labor willing to spend its hours and its eyesight on the task of shaping and polishing diamonds so tiny they would once have been sold for industrial use at a quarter the price polished goods commanded.

The Continental diamond trade was represented by Nathaniel Feinberg. As with India, the Continental interests were cutters and polishers rather than producers of rough diamonds. They had less power in the diamond cartel than the owners of the gem-producing diamond mines themselves. Those mines were the treasure and bane of the diamond cartel's existence, for there were more than enough mines to fill the world demand for gems.

Australia had used its own geologists, rather than ConMin's, to explore the vast Kimberley Plateau. The Argyle diamond mine had been the result. Because the remote Argyle stike was monstrously expensive to develop, Australia sought outside capital. Once the banks learned that Australia wasn't a member of the diamond cartel and thus had no guaranteed market for the Argyle's output, the banks withdrew.

The game hadn't stopped there. India, unhappy

with the cartel, had offered to guarantee a market for Argyle's melee diamonds. The banks were approached again, guaranteed market in hand. Before the loan went through, the Indian government was privately informed that DSD would undercut India's markets by flooding them with below-cost stones of the same size, quality, and cut as India would produce from the Australian mine. DSD and ConMin were rich enough to absorb the losses indefinitely. India was not.

No single diamond-producing country could survive a contest with the contents of DSD's London vaults. India withdrew its offer to finance the development of the Argyle mine, and Australia did what every other individual or nation with a diamond mine had done. It cut a deal with ConMin.

Ian McLaren was Australia's representative to DSD. He watched van Luik warily, and with good reason.

Van Luik opened the Moroccan leather folder in front of him, signaling that the session was open. Immediately everyone began passing single sheets of paper to the head of the table. Each month the mining countries put forth a projected production figure, and each month the cutters and polishers stated their expected needs for raw material. It was up to van Luik to reconcile those two sides of the diamond equation.

He collected the "prayers" of each cartel member, but the papers were a formality. The same figures had been faxed to van Luik the previous day. In any case, the prayers were futile. He had known for the past week how the next three months' output of DSD diamonds would be distributed.

Swiftly van Luik lined up sheets from producers opposite those from buyers and compared amounts with the agenda in his head. There would be some very unhappy people leaving the building today. It wouldn't be the first time, and van Luik wasn't fool enough to believe it would be the last.

"Mr. McLaren," van Luik said abruptly, "DSD can't at this time provide a guaranteed market for the undeveloped Ellendale pipes. As you know, the gem content of Ellendale was very high for a pipe mine. Somewhere in the neighborhood of sixty to eighty percent, was it not?"

"Yes, but—"

"Are you not aware," van Luik interrupted, "that the market has barely recovered from the disaster of 1980? This most definitely is not the time to bring a new gem mine into production."

"Then could we anticipate a price increase on our industrial diamonds?" McLaren asked curtly.

"Regretfully, no. If the price of industrial diamonds goes much higher, Japan would be tempted to begin mass-producing them in their labs, and then Australia would be left with a hugely expensive, hugely unprofitable mine and no way to repay the cost of its development."

"But—"

"I will be at the Argyle mine shortly to discuss long-range planning for its product. Be assured Australia's interests are DSD's interests as well. For the moment, the last thing either of our interests require is one more gem diamond mine."

Without waiting for a response, van Luik slipped McLaren's prayer to the bottom of the stack and addressed the problems created by the next sheet in line.

"Mr. Singh, you will receive two thirds of the melees you requested."

"My cutters would be most grateful if a greater proportion of our sights were made up of larger rather than smaller melees, which are the dregs of the diamond trade."

"You have the only workers capable of turning a profit on the smaller melees," van Luik said. "However, if India would like its allotment reduced, DSD will comply. China has made inquiry about the melee trade recently. We told them our entire output of rough was allocated at present. Naturally we assured them that we would keep their interest in mind, should the situation change."

Singh's face went very dark beneath his stark white turban. Yet when he spoke, his voice was flat and calm. "India has no objection to the kind or quantity of diamonds it will receive in the next three months from DSD."

"Excellent. Your cooperation will be remembered. Mr. Feinberg, your associates' requests will be met in full."

Feinberg nodded.

"Mr. Yarakov, the market for larger gems is just recovering from the disastrous speculation of 1980 and 1981," van Luik said. "We regret that we can handle no more of your output."

Yarakov looked angry but said nothing.

Van Luik paused, obviously expecting an argument. When none came, he said, "Mr. Aram, your requests are unreasonable. If we allocated you that many melees, India and the Soviet Union would have little work for their own polishers."

Van Luik's dry, soft voice carried easily through the big room, for none of the men moved or muttered among themselves. Even Moshe Aram said nothing. In the 1970s, Israel had cut eighty percent of all melees. But in the early 1980s, Israel had been instrumental in the diamond speculation that had nearly broken DSD's hold on the diamond market. ConMin hadn't forgotten. Or forgiven. The cartel had exacted extraordinary retribution, canceling the precious sight invitations of 150 *diamantaires* and thereby gutting the diamond industry in Tel Aviv. Soviet and Indian markets now received the majority of the melees.

"You will receive thirty-seven point six percent of your melee request," van Luik continued. "The Soviet Union will receive eighty-nine point eight percent of its request. Those amounts will be evenly divided among the next three sights in London. How you divide it among your *diamantaires* is, as always, a matter of your own discretion."

"You have punished us long enough," Aram said roughly. "We have done as you wished. We have altered our banking regulations and raised the margin requirements on sight boxes. Our cutters can no longer speculate. What more do you want from us, that we tear down Ramat Gan? What gives you the right to bleed the economy of a small, struggling, democratic nation and send our lifeblood to men who persecute Jews in the Soviet Union?"

"DSD trades in diamonds, not ideologies," van Luik said neutrally, shifting Israel's prayer to the bottom of the pile as he spoke. "You may, of course, ask for an increase in your allotment at this group's next advisory meeting.

"But—"

"The neutrality of DSD is well known," Nan Faulkner said dryly, cutting off another angry eruption from Aram. "Somehow, both sides in World War Two managed to get their hands on industrial diamonds. Nothing has changed since then."

Faulkner stubbed out her cigarillo and gave van Luik a level look.

"It's also well known that what happens in these advisory meetings has a ripple effect that goes far beyond the diamond market," she continued. "You may not consider ideology, but each government represented at this table does. If the Israeli cut stands, I'll be forced to recommend that our American sight holders substantially lower their requests."

Van Luik was surprised, but he did not show it. "You may naturally do as you wish. However, in your country the sight holders are also free to go against your recommendations. In that case DSD would naturally cater to the requests of its most immediate market—your retail jewelers."

Faulkner's smile was as cold as the glass of ice-water she drained before answering. "Yeah, that's the problem with a real democracy," she said, lighting another cigarillo. "But I tell you, it wouldn't take much effort to raise the taxes on diamonds at each stage—imported rough, loose polished stones, and finally set stones. In a year or two, diamond jewelry would go up in price, say, sixty percent in the American marketplace. Luxuries are just that, babe. Luxuries. If they get too high-priced, people go without.

"As for the sentimental trade," Faulkner continued, cutting off the words she sensed forming on van Luik's tongue, "lots of Americans would follow Princess Di's example and have colored gems in their engagement rings, especially if the jewelry manufacturers launched a campaign based on treating your loved one like royalty. At the same time, there might be a grass-roots political movement to boycott apartheid's diamonds."

"No aspect of Consolidated Minerals, Inc., has ever supported apartheid," van Luik said flatly, "and that most definitely includes DSD."

"Tough luck. People associate diamonds and the diamond cartel with South Africa. Within five years at most, fifty percent of your American market would dry up. Maybe even seventy-five percent."

Faulkner smoked her cigarillo and said no more. She didn't have to. U.S. sales accounted for more than a third of all gem transactions in the world—the most profitable third.

"There is always Japan," van Luik pointed out.

"There sure is," Faulkner agreed, her voice hearty as she picked up the pitcher of icewater and began to pour. "The U.S. led them into buying diamond engagement rings. We can lead them right out again. That leaves you with half your former world market, which means that every country at this table just took a fifty percent cut in pay. Hardly worth it just to jerk Israel's chain one more time, is it?"

"Remember, Ms. Faulkner, Consolidated *Minerals* controls more than diamonds."

"Which is the only reason there hasn't been a grass-roots campaign against diamonds in the U.S. before now," Faulkner back, setting down the water pitcher with a thump. "You need our diamond markets, and we need your strategic minerals. So let's cut the bullshit and find a more generous compromise than you've suggested so far."

Van Luik could count his heartbeats in the stabbing pain behind his eyes. He had warned his superiors the United States might be difficult if they squeezed Israel too hard. They hadn't listened. Now they would have no choice.

"Perhaps the loss of jobs and foreign exchange in Israel could be compensated for in another way," van Luik said, looking toward Singh.

"Forget it," Faulkner said. "Israel doesn't need any favors at India's expense. Why not take it out of the Bear's thick hide? The Soviet share of the melee market has gone up by about ten percent every six months for the last nine years."

Yarakov turned on Faulkner and spoke before van Luik could. "As a result of recent political changes in our country, the Soviet Union has employment and foreign exchange problems of its own. Your country supports *glasnost* in the world press, but we still have to pay for American wheat with American dollars."

"Take your restructuring even further," Aram suggested in a hard voice. "Incorporate your farms. Then you'd be up to your ass in wheat, just like America."

"Gentlemen," van Luik said sharply, pinching the bridge of his nose, "I believe the basis for compromise exists. Russia will continue cutting an increasing proportion of the larger melees, because the Soviet Union does a better job than anyone else for the same money."

Aram looked unhappy but kept silent. What van Luik said was the truth, no matter how unpalatable.

"The Soviet Union will guarantee a good price on melees for Israel's artisans to fashion into jewelry," van Luik continued, giving Yarakov an unflinching stare. "In turn, Israel will agree to train a number of Soviet craftsmen in the art of creating luxury jewelry."

He turned toward Nan Faulkner. "Does that seem a satisfactory compromise?"

"Ask Moshe. It's his country," Faulkner said, blowing out a pale stream of smoke. "The United States would have no objection so long as the net result doesn't hurt Israel's position within world economies."

Van Luik nodded and felt a tremor of relief. Faulkner was the key. Her tacit acceptance of the compromise meant that markets rather than ideologies would rule again today.

"Mr. Aram?" Van Luik turned toward the Israeli.

"We would require a twenty year noncompetition agreement," Aram said sharply. "We taught the Russians how to cut melees and look what happened. They're running us out of the market."

"Five years," Yarakov said, looking at his blunt hands rather than at Aram.

"Fifteen."

"Five."

"Thir—"

"Five!" Yarakov interrupted impatiently. "That is my final offer."

"That might be *your* final offer, babe, but can you kill a deal like this without Moscow's approval?" Faulkner asked. She tipped her glass of water from side to side, making the ice inside click softly. When Yarakov was silent, Faulkner turned to Aram. "How does twelve sound to you?"

Though Faulkner's voice was casual, there was nothing casual about her suggestion, and Aram knew it. He hesitated, then nodded. Yarakov didn't look happy either, but he nodded also, sealing the agreement.

"Ms. Faulkner, your requests are disappointingly modest," van Luik continued.

"So is the market."

"We disagree. DSD studies indicate an increasing demand for luxury jewelry worldwide. We have added twenty percent to your request. "We are confident that the American market will be able to absorb it, particularly with the new advertising campaign American jewelers will be launching soon."

Faulkner knocked the ash from her cigarillo and looked skeptical.

"The theme of the campaign is, 'The time to show her is now. Give a diamond as important as your love.' The stress will be on mounted diamonds in excess of one carat."

Faulkner shook her head, making the high-quality diamond studs in her earlobes glitter. "It will take time for such a campaign to have an effect. Meanwhile, we'll have expensive diamond jewelry up the gazoo. Give us a year's grace."

Van Luik made a note on the paper in front of him. "Three months' grace, Ms. Faulkner. If your sight holders don't like the contents of their parcels, they may, as always, refuse them."

Faulkner stubbed out her cigarillo and said nothing.

"Are we in agreement?" van Luik asked, looking around the table. There was no dissent. *"Mazel und broche."*

There was a muttered chorus of *"Mazel und broche."*

Even Nan Faulkner said the traditional words before she shoved back her chair and stalked out of the room, mentally preparing her report for the Secretary of Defense. Of one thing she was certain. She would conclude with a home truth: Another gem diamond mine was definitely needed, a mine controlled by the United States, not ConMin.

15

◆

ERIN LOOKED UP FROM THE REMNANTS OF HER dinner as Cole approached her. Around them was the hum of a busy restaurant. She barely heard it. She watched his lithe walk with an unconscious intensity. It was the same way she listened to his words, looked at his eyes, breathed the air that had touched him. . . . Last night she had fallen asleep in his lap with the hard proof of his arousal against her hip. Today she had awakened fully dressed and alone in the bed. The intense sexuality that was as much a part of Cole as his big hands was fully controlled.

The realization still rippled through Erin's mind at odd moments, rearranging everything in its wake, leaving a feeling that was both peaceful and shimmering with an odd anticipation.

Yet even as the feeling radiated through her, she knew she was reading too much into Cole's restraint. He wanted her, and he was intelligent enough to know that pushing her sexually would guarantee that he didn't get her. She was edging toward wanting him, and she was intelligent enough to know the emotional risks involved. Cole Blackburn didn't strike her as the kind of man who would let himself be vulnerable to love. She wasn't the kind to give herself to a man without loving him.

"Ready?" Cole asked, holding out his hand.

Erin stood and slid her hand into his. "Did you get them?"

"They're strapped to my waist. I got a room at a different hotel and left our stuff in it."

"My camera bag?" she asked.

He smiled slightly. "It's safe in the room. And no, you can't take pictures yet. No one watching you with a camera would mistake you for a tourist."

She sighed.

He squeezed her hand. "We'll rent a car using the new passports and leave tomorrow morning. Once we're out of the city you can take all the pictures you want."

"That's a rash promise. I'm going to hold you to it."

Laughing, Cole and Erin walked out of the restaurant hand in hand, looking like a couple having a relaxed night on the town. Outside it was warm, humid, and smelled like a city enclosed by a greenhouse.

As the two strolled beyond the circle of illumination thrown by a streetlight, they all but disappeared. Cole was wearing lightweight cotton slacks, shirt, and shoes. They were black. Erin was wearing the same. Cole had insisted on dark colors at night and khaki during the day. Since he had bought everything—including the nylon duffels they were using as luggage—she hadn't complained. All she had of her former baggage was a single camera bag and the diamonds belted around her waist beneath her clothes.

A breeze stirred vaguely, bringing the scent of the sea.

"Now will you let me go see the Indian Ocean?" Erin asked.

"Timor Sea, actually."

"Sold."

Cole laughed softly and looked down at the woman who walked so gracefully by his side. She had been different since she had fallen asleep in his lap. Her relaxation with him and her gentle verbal teasing only increased his desire. So did the frank approval in her eyes when she watched him.

"Come on," Cole said. "There's a way down to the sea over here."

Ahead of Cole an unlighted, zigzagging walkway tunneled down through lush growth to the nearby water. They were only a few feet from the coarse sand beach when Cole stopped short, muscled Erin against the trunk of a tree, and pinned her in place with his body as though they were lovers too impatient to wait for privacy. After a reflexive instant of fear at being manhandled, Erin relaxed. Cole's predatory attention wasn't on her. It was on the path behind them that led back up to Darwin's sidewalks.

"I thought I heard somebody behind us," Cole said against Erin's ear.

The strength and weight of his body kept breaking over her with each breath she took. Only a small part of her response was a residue of old fear. Most of it was new desire.

There was just enough light from the waxing moon for Erin to see the strong tendons in Cole's neck, the black beard stubble that was a shadow beneath his skin, and the deep, steady beat of life in his throat. The pressure of his body was impersonal rather than sexual, protective rather than seductive. She told herself it was better that way.

She didn't believe it.

"Come on," Cole said in a voice that was barely a thread of sound. "Farther down the beach there's another way back up to the sidewalk."

Their shoes made a thick, gritty sound in the coarse sand. To their right the sea lapped rather than broke over the beach. Clouds with blurred edges ran like buttermilk over the sky, soaking up moon and stars until nothing remained but a vague haze and a dissolving ripple of moonlight on the water. Intense shadow flowed out from the land where trees overhung the sand. The densities of light and shadow fascinated Erin. They were unlike any combination of dark and bright that she had ever seen.

"Wait here," Cole said softly. "If you see anyone or anything move ahead, yell my name and come running."

"Where are you going?"

The only answer was the whisper of steel being drawn from the leather sheath Cole wore at his wrist. Like another shade of darkness he glided back the way they had come. Erin stared into the night intently, trying to see where Cole had gone.

Hands shot out of the darkness, grabbing her. Before she had a chance to panic, she was following the self-defense routines that had been drilled into her until they were as much a part of her as her memories of Hans.

The man who grabbed Erin made a triumphant

sound that ended in a grunt of pain as her heel connected with his kneecap. He spun aside, hanging on to her with only one hand, grabbing his knee with the other. As she yelled for Cole, she tried to numb her attacker's wrist with the edge of her palm, but he yanked her off balance as he fell. She went down as she had been trained to do, loosely, rolling instantly to her feet, poised to run, for escape was always the best defense. The man's hand shot out and wrapped around her ankle. Reflexively she kicked him in the face. He bellowed in pain.

Suddenly men were swarming all over her, grabbing at her hands and feet. She used everything she had ever learned, knowing even as she fought that there were too many for her to win, that they were too strong, and, worse, that they weren't unskilled fighters themselves. She had taken her captor by surprise when she had defended herself effectively. The other men couldn't be surprised in the same way. They had seen what had happened to their friend and they were overwhelming her by sheer weight.

Erin kept on fighting silently, savagely, because she had promised herself seven years ago that she would kill or die before any man raped her again. Suddenly she took a blow to the diaphragm that literally paralyzed her, driving the breath from her body. She barely heard one of her assailants give a high scream of pain in the instant before he reeled away from her and slumped unconscious into the sand. There was another flurry of motion as a man was lifted up and flung away. He landed hard and lay gasping for air.

The three remaining men abandoned Erin and looked around frantically, trying to find the invisible attacker.

"Run!" Cole ordered.

For an instant Erin didn't recognize his voice. There was a flatness in it that she had never heard before. She sensed motion to her left and turned her head.

"Damn it, *run!*"

Cole looked huge in the nebulous light. His hands and his body made sinuous, almost hypnotic motions as he waited for the men to attack him. With each continuous motion he shifted balance smoothly, always poised to attack or defend in any direction, never giving away his intentions. The knife he held had the dull shine of mercury. Slowly he backed away, trying to draw the men from Erin, who hadn't gotten up.

The men rushed Cole in a ragged line. Erin saw the sudden gleam of steel blades as two of the men drew knives. She tried to call out, to warn Cole, but there was no air left in her body. She fought against herself as she had fought against the men, trying to drag air back into her lungs so that she could do more than lie helpless on the cold sand.

Cole watched the oncoming men, picking the order of his targets with the cool precision of a man who is used to being on the wrong end of the odds in a fight. He knew that he had two advantages. The first was that he didn't have to worry about injuring a friend by mistake. The second was that the men would expect him to defend himself rather than attack them.

The two men holding knives came eagerly forward, keeping just enough distance between them so that Cole could fight only one at a time. He had already chosen his target—the bigger of the two, the man who moved and held himself like a fighter. Cole feinted toward the smaller man, then pivoted and leaped toward the bigger one. Cole's left hand slapped aside the knife. Simultaneously the edge of his right hand delivered a chopping blow to the man's throat. The attacker went down, choking, a threat no more.

Using the momentum of his turn, Cole lashed out with a high, powerful kick to the smaller man's head. There was a thick sound as he connected. The smaller man attacker went face down in the sand and stayed there.

One man remained standing. Two others had staggered back to their feet and were closing in again.

"Erin!" Cole said.

She tried to answer but couldn't, for there still was no air in her lungs.

"Erin."

Only silence answered him. He looked at the three attackers who were still standing. "You're dead men."

With an inarticulate sound one of three reached inside his windbreaker and drew out a long, oddly shaped gun.

Suddenly Cole bent, straightened, and turned in a blur of motion, sending sand hurtling into the man's eyes as the two unarmed men leaped forward. Cole rolled with the attack, taking the blows in order to get in close and finish off at least one of the attackers before the gunman got his vision back.

Erin struggled to her knees, sobbing wrenchingly as breath slowly trickled into her lungs. She saw Cole go down beneath the two men and heard the man with the gun cursing in a heavy Cockney accent. He was on his knees, clawing at his eyes and swearing, temporarily blinded. She hadn't the strength to stand so she did the only thing she could. She crawled closer, gathered a double handful of sand and flung it in the man's face. His frantically moving fingers ground the new sand into his eyes. Screaming curses he came to his feet, flailing around with the gun.

Even as Erin thought of making a grab for the gun she knew she was still too weak. She dug out more handfuls of sand and threw them into the man's face. Grunts and curses came from the darkness beyond, followed by the unmistakable sound of a breaking bone. In the sudden silence the metallic click of the gun being cocked was like thunder.

"Get down!"

At Cole's command Erin flattened out, rolled over and over, and then hugged the ground as the blinded man began firing wildly, shooting in the direction the sand had been coming from. She had expected shattering noise from the gun. All that came were thick spitting sounds.

Cole had also thrown himself to one side, knowing that the next bullets would be aimed in the direction that his shout had come from. Instants later two bullets kicked sand where he had been, proving that while the gunman was temporarily blind, he wasn't deaf or stupid.

Erin lay utterly motionless, trying not to breathe, knowing that any sound she made would send a bullet in her direction. Because it was so quiet, she thought that Cole was also hiding by not moving. Then she caught a suggestion of motion from the corner of her eye. She turned her head very carefully. It took all her self-control not to cry out at what she saw.

Slowly, inexorably, timing his movements so that they were covered by the faint lapping of the waves, Cole was easing closer to the gunman.

Fear washed coldly through Erin. If Cole made one mistake he would be shot down before he could do anything to prevent it. It was the same for her in this lethal game of blindman's buff. Only if they were motionless would they be safe. Yet only if they moved could they ultimately survive; the gunman wouldn't remain blind for more than a few moments.

Erin dug her fingers farther into the coarse sand, gathering grains to fling into the gunman's eyes. She looked from the gunman to Cole, measuring the distance yet to be covered. Cole's head moved once in an emphatic negative gesture. He had seen her hands clenched in the sand. He didn't want her to move suddenly, calling down bullets on herself before she had any chance to get away.

Cole slid nearer, trying to get close enough to grab the gunman, who stood between himself and Erin. If Cole threw his knife or hit the man with a flying tackle, there was a very good chance that the man would topple, gun blazing, right onto Erin. This meant Cole had to be within arm's reach of the man, so close that the sound of the waves no longer offered any cover for his movements, so close he couldn't even breathe without warning the gunman of his presence.

Erin's hands closed with such force in the sand that her fingers ached. Slowly she began gathering herself with a series of small movements. Cole's heart hesitated, then slammed hard as more adrenaline pumped through him. If the gunman sensed Erin's movement he would turn and shoot before Cole could do anything. If she would just lie still, she would be safe. But she wasn't lying still. She was trying to get close enough to fling more sand into the man's eyes.

The gunman had his back partially to her and his head turning. He was poised to spin in any direction, his breathing ruthlessly controlled, listening like a cat at a mouse hole. The silenced gun wove from side to side, covering as wide a field of fire as possible.

Erin saw the glitter of moonlight in the man's eyes as he turned toward the water. She was afraid his vision was rapidly returning. Cole was silhouetted against the pale gleam of the sea, a target too big to miss even with blurred vision.

She threw sand and rolled aside in the same violent motion. The gunman spun toward her, firing before he could see a target. The bullet hit the sand, spraying grit. The gunman whirled back around toward the sea, warned of an attack more by instinct than by any noise Cole made. The gun spat again.

Cole grunted just before the base of his palm smashed against the man's nose with a driving upward blow. The gunman's head snapped backward and blood poured blackly in the moonlight. The man crumpled without a sound to the sand.

"Erin! Are you all right?"

"Yes. Just shaken."

"Watch the pathway we came down."

Cole picked up the gun and checked the load with a few swift motions before he sheathed his knife. Methodically he began checking the other four men for signs of consciousness.

"Anyone coming?" he asked Erin as he bent over the first man and made a swift, hard motion with his right hand. The man didn't move in response.

"No. W-what are you doing?"

"Making sure they're not faking it."

Cole's method was ruthless and effective—stiff-ened fingers driven into the groin. No conscious man could take it without a reflexive whimper and a convulsive movement to protect himself. Numbly Erin watched. She was trembling in the aftermath of adrenaline, but she felt almost unnaturally calm. She had been through sudden violence before, survived it, and adjusted to the reality that she would never expect the world to be a safe place again. This time the violence had been much easier to bear. She had managed to defend herself. She had fought and she hadn't even been injured. Her mind was safe, too. She didn't have any naïve belief in personal safety to lose after the attack. It was all old news. Later she might cry and shake, but not now. Now she was emotionally numb. Surviving.

The fourth man groaned and curled up at Cole's blow. Erin flinched.

"Still clear?" Cole asked her.

"Yes. Shouldn't we get the police?"

"That would put us out of commission as effectively as these men tried to."

Cole yanked the fourth man into a sitting position. "If you can hear me, open your eyes or you'll get another shot to the balls."

The man's eyes opened.

"Who was the target, me or the girl?" Cole asked.

The man said nothing. Cole's hand moved once, hard. The man made an odd sound and jerked convulsively.

"Who was the target?" Cole repeated.

"You," the man groaned.

Relief went through Cole. He couldn't expect to

protect Erin for long from outright assassination attempts. Mayhem was different.

Cole turned and threw the pistol into the sea. "A hit?" he asked.

The man made a hoarse sound. "Just a kneecapping."

Erin's breath came in harshly as she realized that the point of the attack had been to maim Cole permanently.

"Who hired you?" Cole asked.

"Don't know."

Cole believed him. It was typical of thugs not to know any more than the name of the target and how to get to him. Cole pressed his thumbs into the man's neck until the carotid arteries closed down. Unconsciousness swiftly followed. He opened his hands, releasing the man.

"Anyone else coming?" Cole asked.

"No."

"We'll go up the other way just the same. There was somebody back on the first path, but he didn't mix in the fight."

"Why?"

"He may be calling the cops. Let's go."

Cole got to his feet and bent to help Erin up. His normally smooth motions were marred by a slight hitch at every other step. She thought she saw the slick gleam of blood on the dark fabric above his left knee, on the inside of his thigh.

"Are you hurt?"

He grunted.

"Cole," Erin said urgently.

"He didn't kneecap me, thanks to you. I'll only limp for a day or two instead of the rest of my life."

"But—"

"Later. Shock is a good anesthetic, but it wears off fast. By then, I want us to be in a safe place."

"Is there one?"

Cole turned away without answering, which told Erin more than she wanted to know.

16

◆

"I STILL THINK YOU SHOULD LET ME TAKE YOU TO a doctor," Erin said unhappily.

Cole walked into the hotel room, saying nothing. His leg ached and was bleeding, but he knew the wound itself was little more than a burn. All he needed was some help cleaning and bandaging his thigh.

Erin shut and locked the door behind her. The hotel room was small and modestly furnished. Her old camera bag and new duffel were on the bed, as was Cole's new duffel.

"Let me help you to . . ." Erin's glance went to his thigh. "My God!"

"Don't go all soft and useless on me now," Cole said. "It's just blood."

Moisture shone darkly against Cole's slacks. If the cloth had been any color but black, it would have been impossible to conceal the fact that he was wounded. As Erin watched in horror, a bright scarlet rivulet slid from beneath his cuff onto his shoe.

"Unless you're planning to leave tracks all over the carpet, you'd better go into the bathroom," she said in a voice that was too high and thin.

Cole walked unevenly to the bathroom, lowered the toilet lid, and sat down to remove his shoes and socks. Without a word Erin sank to her knees in front of him, pushed his hands away, and began pulling off his shoes. Blood dripped onto her fingers. She made a low sound of distress and tried to work faster.

"Relax, honey," Cole said. "It's not serious."

"Just a scratch, right?" Erin shot back, angry because he was hurt and there was nothing she could do to change that. "I've got news for you, big man. Scratches don't bleed this much."

"Blood isn't spurting with each heartbeat, so the bullet didn't get anything important. As for the mess —hell, it's not like you don't see blood regularly."

"I only hunted whales once."

"I was talking about your period."

Erin gave Cole a glittering look. He smiled. She let out a pent-up breath and shook her head.

"Has anyone ever told you that you're impossible?" she asked, bending over his feet once more.

"Nope. Want to be the first?"

She made a sound that could have been exasperation or amusement, but her hands were much steadier now. Cole was right. Blood wasn't an unfamiliar sight to her.

By the time Erin had his shoes and socks off, Cole had unbuttoned his shirt and tossed it beyond reach of the blood that seemed to be sticking to everything. With quick motions he unzipped his slacks and began removing them. At the scrape of cloth over the wound, his breath hissed between his teeth.

"You're hurting yourself. I'll cut off the pant leg."

"No. I don't want to waste time shopping again. I'll have to wear these pants on the airplane."

Erin looked up. "Does that mean we're going back to California?"

"No. We're going to Derby. With luck, they'll waste their time looking for us between Darwin and Abe's station while we come in from the other side. Get a pillowcase, honey. I'll rip it up for bandages."

"I've got a first-aid kit in my camera bag."

By the time she got back to the bathroom, Cole was standing in his jockey shorts, one hip propped against the washbasin as he tried to examine the red slash across his muscular inner thigh. To Erin's adrenaline-heightened senses, the naked strength of his body was suddenly, violently attractive. She remembered the terrible feeling of rage and helplessness she had known when she went down beneath the attackers. Then she had heard Cole's voice promising vengeance for her hurt, and she had known—really *known*—that this time she wasn't fighting alone. This time a man was going to use his strength to help her rather than to brutalize her.

Cole turned toward Erin. As he moved, light fell across him at a different angle, creating new shadows and highlights. For a crazy moment Erin wanted to grab her camera and catch the supple strength and masculine textures of Cole's body. He was . . . beautiful.

The thought stunned her.

"Sit down," she said huskily. "Let me help you."

Cole's eyes narrowed at the change in Erin's voice, a softness where before there had been only the clipped irritation and anger of an adrenaline backlash.

Now she was looking at him as though she had never seen him before, her extraordinary green eyes clear and wide, approving of him with an intensity that made his heart pound heavily.

Silently Cole sat down on the toilet seat. Erin rinsed out a washcloth in cold water before she bent over him. The enforced intimacy of the contact made her feel weak. She tried to think of Cole as a man who needed help rather than as a powerful, nearly naked warrior whose thighs she was kneeling between.

Then Erin saw his wound and forgot about Cole's lack of clothes.

"It always looks worse than it is," Cole said, seeing the pallor of Erin's cheeks.

"But the blood—"

"I saw your pictures of the whale hunt. You had to be ankle deep in blood to get those shots."

Erin remembered shooting roll after roll of film and then being violently ill. Afterward she had reloaded her camera and gone back to work.

"I threw up all over the place," she admitted as she pressed a cold cloth against the wound, stopping the slow oozing of blood.

"You do and you clean it up, honey. Blackburn's First Rule of Housekeeping."

Glancing up, she saw his amused gray eyes and wondered how she had ever thought they were bleak or cold.

"Right," Erin said. "No throwing up. Besides, you're smaller than a whale. Barely."

She caught the flash of his smile as she bent over him once more.

"Hurt?" she asked, increasing the pressure.

"What do you think?"

Her smile turned upside down. "It hurts."

The back of his index finger brushed lightly down her cheek. "I've felt a lot worse." His breath came in as she shifted the cloth. "I've felt better, too," he admitted wryly. "Burns are the worst for pain."

The pronounced tendency to tremble that was the result of adrenaline and anxiety faded from Erin's hands. While Cole held the compress in place, she went to work cleaning up the muscular length of his leg.

"Well, no one can say you aren't a red-blooded American male," Erin muttered as she rinsed out the washcloth for the fifth time. "Hairy, too."

Cole laughed.

Erin tried futilely to smile. Soon she would have to clean the wound itself. No matter how gentle she was, it would hurt him.

"Just what I thought," he said, lifting the compress to check. "Shallow and messy. No big deal."

"How can you tell?" she asked through clenched teeth. "You can't even see all of it."

"I know how it feels when something cuts muscle and grates on bone. This did neither. But if it bothers you that much, I'll get in the shower and clean it up myself."

Erin paused in the act of turning on the hot water in the sink. She glanced at Cole. The bathroom light poured over him, outlining every ridge of muscle, sinew, and bone. He literally filled the alcove where the toilet was.

"There's no way something could draw blood on you and *not* cut muscle," she said, wringing out a hand towel in the hot water with quick, angry motions, hating what she would have to do next.

"You slap that over my thigh and I'll turn you over my knee," he warned.

"Try it, big man, and you'll end up on the floor."

"Feeling feisty, are you?"

Erin's hands paused. She realized that Cole was right. The knowledge that she had come through violence intact was fizzing slowly through her, permeating years of fear, changing them, changing her. Part of her felt she could take on any man and throw him ten times out of ten. Common sense told her she was insane even to think about it. She let out a long sigh.

"First time on the winning side?" Cole asked.

She nodded.

He smiled crookedly. "Don't let it go to your head, honey. If a hit had been ordered, we'd be face down in the sand. You should have run like hell when I told you to."

Shaking her head in silent disagreement, Erin knelt between Cole's powerful legs. Her hair gleamed in shades of mahogany and copper and gold as she moved. His breath came out in a rush as the warm towel draped almost tenderly over the wound. Her hands worked slowly, gently, carefully, cleaning the angry furrow.

"I mean it, honey. You should have run," Cole continued quietly, stroking her gleaming hair with his hand. "It's the first rule of self-defense."

"You should have taken your own advice."

"It didn't apply to me. I wasn't defending myself."

Her breath came in. "I know. You were defending me."

Beneath Cole's palm Erin's head turned. He felt the warm touch of her kiss against his hand in the instant before she rose to rinse the towel under the faucet once more. She wanted to thank Cole for defending her but didn't know what to say that wouldn't sound hopelessly naïve and foolish. He had fought for her when she had been helpless. She didn't have any words to tell him how much that meant to her. She was still discovering it herself.

Erin was certain about one thing, however; she could not have left Cole Blackburn to die while she ran away, unhurt.

She knelt once more and resumed cleaning the wound. Hot tears gathered at the back of her eyes when Cole's breath hissed out and he began cursing in a low voice.

"I'm sorry," she whispered, hating the knowledge that she was hurting him. As gently as possible she blotted the wound, trying to see how deep it was and if any cloth from his slacks was imbedded in his flesh. "Can you turn more to the left?"

Cole's leg bent. He braced his foot against the washbasin and wondered if Erin had the slightest idea what it was doing to him to feel her hair slide against his uninjured thigh, to feel her hands on his bare leg as she steadied herself, to feel her breath against his naked, sensitive skin. At least her unintentional seduction was taking his mind off the bruised, burning pain radiating from the shallow wound. He had been lucky as hell to get away with such a minor injury and he knew it.

"How's that?" he asked, shifting until light fell directly on his inner thigh.

"Good."

Erin put her hand on Cole's thigh to hold him in place. With an effort she forced herself to concentrate

on his wound as though it were an object seen through
a camera lens. She bent closer, peering at the scarlet
furrow. No matter how she turned, a shadow still fell
across the wound, concealing its depth. Caged between his legs, she shifted awkwardly, almost leaning
against his torso in order to see from a different angle.
The motion sent first her shoulder and then her hair
sliding across his groin.

A shaft of desire went through Cole, tensing his
whole body in an instant.

"Does that hurt?" she asked anxiously.

"Not . . . quite."

Cole's voice was thick and his eyes were focused
on Erin's hair, not on her hands. He wondered if silk
or satin or fire came in that particular shade. Her hair
felt like all three when it slid down over his skin, the
strands cool and silky, yet somehow warm at the same
time.

"Lift a bit higher if you can," she said, pressing
gently with both hands against his thigh. "That's
good." She looked at the wound and let out a long
sigh of relief. "You're right. It isn't serious. It must
hurt, though."

Cole didn't bother to deny it. "Have any bandages in that kit?"

"In your size? I doubt it," she said dryly, starting
to get to her feet.

"Stay put, honey," he said, holding her gently in
place against his body. "I can reach it."

When Cole leaned forward, he all but surrounded
Erin. She felt the supple power of his leg beneath her
hands, felt the soft abrasion of his body hair against
her wrists, and sensed the quintessentially masculine
heat brushing against her arm. Sensations shivered

from her breastbone to her knees, shortening her breath. Carefully she drew in air, telling herself that she must be mistaken. She couldn't have felt what she thought she had felt. Cole couldn't be aroused.

A tube of antibiotic ointment appeared at Erin's eye level. She took it, carefully blotted the wound again, and began smoothing ointment over raw flesh. Cole hissed a string of words in a foreign language. She was grateful she didn't know the translation.

With each light brush of Erin's fingers against his body, Cole's pulse leaped. The burning of the wound didn't compare to the way she set fire to his blood. Because there was nothing he could do about either fire, he kept cursing in the kind of Portuguese used in the diamond fields of Brazil, blasphemies that could etch steel.

As Cole cursed, he told himself it was a simple case of the oldest aphrodisiac of all—adrenaline. He had felt it before, the aftermath of ambush, the vivid, almost overwhelming rush as he knew that he had survived, and then the sexual hunger that was his body's way of celebrating being alive. If Erin had been any other woman he would have pulled her onto his lap, burying himself in her until he came with a violence to equal his arousal. But she wasn't any other woman. She had been brutalized to the point that she might never invite a man into the hot, sleek depths of her body.

Grimly Cole tried not to think about the delicate hands that felt so tantalizing on his skin. Like Erin's breath, warm and sweet. Like the scent of her. Like her breasts brushing against his leg when she bent even closer, trying to reach the back of his thigh. The soft resilience of her breasts was a brand against his naked skin. He flinched and swore, wondering why this one woman among all women aroused him to the point of pain.

"Whatever happened to the strong, *silent* type?" Erin said unhappily, biting her lower lip.

"Do you believe in the Easter Bunny too?" He hissed another curse between his teeth.

By the time Erin was finished, her lip had tooth marks in it but there was almost no fresh bleeding along the wound. Two square bandage pads appeared at her eye level.

"Don't believe the advertising on the wrapper," Erin said. "These stick just like the old kind."

As she shifted position to put the first bandage in place, she brushed intimately against Cole, who drew in his breath hard. Erin froze against him, thinking she had somehow hurt him again.

"You should put the bandages on yourself," she said unhappily. "I'm too clumsy. I don't want to hurt you any more."

Cole looked down at the woman curled between his legs, her eyes haunted and yet so beautiful it came as a shock of pleasure each time she looked at him.

"You're not a bit clumsy." He dropped the bandages into her lap. "And I like having your hands on me."

Her head snapped.

"How about you, Erin?" he asked, watching her intently. "Do you like having your hands on me?"

"I don't like hurting you." Tears filled Erin's eyes, magnifying their beauty. "I'm sorry, Cole. I really don't mean to hurt you."

His fingertips brushed the length of her right cheekbone. "Such a tender little thing to be so brave."

"I'm not brave. I was so scared I was shaking."

"What do you think courage is, honey? It's being scared and getting the job done anyway. The rest of it is just bells and whistles. Useless."

Calloused fingertips caught the tears that trembled on the edge of release. Cole brought his hand to his lips, tasting the clear, diamond-bright drops.

"Salty and very, very sweet. Nobody has ever cried for me, Erin. Not one person on earth."

She closed her eyes, unable to bear the intensity in his. When she opened them again, it was to concentrate on Cole's wound. She smoothed the bandages over his leg, trying not to hurt him. It was difficult. Her concentration kept splintering over his words and the fact that she was kneeling between the legs of a man who was nearly naked and fully aroused, yet wasn't touching her in any way.

But what really ruined Erin's concentration was her own lack of fear. She should have been terrified by his strength and his arousal. She wasn't. She was restless, nervous, jumpy, and alert, but she wasn't afraid.

"That should do it," Erin said in a husky voice.

Hurriedly she stood and walked into the bedroom. She didn't hear Cole get up, didn't hear him follow her, but she knew he had. His hands settled on her shoulders and squeezed lightly.

"Thanks." His voice changed, becoming harder. "But honey, the next time I tell you to run, *you damn well better run.*"

"I couldn't have run even if I'd wanted to," Erin said, exasperated and angry. "That bastard hit me so hard I couldn't breathe for—"

"He hit you?" Big hands spun Erin around, stopping her words. "Where?"

"Here," she said, pointing just below her breast-bone.

Without a word Cole began unbuttoning Erin's blouse.

"Cole! What do you think you're doing!" she said, pushing futilely at his hands.

"Hold still."

It was the same flat voice that Cole had used on the attackers. Erin obeyed instantly, but it was from surprise rather than fear. With a feeling of disbelief she watched her blouse separate beneath Cole's deft fingers. She opened her mouth but no words came.

"Does this hurt?" he asked impersonally.

Erin felt the exquisitely gentle probing of his fingertips along her ribs. Odd shivers of response marched over her skin, leaving a wake of goose bumps.

"Does it hurt?" Cole asked again, looking into her shocked eyes.

Her mouth opened but she couldn't even take a breath. She shook her head in a negative.

"This?"

Warm, slightly rough fingertips moved along her ribs to her breastbone.

"A little," she whispered.

She saw Cole frown and felt the pressure of his fingertips increase.

"Now?"

"That hurts a little more, but still not much."

Erin watched Cole's face as he touched her. His eyelashes were very thick, very black, making his eyes appear like clear crystal touched with tiny shards of blue and green. The intense black of his hair was reflected in the heavy shadow of beard darkening his tan skin.

"Take a deep breath," he said.

Erin breathed in.

"Again. Deeper." Cole watched her face closely but saw no sign of real pain. Her ribs rose reassuringly beneath his hands, telling him she was able to fill her lungs in a normal way. "Does it hurt now?"

"Some, but not enough to interfere with breathing. Really. I've been hurt much worse tripping over camera equipment."

Cole smiled slightly but kept probing. "Ribs?"

She shook her head.

"Here?"

"Ouch!"

"That's what I thought. Your ribs are okay but you took a shot to the diaphragm." He traced the beginnings of a bruise with his fingertips. "You're going to be wearing a rainbow for a few days." He turned her around so that her back was to him. "You hurt anywhere else?" he continued, running his hands over her slowly. "Spine? Kidneys?"

"No."

"Sure?" he asked, kneading Erin's lower back gently, searching for any signs of soreness, any flinching away from his light, probing touches.

"I'm sure."

"Let me know if that changes."

Cole turned Erin around and calmly began buttoning her blouse once more, trying very hard not to notice the taut swell of her breasts beneath her bra and the soft heat of her skin. When his hands were between her breasts, she took a swift, involuntary breath. Inevitably his hands brushed against her.

Erin felt the accidental touch and held her breath, waiting for him to take advantage of the moment. She had no doubt that he wanted her. He couldn't hide his arousal while standing in front of her wearing jockey shorts that were becoming less concealing with every one of his heartbeats.

Without a pause, Cole kept buttoning Erin's shirt.

She closed her eyes and told herself that she was relieved, not disappointed. Cole's past might have been as shadowed as a midnight jungle, but his deepest instincts were honorable. He would protect rather than brutalize. Yet there was no doubt that he could, and would, fight with disciplined savagery if the need arose.

And that was the key, Erin realized. Discipline. More than any man she had ever known, even her father, Cole was in control of his mind, of his body, of his instincts—of himself. The certainty of his self-control raced through her, more heady than wine, leaving a curious warmth in its wake.

"Be sure to tell me if you start hurting," he said again, turning away from Erin. "I'm going to wash out my slacks."

"Cole?"

Erin's voice dried up as she watched him turn toward her once more. He was so much bigger than she was, so much stronger, nearly naked, and his eyes were smoldering as he watched her.

"You better lie down, honey. You look a little strung out."

For the space of one breath, two, Erin didn't answer. Then she went to the bed and lay down. As she closed her eyes, the sound of running water came from the bathroom.

17

◆

WITH QUICK, STRONG MOTIONS COLE SLUICED blood from his slacks. When the water no longer ran pink, he wrung out the slacks, rolled them up in a towel and squeezed, blotting up water. A snap of his wrist shook them out. He tossed them over the shower rack to dry, picked up his shirt, and put it on. He took a lot of time, long enough for his fierce arousal to subside.

When Cole came out of the bathroom, Erin was lying wide-eyed on the bed, staring at the ceiling, because every time she closed her eyes she saw a picture of Cole, his chest naked but for the black wedge of hair that tapered to a line and vanished behind the white of his underwear. Her eyes snapped open.

"I can't sleep," Erin said. "Every time I close my eyes I see . . ." Her voice died.

"The fight?" Cole asked.

She shook her head. "You."

The corner of his mouth turned down. "And that scares you."

"Not . . . quite."

Cole didn't miss the exact imitation of his earlier words. He crossed the remainder of the room and stood by the bed, watching Erin with crystalline intensity. "Are you trying to tell me something?"

Her head turned toward him, revealing brilliant green eyes and a smile that hovered on the edge of turning upside down. "I liked you better without the shirt."

"Did you? I got the feeling it made you uneasy as hell."

"There's rather a lot of you," she said, watching him through thick, lowered lashes.

"You noticed," he said dryly.

When Erin realized where she was looking, she blushed to the roots of her hair. "You're making this hard for me."

"No. That's what you're doing to me. Again."

"I noticed," she muttered.

Cole laughed, surprised as always by Erin's combination of innocence and resilience. The laughed ended as his breath came in with a soft, ripping sound. Erin's hand was on his leg, her fingertips light against his skin as she traced the edge of the bandage.

"That's dangerous territory, honey."

"It's all I can reach from here."

"If I get any closer, I'll be in bed with you. Is that what you want?"

"I . . ." Erin's voice died. She swallowed and tried again. "I don't know. All I know is I like touching you. I like looking at you. I like it when you hold me. I like it when you kiss me. I like the taste of your skin. I like the feel of your hands on me." She looked at Cole in unconscious appeal. "I want you more than I ever thought I'd want any man. Is that enough?"

"It's a hell of a start," he said in a low voice. "Move over, honey. Let's find out what else you like."

Wondering if she had made the right choice, Erin made room for Cole on the bed. She felt the mattress give deeply as his weight settled on it. Torn between fear and desire, she closed her eyes and waited for him to pull her into his arms. When he didn't, she opened her eyes. He was unbuttoning his shirt and watching her with an intensity that made her breath shorten.

"Cole?"

"Whatever you want," he said simply, throwing the shirt aside. "But you have to tell me, Erin. I won't take a chance on guessing wrong and frightening you."

She gave an odd laugh. "Some of the things I want with you already frighten me."

He smiled slowly. "Sounds interesting. Should we begin with them or save them for last?"

"I think . . . a kiss."

As Erin spoke, she looked at Cole's mouth with unconscious hunger. He saw and hoped that his self-control was as good as he had always thought it was. Deliberately he lay on his back, laced his fingers together, and put his hands behind his head.

"Then why don't you come here and kiss me?" Cole said.

Surprised, Erin hesitated. Despite his words about not frightening her, somehow she had expected Cole to quickly take the lead. That he hadn't both reassured and tantalized her, for as he lay on his back there was no doubt of his own arousal. Slowly she turned onto her side and bent down to Cole's mouth.

The kiss was gentle, almost chaste, until she ran the tip of her tongue along his lips. The taste of him was even better than she remembered, hotter. The feel of his tongue caressing her own made streamers of sensation uncurl in the pit of her stomach.

Erin didn't know how long it was before both of them were breathing quickly and she was making small sounds at the back of her throat with each deep, slow stroke of his tongue. At every breath, every heartbeat, she joined her mouth more deeply with Cole's, lured by the hot pleasures of his kiss. Slowly her hands began to explore his arms from his strong wrists to the hard swell of biceps and shoulders to the surprising, exquisite softness of the hair beneath his arms.

For long moments Erin savored her discovery before her fingers moved on. She threaded through the intriguing fur on Cole's chest, stroking and kneading the flesh beneath, silently telling him just how much she enjoyed his masculine textures and strength, drawing a nearly soundless groan of pleasure from him when her fingers skimmed the flat disks of his nipples.

"Did you like that?" Erin asked, touching his nipples again, feeling them change as they drew into tight nailheads.

"I'm not sure," Cole said in a low voice. "Why don't you try it five or ten more times?"

For an instant she didn't understand. Then she did, and laughed. "You're teasing me."

"I would have sworn it was the other way around. But I'll forgive you if—"

Cole's voice broke as her hands skimmed down to the elastic band of his underwear and stopped. When Erin reversed direction and went stroking back up his chest, he had to bite back words of disappointment. Slowly she bent and tasted first his neck, then the median line of his body to his breastbone. With great care she closed her teeth over a sleek swell of muscle. His breath broke again and she smiled.

"I like that," she said. "I like knowing I can affect you."

"Then run your hands a little farther down and watch the fireworks," Cole offered, smiling despite the need that made his whole body clench.

Erin's laughter was like soft flames licking against his stomach. For a few moments there was only the sound of skin sliding over skin and Cole's quickening breaths as she stroked his chest.

"Cole?" she whispered against his neck, "would you touch me too?"

He unlocked fingers that ached from the pressure he had exerted to keep from reaching for the soft temptation of Erin's body.

"Where?" he asked huskily.

Erin made a puzzled sound against his skin.

"Where do you want to be touched?" Cole felt the heat of Erin's blush where her cheek lay against his chest. He laughed softly. "Good. That's one of the places I'm dying to touch."

But he teased her first, caressing the hollows beneath her slanting cheekbones, fitting the warmth of her neck into the hard curve of his palm, massaging her arms from shoulders to fingertips until her eyes closed and his name came from her lips in a sigh of pleasure. He kept stroking her until she began to twist in slow motion against his hand, wanting him to touch the breasts whose nipples were growing hard with her own arousal.

"Cole, please," Erin said, her voice husky.

"Please, what?"

Instead of answering, she took his hand and drew it over one breast. The first instant of contact made her shiver. Instinctively she moved against him, trying to ease the sensual ache as her nipple hardened in a rush. Cole felt the change in her, saw it, and the force of his own response made his hand shake. Slender fingers closed over his, but not to push him away. Slowly she pressed him closer and yet closer, moving against his hard palm.

"Do you like that?" Cole asked, trying to make his voice gentle, and failing. His tone was like his body. Too hard, too hot, too obviously aroused.

"Yes, but . . ."

He set his jaw and lifted his hand, freeing her. Immediately her arms moved as though to shield her breasts if he changed his mind.

"It's all right," Cole said. Then he realized that Erin wasn't withdrawing, she was trying to unbutton her blouse but her hands were trembling. A wave of desire clenched his body, shaking him with its intensity. He took Erin's hands, brushed his lips over them, and smoothed her fingers against his chest. "Let me."

"I'm sorry, I don't know what's wrong. I'm shaking, but I'm not scared. Really I'm not."

"Look at my hands."

She looked, saw the fine tremor in his fingers, and made a sound of surprise.

"Yeah, it shocked me too," he said. "I've never wanted a woman until my hands shook."

Erin's eyes widened. She glanced back to Cole's face and saw that he was watching her, half expecting her to panic.

"Should that make me nervous?" she asked.

"Why not?" he muttered. "It scares the hell out of me."

Deliberately Erin glanced down the length of his torso. "Um, I don't know how to put this, but that doesn't look like fright."

He laughed and the claws of hunger loosened in his groin. His fingers eased between the warm folds of Erin's blouse, pushing aside the dark cloth until he could see the smooth rise of her breasts beneath a rose-colored bra.

"Should I stop now?" Cole asked, sliding a fingertip beneath the edge the bra, skimming the rising and falling of her breasts. "Or do you want me to touch you the way you touched me?"

Before her courage deserted her, Erin reached up and undid the front fastening of her bra. For the space of two breaths Cole simply looked at her and counted the pulse hammering in his body. Her breasts were more beautiful than he had expected, full and high, and her nipples were flushed deep rose with desire. Her skin was flushed as well, bringing into stark relief the fine white lines of old scars.

Realization hit, bringing Cole under control in a freezing rush. "He used a knife on you!"

It took Erin a moment to understand what Cole meant.

"I forgot about the scars," she whispered. "They're so much less ugly than they used to be, but I understand if you don't want to—"

Erin's voice broke as the tip of Cole's tongue traced first one scar, then another, then another, touching her so gently that tears gathered and overflowed onto her cheeks. His words were another kind of caress, a glittering fire licking over her mind and body, telling her that she was beautiful, softness and heat, sweetness and hunger, a burning all the way to his soul.

The restraint and unexpected tenderness of Cole's caresses unraveled Erin. She forgot the past, forgot the future, forgot everything but the exquisite sensations radiating through her body with each touch of Cole's hands, his body, his mouth, until she was breathless and whimpering softly, twisting against him in slow motion.

Cole felt her response in the heat of her skin, tasted it in the fine mist he licked from between her breasts, heard it in the soft, broken cries that were his name. Her sensuality was as unexpected as it was uninhibited. Blood hammered through Cole so fiercely he could barely breathe. He bent to her breasts once more, tugging on a hard peak with his mouth even as his hand slid down her body, undoing her clothes, pushing them to her knees, then returning to find the softness and heat that had been hidden beneath cloth.

When his hand curled possessively around the tangled thatch of hair, she went rigid. Even as he started to retreat, he felt Erin's sultry response. A wild answering heat swept through him, making him groan with the knowledge that it was pleasure, not fear, that had tightened her body. He moved his hand again, sending his palm over the sensitive flesh, drawing forth another passionate shudder. Unable to stop himself, he slid one finger between sultry folds of skin and caressed even softer, hotter flesh.

"Cole!"

"I'm right here," he said, teasing the hard peaks of Erin's breasts with his tongue while his finger slowly withdrew from her body, only to return even more deeply. "Do you want me to stop?"

Erin laughed a little wildly; then her breath broke in a cry of surprise as pleasure burst, sending heat shimmering over her. Instinctively she moved, seeking Cole's touch once more, needing it with a force she neither understood nor questioned.

"Is that yes or no?" he asked, biting her nipple with exquisite care.

Another shudder of pleasure ripped through Erin, taking her voice. "Yes," she managed finally. "I mean no."

Her eyes opened. Their smoldering color was more beautiful than anything Cole had ever seen, even the green diamond she had given him.

"Don't stop," Erin said in a husky voice.

"Does that mean I can finish undressing you?" Cole asked, his voice as caressing as his hand.

Erin looked down the length of her own body to the dark masculine hand nestled between her legs. She made an odd sound, not quite laughter and not quite embarrassment.

"All I'm really wearing is you," she said. "I . . . like it."

Cole set his jaw against the force of his own response. Erin's honesty and sensuality kept taking him by surprise, stripping away his control with every hot word, every hungry movement, her eyes a green fire burning through him. He tried to be gentle as he discarded the rest of their clothes, but he knew he was moving too quickly, almost clumsy with the violence of his own need. He saw her head turn slightly and knew the exact instant she saw that he was as naked as she was, lying on his back, unable to hide the extent of his arousal.

Closing his eyes, Cole prayed he wouldn't have to find out if he could keep the promise he had made to her: *We could be dead naked and you could be all over me like a hot rain, but if you changed your mind I'd get up and get dressed and that would be the end of it.*

"Cole?" Erin whispered.

His eyes opened. "Frightened?"

Slowly she shook her head.

"Sure?"

She nodded.

"Then what is it, honey?"

Unable to bear his intent look, Erin bent and brushed her mouth over Cole's shoulder while she asked her question. "Is it all right if I touch you?"

"Any time, anywhere, any way you want."

Her hand slid hesitantly down his body. "Even here?"

His breath broke. "Especially there."

Her fingertips were cool, uncertain, and incendiary as they traced the hot, unfamiliar textures of his desire.

"I can feel your heartbeat," she whispered, curling her hand around him.

Cole shuddered and groaned.

"I'm sorry," she said instantly, withdrawing.

"Do it again and I'll forgive you." His breath came in with a ripping sound as Erin's hand returned to his hard, aching flesh. "Yes, like that. Just . . . like . . . that."

In an agony of pleasure, he pressed rhythmically against her caressing hand, once, twice, three times before he managed to bring himself under control again.

"There's another way to tease each other," he said finally, his voice low and almost rough. "A way we'll both enjoy." He saw her expression and smiled. "I said tease, not ease. I won't take you, honey. You'll have to give yourself to me every inch of the way. Do you believe me?"

As Erin nodded, Cole lifted her and settled her astride his hips. Her breath broke as she felt him lying between her legs, pressing against her without entering her, sending streamers of sensation coursing through her with each small movement of their bodies. When he rocked her hips gently, sliding her over his hard flesh, a low ripple of sound came from her lips. He rocked her again and fought not to lose control. He released her hips but the rocking didn't stop for she couldn't stop, her breathing rapid and broken, her body shaking, urgent, driven.

"Cole," Erin whispered, reaching for him, trying to complete the union of bodies she had never expected to want, much less to need until she was wild with it. "Help me."

His hand moved, covering hers, guiding her. "Like this," he said, pulling her mouth down to his. *"Like this."*

Their mouths and bodies joined at the same time. A low sound of pleasure came from Erin as she settled over him, feeling him fill her slowly, never taking before she could give, until finally she could get no closer and he could get no deeper. She tried to speak, to tell Cole how incredible the sensation was, but when she lifted her mouth from his, the motion tightened her around him even more.

Words burned into silence as she moved again, deliberately measuring herself and him at the same time, pleasuring both of them, feeling the world slide away with each motion, each breath, until Cole made an anguished sound and went rigid beneath her. She felt the intimate pulses of his release deep inside her and shivered in return, feeling as though she were balanced on the brink of something elemental, unknowable.

Then his hand moved, searching through her sensual heat, finding the focus of her need. He stroked the satin nub, caressing her until her eyes went wide with surprise as intense pleasure burst through her, drawing a ripple of sounds from her lips as her body convulsed delicately around him. He drank the sounds with a kiss and held her until they could both breathe evenly once more.

And even then he held her, for he had tasted the salt of tears as well as passion on her lips.

"Honey?" Cole asked, kissing Erin with a gentleness that was at odds with his harsh voice. "Did I hurt you?"

She shook her head.

"You're crying."

"Am I?" Her hand moved to her cheek. She took in a shivering breath. "I am." With a sigh she smoothed her cheek against his chest before burying her face against his neck. "I'm happy, Cole. I never expected to be. Not this way. I never expected to fall in love after Hans. Then I met you."

Cole's hand hesitated as it stroked down the elegant line of Erin's spine. "Don't mistake what we have as lovers for love. You can get hurt that way. I don't want to hurt you, Erin."

For an instant her eyes closed. She hadn't expected Cole to return her love, but she had hoped.

"I believe you," she said, letting out a long, shaking breath. "Unfortunately, I'm not a halfway kind of person. But don't worry. I'm not expecting any deathless promises from you. That doesn't mean I won't try to trip you and beat you to the floor from time to time."

He laughed in surprise and brushed a kiss over Erin's hair. "I'll look forward to it."

Erin touched his hot skin with the tip of her tongue, tasting him almost secretly. Then she gave a long, shuddering sigh and relaxed against him. Within moments she was asleep.

The trust implicit in the utter relaxation of Erin's body sank into Cole, sliding past defenses he didn't even know he had, shaking him as deeply as passion had. For a long time he lay quietly, smoothing his hand over Erin's hair and back, thinking of the past and the unknown future.

But most of all Cole thought about how he would keep Erin alive when ConMin got serious about canceling her ticket to ride on the diamond tiger.

18

Hugo van Luik sat in the half-light of his study, holding the phone in one hand and trying to think. But it was hard to think while Jason Street poured Australian slang into one ear, the night poured silence into the other, and painkillers blurred all distinctions.

Frowning, van Luik stared through the open door to the bedroom across the hall. Limned by light from the street, his wife stirred and rolled over in bed. Her hair was a pale silver glow in the darkness. If she was awake, she hadn't called out to him. Thirty-eight years of marriage had taught her to leave her husband's business to him. If the problem that loomed in the middle of the night took five minutes or five days, she rarely commented. Or perhaps she simply didn't notice.

Van Luik sighed soundlessly. Once he had relished alarms and intrusions at odd hours. Such things were proof of his importance to the plans of corporations and nations. Now he regarded the job at hand—

that of bringing the elusive Cole Blackburn to bay—as an imposition. Van Luik was tired of trials. He simply wanted it done. Finished.

"Are they still in Darwin?" Street asked across the thousands of miles.

"They checked out of the hotel before the men found them. No one checked into any other Darwin hotels under the names of Blackburn or Windsor. No one rented a vehicle under those names. And we believe Blackburn might be wounded."

"Gunshot?"

"Yes."

"Then he'll avoid doctors."

"We are assuming the two are still in Darwin."

"Maybe," Street said. "And maybe they're using false papers. Her father would be able to get them anything along that line they wanted."

"Agreed. I have asked McLaren to enlist his contacts in ASIO. They will use photos to assist the search."

"McLaren, eh? Was he the wanker who hired the girls Blackburn chewed up?" Street asked sardonically.

"The man is a formidable brawler, from all accounts."

"What do you expect them to say, that he fought like an old woman?"

Van Luik bit back a curse as pain stabbed. "Next time, you will take care of the matter yourself."

"With pleasure, mate. But first we have to find the bastard."

"What is the best way for him to reach the Windsor station?"

"There are only two ways. You rent a plane and

fly in or you rent a Jeep and drive. I'll bet on the Jeep. He'll need it at the station anyway."

"What about a bus?"

"To the station? Not a chance. It's way off the only highway."

"Could he walk there?"

"Not this time of year, mate. He'd be dead of heatstroke before a day, and the tart would pack it in after a few hours. Tell McLaren to shut down Darwin's rentals. I'll take care of Derby."

"Derby?"

"It's the only other place in northwestern Australia you can rent a Jeep. This isn't bleeding London."

Silence, followed by: "Street?"

"What."

"Find them. Make certain they discover nothing before the monsoon makes it impossible to prospect. Failing that, destroy the mine."

"What if it's the size of bleeding Argyle?"

"We think not. We have reason to believe it is a pothole placer deposit of the sort that could be destroyed quite easily."

"What makes you think so?"

Van Luik grimaced and counted his heartbeats in the excruciating pain behind his eyes. "You have your faults, Mr. Street, but geological incompetence isn't one of them. Do you really believe Abelard Windsor could have hidden something the size of Namibia's beach deposits from you for the past ten years?"

"Not a chance, mate. Not one bleeding chance."

Grimly van Luik pursued the main point. "The wet may be enough of a delay for our purposes. Many things can change in the span of five months. Important things. Things that are crucial to maintaining the balance of power within the cartel. *Keep Blackburn off the station.*"

"That could be real tricky, mate. Accidents happen. I might end up killing the girl trying to stop him."

"What is the English saying, beggars cannot be choosers?" Van Luik pinched his nose. "Whatever happens, make certain it looks like an accident. If you end up killing her, it would be far better if the body disappeared. I will be waiting for your call."

Street started to speak, heard the click as the connection was broken, then hung up hard. After a moment he redialed, waited, and spoke again.

"G'day, luv. You got any Yanks asking after your Rover?"

"No Yanks, just a Canadian pair wanting to see Windjana."

Street hesitated. "Canadian?"

"Right."

"Man and a woman?"

"That's right. Name's Markham."

"When did they make their reservation? Last month?"

"Called from Perth a few hours ago. They're catching the Ansett flight. Why?"

Street thought quickly. He could assume it was simple coincidence that a pair of Canadians got a sudden urge to see Western Australia's bleak outback wilderness. He could assume it was simple coincidence that Windjana Gorge was in the direction of Abe's station. He could assume Blackburn and Erin were still hiding out in Darwin, nursing a wound.

Street could assume all those things, but he would be a fool not to at least get a look at the couple.

"Luv," he said, "I'd really like them delayed. Say until tomorrow morning."

"What's in it for me?"

"Fifteen centimeters of the best you'll ever get."

"Cocky bastard, aren't you?"

"You should know," he retorted.

"When you going to pay up?" she asked, laughing.

"I'll be there before dark."

"I'll be waiting."

Street hung up smiling and feeling an anticipatory ache in his crotch. Nora was the prettiest single girl in Derby, which meant that she was only as plain as a termite mound rather than as ugly as a burned stump. But she had her oddities in bed, which put most men off. Not Street. He found her inventiveness stimulating.

Whistling softly, he began packing a small rucksack, hoping Cole Blackburn—if it was him—chose the overland route instead of flying in. There were very few roads between Derby and Crazy Abe's station.

Jason Street knew every meter of them.

19

◆

DERBY HAD THE FEEL OF A TOWN ON THE DOWN-hill slide from exhaustion to extinction. The buildings rested unevenly on stilts, as though the wide plain at the edge of the ocean flooded regularly. Although Derby's street was wide enough for multiple lanes of traffic in both directions, only one lane in each direction was paved. The parkway between the lanes was planted with grass and baoboab trees with their gross trunks and spindly branches that resembled roots. The patchy pavement asphalt was soft from the heat. No cars, truck, or buses were moving. The climate sapped people of all but the ability to sweat.

Darwin had been hot, but air-conditioned and modern. Derby was hot and primitive.

The Rover for which Cole and Erin had waited eighteen hours was as unimpressive as the town itself. The vehicle was a well-used, shambling, rattling sort of reliable wreck, filled with junkyard odds and ends, toolboxes and tarps, spare tires and jacks, metal mesh, and God knew what else, all of it stored in cabinets held shut by nails stuck through hasps. A railed cargo platform ran the length of the top. The fenders were loose, but the steel mesh that separated cargo from passengers was securely fastened and strong enough to hold back a bull.

Cole was giving the Rover a thorough vetting before they left town. Between Derby and Fitzroy Crossing several hundred kilometers down the Great Northern Highway, there were no towns, no settlements, no service stations, no crossroads, no tow trucks—nothing but the spinifex, gum, and wattle wastes of Western Australia.

Erin stood in the miserable shade cast by the overhang of a tin roof and watched Cole check out the Rover's engine. If his wound bothered him, he didn't show it. Nor had he shown it that morning, when he had awakened her with kisses and touches that had melted her until their bodies were joined in an intense pleasure that made pain impossible.

Smiling at the memory, Erin ignored the sweat that gathered beneath her sleeveless, scooped-neck T-shirt and trickled down toward the shorts that had already begun to turn an unappetizing shade of brown. Despite Derby's incredible humidity, the air was thick with a rust-colored dust. Flies descended in the pause between gusts of sultry air. Automatically Erin waved the persistent insects away from her face. Cole did the same as he bent over the Rover's grimy engine.

The heat kept taking her by surprise. She was grateful that Cole had insisted their clothes largely consist of shorts, tank tops, bikini underwear, and thongs. The only concession to Western dress was socks and sturdy walking shoes. The floppy cabbage-leaf cloth hat she wore, her nearly black sunglasses, and the crisp nylon travel bag at her feet were all new. Even the Canadian passport in the bag was new, at least to Erin, although it had a well-used look about it. Cole had produced it, along with one for himself, after they arrived in Perth. Mr. and Mrs. Daniel Markham of Nanaimo, British Columbia.

There had even been a well-worn gold wedding ring for Erin to wear. It was inscribed with her mother's name. The realization that she was wearing her mother's wedding ring disturbed Erin. Family photos had also come with the passports, photos of Erin's grandmother, Bridget McQueen Windsor. When Erin first had seen the photos, passports, and ring, she wondered if Nan Faulkner knew what Matthew Windsor had done, or if her father was putting his lifelong career at risk in order to make up for the misjudgment of seven years ago.

There had been no answer to that question, simply a note from her father that said: *This is all I could find of my father's life in Australia. Be careful, Erin. I love you. Dad.*

The gold ring smoldered in the tropical light, reminding Erin of the photos tucked within her nylon bag. She leaned over, rummaged in the duffel, retrieved the envelope, and stood upright again.

Erin went quickly through the photos, then more slowly. They dated from the time when both Windsor brothers were young and exploring Australia's wild outback together. The black-and-white images showed a land that was sparse, spare, bleak. Yet the men were always smiling, especially when Miss Bridget McQueen was in the photo.

One picture in particular held Erin's interest, a

photo of the young Bridget wearing an old-style dress and standing on a rocky rise with thin, peculiar trees and strangely shaped rocks all around. Bridget was radiant, mischievous, and impudent as she looked up from beneath long lashes at the invisible man who was taking her picture. Off to one side was a man with dense, straight eyebrows, unkempt hair, and a look of raw longing on his face as he watched the young woman whose unbound hair lifted on the breeze.

On the back of the photo was written *Some love for silver, some love for gold,/We love for the heat that never runs cold.* The writing was even, elegant, and old-fashioned. Perhaps bad poetry and careful script had run in the Windsor family.

"That's it," Cole said. "Let's hit the road."

The Rover's hood slammed into place, underlining Cole's words. Erin stuffed the pictures back into their envelope and put it in her camera case. As she bent over, her head poked beyond shade into sunlight once more. The heat was suffocating. She had to force herself to drag the thick air into her lungs. It felt as though she were sucking oxygen through layers of used sauna towels.

And this was spring, not summer. Erin tried to imagine what Derby would feel like under the full weight of a summer sun. She could not.

The interior of the Rover seat was as hot as it was dusty. The engine fired quickly on the first try. Erin sat and sweated.

"You were right," she said.

"About what?"

"Sweating. It doesn't help."

Cole smiled a bit grimly. "I'd rather have been wrong. I hate this bloody place during buildup."

As the Rover began moving, the steady flow of air from the open windows helped to cool Erin. After fifteen minutes the heat and humidity no longer seemed remarkable or shocking to her, simply enervating. Derby disappeared in the side mirror, a sorry group of low buildings strewn across the flat landscape like God's afterthought.

The alien quality of the land was more subtle in its impact than the heat, but ultimately more powerful. To Erin, accustomed to Alaska and California, the area around Derby was like being on another planet. The land was utterly flat, unbroken for as far as the eye could see. No mountains rose in the heat-hazed distance, no hills, not even hummocks. The trees were few and stunted. If grass grew at all, it grew in sparse clumps. The iron-red soil showed through the spare veneer of plants.

Slowly, however, Erin became captive to the land, absorbing its shapes and textures, its heat and humidity and flatness, the alienness that was both subtle and overwhelming.

Cole's glance flicked to the rearview mirror. The heat haze made it impossible to be certain, but he thought there was a vehicle behind them. As no side roads had come in, the other car must have come from Derby. He frowned, looked in the side-view mirror, and picked up the speed imperceptibly.

Scattered termite mounds began to appear, sometimes thickly, sometimes not. There was no obvious reason for the variation in density. Most of the mounds were knee-high spikes that resembled the air roots of mangrove trees. The bigger mounds were six feet or more tall and wide at the base. The great dry globs of reddish earth looked for all the world as though miniature castles had been built of rust-colored wax, only to have the punishing weight of tropical sunlight deform the wax until nothing remained but the slumped ruins of the original design.

The air seethed with heat and moisture. To the right and to the left of the Rover, the sky was a heat-misted blue. Directly behind was a distinct river of clouds of every color, from white to blue-black. As it moved, the river widened until it resembled a huge, barely opened fan laid across the empty sky, yet still the clouds came on, churned out by an invisible source.

"There aren't any mountains or storms, so where are the clouds coming from?" Erin asked finally.

"The Indian Ocean."

Absently Erin plucked at the tank top that had become a damp, faithful shadow over her body from neck to waist. Cole caught the motion from the corner of his eye and turned for a better look. She had taken his advice and kept her clothes to a minimum. That minimum didn't include a bra. The damp cotton clung to the full curves of her breasts and peaked unmistakably over the darkness of her nipples. The temptation to slide his fingers between cloth and skin was so sharp that Cole looked away.

More sensed than seen beneath the brilliant sunlight, lightning danced behind the Rover. No rumble of thunder followed.

"I thought this was the dry season," she said after a time, looking over her shoulder.

"It is."

"Then why is it raining?"

He grunted. "It isn't."

Erin blew a wisp of hair out of her eyes with unnecessary force. "Not here. There."

"Just a tease. When the wet comes to stay, clouds and lightning go from horizon to horizon and the rain comes down like mountain thunder."

"A tease." She sighed and pulled at her damp, clinging tank top.

"Don't do that. It's too hot to think about what I'm thinking about."

She gave him a sideways look and a remembering kind of smile.

"Quit distracting me and get familiar with the country," he said, handing a map to Erin. But he was smiling too.

Erin opened the map against the sixty-mile-an-hour wind coming through the open windows. Holding the paper across her knees, she matched the map with the landscape of sparse trees and spare grasslands that flashed by on either side. Orienting herself wasn't difficult. The Great Northern Highway was the superhighway of Western Australia, linking Darwin and Perth through almost five thousand kilometers of uninhabited land. The road was only one lane wide. It was the better of the two roads that penetrated the interior of the vast western state.

Out beyond Derby the road divided. The Gibb River Road went north. The Great Northern Highway went east. Once that basic choice had been made, there was nowhere to go but forward or back. There were no other through roads. The Gibb was also one lane wide, but that lane was dirt. It ran north, up onto the Kimberley Plateau, where it dead-ended. There was nothing but scattered stations and mineral claims from one end of the Gibb Road to the other.

When the time came to make the choice, Cole turned onto the Gibb Road. Dust began to boil up from the tires.

"I thought Abe's station was closer to the Great Northern Highway," Erin said.

"It is. But we're tourists going to Windjana, remember?" What Cole didn't add was that it was a lot easier to spot a tail on a dusty road than on a paved surface.

Erin went back to studying the map. Every thirty to fifty kilometers, the map showed spur roads taking off from or merging with the two highways.

"What are these dirt roads named?" she asked. "I haven't seen any signs, and there aren't any numbers on the map."

"They don't have names or numbers. Most of them dead-end out at some station or mine."

A boil of dust ahead caught Erin's eye. Gradually a car appeared in the distance. It was the first vehicle they had seen since they had left Derby. She held her breath as the two cars rushed headlong at each other on the single-lane road.

She quickly learned that although other traffic was rare, it wasn't rare enough for her peace of mind. As the two vehicles hurtled forward, each driver held the single lane until the last possible moment. Neither one slowed down at all. A glance at the speedometer told Erin that the closing speed of the two vehicles was at least 120 miles per hour.

At some unseen but mutually understood signal, each driver turned his left-hand wheels out on the shoulder, making room for the cars to pass with inches to spare. As the vehicles raced by, each driver lifted his right index finger from the steering wheel in recognition.

The third time it happened, Erin let out her breath as the oncoming car roared past in a boil of dust. "This has to be the world's longest-running game of Chicken."

Cole smiled, touched her cheek with his fingertip. His smiled faded as he glanced in the mirrors.

"Why is the roll bar on the front bumper?" she asked finally.

"That's called a bull bar out here and a 'roo bar in the rest of the outback. Most outback vehicles have one."

"Why?"

"Cheaper than fenders," he said. "A bull bar also keeps whatever you hit from getting under the wheels and flipping you over."

"What can you hit besides termite mounds?"

Cole tilted his head toward a handful of rust-colored, bony cows grazing in the limited shade of the stunted trees. "Kimberley shorthorns."

"They're hardly bigger than mule deer," she said.

"They're big enough to kill you, and they're not the only thing running around. This country isn't fenced. Everything roams—kangaroos, feral donkeys and horses, bush bulls. Any one of them could be big enough to get in underneath the front wheels of a Rover."

"Does that happen often?"

"If you drive these roads at night, sooner or later you'll hit something big enough to matter." Cole's eyes narrowed as he looked in the side-view mirror. "That's why a short-barreled shotgun is part of my outback equipment. You can't be certain of killing an animal outright in a collision. Especially a bush bull."

Erin looked at the cattle again. They were slat-thin, pony-size, and ragged. "Is one of those a bull?"

"Probably, but that's not what a bush bull is. A bush bull is a feral water buffalo."

She looked dubiously at the sandy, dusty country. *"Water* buffalo?"

"Up around Darwin they get at least sixty inches of rain a year. Most of it comes in a four-month stretch. Monsoon season. It gets plenty wet then."

"Fifteen inches a month?"

"More in January. Less in other wet months. That's when all the dotted lines on that map turn into huge muddy rivers and every little crease in the land runs liquid. The fords are impassable, and the few bridges that have been built are under water. The un-sealed roads and station tracks are useless." Cole watched the rearview mirror for three seconds and then forced his attention back to the road ahead.

"With all that water, why aren't there dams to ensure a year-round water supply?" she asked. "Then they could at least irrigate hay to feed those poor cat-tle."

"This is the wrong kind of country for dams. Too flat. Even if you built a huge reservoir, the soil is too porous. The water would just soak in and vanish."

As Cole spoke, he glanced into the side mirror and accelerated gradually, hoping Erin wouldn't no-tice.

"Look at the map again," he continued. "The Fitzroy and the Lennard aren't really rivers in the usual sense. They're floodplain channels that are dry until the wet begins. The rest of the time they're chains of year-round waterholes that you could throw a rock across without straining your arm."

Erin gave him a startled look.

"It's true," he said. "The Kimberley's savannah landscape is deceptive. You go through a gallon of water a day just sitting in the shade—what shade there is. This place will kill you almost as fast as a classic Saharan dune landscape. Maybe faster, because it's so hard to believe what's happening. I believe it, though. This climate will grind you flat."

Erin turned and looked out at the empty land racing by. She tried to imagine inches of rain pouring down week after week for four months.

"What happens to all the water?" Erin asked finally.

Frowning, Cole checked his mirrors again, holding the inside mirror with his hand to reduce vibration. The clarified reflection left no doubt. Someone was back there, keeping pace. He pressed down on the accelerator harder.

"Some of it evaporates. Most of it just sinks in and slowly percolates to the sea through rock formations that hold water like a sponge. Limestone is one. Sandstone is another."

Erin remembered the BlackWing maps she had stared at for so long. "Weren't those blue crosshatches on your map limestone?"

Cole nodded, glanced in the rear and side mirrors, and saw no change in the relative positions of the two vehicles. The vague dust cloud far behind them had speeded up shortly after he had. Gently he eased off on the accelerator, slowing imperceptibly.

"Windjana Gorge is an ancient reef," he said.

"The Oscar Ranges are marine limestone. Old, old reefs, and the fossils to prove it."

"But no water?"

"Sometimes you get springs and seeps where the limestone beds have been fractured. The water that flows up is fresh and thousands of years old."

"What if there aren't any springs? Does that mean the limestone doesn't hold water?"

"Not necessarily. When conditions on land are right, water dissolves passages in the limestone and all the runoff water goes straight underground. Eventually you can have rivers slowly flowing through solid rock. That's how you get cave systems like Carlsbad Caverns in New Mexico."

"Do you think something like Carlsbad exists in the Kimberley, just waiting to be discovered like Abe's diamonds?"

Cole heard the excitement in Erin's voice and tried not to smile. "The odds are against it. Caves are ephemeral things. Most of them don't last any more than six million years."

"Is that all? Gosh, maybe we'd better drive faster."

He glanced at the deadpan innocence of Erin's expression and smiled despite the sticky heat he hated and the persistent vehicle. "In human terms, caves last forever, but they're only mayflies compared to diamonds. Those rocks wrapped around your waist might well be the oldest things on earth."

Erin looked startled. "What?"

"It's a long story." Cole glanced into the mirrors.

"This is a long road," she said, smiling.

Erin's smile made Cole wish that they were anywhere else, so long as it was safe; because it wasn't safe where they were. The vehicle behind them had shifted speed every time Cole did. Whoever it was didn't want to catch up or to pass. It could be simply that the traveler had unconsciously paced himself against the car ahead, or it could be something a good deal less innocent.

Either way, Cole could do nothing to lose the other car. There was only one road for the next thirty klicks, and both vehicles were stuck with it.

20

◆

COLE STARED INTO THE MIRROR, THEN GLANCED quickly at Erin, afraid that she had noticed his distraction. There was no point in telling her about the tail. Adrenaline would exhaust her even more quickly than the brutal climate.

The terrain had begun to pitch up very subtly. Cole knew that about ten minutes ahead there would be long, rolling creases in the land. Then the road would fork. The spur would go to Windjana Gorge. The Gibb Road would head on toward the King Leopold Ranges and an eventual dead end at the tiny settlement of Gibb River. Nearly all the Gibb traffic was to stations along the way. No locals went to Windjana in the buildup. Nor were there any tourists in Derby. He and Erin were so unusual that they had been stared at on the street.

Which meant that if the dust cloud turned off at Gibb, everything was fine. If the dust cloud followed the Rover to Windjana, it would be another matter entirely.

"Cole?"

He glanced away from the mirror. "Hmm?"

"How do diamonds get into volcanoes?"

"We used to think diamonds crystallized out of molten rock as it cooled," Cole said. His voice was calm, revealing none of the tension rising in him as he drove toward the Windjana spur. "The inside of a volcano is damned hot. Diamonds would melt there like chips of ice in fresh coffee."

He paused and glanced aside to see if Erin was looking in her side-view mirror. She wasn't. She was watching him, her beautiful green eyes wide and intent, oblivious to everything else . . . including the dust cloud following them.

The first highway sign in fifty miles appeared just as the dirt road divided. The Gibb River Road continued straight ahead. The right fork led to Windjana Gorge and Tunnel Creek national parks. Cole turned right.

"Not too long ago," Cole continued, "a bright lab boy looked at the dark specks caught inside a diamond and wondered what they really were."

"I thought they were carbon. You know, little bits of stuff that hadn't quite made the grade to diamond."

"That's what everyone assumed. Then someone *looked.* The stuff is pyrope, which is a special kind of garnet. You can tell how old pyrope is by measuring its radioactivity. The diamond the lab boy was looking at had come from from a kimberlite pipe that was a hundred and thirty million years old. The diamond and its garnet flaw should have been the same age as the pipe. Instead, they were billions of years old."

"But then how did the diamonds get into the

pipe? Wasn't the magma hot enough to melt diamonds after all?"

"No one knows. My own private guess is that there's a diamond zone somewhere, way down in the earth, past the point where steel pipe bends and melts and rock flows like wax left out in the sun, down where the pressure and temperature are so great that diamonds were squeezed out as the planet itself cooled more than four billion years ago."

Unconsciously Erin's hand went to the cloth belt beneath her shirt where twelve ancient pieces of crystal were concealed.

"When the earth cooled beyond a certain point," Cole said, "the conditions for diamond formation were gone forever. But the diamonds remained, making a thin crystalline veil over the inner face of the earth."

"Then how do diamonds get up to where we can find them?"

"Every so often the crust shifts and a needle of magma explodes through that diamond zone so hard and fast the diamonds don't have time to melt before the rock around them cools. But most of the time, they melt. Only one in twenty pipes holds diamonds."

Erin rode in silence as she imagined a glittering veil billions of years old, a fantastic crystalline residue of the formation of the planet itself.

"What a shame," she said finally.

Cole looked away from the mirrors. "The diamonds that are destroyed?"

"No. The ones that survive to be worn by bimbettes and loan sharks."

He smiled, but it was one of his old smiles. Bleak. The dust cloud had turned onto the Windjana road.

Cursing the necessity, Cole rummaged in his kit bag on the back seat with one hand and drove with the other.

"Can I help?" Erin asked.

"See how fast you can put on your walking shoes," Cole said. "Then steer while I put on mine."

After a swift look at his face, Erin didn't ask questions. She put her shoes on quickly, then held the wheel with one hand while Cole jammed his feet into real shoes. Inevitably the Rover slowed.

"Thanks," he said, taking the wheel again but holding the Rover to a slow pace. "Take the binoculars and see if there's anyone behind us."

Erin adjusted the focus on the glasses and scanned the road behind them carefully. "There's a white car."

"Is he overtaking?"

She waited for the space of a breath. "No."

Cole swore beneath his breath.

"Cole?"

His hands flexed on the wheel as he said flatly, "We've been followed since we left Derby. He's a real cute one. We speed up and so does he; we slow down and he drops back. How many are in the car?"

"It's too far and too heat-wavy to tell."

Cole reached beneath the seat, pulled out the short-barrelled shotgun, and handed it to Erin. "Ever use one of these?"

"Yes."

"Good. Keep it handy, but keep the safety on."

"What are we going to do?"

"Run like bloody hell."

With no more warning than that, Cole gunned the Rover up and over a shallow crest and dropped down

into a long incline. The accelerator hit the floorboard
and stayed there, held flat by his big foot. The vehicle
picked up speed rapidly, its engine screaming at full
revs. The speedometer needle swung around the dial,
touching a hundred and thirty kilometers.

Erin tried not to think about the assorted wildlife
that ranged the unfenced country.

The rust-red road flew beneath the Rover's
wheels. They flashed past the dry ravine at the bottom
of the crease and started up the long incline on the
opposite side. Gradually the incline began to win. The
Rover's speed dropped. Cole kept the accelerator hard
against the metal, keeping track of the dashboard temperature and oil pressure gauges with quick glances,
holding the heavy vehicle to the smoothest part of the
dirt road, and watching the shoulder for wandering
animals.

The Rover topped the second crest before the
dust cloud reappeared in the rearview mirror. Cole
kept the accelerator floored. The road flattened out,
then ducked around a small outcropping of rock, the
first thing Erin had seen in Australia that resembled a
hill.

Cole pushed the Rover to the edge of its capabili-
ties and held it there mercilessly.

The spur road to Windjana narrowed rapidly.
Ruts appeared, and the shoulder looked like a mixture
of rust and sand. The spur snaked off into more sparse
woodland and grass, but there were enough broad
twists and variations in elevation that the Gibb Road
was soon out of sight.

Erin hung on to the shotgun with one hand and
the braced herself with the other. Like Cole, she
watched the gauges on the dashboard constantly.

"How long will the Rover take it?" she asked.

"Not long enough. I'll bet he knows it, too. He's playing us like a bloody fish."

"What are we going to do?"

Cole smiled grimly. "What fish have always done —grab the line and run with it."

"What if it's all a coincidence and he's not really following us?"

"I'll shave my legs and wear a tutu."

The Rover jerked as Cole slammed through gears over a rough patch of road. Erin braced herself as they rocketed along the increasingly rough route. Time after time she was sure that they were going to crash, but each time Cole pulled them through at the last instant. The Rover hammered through dry ravines and skated eerily over sandy spots.

For several miles the only sound was that of the laboring vehicle. Erin glanced at the temperature gauge with greater and greater frequency.

"Cole," she said finally, "we're overheating."

"I know. If there are any tourists or campers around Windjana, we're going to stick to them like a bad reputation. Killing people is easy. Getting away with it is harder, especially when one of the corpses is the daughter of a highly placed CIA officer. ConMin won't want witnesses."

Cole kept one eye on the temperature gauge and the other on the landscape. Both were hot. The ground was rusty. There were more trees here than near Derby, bigger trees, but still not a forest. There were a few very low hills with small outcroppings of rock at their crests.

Nothing was big enough to hide the Rover.

They burst from the sparse open woodland onto a

sandy floodplain. Beyond it a ridge of rock rose like a dark wall into the sky. After the absolute flatness of the land they had come through, the limestone ramparts seemed unreal. A wide slice had been cut through the limestone by the Lennard River. The river itself was invisible, but the gap of Windjana Gorge was eloquent testimony to the power of the wet.

"Can you see any vehicles ahead?" Cole asked as they raced toward the gorge.

"No, but there must be someone there. It's a national park."

"In the middle of bleeding nowhere."

"What about park rangers?"

"This is Western Australia," Cole said. "Tourists out here are on their own."

Erin shaded her eyes and looked harder as they flashed by a faded sign stating they had entered Windjana National Park. The park was deserted, as empty of people as the land around it. There was nothing but an ill-defined parking lot and a few unroofed, sun-bleached outhouses. No place to hide. No witnesses to carry tales.

The road forked. Cole followed a track that veered away from the gorge and the park entrance. The track paralleled the south face of the ancient reef. Fingers of water-eroded limestone fringed the cliff face, creating deep, very narrow canyons. Tall trees grew in a true woodland that followed the shade and runoff line of the ridge. Smaller gums and spinifex grew within cracks and crevices in the cliff, wherever the wind had deposited seeds and enough debris to create soil. Cattle trails were everywhere.

The dirt track bent slightly, following an irregularity in the cliff, cutting off the view behind. Cole swung the wheel hard to the left, sending the Rover off the track and toward the cliff. He dodged the big trees even as he downshifted, letting the Rover skid and wallow just at the edge of going out of control. The trees closed behind the vehicle, shielding it from the road. The ragged, deeply indented cliff face loomed with startling suddenness. Cole braked sharply and shut off the ignition.

"Get a box of shells from my kit," he said, grabbing the shotgun from her as he got out. "Run along the cliff face until I catch up. Move!"

A fitful wind slowly dissipated the dust thrown up by the Rover's frantic passage. Erin ran as quickly as she could through the soft, sandy soil along the cliff face. Within seconds she was sweating from her scalp to her toenails. After a minute she felt as though she were breathing molten lead. By the time Cole caught up and pulled her into another narrow opening in the cliff she felt wrung out and used up.

"I brushed out—tracks. Stay down—out of sight," Cole ordered, breathing hard.

Erin handed him the shotgun shells and nodded, too winded to speak.

He turned and measured the rough water-pitted rock that loomed around them. Without a word he hung the shotgun down his back from the leather sling and began climbing. He tested hand- and footholds carefully, pulling himself upward with the easy, unhurried rhythm of a man accustomed to climbing. In thirty seconds, he was high enough to have a view of the road. He wedged himself into a shaded crevice, unslung the shotgun, and waited.

Five minutes after Cole had positioned himself, a

dust cloud bloomed along the road. The erratic breeze from the gorge scattered the dust quickly. Absolutely motionless, partially concealed within the dense shade thrown by the cliff itself, Cole waited.

A vehicle shot into sight. Cole could see only that the driver was alone and the car was a Japanese knockoff of a Jeep. Without a flicker of hesitation the boxy, enclosed vehicle roared past the point where Cole had turned the Rover into the trees. He glanced at his watch and started counting. The next ten minutes would tell Cole whether his gamble had paid off, or whether he would have to stalk the man, kill him, and bury him in the sand—if the man didn't kill him first.

Erin could hear the passing vehicle even though she couldn't see it. She looked up the rock walls to the blinding blue sky and saw Cole wedged into a black slit. The tension in his body was a silent warning. She flattened against the rough stone and waited.

And waited.

Finally Cole came back down the cliff. "He went by without a look."

"Thank God."

"It's not over yet. We're going back to the Gibb River Road; then we have to cut overland to the Great Northern Highway again."

"Why?"

"Right now he's between us and Abe's station. Assuming he has enough gas to get there—"

"Do we?" she interrupted.

"No," Cole said, and kept on talking. "When he figures out he's lost us, he has a choice. He can go on a shitty little dirt track to Abe's station and wait for us there, or he can cut down to the paved road and hope he beats us to Fitzroy Crossing."

"What's at Fitzroy Crossing?"

"The only gas station for three hundred miles. We'll just make it."

21

◆

COLE AND ERIN FOUND THE GREAT NORTHERN
Highway in late afternoon, unsure whether they were
ahead of or behind their pursuer. Cole ran the Rover
up to its top speed and held it there. After the rough,
unpaved spur road, the Great Northern's sealed surface seemed eerily quiet, almost unreal, no hissing of
grit pelting over the frame and spinning away from the
tires in red turmoil.

The land was flat again. Pale-barked baoboabs
loomed above the much smaller gums like goblins rising from a shallow, dusty, light-green sea. The highway's single lane had more traffic than the Gibb Road.
They met an oncoming vehicle about every twenty
minutes. Most of the traffic was cars or small trucks.
Occasionally a diesel hauling three freight trailers behind would come howling down on the Rover. The
first time Erin saw one coming, she made a sound of
disbelief.

"What in God's name is that?" she demanded.

"A road train."

"A road train," Erin repeated, not understanding.

"A truck hauling three trailers," Cole explained. He lifted his foot on the accelerator, bringing the Rover down to sixty miles an hour.

"How big is it all together?"

"Can't tell head on. Some of the rigs are a hundred feet long."

For a minute Erin was silent. The road train hurtled closer and closer, filling the single-lane road to the edges, sending clouds of grit boiling up from the dirt shoulder on both sides. It was going as fast as the Rover.

"There isn't enough room for both of us," Erin said.

"No worries, love," he said, smiling as he used the common Aussie reassurance. "There's plenty of verge."

With that Cole whipped the Rover to the left, putting two wheels off the road into the dirt. The road train did the same with its left-hand wheels. The Rover bucked and rattled with the force of the road train's passage. The road train hurtled past.

Sunset was a swift, slanting cataract of light that turned clouds from cream to crimson to ink with startling suddenness. No sooner had Erin started to admire the colors than they vanished.

Cole flipped on the headlights, then threw a second switch on the dashboard. A powerful spotlight mounted above the windshield cut a wide swath through the darkness ahead, reaching out half again as far as the headlights.

"Cow on the right," Erin said, catching a flash of light that could only come from the reflective pupil of an animal's eye.

"Bloody stupid animals," Cole muttered, braking hard and simultaneously turning off the overhead spotlight. "May they all go to those great Golden Arches in the sky."

"As in hamburgers?"

Cole grunted, slid the Rover past the cow in a shower of dirt, and drove on, picking up the speed he had lost. He drove hard and fast, but he never outran his lights, for at dusk Kimberley shorthorns began wandering out of the bush's thin shade to graze along the road's edge, where water from the blacktop ran off to create relatively lush feed.

As it grew darker, spotting shadows looming at the edges of the Rover's headlights became a kind of adrenaline-filled game that distracted Erin and Cole from the clinging heat that hung on far longer than sunlight had. Overhead a carpet of stars emerged. The sky was as alien as the land had been. Except for the Southern Cross, the stars were evenly spaced and of the same brightness.

Time and again Cole braked, reached up to turn off the spotlight, and cut the headlights down to low. Dense shadows moved slowly across the road ahead. When one of the cows turned toward them, its eyes flashed eerily in the light.

"Why do you turn down the lights?" Erin asked finally.

"It blinds the cattle. They freeze if they're on the road, and if they're not, they're as likely to jump toward the light as away from it. I stay off the horn, too. It panics them, and a panicked cow will run right into a car."

Then, although Erin had promised herself she

wouldn't, she heard herself asking, "Any lights behind us?"

"No."

"Could he be running without lights?"

Cole smiled coldly. "I hope so. That little Tojo he was driving doesn't weigh much more than a cow."

In the darkness ahead, what at first had seemed an extension of the star-packed southern sky resolved into a cluster of artificial lights. They were the first fixed lights Erin had seen on the landscape since leaving Derby behind.

"Fitzroy Crossing?" Erin asked.

"Nothing else is out here."

Fitzroy Crossing was the place where the Great Northern Highway's single lane crossed the Fitzroy River. That, and year-round water trapped in the huge billabongs gouged out by floodwaters, supported a town of a few hundred whites, a varying population of Aborigines, and uncounted crocodiles.

Cole drove into a ramshackle service station, shut off the engine, and said as he got out, "Stay in the car. If you see anything that makes you nervous, hit the horn. The shotgun is under my seat."

"I'm a lousy shot."

Cole's teeth flashed whitely. "Doesn't matter. The barrels are just long enough to be legal and just right for close work against superior odds. The load is double-aught buckshot. Just point, pull the trigger, and watch the odds improve."

Without a word Erin reached under the seat and put the shotgun across her lap. Cole filled the gas tank and the spare fuel cans that had been depleted by high-speed driving, added oil and water, checked various cables, hoses, and reservoirs, and finally went inside to pay.

Erin kept looking around but saw no one except an Aborigine with grizzled hair on top, thickly calloused feet on bottom, and a freeform castle of Black Swann beer cans piled to one side. When Cole emerged from the combination grocery store, café, and bar, he was carrying a stack of sandwiches and lukewarm soft drinks from an overmatched refrigerator. He stopped for a moment, exchanged a few words with the Black Swann castle builder, left a sandwich, and came back to the Rover.

Moments later Cole and Erin were on the road again. She had the distinct feeling he was glad to be out in the darkness once more.

"There's a roadside park thirty klicks north," Cole said. "We can use the picnic tables as cots, if nobody beats us to them. Or we can push on to the station."

"Which is safer?"

Cole shrugged. "Little white Japanese vehicles are common here. The town is full of them. If our bird dog got smart and cut across the Tunnel Creek road instead of turning around and going over his backtrail to catch us, he's probably ahead of us. He'll assume we're going to push for Abe's station, where we have help. It's damned easy to set up an ambush at night out in the bush."

"I've always wanted to sleep on a picnic table."

He laughed softly. "Don't worry, honey. I've got a tarp and sleeping bags in back. We'll hollow out a place in the sand and sleep like babies."

They saw no other traffic until ten minutes later, when oncoming headlights flashed into life about a half mile ahead. The height and number of the lights told Cole that the oncoming vehicle was a road train. The headlights of the rig were a white blaze. Its searchlight reached out toward the Rover like an accusing finger.

Automatically Cole lifted his foot from the accelerator and began checking the shadows at the edge of the spotlight with unusual care, seeking the eerie flash of animal eyes. Erin tried to look away from the oncoming lights and concentrate on checking the shoulder for range cows, but the cone of brilliant light nearly blinded her.

The distance between the two vehicles closed rapidly. Cole grunted and switched off the Rover's spotlight. The road train didn't return the courtesy. It bore down on them, growing bigger and more blinding by the instant.

"Christ, must be a million candlepower on that bastard," Cole muttered. "He could jacklight deer on Jupiter."

Angrily Cole lifted his hand to shade his eyes from the blinding glare. At the same time he let the Rover drift farther out onto the shoulder, giving the oncoming vehicle most of the pavement. The road train gave way as well but didn't slow at all. It bore down on them like a runaway freight train.

"Is he forgetful or just rude?" Erin asked as she slapped the spotlight switch on and off in an unsubtle reminder.

Two hundred yards away the huge, dazzling spotlight flicked off.

"About time, you stupid son of a bitch," Cole said.

No sooner had their eyes begun to adjust than the

huge spotlight exploded into life again. Its brilliant blue-white beam pinned the Rover's windshield as the huge road train roared straight toward them, no room to swerve, no place to hide, and the light like a knife in Cole's eyes. Blindly he yanked the wheel hard left, sending the Rover careening wildly over the savannah, dodging chest-high termite mounds and splintering small gums on the bull bar.

After a few hundred yards the Rover clipped a big termite mound, went sideways, caromed off a swollen boab trunk, climbed a smaller termite mound, and almost rolled over. The front wheels cleared the mound before the Rover stopped moving and hung canted, off center, helpless, its engine racing.

During the final moments of the wild ride, Cole's head had been slammed against the side window. For an instant he sat stunned before he killed the lights out of reflex and shook his head roughly, trying to focus. Images came in twos and fours. He shook his head again. It didn't help.

There was a screaming from the highway as the road train's brakes locked up and burned rubber.

"Erin?" he asked hoarsely. "Are you all right, honey?"

"Shaken," she said, her voice ragged, "but nothing permanent."

"Take the shotgun and run."

"But—"

"Do it!"

Shotgun in hand, Erin opened her door and scrambled out into the dark. She ran around to Cole's side of the Rover and levered the door open.

"I said—" he began.

"I'm not leaving you like a staked goat!" she

cried, over the sound of the road train's howling brakes. "Get out!"

Cole rolled out of the seat, found his feet, and staggered forward. Erin caught him and levered him upright with her shoulder. As soon as he was standing he broke into a ragged run, depending on Erin to guide him through the multiple images of night.

After a few moments, four became two and then, sometimes, one. Cole's stride lengthened. In the back of his mind, he heard the road train's brakes shrieking and rumbling, then an ominous silence as the huge mass finally ground to a stop.

A powerful spotlight began sawing back and forth through the bush like a white sword. It was off to their left, but the next sweep would catch both the Rover and them.

Without warning Cole yanked Erin off her feet, pulled her down behind a termite mound and completely covered her with his body, praying that his dusty khaki clothes would provide adequate camouflage for both of them. Then he realized what he had done—dragged her down and overpowered her just as Hans once had.

Face down in the dirt, Erin fought for breath, but she didn't panic. It was Cole who was pinning her down, Cole who had never hurt her, Cole who had fought for her when she had been helpless. Cole had never used his strength to humiliate, hurt, or violate her. He had brought her pleasure, not pain, a wild sharing of bodies that enhanced rather than destroyed all that was human in her.

As Erin's body relaxed, Cole let out a long breath and spoke in a soft, low voice. "Don't move. Don't look up. Your eyes catch light just like any other animal. Understand?"

"Yes."

Very gently he brushed his lips over her cheek and whispered, "You're quite a woman. As brave as your photos. Now I want you to be as smart. No matter what happens, *stay put*. I'd hate to kill you by mistake. Can I count on you not moving?"

"Yes."

Erin felt Cole's weight slide slowly from her. The forgotten shotgun was eased from her grip. There was the brush of skin against skin, a whisper of cloth against spinifex . . . then silence.

Cole belly-crawled away while the spotlight swept the night. An edge of the light touched the Rover, rushed by, then returned, pinning the vehicle in a tunnel of blazing white light. The Rover looked like some primeval outback beast perched on its haunches with its nose pointed into the air. Carefully not looking at the light, Cole crawled closer, knowing that the road-train assassin would have to get out to check his handiwork.

When the searchlight swept toward Cole, he closed his eyes completely to protect his night vision and prevent any flash of his own eyes giving away his position. The searchlight swept on, restoring darkness beyond his closed eyelids. He opened his eyes. After several minutes he saw a shadow flicker off to his left in the pale moonlight. It could have been simply a trick of his eyes, which were still given to double images.

And it could have been a man.

Cole froze, then turned his head very, very slowly. Nothing moved, yet he was certain someone was out there. The man was a creature of the outback, sliding from shadow to shadow, cover to cover, moving with the silence and assurance of a king mulga. Cole blinked his eyes, trying to clear them of extra images.

The assassin disappeared in shadows, then reemerged a moment later, closer to the Rover but too far for any kind of accuracy with buckshot. Night shooting was tricky at best. A short-barreled gun and a head that was ringing like a savagely struck bell weren't helping Cole at all.

Suddenly the man was silhouetted against the Rover's window. Cole came to his feet in a silent rush, threw the shotgun to his shoulder, and fired in one smooth motion. A tongue of orange-white flame bloomed in the night. The blast covered the metallic sound of the pump gun's action. Cole fired again just to the right of the place the man had been, racked in another round instantly, and fired to the left of his first shot. As he pumped again he leaped to the side, knowing that his muzzle flashes were a beacon telling the assassin where to shoot.

The sound of the shots rolled through the night like thunder. Off to the right birds cried their disturbance. Gradually silence returned to the bush. There was no scream of pain, no return fire, nothing to show whether enough of the buckshot had found a target to make a difference.

Cole waited, neither moving nor breathing, listening with every nerve ending. He caught the faintest suggestion of cloth against spinifex, a bare hint of boot against soil, a blurred shadow retreating. Cole threw himself to one side, rolled over several times, and fired again. Then he rolled back in the other direction and waited.

Silence.

Cole eased three more fat shells into the magazine of the shotgun before he moved silently in the direction of the road train. He felt a sudden flash of sensory memory—a night thick with heat and humidity and the silent jungle all around, too silent, telling of predators on the move. Kill or be killed. Live or die. Nothing new.

But this time it was different, more difficult, for he was protecting more than his own life. He cocked his head, listening to make sure Erin had not betrayed her hiding place. He heard only silence.

Motionless, Erin lay and listened to the silence, fighting the urge to call out Cole's name. She had stalked animals in the wilderness with her camera, she had watched wolves hamstring and bring down moose, but never before had she lain in cover and waited for men to kill or die. Futilely she wished she had something more deadly at her command than her own clenched fists.

A door slammed. The road train's diesel growled and revved. Gears clashed violently as the train began to retreat, picking up speed with every second. The spotlight and headlights went out, as though the fleeing assassin was afraid of drawing any more fire.

Warily Cole retreated in the direction of the Rover. When he was close to where he had left Erin, he whispered her name.

"Over here," she whispered in return.

A moment later Cole slid down beside Erin, pulling her into his arms, holding her until she stopped shaking, being held in return. Long after the first rush of adrenaline-induced trembling passed, he continued to hold her, stroking her as he listened to the night.

Slowly the small sounds of insects and nocturnal life returned, telling Cole that no one had been left behind on the road to sneak closer to the Rover and wait in ambush.

"You've been itching to drive all day," he said quietly. "Feel up to it now?"

Erin nodded.

"Stay here while I take a look around. If it's clear, try getting the Rover off the mound."

"Why wait around?" she demanded. "He could be setting up another ambush down the road."

"He was heading toward Fitzroy Crossing. We're not."

"What if there were two of them and one took off and the other one stayed behind?"

"He's not that stupid."

Erin's breath came in quickly. "You sound disappointed."

Cole's teeth glinted coldly in the moonlight. "There's nothing I'd like better than to put that bastard in the ground." His smiled vanished. "They weren't after just me this time. You came too damn close to buying it under that road train's wheels. As far as I'm concerned, it's open season from here on out."

Before Erin could say anything, her mouth was claimed in a swift, fierce kiss that ended as suddenly as it had begun.

"Five minutes," Cole said. "If I'm not back and you haven't heard anything, try to get the Rover off that hump. I'll catch up before you get to the road."

Erin waited what she judged was five minutes, then made her way to the Rover. She had to climb in at an awkward angle, but once behind the wheel she started the engine easily. The gear box had been designed for a man. A strong one. Erin wrestled the shifter into reverse gear and fed gas. The Rover dragged a few inches off its high point. She shifted into first, inched forward, then quickly went into reverse. This time the front wheels caught and held traction.

No sooner did the Rover groan and thump free of the mound than loose soil threatened to bog the wheels. Erin shifted into low range and tried again. The Rover eased forward. She made a very slow turn without lights, heading back toward the road. Cole materialized from the shadows beside her door.

"I'll drive," she said quickly, stopping. "You ride shotgun."

Cole went around to the other side and climbed in. "You drive to the station turnoff. I'll take it from there."

"No camping out on picnic tables?"

"Not tonight. We're going to ground in the bush until I stop seeing double."

"Wouldn't we be safer at the station?"

"Safer?" Cole laughed, but there was no humor in the sound. He turned and looked at her with eyes that glittered like ice in the reflected light of the dashboard. "Haven't you figured it out yet? The station isn't safety—it's the hunting ground of the diamond tiger."

22

◆

Cole came awake before the first stars began fading from the crowded southern sky. The air was humid, fragrant, filled with the subtle rush of awakening life. Erin stirred sleepily and snuggled closer to him, enjoying the resilient heat of his body in the cool of pre-dawn. He shifted until he could put both arms around her.

The headache that had plagued him didn't return with his movement. Nor did it return with the sudden quickening of his body as he felt the softness of the woman pressed against him. He was tempted to awaken her as he had yesterday morning, bringing her from sleep to abandoned sensuality, bypassing inhibition and fear, touching the intense passion that had been buried for years within her.

Even as Cole told himself all the reasons why he shouldn't, his hands were moving over Erin, pushing away the frail barrier of clothes, seeking the sleek center of her, finding it. He caressed her slowly, felt her body's sultry response, and wondered what her dreams were like.

Her breath broke and her eyes opened, gleaming enigmatically in the star-filled night.

"This is becoming a habit," Erin murmured, smiling and stretching languidly against him.

"I'll stop."

"Really?" Her hands slid down Cole's body, finding and caressing the hard male flesh that rose eagerly to meet her. "When?"

"Whenever you want."

Erin looked up into the pale blaze of his eyes and knew that Cole meant it. He would stop right now if that was what she wanted. But she didn't. Barely awake, operating at the level of deepest instinct, she wanted him.

His hand moved and heat burst in the pit of Erin's stomach, shaking her. His touch slid deeply inside her until the heel of his palm grazed the exquisitely sensitive nub concealed between hot folds of skin. Her lashes half lowered and her breath unraveled. Splinters of pleasure shivered through her, melting her in his hand. She looked into his eyes and knew only the truth of her love for this man.

Cole made a thick sound of pleasure as Erin urged him over on top of her and he joined their bodies as completely as he could, moving in slow counterpoint to her until pleasure overwhelmed both of them. At the last instant he covered her mouth with his own, drinking her wild cries even as he poured himself into her. Then he held her until their breathing evened out and their heartbeats slowed. He felt the boneless relaxation of her body as she drifted into sleep once more.

"No, you don't," he said. "It's time to get up."

Erin murmured and separated herself from Cole with a slow reluctance that sent currents of passion searching through him once more. Ignoring the delicate talons of desire, he dressed quickly, rolled sleeping bags and tarp, and stuffed them in the Rover. Then he scrambled up a steep slope and stood in the moon shadow of a hilltop outcropping.

The track leading to Abe's station was below and to the right. The vague road was barely discernible in moonlight. In some places, it vanished in the thin bush cover. Only someone who was familiar with the track would have been able to follow it—or someone like Cole, whose memory was remarkable.

The dusty, rutted track was deserted. The predawn darkness was silent.

"I guess the bastard finally had enough," Cole said as Erin climbed up and stood beside him.

"Thank God."

Cole's smile flashed whitely. "God had nothing to do with that one."

"How's your head?"

"Still there."

"Hold still."

He stood motionless while Erin's fingertips searched lightly through his hair just above his right temple. His scalp prickled in elemental response as his whole body tightened.

"The bump is almost gone," she said after a moment.

His fingertip traced her cheekbone. "Come on. Back to the Rover before I do something foolish again." His voice had an unmistakable roughness to it as he added under his breath, "Woman, you have the damnedest effect on my self-control."

Erin followed him, picking her way carefully in the tricky light. The first few steps down the slope were steep and crumbly. She slid, caught herself, then slid again until her walking shoes found better purchase. All around her spinifex gleamed in lines of silver that shifted and rippled with the hot breeze. Somewhere in the distance an animal gave an odd, resonant cry.

"What's that?" she asked.

"Cow talking to the moon."

Another urgent cry came on the wind.

"Moon talking back to the cow?" Erin said dryly.

Cole smiled. "You learn fast."

The two doors to the Rover closed as one, sounding loud in the stillness. Cole started up and eased the Rover back onto the rough, rutted track, using only moonlight until they were down on flat land again. As the Rover bumped forward, Cole could see signs where a larger vehicle had taken the track, leaving behind crushed spinifex and broken brush. There were other signs of recent traffic as well, tire tracks not yet blurred by the wind.

"Lots of traffic," Erin said.

"You have good eyes."

"Nervous eyes, after yesterday."

"So far I haven't seen anything unexpected," Cole said. "Just the sort of tracks you'd see on Abe's driveway."

"Some driveway. Must be sixty kilometers long."

"As the crow flies—or the cockatoo, since we're in the Kimberley. The narrower tread marks belong to something with a wheel base smaller than the Rover's.

Probably one of the old Jeeps that Abe kept around. He had three of the damn things the last time I was here. He just kept cannibalizing to keep one of them going."

"Then you don't think anyone's at the station right now?"

"Some people from BlackWing will be there. At least they damn well better be, or our prospecting won't get off the ground before the Wet. Sarah might be there. Maybe some of her kids and grandkids. The men probably went walkabout after Abe died."

"Who's Sarah?"

Cole smiled strangely. "Nobody knows. She was a child when Abe and his brother first pegged out their pastoral lease. Her tribe had either been wiped out by disease and war, or they had just gone walkabout and left her. She stayed with Abe."

The Rover lurched and wallowed. Erin braced herself on the dashboard as Cole downshifted into low gear and crawled over the deeply rutted, concrete-hard remains of a dried-out bog.

"Do you think Sarah knows about the mine?" Erin asked.

"I doubt it. If she did, she wouldn't care. Diamonds are a modern passion. The Aborigines have no use for modern things."

"Surely life changed after the English came?"

"The English haven't been here very long. The first Australians drove cattle to the Kimberley from Queensland a little more than a hundred years ago. The trek took two years. They started out with ten thousand head and lost more than half, so nobody was in a bloody great hurry to do it twice. There's been more settlement out here in the last twenty years than there was in the first hundred."

The Rover staggered and slithered over what could only have been a muddy patch of ground.

"A seep," Cole said.

"Water?"

"It happens, you know."

"You could have fooled me. That's the first free fresh water I've seen since I got to Australia."

Cole swerved the Rover as an animal the size of a small dog flashed across the track.

"What was that?" she asked.

"A wallaby."

Erin stared into the night. She saw nothing. She sighed and settled back again. "Did Abe ever talk about his brother?"

"Not to me. Not directly. According to local legend, after your grandfather left with Bridget McQueen, Abe went native for a time. He learned the language, lived the life, and became a kind of god or devil to the Aborigines who migrated through the station. He sat at their fires, they pledged young women to him, and saved him the choice parts of lizard and croc."

There was silence for a few moments while the Rover groaned and bumped along the track.

"Did you like Abe?" she asked.

"I respected his toughness. I admired his knowledge of the land. But like him?" Cole shrugged. "No one liked Abe, least of all the people who knew him best—the Aborigines. You don't *like* your gods or devils. You just live with them the best way you can. He was obsessed with sex, but he hated women more than any man I've ever known."

"Then why did he leave me the station? He could have willed it to Dad or Phil."

Cole's sideways glance was a pale glitter against the dark planes of his face. "Maybe Abe didn't hate them enough."

"What do you mean?"

Softly Cole began to quote from "Chunder": " 'I'm going down alone/Where the black swan floats/O'er a dead sea's bones./Stone woman giving me hope,/Secrets blacker than death/And truth it's death to speak./ But I will speak to you./Listen to me, child of rue./You will curse the day/As I cursed my queen lady.' "

The words spoken in a man's deep voice beneath the vast Australian night sounded very different than those same words read mockingly in an expensive Los Angeles hotel. A frisson of unease rippled through Erin.

"What had women ever done to him?" she asked.

Cole's mouth turned down in a hard smile. "Oh, probably the usual thing."

"Which is?"

"Screwed him over."

"From what you've said about Abe, being screwed was his idea of a good time."

"There's a world of difference between screwing and being screwed."

"I know," Erin said bleakly.

Cole remembered Hans. "Sorry, honey. I wasn't thinking." He smiled bitterly. "It's a pity Hans didn't meet Wing's sister. They were made for each other. But Justice is blind and Mercy is an unpredictable whore."

After a moment of silence, Cole went back to a safer subject.

"I don't know what happened to sour Abe on women. He never talked about it. Looking at those pictures of yours, it's probably as simple as two brothers wanting the same woman and only one of them getting her."

"Grandmother?"

Cole nodded. "After Bridget left, one of Abe's white neighbors asked him why Nate Windsor had gone to America. Abe worked the man over with a stockman's whip. If Abe hadn't been so drunk at the time, he probably would have flayed the poor bastard alive. The same thing happened every time your grandfather was mentioned. Abe went into a murderous rage. After a while, people stopped talking about Nate Windsor and started talking about Crazy Abe."

The track disintegrated into braided ruts climbing a hill. Cole killed the headlights before they could show over the rise. Bucking, sliding, shuddering, the Rover crabbed uphill. As soon as they reached the top, Cole turned off the engine. Down below in a windswept hollow, lights gleamed in the darkness.

"What is it?" Erin asked.

"The station house."

"It looks pretty busy for this early."

"During buildup, you get up before dawn if you want to get anything done. It's too damn hot otherwise."

Cole pulled a box of shotgun shells from his kit and dropped a dozen of them into his pocket. "I'm going to make sure there aren't any surprises. If it's all right for you to come in, the house lights will flash twice. Give me an hour. If I haven't signaled by then, get back to Fitzroy Crossing, call your father, and camp with the local police until he arrives."

"What about you?"

"That's my problem. Staying alive is yours. Whatever happens, don't come in after me! Once I leave the Rover, I'll assume everything that moves out there is an enemy."

"Cole—" Erin began.

"Promise me you'll stay here," Cole interrupted urgently, leaning toward her. "I could get killed worrying about you."

She felt the heat of his breath and the gentle caress of his mouth.

"Promise me," he whispered.

She shivered as the taste of him spread like wine across her tongue. "Yes."

The sound was as much a sigh as a word, but Cole understood. The kiss changed for an instant, becoming less gentle, more consuming. Then the Rover door opened and he was gone. The night closed around Cole, concealing him.

He moved silently down the slope, using natural cover to conceal his outline. It took him twenty minutes to reach the compound. When he was within ten yards of the house, he crouched near a slender gum and waited.

Nothing moved. Even the wind was still. From behind the house came the hum of a large generator. On the roof a satellite dish stood ready to receive invisible messages. Another array of electronic gear was nearby, ready to send messages.

Cole circled the house at a distance. Two new one-ton pickup trucks were parked in back, gleaming among the rusted carcasses of old Jeeps. Nothing stirred in the darkness except the slow expansion of cigarette smoke giving away the position of a hidden guard. Bypassing the man, Cole eased toward the kitchen window. He had nearly reached it when the back door opened an arm's length away.

Cole's night vision was ruined by the sudden outpouring of light. Too close to do anything except attack, he stepped forward soundlessly. As the door closed he snaked his arm around the person's throat.

"Don't talk. Don't move," Cole said very softly.

Even as the words left his mouth, an exotic perfume bathed his senses, the scent as familiar as the delicate perfection of the bones and flesh lying helplessly within his grasp.

"Hello, Lai," Cole said softly. "Long time no see. But not long enough."

23

◆

After hours spent dodging stock along the Great Northern Highway, Jason Street reached his satellite office in Kununurra. When he parked and walked to the office door, no one questioned what he was doing out and about in bush clothes that looked as though he had crawled like a mulga over the land. No one questioned the oozing reddish burn that showed just beneath the short, ragged right sleeve of his shirt. No one questioned him at all for the simple reason that Kununurra rolled up its few narrow streets and went to bed shortly after the sun did. The only exception to the general lifelessness was in the beer halls in town and on the tribal land at the edge of town where Aborigines gathered around a huge bonfire and drank themselves into a modern version of their ancient Dreamtime.

Street's office was stale and stifling. He paused only long enough to turn on the air conditioner before he headed for the computer. He keyed in a code, lit a cigarette, and looked at the messages that had piled up while he had chased all over the outback. The crop was about what he had expected—one of his security guards had shown up drunk for work at a mine, another client was complaining that his latest fee was too high, and a mining consortium wanted his opinion as to whether their latest decline in profits was due to a falling off in the quality of the ore itself or to high-grading by the workers.

Hugo van Luik had called.

Street cursed a stream of smoke, coughed, and looked at his wristwatch. Van Luik was probably still in his Antwerp office. Street picked up the phone that had a scrambler connected, entered the number, and waited. Van Luik answered on the second ring.

"G'day, mate," Street said, his Australian intonations making the words sound a good deal more cheery than he felt.

"Is it done?"

"Next time you send me on a hunt, you might tell me I'm after a real tiger."

"Have I ever sent you after small game?"

"Jungle bunny rebels and wog smugglers are one thing. This Blackburn-Markham bloke is another. He's too good to be just a diamond hunter. You're certain he isn't CIA?"

"Regrettably, yes. A deal might have been struck with the CIA."

Street swallowed a yawn and rubbed his scalp where sweat had dried into a dirty crust. "Well, he's at Abe's station by now."

"Mr. Blackburn is a very lucky man."

"Lucky?" snarled Street, angry at the insinuation that he was doing less than his best work. "From where I sit, it looks more like he's one smart tough bastard. Passport in another name, driver's license, the lot."

"What went wrong?"

"Bloody everything, that's what. He vetted the Rover like he was looking for fleas. He found everything that could go wrong and fixed it. Took him hours. Nora wanted to hire him as a mechanic. So much for an 'accidental' breakdown."

"Go on."

"Oh, I did that, too. Chased them all over the bleeding back of beyond. Blackburn spotted me once I turned onto the dirt road. He ran for Windjana. My vehicle had more legs than Nora's old Rover. I figured to catch them at the park. Rented car breaks down and two Yank tourists wander off and die in the outback, just like Crazy Abe. Bloody sad and all that, but the outback has killed better men before and will kill them again. No worries, mate. Not a one."

Van Luik's breath came in hard at the thought of the inquisition that would have followed Erin Shane Windsor's death, no matter how innocent the circumstances might have seemed. Yet even as sweat pooled along his spine, van Luik admired the tempting, brutal simplicity of Street's plan. All problems solved in one stroke.

"What happened?" van Luik asked after a moment.

"Blackburn hid somewhere in Windjana until I went by. Then he doubled back again to the Gibb and retraced his trail until he found a spur road that connected with the Great Northern Highway. As soon as I was sure I'd lost him I went on to Fitzroy Crossing, where he had to stop for petrol. When I got there, one of the road trains was parked for a bit of tucker. It was dark and no one was about except the plonkos. I decided to have a go at flattening the bastard. I jiggered the ignition and went looking for Blackburn's headlights. Thought I had him, but he's bloody quick. He went rocketing into the bush, banged about, and pranged on a termite mound."

Street paused to stub out his cigarette. Van Luik said nothing.

"Took me awhile to bring that bloody great road train to a stop. Then I had to get back to the Rover. Took me awhile to do that, too. I wasn't about to have a go at Blackburn on the rush. He's too cute by half. Bloody good thing I tiptoed. He had a sawed-off shotgun. Nearly did for me right there."

"Could he identify you?" van Luik demanded.

"Not a chance. It was dark and I didn't get that close. If I had, I'd be dead."

"The girl?"

"Never saw her."

"Could she have been hurt?"

"I checked the Rover before he tried to blow off my head. She wasn't inside. He could have carried her off somewhere in the bush. He's bloody big."

"Is there any chance that you will be connected with the stolen vehicle?"

Street laughed curtly. "The dole had just come in. Those Abos wouldn't have recognized their own mother."

"Explain," van Luik demanded.

"The Australian government pays off the Abos for being born, and the Abos take their cut of the dole to the nearest bottle shop and buy enough beer to make them forget they were ever born at all. No one white and sober saw me."

"Where are you now?"

"Kununurra. I'll go to Abe's station as soon as I'm called in to appraise the leases. Tomorrow, probably, if the file clerk pulls out her finger. Day after for certain."

Van Luik let the silence build before he said carefully, "Your government is being recalcitrant about having you officially appraise the Sleeping Dog mining leases, despite the fact that you have negotiated Abelard Windsor's contracts with ConMin and DSD for the last ten years."

"Bugger all!" Street snarled. "Has she moved on getting the will recognized yet?"

"Matthew Windsor did. He, of course, is in a position to see that matters proceed at a brisk pace."

Street lit another cigarette, blew smoke, and said, "We can't wait until I get the green light on appraising the leases. Blackburn's partner has put enough high-tech prospecting equipment at the station to make me nervous."

"We are negotiating with the Americans about the appraisals," van Luik said finally. "They are divided. I expect your permission to come through shortly."

"It better, mate. I've got some of the station Abos watching the countryside for any prospecting, but they could go walkabout at any time."

"Pay them more."

Street made an impatient sound and wondered how he could explain Australia's natives to a man as urbanized as van Luik.

"Money doesn't work real well with Abos. Fear does. So long as they think I'm Abe's shadow, they'll obey me. But if I lean too hard, they'll go walkabout."

Van Luik breathed in slowly before he spoke with great care. "If Erin Windsor brings that mine into production, you are a dead man. *Mazel und broche.*"

The connection went dead. Street looked at the receiver and snarled, "But what if I'm the one to bring the mine into production, you stupid sod?"

Street laughed, then winced at the pain in his arm as he tossed the receiver into the cradle.

"Choke on your *mazel*, old man. Rack off and die."

24

◆

Erin awoke disoriented, wondering where she was. The steamy heat, the lack of a mattress beneath her, and the lairlike smell of the room itself brought everything back. She was at the Windsor station, sleeping in her great-uncle's bedroom. Or what was left of it. Cole had taken one look at the bed and thrown it into the back yard, mattress and all. He had brought in sleeping bags and pads from the Rover. Without a word he had set up two pallets in Abe's room and settled down to sleep next to her with his body blocking the closed door.

Lying motionless, Erin remembered the currents of barely controlled emotion she had sensed in Cole when she had come into the station house. He had introduced her to a Chinese woman called Lai, a woman whose hungry black glance had been all over Cole like hands. He hadn't introduced Erin to the six other men at the station who were also Chinese. They understood no English—or, if they did, they kept it to themselves.

Lai knew English. Erin suspected that the Chinese woman also knew Cole Blackburn. Or wanted to.

Restlessly Erin rolled over on the hard floor, tired but no longer able to sleep despite the exhaustion of her body. The sleeping bag Cole had used was pushed to the side, empty. The door was closed. She looked at the door and wondered if Cole was with Lai of the hungry eyes and exquisitely fragile body. The thought of him alone with the Chinese beauty made Erin's mouth flatten and turn down with a jealousy she was too honest to deny.

"Erin? The helicopter is almost ready." Cole's voice came from the other side of the closed door.

She sat up quickly, then groaned. The door opened with a bang. Cole stood there looking as dangerous as a drawn gun. His bleak gray glance flashed over the room and found nothing but the grim accommodations that Abe had preferred.

"What's wrong?" Cole asked, looking intently at Erin. Other than the mussed, gritty tank top and shorts, she seemed fine.

"Nothing. I'm just a little stiff after sleeping on the floor."

Slowly Cole relaxed. "The princess and the pea, huh?"

"More like a bowling ball."

He helped her to her feet, then held her close, giving her a hungry kiss that made her forget all the aches.

The sound of someone moving just beyond the open door was as startling as a shot. Although Cole's back was to the doorway, he didn't have to turn to identify the eavesdropper. He knew that Lai had followed him from the kitchen when he had come to awaken Erin.

"What is it, Lai?" he asked without moving.

Erin's eyes widened at the change in Cole. The difference was shocking. The sensual heat and gentleness were gone. In their place was a leashed, violent emotion that could have been anger or something close to desire. When she tried to ease away from the intimate embrace, he held her in place as much with his glance as with his hands.

"Chen Wing has called," Lai said. "He asks to speak with you."

Lai's voice was hushed, soft, controlled, but her eyes hungrily watched Cole's body. For just an instant she glanced at Erin as though measuring her for a shroud. Then Lai lowered her eyes and waited with the outwardly patient obedience peculiar to the Chinese culture.

Uneasiness moved in waves over Erin's skin. Any doubt she might have had about the currents running between Cole and Lai was gone. Cole and Lai knew each other.

Intimately.

"Tell him I'll be there in a minute," Cole said.

Lai turned and walked away, her high heels clicking on the wooden floor. Her obedience might have been that of a traditional Chinese woman, but her clothes were an elegant synthesis of West and Orient. She wore the traditional black silk slacks, but they weren't baggy. They fitted with a perfection that only personal tailoring could ensure. Her blouse was also silk, also black, and unbuttoned to a fashionable depth that showed the swell of her golden breasts. Her burnished black hair hung in a smooth curtain that came to her hips.

The photographer in Erin reluctantly concluded that she had never seen a more attractive female.

"She's stunning," Erin said finally.

"Yes."

The word was like Cole's expression, utterly neutral. Erin had no way of knowing what emotions lay beneath the surface. She knew only that emotions were there, shielded with every bit of Cole's considerable self-control.

"How long have you known her?" Erin asked before she could stop herself.

"Long enough."

"For what?"

"I'll go talk to Wing. Bring me some coffee, would you? It may take awhile." Cole stopped at the door and looked over his shoulder. "In any case, from now on don't be out of my sight for more than three minutes at a time. And never be out of calling distance. Understand?"

Erin blinked. "Don't you trust Lai and those men?"

"I don't trust anybody. That's why I'm still alive. Stay close to me. Always. If I have to come looking for you, I'll come ready to kill."

Cole strode through the shambles of the house to the room Wing's men had gutted and turned into a communications center. Everything Cole would need to talk to Wing or to transmit and receive computer information was already in place.

Cole picked up the phone. "Hell of a job, Wing. I was expecting to tap out my messages on a computer."

"Thank you. I regret the delay in the bedding and in the improved plumbing. Lai has promised to redouble the efforts of the men. Is everything working?"

"New generator, transmitter, receiver, modems, computers, fax, and some stuff I haven't even had a chance to play with yet," Cole said, looking around. "You must have had a small army for the installation."

"There were several bush pilots who were more than willing to haul people and supplies at triple rates, despite the lack of a decent landing strip. I also took the liberty of beginning the survey immediately. The findings are being processed as we speak. If you have any reason to suspect the technician's competence or the pilot's navigational integrity, the helicopter stands ready to repeat the entire sequence."

"Why did you start without me?" Cole asked bluntly.

"We learned that someone else has been quartering the Windsor station by helicopter. I have to assume they are after the same information we are. Under the circumstances I had no choice but to go ahead on the survey."

"Who was it?"

"We're still working on that. The helicopter was rented by International Mining Security Advisors Ltd. The company is owned by an Australian called Jason Street and takes contracts from various mining interests to advise on or to create security for their mines. Unfortunately, IMSA's security is quite good. We can't find who hired IMSA to do the survey. The technician simply had his orders and followed them."

"Does IMSA own any mines in Australia or any interest in an existing mine?"

"No."

"Does it do a lot of work for the diamond cartel?" Cole asked.

"A modest amount. Something less than twelve percent of its net profit. Interestingly enough, Mr. Street was formerly with ASIO."

"Formerly?" Cole asked sardonically. "Once sworn, never foresworn."

"We are aware of that probability. In any case, as the Australian government finally is being brought to the point of cooperating with BlackWing on this venture, I doubt that Mr. Street is a direct threat to your operation in the long run."

"Keep after IMSA and Street," Cole said flatly.

"Agreed." Wing took a breath. "Lai said you were injured."

Cole gave Lai a narrow look. She watched him as though he were a god walking among men. Once he had trusted that look. Now he recognized it as another part of her sexual allure, an act that was as carefully constructed as the silk clothing she wore.

"A bullet burn on my thigh from Darwin," Cole began.

"Ah, yes, Darwin," Wing murmured. "You haven't mellowed, have you? Uncle Li was quite gratified. The local police are quite mystified."

"Good."

"Lai mentioned another incident . . . ?" Wing probed.

"Road train tried to flatten us near Fitzroy."

"Anything that needs—er, explaining to the local authorities?"

"No. I missed the bastard."

"I see." Wing hesitated. "As you requested, I

have pressed for the details of Abelard Windsor's death. Everything seems within reason. He was never a very stable man, I take it. He walked out into the bush with a can of Fosters in one hand and a shovel in the other and was never seen alive again."

"Probably the climate pushed him over the edge," Cole muttered. "Jesus, I hate buildup." He wiped sweat from his forehead. "Anything else?"

"No."

"Who looked for him?"

There was the sound of Wing rustling through papers. "It appears the people on the station who might have noticed Mr. Windsor's absence were quite drunk themselves. Finally one of the Aborigines—Sarah is her name—sobered up enough to realize that something was wrong. She called Jason Street. By the time he returned to the station, it was too late."

"Returned? Does he live here?"

"He and Mr. Windsor often drank together for extended periods. If gossip is to be believed, they shared other tastes in common. Apparently Mr. Street is fond of women of color. He is also a formidable fighter. It was Mr. Street who found our people going through the station house. He killed two of them without sustaining any particular injury himself."

Cole's eyebrows went up. "Two of them, huh? Tough bastard. What did the Australian cops think of that?"

"Nothing. Mr. Street caught the people in the act of burglary, they attacked him, and he killed them. Regrettable, but they were only wogs after all."

Cole heard and understood the undercurrent of rage in Wing's voice. Many Australians, especially in the outback, had little use for nonwhites. Chinese, in particular, came in for discrimination.

"What did the autopsy say about Abe?" Cole asked.

"If there was an autopsy, the results weren't included in the report. There was simply a statement that death came as the result of heat prostration. It was quite some time before the body was discovered. Considering the climate, I doubt there was a great deal left to work with."

"I don't like Street's name turning up so often."

"Noted, but not really meaningful. There are so few people in the Kimberley it is unavoidable that the same names would crop up repeatedly, particularly in that Mr. Street was as close to a friend as Mr. Windsor had. Mr. Street even negotiated the Sleeping Dog contract with DSD. Undoubtedly he will be the man designated by the Australian government to appraise the state of the various Windsor leases."

"Keep Street out of here," Cole said flatly.

"We're trying. Unfortunately, while certain members of ASIO are being reasonably cooperative with us, the Australian government itself shows every indication of being lobbied by various powerful members of the cartel."

"Are you certain Street doesn't belong to Con-Min?"

"We have found no convincing proof he is Con-Min's, and we are looking very diligently. I think Street's attraction for the various members of the cartel stems from the fact that he isn't *our* man."

"Any potential competitor of ours is a potential friend of theirs?"

"Precisely."

"I assume you're taping this," Cole said.

"As always."

"That will save faxing you the list of camera equipment Erin decoyed to London."

"Everything is already at the station. We removed it at the New York stopover and rerouted it via a private courier. It arrived while you slept." Wing chuckled softly. "ASIO was most surprised when they took apart the crates in the Darwin customs office. It seems they had erroneously concluded that Ms. Windsor wasn't really interested in photographing their lovely country."

Cole grunted.

"Apparently they expected to find esoteric mining supplies," Wing continued. "Instead they found only ordinary cameras, lenses, and film. Imagine their disappointment—"

"How did you explain all the electronic gear you installed here?"

"It hasn't been installed anywhere. BlackWing's office in Darwin will be undergoing an expansion soon. We simply ordered and warehoused everything in advance to make sure all was at hand when we needed it."

Cole smiled at the satisfaction oozing from every syllable of Wing's speech. Then amusement faded from his expression. "Just one more thing."

"Yes?" Wing said warily, hearing the change in Cole's tone.

"Lai is on the first transport out of here."

"That would make Uncle Li most unhappy."

"Tough shit."

"Lai is experienced in specialized communications and in computer programming with application to mineral surveys. She will be invaluable.''

''Not to me.''

''You sound like a man with an emotional investment in the subject. Perhaps even like a man still in love?''

Dispassionately Cole decided it was just as well Wing was on the other end of a very long communications link. Cole would probably regret delivering Wing in pieces to his too-clever Uncle Li.

''Having Lai rub up against me every time I turn around won't start the kind of fire Uncle Li has in mind,'' Cole said flatly. ''The Chen family isn't going to get their hands on any more than half of my half of the mine. Tell Li I'm disappointed in his estimate of my intelligence.''

''There is no need to irritate him. He had nothing more in mind when he sent Lai than for her to provide you with the best liaison the Chen family has to offer.''

Cole laughed coldly. When he breathed in, a haunting fragrance bathed his senses, calling up buried memories of hot nights and a golden woman crying love as she climaxed beneath him.

Rooting and hooting about love./Mistresses of lies,/Damn their hot cries.

''Liaison, huh?'' Cole said sardonically. ''Is that what you call prostitution in Hong Kong these days?''

There was no answer.

''Listen to me, Wing. Your men—and your thoroughly trained sister—had better treat Erin Windsor's welfare as though it's the only hope for the survival of the Chen clan. Because it is. Tell Uncle Li to read between the lines in my file. Do you understand me?''

''I'm pained that you distrust us so much.''

"Yeah, I'll just bet you are. Right in the ass. Using Lai as bait was a mistake. Goodbye, Wing. I won't call to give you progress reports. I'm sure your obedient little spy will take care of that for me."

Cole broke the connection and turned to the woman who had been standing silently behind him. His face was expressionless as he looked at her, a golden woman standing in the exact center of a nimbus of light from the doorway. He wondered if she had always been like that, with every act, every breath calculated to display her extraordinary beauty. He didn't remember Lai as calculating. He remembered the seething violence of her sexuality, a hunger that had seemed as unforced as the sunlight pouring over her right now.

Grimly Cole measured how young he had once been, and how old Lai had been. Without warning his hand flashed out and closed almost gently around Lai's throat. She stood motionless but for the sudden, heavy beat of her pulse beneath his thumb.

"I trust you heard everything," Cole said.

"Yes," she said softly.

"You'll tell your men."

"Yes."

Gray eyes measured the delicate, perfectly formed woman standing before him. Once he had dreamed of having Chen Lai in his grasp again. Wing must have known that. Certainly Uncle Li had. So the Chen family had made Cole's dream come true. As long as the diamond mine was found, Cole could do whatever he wished to Lai, punish or humiliate or rape her, take anything he wanted from her.

Even her life.

Lai knew her physical vulnerability as well as

Cole did. It was there in the hidden tremors that made her quiver, in the rapid pulse beating beneath his thumb, in the shallow, rapid breaths that touched him across the few inches separating their bodies, in the luminous black eyes that watched him.

But it wasn't fear Cole saw in Lai's glance. She was looking at him as though he were meat and she had been long without food. The delicacy of her perfume was mixed with the primitive, far more heady scent of female desire. Against the thin silk of her blouse, her nipples showed as hard buttons.

She wanted him.

Cole's thumb moved against Lai's soft throat in what could have been either a caress or a threat. "Such an obedient daughter of China."

She lowered eyelashes the color of midnight. "Thank you," she said huskily, moving her chin slowly, caressing the hard hand at her throat. She shifted, easing forward, flowing against him as she lifted her hand and traced the line of his jaw with her fingertips. "We were always very good together, Cole. I have dreamed of you."

Erin came to the doorway holding two cups of coffee. She saw Lai moving against Cole and Cole's thumb caressing Lai's throat. For an instant Erin was too shocked at the intimate tableau to speak.

"Obviously you have your hands full," Erin said tightly. "I'll leave your coffee in the kitchen."

"Stay."

The quality of Cole's voice was like a whip. Erin found herself automatically obeying. That, too, angered her.

"Do you keep pets?" she asked in a clipped voice.

Cole turned away from Lai and focused exclusively on Erin. "Pets?"

"Sit. Stay. Roll over. Pets."

He smiled crookedly, released Lai, and walked over to take a cup of coffee from Erin. "No pets, honey. Nothing would have me."

"Really? I'll bet there's a Venus's-flytrap close by with your name on it."

Cole's laughter was lost as the beat of a helicopter's rotor blades washed over the house, the sounds magnified by the humidity.

"Tell him we'll be out in a minute," Cole said.

The words were for Lai, but he didn't look away from Erin as he spoke. Lai turned and left the room. Not once had she looked at Erin.

Over the rim of the coffee mug, Cole measured the depth of Erin's anger. He regretted it, but now wasn't the time to do anything about it. He was too angry about her lack of trust in him to be civilized on the subject. Cautiously he sipped the black coffee, found it hot but not scalding, and drank it without ceremony. The sound of the helicopter blades diminished to a lazy *whap . . . whap* that told of a machine throttled down to idle.

"Ready to fly?" he asked Erin. "Maybe by the time we get back, Wing's army will have the new plumbing straightened out for a shower and a washing machine."

Cole's casual words infuriated Erin. She considered refusing the conversational gambit, but decided she would appear even more foolish than she already felt after displaying her jealousy.

"Just wear your clothes when you shower," she said, trying to sound as matter-of-fact as he had. She didn't succeed. She had never been a very good actress. "A shower gets the clothes clean enough. I did it all the time in Alaska."

"Washing clothes with you in them, huh? Sounds like fun."

The sensual teasing was unexpected, baffling Erin even as it made her more angry. "It's a game for one," she said in a clipped voice. "Like solitaire."

"That doesn't sound like fun."

"Don't worry. I'm not the only woman in the Kimberley whose clothes need washing."

"You're the only one whose clothes I want to wash."

Erin's breath came in hard. "My God, Cole, I know I was stupid to talk about love, but even stupidity has its limits. I'm not blind! If I had come in a few minutes later, Lai would have been all over you like a rash."

"But I wouldn't have been all over her."

"Bullshit," Erin said angrily.

The sunlight that had changed Lai into a diminutive golden statuette sent streamers of fire through Erin's hair and transformed her eyes to brilliant green gems. Unlike Lai, Erin was unaware of her own allure, her color and heat and shimmering life. Cole wasn't. He wanted Erin until he had to look away or reach for her; because if he reached for her now, she would refuse him. Cole didn't trust his own temper if that happened. He was never at his best during buildup and he knew it.

"Don't let Uncle Li get away with it," Cole said, when he could trust his voice not to betray his rage.

"With what?"

"Putting Lai between us."

"You should have thought of that sooner. You sure as hell didn't mind where Lai was standing a few minutes ago."

Cole made a throttled sound. It had been a long time since he had lost his temper, but he felt it slipping now. His head ached, the scab on his thigh pulled with every motion, he hadn't slept more than a handful of hours since Los Angeles, the temperature was well over one hundred, the humidity wasn't far behind, and now Erin was watching him like a stranger, as wary and distant as though she had never lain across his naked body and whispered her love.

"Look—" he began harshly.

"I did," she said, interrupting. "Unlike you, I didn't like what I saw." Then, before she could stop herself, Erin asked. "Who is she?"

"Wing's communications specialist," Cole said through his teeth.

"You know what I meant. Who is she to *you*?"

Cole slammed his coffee mug down with enough force to shatter it. Before the pieces hit the floor he took a long stride forward, coming so close to Erin that she had to tilt her head back to see his eyes. Nothing in them comforted her, but she didn't back up an inch.

"To me," Cole said in a low, savage voice, "Lai is a living, breathing reminder of how rock stupid a man is to trust a woman's cries of love. Abe had the right idea about women. Fuck them, but don't love them."

Abruptly Cole turned and headed toward the back of the house.

"Lai knows where your new camera gear is. Get it and be out back in three minutes."

25

◆

BEFORE ERIN COULD SAY SHE HAD NO INTENTION of asking Lai for anything, Cole was gone. Angrily she walked to the bedroom, grabbed her battered camera bag, and went outside.

The violence of the sun brought Erin up short. It had been hot and sticky in the house. It was insufferable outside, a steaming sauna with no walls and no exit. Flies flocked to her. She waved them away automatically and walked toward the helicopter that was crouched off to the rear of the house. If the aircraft had ever had doors, they had been removed.

Cole was talking with the pilot. After a moment the man climbed down and let Cole into the pilot's seat. He looked at gauges and brought up the revs. The rotors whirled more quickly, sending billows of grit into the sky. The artificial wind scoured over the ground where Abe had made an informal dump of station trash. Beer cans went bouncing and flying out of the yard, only to become tangled in bunches of spinifex.

When Cole was finished with his preflight check, he gestured Erin over. His mouth flattened as he noticed that she carried only her old camera bag. Photography was not just her profession, but her passion—yet she wouldn't even ask Lai where to find the rest of her camera equipment. That told Cole how angry Erin was, which told him how little she trusted him despite her whispered protestations of love.

Erin's reaction made Cole furious even as his mind told him not to lose his temper again.

Don't let Uncle Li get away with it, Cole told himself savagely. Divide and conquer is the oldest game of all.

Because it worked. Especially in the hellish climate of Western Australia in the time known as buildup. But even knowing his opponent's tactics didn't change the emotions snaking through Cole, testing his control. Uncle Li had an uncanny instinct for the jugular, the crotch, the Achilles heel. Cole hadn't known until this moment that he was Erin's vulnerable point.

He had just found out she was all three of his.

God damn Uncle Li.

"Buckle up and put on the headset," Cole said curtly over the helicopter noise. "There are sunglasses and sunscreen in the seat pocket. Use them."

Erin stepped up into the chopper, put on her safety harness, and began looking over the headset. There was no switch for speaking.

"Voice activated," Cole said loudly as he put on a pair of dark glasses.

She nodded, put on the headset, adjusted it, fished out her own sunglasses, and settled them on her nose. The relief from the intense light gave the illusion of coolness. Unfortunately, it was only an illusion. She reached for the sunscreen, which was also an insect repellent.

"Ready?" asked Cole.

His voice came clearly through the headset. Erin nodded again. Cole grimaced at her unwillingness to talk to him but made no effort to change the situation. His own temper was still too raw. He hadn't been this angry since Lai had aborted his child.

The realization shocked him.

Cole brought the revs up until the helicopter was quivering like a greyhound waiting to be released. An instant later the chopper leaped into the sky.

When Erin finished applying the sunscreen, she sat and stared out the window, seeing nothing of the land and too much of a delicate, extraordinarily beautiful face, eyes like black tears watching Cole, worshiping him—and Cole's hand caressing the graceful line of Lai's neck, touching her as though she were made of fire, watching her burn. With a sense of bafflement and surging anger, Erin wondered if all males were untrustworthy or if she simply had wretched taste in men.

Don't be ridiculous, she told herself angrily. Cole doesn't owe me anything but his expertise as a diamond prospector. He didn't make any promises, not even the implicit one of saying he loves me. He didn't talk about what would happen after we found the mine or gave up looking for it. It's rude of him to lust after another woman while I'm in the house, but it's hardly the first time in history something like that has happened.

Nothing new. No big deal. A close brush, but this time I got away intact. Once I get out of this hell-

ridden climate and get a full night of sleep, I'll laugh
about the whole thing.

Beneath her bracing thoughts, Erin sensed darkness condensing, depression growing one slow drop at
a time, draining light from her. Knowing her response
was irrational didn't change it, any more than knowing she had been the innocent victim in an undeclared
war seven years ago had changed the extent of her
psychic and physical injuries afterward.

At least Cole didn't keep score with a switch-
blade. Any scars he left on her wouldn't show.

There was little comfort in the thought, but the
past had taught Erin to accept small comforts. Better
she found out about Cole now than later. Better the
dreams stop now than later.

Better if she had had the sense never to dream at
all.

"We'll fly the east edge of the station first," Cole
said finally, breaking the silence. He dropped a map in
Erin's lap. "Then we'll do the north leg. Dog One is
on the northern edge. I'll keep the chopper at about a
thousand feet and go slow."

He paused, but Erin said nothing.

"I've never had a chance to see the station from
the air," Cole continued, trying to keep the irritation
out of his voice. "Sometimes you can pick up things
you'd miss on the ground. While we fly, try to match
features down there with the map."

Erin nodded to show that she had heard, unfolded the map, and forced herself to focus on it
rather than on her foolish feeling of betrayal.

As the chopper bored through the sky, Erin concentrated on the landscape below. The variation in the
ground surface surprised her after the unrelieved flat-

ness of the area around Derby. On Abe's station there
were low ridges and blunt pinnacles of black rock. In
between, there were narrow grasslands and sparse
trees. At very rare intervals there were startling bits of
vivid green. Cattle trails braided around the fragments
of green.

"Seeps and small springs," Cole said finally, seeing Erin's interest. "The black rocks are Triassic limestone outcroppings."

She nodded absently, absorbed in the landscape
below.

When Erin didn't answer him, Cole turned and
looked intently at her. The line of her shoulders wasn't
as stiff as it had been when she had gotten into the
helicopter. Her mouth was more relaxed, too. She was
wrapped up in the land rather than locked in anger at
him.

To Erin it seemed like a long time before the helicopter reached the edge of the station and turned
north to fly the east leg of the boundary. As she
watched, more ridges and shallow troughs appeared.
There were red rock hills in broken array, like a rumpled blanket thrown over the land. Roads were nonex-
istent. Even ruts didn't show. The vague, random-
looking lines she saw from time to time could have
been cattle trails or simply runoff channels for the few
months of the year when free water existed in the
land. There were no buildings, no canals, no windmills, nothing to suggest that civilized man had ever
existed out here or ever would.

Occasionally Erin spotted Kimberley shorthorns
or kangaroos below. Cow and kangaroo alike fled as
the thunderous dark shadow of the chopper skimmed
the rugged land. Once she saw a small blackened cir-

cle surrounded by a ring of something that reflected sunlight in countless small silver-white flashes.

"What's that?" Erin asked.

Cole looked away from an intriguing geologic anomaly on the landscape and glanced where Erin's finger was pointing. "Aborigine camp," he said. "The black is where the bonfire was."

"What about the shiny halo?"

"Broken beer bottles and smashed beer cans."

If anyone had been there last night or a week or a year ago, there was no one in sight now. There was nothing but the chaotic, untamed land.

"Where are the natives?" Erin asked.

"They could have been gone since last night or since the last wet. I can't tell from up here."

"Where are their shelters?"

"In the dry, they don't need any. In the wet, they use natural stone overhangs, unless they're on reservation land. Then they'll use houses the government built for them."

The helicopter bore along its northern heading, not having completed even one leg of the Windsor station's huge rectangle. As the minutes went by, the sheer scale of the station seeped into Erin. With it came an intimation of the relentless demands the land would make on anyone who dared to walk its seamed face.

The depression inside Erin slowly grew, fed by more than her own certainty that she had once again misjudged a man's intentions. This time it was the land she had misjudged. Despite all she had been told, she hadn't believed that Australia could be as harsh, as empty, as protective of its secrets as Alaska had been. She hadn't believed that the tiny spot called the

Windsor station would be physically taxing to explore. There was no ice, no untamed rivers, no jungle, no mountains, not even a real forest—nothing to hide the nature of the country itself. Surely Abe's diamond mine could not be all that well concealed.

Erin hadn't understood how sere the land was, how inhospitable to life. Alaska had the ocean and rivers full of salmon to provide a wealth of food for its natives. The Kimberley Plateau had neither ocean nor reliable rivers. It had no herds of migratory animals, no flocks of edible birds, no flora rich with berries and seeds.

Most of all, the Kimberley had no dance of clean, fresh water.

The longer Erin watched Windsor station unfold beneath the helicopter, the deeper her depression became. She had been naïve about more than Cole Blackburn.

"My God," she said finally. "How does anyone survive down there?"

"Carefully."

She shook her head.

"It's not as hopeless as it looks," Cole said. "There are small seeps to drink and big snakes to eat."

The sound Erin made could hardly have been called a laugh. "When you told me how static the Aborigine culture had been until the white man came, I didn't believe it. I do now."

He gave her a questioning look.

"When you told me the natives had been walking for forty thousand years over the biggest, purest deposit of iron ore on earth but they hadn't discovered metalworking, I wondered why. When you told me they had literally walked over huge, pure gold nuggets and never hammered earrings or icons or even bracelets from the gold, I wondered why. I also wondered why they didn't domesticate any animals, invent weaving or shoes, or have any kind of written language.

"Now I don't wonder. They were lucky to survive long enough to bear children who would also be lucky to survive and bear children, who would also be lucky to survive, world without end, amen."

"That's the buildup talking," Cole said, looking at Erin's flushed face and sweat-slicked skin. "When it's this hot and sticky, life doesn't seem worth the trouble to live. Once it rains you'll feel different about the Kimberley."

Erin looked from the ground to the sky. The odd, distinct river of clouds that poured in daily from the distant Indian Ocean had gradually become more than a dark column. It had widened at the edges until it was a hazy lid over the land. Distinct thunderheads billowed in slow motion, lazily eating the hot sky. Searing white on top, slate gray on the bottom, the clouds promised an end to the claustrophobic humidity and heat.

"I wish the clouds would quit strutting and get down to work," Erin said.

Cole smiled crookedly. "No, you don't. Once the wet sets in, we won't be able to go prospecting. We'll be grounded."

As he spoke, his gray glance went over the gauges. Frowning, he flicked his index finger against the fuel gauge. The needle wavered, rose, then fell steeply, only to rise once more, indicating a nearly full tank.

"Problems?" Erin asked after a moment.

"The pilot told me this gauge wasn't very reliable on the top end. If I hadn't checked the fuel level manually, we'd be heading back right now."

"What about the bottom end?"

"He didn't say." Cole glanced at Erin. "Don't worry, honey. The chopper is mechanically sound."

"How do you know?" she retorted. "You didn't have time to go over it the way you did the Rover we rented."

"The pilot had just flown in from Dog Three. He topped off the tank because he was expecting to fly us all over the station. I made sure he didn't have a chance to bugger anything after he found out he was staying behind."

Cole's casual anticipation of sabotage startled Erin. "You really don't trust anyone, do you?"

He shot her a sideways glance. "Neither do you. You don't even trust me."

"I trust you to find the diamond mine," she said evenly.

"But not to keep my hands off Lai, is that it?"

"That wouldn't be very bright of me, would it, considering the touching scene this morning?"

"Erin, for Christ's sake—"

"Forget it," she interrupted tightly. "All you promised me was your best effort at finding a diamond mine. The rest of it was just proximity and adrenaline. Subject closed."

"Shit, lady, you're really trying to make me lose my temper, aren't you? If you think—"

Erin yanked off her headset.

Cole came within an inch of grabbing the earphones and slamming them down over Erin's stubborn head. The ease with which she set fire to his temper amazed him. Even as he told himself to cool off, sweat trickled into his eyes. He wiped his face on his bush shirt and his palms on his shorts. Within moments, his skin was sticky with sweat once more.

It would get worse before it got better, hours and days and nights and more days of relentless heat, stifling humidity, the sun a hammer flattening everything, the air a torpid beast suffocating whatever survived the sun's savage onslaught.

"God *damn* this weather," Cole said viciously.

Erin didn't hear him. Her headset remained in her lap, allowing the helicopter's noise to cut her off from the man to whom she had given too much of herself. But that was the way she had always been—all or nothing at all, life taken at full tilt or full stop, nothing in between. Even Hans's brutality hadn't changed that. Nothing would. It was simply the way she was.

The world shifted sharply as Cole changed the heading of the helicopter, turning it onto the short north leg of the station's nearly rectangular holding. After a startled look at Cole, Erin positioned the map to match the new direction and looked down at the land once more, watching for something new, something different, something to lift her spirits.

She saw only ground that was seamed, worn, bleached, a land lying exhausted beneath the combined weight of humid air, sunlight, and incomprehensible time.

Unhappily Erin acknowledged that in many ways Crazy Abe's legacy was as much a disappointment as finding Cole in Lai's arms had been. Both Cole and the legacy had seemed to promise Erin a new world in which to slough off the dead weight of the past, freeing her to explore the possibilities of life. Both legacy and man had promised her hope. Both had proven to be less than they seemed. Crazy Abe's legacy was a steamy, dusty, time-ridden hell. Cole Blackburn was a man who couldn't resist the lure of one woman even while he was another woman's lover.

Broodingly Erin unfolded another panel of the map, held it against the hot air boiling through the open doors of the helicopter, and went back to the solitary game of matching land features with marks. The only marks on the map that seemed useful were those Cole had carefully written in. His symbols indicated the rare seeps and important geological boundaries, the dry watercourses, and the random lumps of limestone poking through the rusty surface, bringing relief to a land worn nearly flat by time.

A line of compact gum trees showed rather startlingly green against the landscape, catching Erin's eye. She looked more closely, saw that the trees traced an otherwise invisible watercourse between two ragged black lines of limestone, and checked the map. Frowning, she looked down again. After a moment she picked up her headset and put it on once more.

"Are we still flying the northern leg?" she asked.

Cole shot Erin a glance. Behind the sunglasses her eyes were unreadable shadows. "Yes."

"Headed for Dog One?"

"Yes."

"Then we have a problem." Erin pointed to the trees and then to the map. "The northern boundary is here. Dog One is here. We're here."

"And right here," Cole's finger stabbed the map, "is something I want to look at."

"What?"

"Those limestone ridges. I suspect they're the remnants of an ancient reef, but they could have been formed in some other way."

"What difference does it make?"

For a moment Cole was tempted to ignore Erin's cool pursuit of geological facts and require that she speak about something more personal. He ignored the temptation. If Erin distanced herself from him any more, she would be brought down and dispatched as quickly as a lone lamb discovered by a wolf pack. They must stand together—if not as lovers, then as business partners.

"If the ridges were part of a reef, the coastline was nearby," Cole said evenly. "Where there's coast, there's beach. I'd love to find another Namibia. Except the beach sands here would have been changed to sandstone, unless the sandstone has already been eroded away a grain at a time, making loose sand once more."

"Is that possible?"

"Where do you think the sand in the deserts came from, if not from rock?"

Erin blinked. "I never thought about it. You mean sand becomes sandstone becomes sand becomes sandstone?"

"World without end," Cole said, echoing Erin's earlier words. "The surface of the earth has been recycled again and again as continental plates meet and devour each other. Nothing survives subduction intact, not even diamonds. But the Kimberley Plateau hasn't been devoured for a billion and a half years. It's the oldest land surface on earth, which means the diamonds that were eroded out of their mother pipe could still be around somewhere, rounded off and gathered into placer pockets, waiting to be found."

Cole twisted the collective control, dropping the helicopter toward the ground between the ragged ranges of hills. As the chopper descended into a clearing in the gum trees, dust and grit boiled up from the ground. As soon as the rotor settled into a lazy rhythm, Erin reached for her harness. Cole's hand locked around hers, preventing her from moving.

"Wait."

Eyes narrowed against the brilliant light that penetrated even the sunglasses' deep orange tint, Cole looked at the patches of dappled shade thrown by trees and at the more impenetrable shadows thrown by rocky knobs. One of the shadows separated and began to move toward them. Cole returned his hand to the controls but made no other movement.

"See it?" he asked.

For a time Erin stared at the dappled light and shade beneath the gum and acacia trees. Then her breath came in as she recognized the dusty black hide and thick curving horns of a water buffalo. The animal lowered its head, preparing to drive off the interloper.

"My God," she breathed. "It's huge!"

"Mean, too."

Cole brought up the revs and held the helicopter at a hover a few feet off the ground. The sudden sound and movement made the water buffalo cautious. It stopped and watched balefully.

"Are there any more around?" she asked.

"No. The bulls are solitary except at mating time."

"Like men," Erin said coolly.

The bull charged before Cole could answer. He

raised the helicopter until the skids were ten feet off the ground. The water buffalo passed beneath the hovering craft, slowed, and slewed around to face its elusive enemy. Cole held the chopper in a position that sent the maximum amount of dust and grit in the animal's eyes. After a few minutes the bull turned and trotted away in disgust.

"Reminds me of Abe," Cole said over the noise of the engine. "Angry, alone, and working hard to stay that way."

"When Abe's anger wore thin, he must have been a desperately lonely man."

"What makes you think it ever wore thin?"

"Anger always does."

Cole looked closely at Erin's face, but her sunglasses still concealed any emotion she might have felt.

"Is that why you left Alaska?" he asked. "Did your rage at life finally wear thin and you were lonely?"

Erin tilted her head as though considering the question. "I suppose that's part of it. What's your excuse, Cole? What did life do to you that turned you into a solitary rogue?"

"I trusted a woman who said she loved me."

Erin became unnaturally still. "Lai?"

"Lai," he agreed.

"What happened?"

"The usual. She didn't love me."

"Did you love her?"

He shrugged. "What's love? I wanted her."

Turning away again, Erin looked out the window at the bleak landscape of her legacy.

Cole landed the helicopter and cut back on the revs while he watched the bush where the bull had disappeared. Nothing moved but leaves tossed by the rotor's artificial wind. After a time he throttled down to an idle. No shadow came drifting up from among the trees to challenge the helicopter's right to land.

"Stay here," Cole said.

Erin would have argued, but without the fanning action of the rotor, the heat was rapidly becoming insufferable. She had no desire to get out and slog over soft ground beneath the full weight of the sun for no better reason than defying Cole.

Keeping one eye on the bush where the bull had disappeared, Cole walked toward one of the many nondescript dark rocks that poked through the soil. The sound of steel on stone rang through the wilderness as he chipped off a sample with his rock hammer. Beneath the rough black exterior, the stone was a smooth shade of cream. He took samples from other black rock knobs before he returned to the helicopter. By the time he climbed in, he was as wet as if he had been swimming.

"Well?" Erin asked.

"Looks a lot like the Windjana formation, which means a reef. I won't know for sure until I look at these under a microscope."

"Do you have one?"

"Back at the station. Wing is a thorough man. What he doesn't think of, Uncle Li does."

"Anything to keep their diamond prospector happy, is that it?" Erin asked, trying to keep the acid from her voice.

"That's it," Cole agreed curtly. "Unlike some

people, the Chens know just where their bread is buttered."

The chopper leaped into the hot, wet air and climbed to a thousand feet. Ten minutes later they descended near an irregular depression. Gradually Erin realized that the hole was man-made rather than natural. A tunnel gaped off to the side.

"Dog One," Cole said laconically.

As soon as he turned off the engine, heat wrapped around them in a thick, invisible shroud. Cole peeled off his bush shirt and dropped it behind the seat. Erin plucked at her own top, trying to create a breeze.

"Take it off," he suggested. "We're the only people in a hundred miles."

Erin shot him a sideways look. "I'll survive."

"Suit yourself."

Cole bent and reached behind her seat. She looked everywhere but at the swirling masculine patterns of hair that covered his chest. When he straightened, he was holding a large canteen. He unscrewed the top and handed it to her.

"Drink."

The water was warm and a bit stale. Erin quickly drank her fill and handed the canteen back to Cole. He shook his head.

"More," he said. "You're used to Alaska. Until your body gets used to the Kimberley, you'll have to drink much more water than you think you need."

When Erin had drunk enough for Cole's satisfaction, he took the canteen and drank too. Only then did he get out and walk toward the hole in the ground that was the only sign of Sleeping Dog One's existence. He didn't look behind to see if Erin was following. She yanked off her harness, grabbed her camera case, and dropped to the sunstruck ground. Instantly beads of sweat gathered all over her skin. She felt as though she had just stepped into a muggy pizza oven.

There were no signs, no stakes, no fences to indicate that the land held anything but the random debris of a failed mining effort. Dog One had been worked, but never in a concerted way. A rusty wheelbarrow stood on its pitted wheel beside the entrance. A pick and shovel lay discarded in the spinifex. The ore dump was so close it had eroded into the mine's entrance, threatening to seal it.

"Doesn't look like much," Erin said.

"It isn't."

Inside the tunnel mouth, out of the sun, the air was a bit cooler. Erin pocketed her sunglasses and let her eyes adjust to the darkness. When she turned and looked back toward the entrance, the violent contrast of sunlight and the black outlines of the roughly hewn mine fascinated her. Without looking away, she dug her camera out of the bag and went to work, trying to capture the elemental difference between dense velvet shade and a sun that made her believe in hell.

In Alaska light and darkness had been divided into huge, nearly seamless blocks of time. In Australia, they were shards left over from a primordial explosion. The difference compelled Erin in a way she could express only through photographs. Lost to everything else, she looked at the black and incandescent world through the camera lens.

After going farther into the tunnel, Cole turned to see what was keeping Erin. When he realized what she was doing, he switched on the electric lantern he had brought and gave his attention to the tunnel wall itself. The shoring was rude but still quite effective. With mining, if with nothing else, Abe had been a careful man.

Satisfied that the tunnel was reasonably safe, Cole went farther in, descending with each step where Abe had followed the lamproite sill to a point where it spread out in a lateral dike. Nothing had changed since Cole's last visit to Dog One. The walls were still dull lamproite except where Abe had misjudged the slope of the ore and had had to backtrack. The tunnel ended abruptly where Abe had lost the lamproite dike and given up, for the quality of the diamonds simply didn't repay the work of digging them out. Only gem diamonds repaid the cost of mining.

As Cole retreated, he studied each dead end where the tunnel strayed from the line of the lamproite intrusion. He scrutinized the walls of these failed tunnel offshoots carefully, looking for any sign that Abe had accidentally cut across a paleo-streambed, a paleo-beach, or any stratum that might have been laid down by moving water. Cole saw nothing that interested him.

Erin's voice floated back through the darkness. He shone the light on his watch, saw that an hour had passed, and shook his head in amusement as it occurred to him that he had finally found a woman who wouldn't be bored on a prospecting expedition.

"I'm coming," he called. He flashed the light back the way he had come and walked quickly.

"Find anything?" Erin asked as Cole emerged from the darkness, pushing a perfectly shaped circle of light before him.

"Nothing new."

As Cole walked forward, the light glanced off a small pile of rubble pushed against a wall. There was a dark shimmer to the little mound that intrigued Erin.

"What's that?" she asked.

Cole played the light over the mound again and said calmly, "Diamond ore."

Erin made a startled sound and bent down to scoop up a handful of the rocks. In the yellow light of the electric lantern, the ore looked as common as mud. The few tiny crystals embedded in the shards of ore were the color of camp coffee and nearly as opaque.

"These don't look anything like diamonds," Erin said.

"You're thinking of gem diamonds. Those are bort."

For a few more moments Erin studied the fragments of ore and minute, ugly diamonds. "I don't see any green crystals."

"If there were any, Abe would have been buried in diamond buyers. But they rarely came out here."

"Didn't Abe ever leave the station?"

"Abe never went beyond the store in Fitzroy Crossing. He had plenty of money for equipment and food and Fosters lager. That was as much as he needed from civilization."

"He really didn't like people, did he?"

"People hem you in and betray you," Cole said. "There's a freedom out here that's addictive."

"You and Abe were a lot alike. Once burned, forever shy."

"You should know, honey. You're backing away from the fire as fast as you can." Cole flashed the light toward the entrance. "There's nothing for us here. Let's go."

Without a word Erin turned and began walking toward the searing sunlight that waited at the mouth of Dog One's tunnel.

26

◆

"No," MATTHEW WINDSOR SAID. "STREET HAS worked too many sides of the political fence. I don't trust him."

"ASIO vouches for him," Nan Faulkner said curtly, stubbing out her cigarillo. "So does MI-Six."

"MI-Six has vouched for a lot of traitors."

Faulkner swore, lit another cigarillo, and watched the man who sat opposite her broad teak desk.

"I could make it an order," she pointed out, exhaling a stream of smoke.

"You've got my resignation. Use it."

"I'd rather use you." She drummed her fingers impatiently on the desk, then reached a decision. She opened the belly drawer, pulled out a battery-operated tape player, and set it on the desk. "Listen to this."

She punched a button and the tape began to play.

Windsor looked sharply at Faulkner, then listened intently. The first voice was male and unfamiliar. The second voice was Cole Blackburn's. The conversation made it clear that Cole had been employed to find the diamond mine regardless of whatever it cost—including Erin's life.

"I recognized Blackburn's voice," Windsor said when the tape became silent. "I presume the other man was Chen Wing?"

"A good guess." She smiled thinly. "But then, you're good at what you do. Yes, it was Wing."

Windsor waited.

"You're not stupid, Matt," Faulkner said impatiently. "You know what this means."

"Tell me what you think it means."

"Cole Blackburn isn't the loose cannon we thought he was. He's in the pay of an ambitious Hong Kong clan run by a cunning, ruthless old bastard who happens to be Chen Wing's uncle." Faulkner waited, but no comment came from the big, impassive man who sat opposite her. She exhaled smoke and made a disgusted sound. "Your daughter's life is on the line and you have nothing to say?"

"Erin's life has been on the line since she was named Abelard Windsor's heir."

"Shit." Faulkner sucked in hard, making the cigarillo's narrow tip glow. "We made a mistake not taking Blackburn out of the game, and you know it."

"No, I don't know it. Nothing I just heard proves he signed up as Erin's assassin."

Faulkner gave him a look of disgust. "Wing says nothing matters after the mine is found, and Blackburn doesn't say squat about it."

"That doesn't prove he—" Windsor began.

"Jesus, Matt," Faulkner interrupted angrily. "I thought you'd be happy to hear we're sending a bodyguard in for your daughter. Otherwise she'll die as soon as the mine is found and the Chen clan will control half of the mine outright and you know it as well as I do."

"The Australian government—"

"No!" Faulkner said, cutting across Windsor's words. "The Aussies won't lift a finger. The boys down under would be more than happy to stick it up the cartel's ass and break it off. They're still mad as hell about the Argyle mine."

"That doesn't mean Blackburn is an assassin. He's spent his whole life avoiding being owned by anyone or anything. Why would he suddenly change his pattern?"

"Money," she said succinctly.

"He's been offered money before. Lots of it. He turned it down."

"Pull your head out of your ass! If Sleeping Dog Mines is half what we suspect it is, a whole lot of set patterns will change real quick. If Blackburn is somebody's mole, this would be the score that would bring him to the surface."

"I still don't buy it."

"I'm not selling," Faulkner said coldly, "I'm telling. Europe is going through the biggest economic restructuring since they scragged the czar, the Soviets are flat starved for international currency, and the cartel is the biggest cash cow they have. If the cartel goes under, so do the Soviets. We don't want that to happen, babe. We have to control that fucking mine!" She blew out a dense burst of smoke. "I've taken a lot of flak over your refusal to recommend Thomas as your daughter's diamond expert."

"Thomas is CIA."

"You bet your ass he is. That's the whole point."

"No. The point is he would trade Erin's life for

the mine any time he got an offer." Windsor watched Faulkner, seeing the new lines of strain. "Who's squeezing you?"

"You know better than to ask. I sure as hell know better than to answer."

Faulkner smoked in tight silence for a few moments before she closed her eyes and went on wearily.

"I shouldn't tell you this, but if I can't trust you I might as well cut my throat and get the waiting over with." She stubbed out her half-smoked cigarillo. "Either we give Jason Street a letter of introduction to Erin or we can forget all the strategic minerals we've been getting from ConMin. South Africa won't sell them to us. Neither will the Soviets. Which means the U.S. will be shit out of luck real quick."

Silence was Windsor's only answer.

"Say something, Matt."

"Like what? I'm having a hard time believing that ConMin is willing to go that far over a diamond mine that may or may not exist!"

"Oh, they're willing. Not eager, mind you, but willing. You know where Erin is. Call her. Use my phone."

"No."

Faulkner looked across her desk in blank disbelief. "What?"

"I was ambitious once. I came close to destroying Erin by using her as an unwitting source of disinformation for a Soviet agent known as Hans Schmidt."

Faulkner sat very still. She had read the file and wondered about Windsor's role. Now she knew.

"I told myself it would be all right," Windsor said. "I'd gone over Schmidt's file until I had it memo-

rized. I'd questioned other sources. If he wasn't a Soviet, he would have been everything a father could
want for his daughter—intelligent, strong, ambitious,
a real comer. He seemed very much in love with Erin.
She was certainly in love with him."

"And if you doubled him," Faulkner said, "you
would have had a direct pipeline to the Kremlin at a
time when the U.S. was spending too many days on
yellow alert."

"Yes," Windsor said simply. He closed his eyes
for a moment, knowing he couldn't conceal the old
echoes of pain, rage, and shame from Faulkner's
shrewd black eyes.

She sighed. "Don't blame yourself. You had no
way of knowing Hans got off by cutting up girls."

"No, but if I had told Erin that Hans was a Soviet
agent, she would have broken the engagement. As it
was . . ." Windsor's voice faded.

"As it was, your daughter ended up in the hospital. It wasn't your fault. And you got even," Faulkner
pointed out with a thin, cold smile. "You got even but
good."

There was silence for the space of several breaths.
Faulkner waited. Finally Windsor began talking again.

"I'm no longer sure about absolute right and absolute wrong," he said slowly. "I did what I thought
was right, what was necessary, what was useful, and I
got a little gold star in my file because the information
Erin innocently passed on to her loving fiancé threw
the Soviets off the scent of our secret negotiations
with Iran for a whole three weeks."

"Every hour of that time was vital," Faulkner
pointed out. "We made some real gains, Matt. We
came very close to getting the moderates in power."

"Close, but no cigar. For that my daughter was beaten, raped, and tortured by a sadist. Erin hasn't trusted or loved me or any other man since that day. Seven years. She's not even thirty. She's got a whole lifetime of nightmares and distrust and loneliness ahead of her."

Faulkner grimaced but didn't disagree.

"Every second I stayed with her in the hospital," Windsor said quietly, "I swore that I would never knowingly use an innocent—*any* innocent—again. Ours is a game for informed, consenting adults." He met Faulkner's dark glance. "The answer is still no."

The door to Faulkner's office opened. Two men came in and stood at either side of Windsor. With a great effort he throttled the rage that made his body rigid. If he lost his temper, there would be no chance of helping Erin at all.

"House arrest?" he asked in a clipped voice.

"I'm sorry," Faulkner said simply. "A letter went out to your daughter yesterday. Jason Street will be on the Windsor station by tomorrow. Erin will be safe."

27

◆

HUGO VAN LUIK HAD FORGOTTEN HOW GODFOR-
saken diamond grounds and diamonds mines could
be. The Argyle mine was in a place so desolate and
remote that workers were flown in, given room and
board, and then flown out at regular intervals, like
military personnel at a hardship post. The place was a
bleak paean to technological efficiency, an orderly assembly of barracks and mess halls, power shovels, ore
crushers, conveyor belts, and x-ray tables. Argyle produced diamonds with mechanical regularity, even if it
crushed some promising gemstones in the process.

Van Luik only wished the process crushed more.
Diamond grit was useful. At the moment, gemstones
were not.

Sighing, van Luik leaned back into the Otter's
uncomfortable seat. He was relieved to have the oblig-
atory visit to the Argyle mine behind him, complete
with still photos of men in suits shaking hands and
smiling into the camera. Van Luik no longer cared for
the politically important process of pressing flesh and

giving personal assurances to strangers that their lives were important in the international economic scheme.

Yet he had played his role with all the skill of the actor he had once wanted to be. He hadn't endured the tour out of respect for the Argyle mine and its huge output of muddy industrial bort or its modest numbers of tiny pale-pink or straw-yellow gemstones. A Japanese syndicate had recently been sniffing around Argyle, considering the purchase of the mine. Van Luik wished them well.

Anything that would keep the Japanese from experimenting with better and cheaper ways to produce industrial diamonds was a plus for ConMin. If the Japanese purchased Argyle, it would be something of a relief. They would be more sophisticated and less impatient with the delicate balancing act among the diamond cartel's members than Australia was.

Closing his eyes, van Luik tried to ignore the exquisite tendrils of pain infiltrating the area behind his eyes. The plane bucked in the torrid, seething currents of afternoon air. The buildup was on, bringing with it a wet heat that exacerbated van Luik's headaches and made the blinding tropical light a constant source of pain. He closed his eyes and endured.

Not until the twin-engine Otter banked over the shimmering, man-made sprawl of Lake Argyle and lined up for a landing at Kununurra did van Luik open his eyes, mop his flushed face and sweaty neck with a handkerchief, and prepare to deal with the real reason he had come to Australia.

Grimacing at a deep thrust of pain, he squinted out the window. River swamps, low-rising red rocks, scrubland, and a town like a crusty rash spread below him. As the plane descended, the temperature rose.

The climate was as close to hell as a living man could expect to endure. It made van Luik question the sanity of the English settlers who had chosen Western Australia for their home.

The Otter touched down smoothly on the sun-softened tarmac and taxied to the mining company tiedown next to the small tin-roofed passenger terminal. The cabin steward popped the door and lowered the stairs.

"There's your flight, right on time, sir," the steward said, pointing to an aircraft that had appeared in the south and was headed straight in for a landing. "It will leave in ninety minutes."

Van Luik grunted his understanding and headed for the terminal. The real purpose of his visit would take only a few minutes, but he expected it to be no more pleasant than his tour of Argyle had been. Given a choice, he would never have taken the chance of being seen with Jason Street.

But van Luik had not been given a choice. Part of the reason was that the letter he carried was too important to be entrusted to any ordinary courier. The more pressing part of the reason was that van Luik's employers were unhappy with his handling of Abelard Windsor's legacy. Being dispatched as an errand boy without benefit of company planes and executive luxury was an indication of just how deep ConMin's displeasure went. It said quite clearly that if the matter wasn't resolved to ConMin's satisfaction, Hugo van Luik was as expendable as Jason Street.

The Dutchman felt a damp chill as he walked into the heavily air-conditioned building. The change in temperature was welcome, but it caused an excrutiating lance of pain behind his eyes. There were a half-dozen people in front of the Ansett airlines ticket counter—two barefoot Aborigines in jackaroo hats and denim pants and an outback wife with a screaming baby and two shrill, relentlessly quarrelsome children.

Van Luik headed for the louvered swinging doors beneath the sign that said PUB. The interior was mercifully dim. Jason Street sat on one of the five stools that lined the zinc bar, talking to the dumpy woman who was the bartender. Unhappily van Luik eyed the big man in his dusty khakis and unpolished boots. A broad-brimmed hat with a snakeskin band was pushed back on Street's head, revealing a sharp demarcation between his weathered face and the untanned skin normally covered by the hat.

"Now there's a weary tourist if ever there was," Street said. "Hey, mate, might you be interested in an outback tour?"

Van Luik forced himself to smile. "Not at this time, but I'll be bringing my wife on my next trip. Perhaps we could work out an itinerary that would not be too strenuous?"

Street smiled and turned to the barmaid. "Two ales, luv, and one for yourself too."

The woman produced two cans of Castlemain ale, pulled the metal tabs on them, and slid them across the bar. Street picked both up and led van Luik to a small table in the darkest corner of the little pub. Behind him, the barmaid pulled the tab on a third can and retreated to a chair behind the cash register.

"Here you go, mate," Street said.

"I am not your mate," van Luik said in a vicious tone that went no farther than Street's ears.

Street slouched in a chair, took a pull from his

drink, and grinned. "Bit irritable, aren't we? Heat getting us down?"

The Dutchman turned his back on the rest of the room so he couldn't be overheard. "Speak softly, *foutre*."

Street knew enough French to know he had been insulted. He smiled more widely. "What are you going to do, mate, fire me?"

"There are dozens of security consultants in the world," van Luik retorted. "Are you certain I haven't already hired your replacement?"

Street's smile turned cold. "Send him on. I'll even give him the first shot. But he'd better be good, because he won't get another. When I've cut him up for the flies I'll come for you. You understand, *mate*?"

They glared at one another for a long moment. Finally, van Luik broke off the contact, picked up the can, and drank. The ale was lukewarm and bitter. "What progress have you made?" he asked.

"No progress to make until I get on the station, and you bloody well know it."

"I assume you have something more effective and deniable than a car smash in mind," van Luik shot back.

Street smiled. "I do, mate. I do."

The pain in van Luik's head had redoubled until his fingers tingled. He flexed his hands but did not lift a finger to pinch the flesh at the bridge of his nose.

"Where are they now?" van Luik demanded softly.

"At the station," Street retorted. "Where else? They've made some short recon trips while information is being collated."

"And?"

"The only shiny stuff they found was their own sweat."

"You're certain?"

"They have rotten radio security," Street said easily. "The scrambler on the satellite up-link is identical to one in my Darwin office. I've read every piece of mail they've sent."

Van Luik took another small sip of ale, wondering why he had the uneasy feeling that Street was lying.

"How is the woman standing up to the rigors of the climate and the land?"

"The buildup got to her real quick. She's short-tempered as a cat in a bath. She and Blackburn aren't as chummy as they were."

"How close were they?"

"Fucking close."

Van Luik grimaced. "Has she made any progress on finding clues in 'Chunder'?"

"She spends a lot of time reading it."

"Good."

"Why?"

"A person does not work on a puzzle that is already solved." There was silence while van Luik fought against the impulse to squeeze the bridge of his nose. "How is Mr. Blackburn holding up?"

"Mean as a snake," Street said cheerfully. "Going on short rations will do that to a man."

"Rations? Is there a problem getting food to the station?"

"Food isn't the problem. Sex is. They're sleeping in the same room but not on the same blanket."

"Your information is quite complete."

"That's my job," Street said coolly. "If you don't believe me, go to the station yourself."

"I will leave that dubious pleasure to you." Van Luik drew a thin parcel from his suit coat and slid it across the table. The packet was wrapped in bright yellow plastic and secured with string wrapped in a figure eight around two buttons. "Do not open it."

Street glanced at the packet. "What is it?"

"Your entree, a letter of introduction to Miss Windsor." Van Luik reached into his pocket and withdrew a sheet of paper. "This is a photocopy."

Without a word, Street took the sheet, read quickly, and looked up.

"Genuine?" Street asked bluntly.

"Does it matter?"

"Not as long as the signature passes muster."

"There will be no difficulty with the signature."

"Bloody hell. Somebody really twisted the CIA's balls." Street shot van Luik a glance. "ConMin? Or was it their own government?"

Van Luik retrieved the copy, stood, and walked out without a word.

It wasn't until the plane was over the vast Pacific Ocean that painkillers subdued van Luik's savage headache. Just as he slid into sleep, the thought that had nagged beneath the pulses of agony surfaced: Street had never before mentioned having any satellite scrambler except the one van Luik had given him.

28

◆

DAWN WAS A SILENT TIDAL WAVE OF HEAT AND savage light. The Kimberley Plateau's big birds of prey spread dark wings and leaped from their boab tree perch into the rising inferno. Erin crouched over first one tripod and then another, triggering the shutters repeatedly, refocusing, triggering again, moving quickly until the rapid *snick snick snick* of the motor drive fed the last thin strip of film and fell silent. Even as Erin reached for the third camera body she had loaded with film, she sighed and knew it was too late. The moment of the predatory kites' dark awakening was past.

She stretched her back, sighed, and began removing cameras from their tripod mounts.

"That's it?" Cole asked, rising from the darkness beneath an acacia tree.

Erin jumped. She had been so intent on her work that she had forgotten Cole was nearby, watching her, shotgun in hand.

"Yes, I'm through for now."

She packed up her camera equipment, shouldered all of it, and looked around at the land that was
slowly, inevitably being transformed by the rising violence of the sun. She was learning new rhythms in this
strange, austere country. One of them was to rise early
and savor the relative coolness. For a few minutes
each morning the sun felt almost welcome.

Almost, but not quite. Despite the fact that dawn
was less than five minutes old, the temperature was
already in the high eighties. The heavy blanket of air
simply didn't let the land cool off, even during the
hours of darkness. Each day was hotter and more humid than the one before. Each day the clouds teased
and muttered but did not deliver rain.

Squinting against the early light, Erin looked up
at the black designs made by the Kimberley kites soar-
ing gracefully in a sky that seethed with light.

"I've always wondered," she said softly, watching
the kites, "whether birds of prey spend so much time
hanging in the sky because they can, or because they
must."

"I suspect they can because they must."

When Cole reached for the straps of the camera
bags, his fingers brushed over the bare skin of Erin's
arm. She flinched and stepped back, saying without
words that she didn't want his touch or his help.

Cole's mouth flattened as he turned away and
started walking. Erin hadn't fought his edict that she
never be out of his sight, but she had made it clear
that theirs was now a business relationship. He hadn't
liked it, but he hadn't tried to change her mind. Pushing her would only drive her farther away.

As they walked the short distance to the station
house, the sounds of unfamiliar birds poured from ev-

ery acacia and gum. Abe's well and stock tank had created a mecca for wild animals of all kinds, making Erin's job of photography easier. In the two days since she had been at the station, she had managed to capture fourteen different varieties of local animal life. She had also learned a visceral appreciation of why predators waited at waterholes in dry country.

It worked.

"Which mine are we looking at today?" Erin asked.

"Dog Four."

"Again?"

Cole nodded.

"Why?" she asked.

"Because it's close to another site I want to look at."

"Isn't Dog Four where we saw the goanna?"

"Yes," he said.

"Good. I'm having trouble getting a handle on the best way to shoot one."

"With a twelve-gauge," he said dryly.

Erin smiled despite her vow to keep the relationship between Cole and herself on a purely business basis. It was difficult now for the same reason it had been difficult in the beginning—Cole's intelligence and quick, deadpan humor were even greater lures for her than any regularity of face or strength of body he had.

He's even bright enough not to try to get in bed with me again, she told herself grimly. Or maybe it's just that sweet, delicate Lai is taking care of his business.

Yet even as the thought came, Erin knew it wasn't true. When she and Cole were at the station, he was always near her. They slept in the same room, they ate at the same table, and they flew the land in the same helicopter.

Maybe it's not just for my safety. Maybe he's afraid to be alone with Lai, she thought.

Erin's mouth turned down. Cole hadn't looked afraid when she had come into the room and seen his big hand caressing Lai's neck. He hadn't looked particularly passionate, either. He had looked . . . suspended, patient, curious, coiled.

Predatory.

A feeling of unease shivered through Erin. Whatever had happened between Lai and Cole in the past had gone deep. Love, hate, or both tangled together, it didn't matter. Cole had given Lai more than his body. He had gotten back the certainty that women were what Abe had called them: mistresses of lies.

Erin stepped from the uncertain shade of the acacia grove into the spinifex. The sun was a steaming, searing shroud enfolding her. Sweat began to stand on her skin and gather in rivulets between her breasts and beneath her arms. Flies came in their ragged squadrons but didn't land on her. The combination of insect repellent and sunscreen the Australians used was effective.

She only wished they had a repellent for the insufferable Kimberley climate as well. Already she could feel herself becoming surly, tense, wanting to lash out at anything within reach. She suspected Cole felt the same way, but he disguised it better. That, too, irritated her, making her want to pry beneath his self-control.

"How long does the buildup last?" Erin asked.

"Until it rains."

She made a disgusted sound.

Cole slanted a sideways look at her. Erin's pale skin was already flushed with heat and burnished with sweat. He took off his hat and dropped it over the burning mahogany of her hair.

"Where's your hat? I told you not to—"

"And I told you I can't work with a damned hat flopping and flapping in my eyes," she retorted, cutting across his words. "Besides, I knew we wouldn't be out in the sun for more than the time it took to walk back to the house."

Erin yanked the hat off and handed it to Cole. He pushed it over her head again.

"Wear it," Cole said. "Two weeks ago you were sitting on a glacier at the other end of the earth, getting ready for winter. Now you're sitting on a stove waiting for summer. Your body is still trying to figure out what hit it."

"Yours seems to be doing just fine," she said resentfully.

"I was in Brazil. Different stove, same temperature, same season. Stop wasting your energy trying to prove you can take the climate as well as I can. You can't. Give me the damn camera gear."

Cole didn't wait for Erin's agreement. He simply stripped the gear from her with quick motions. They finished the walk to the station in silence. When they arrived Lai was waiting at the table that had been set in the shade of a wide white awning. The awning stretched across the back of the house, helping both to shade and to extend the living space. A big white tent had been set up fifty feet beyond the house. The eight Chinese men lived there. They serviced the array of equipment and, she suspected, guarded it as well.

Lai looked like golden porcelain, cool and delicate, perfectly formed within her indigo silk slacks and shirt. She nodded politely before she withdrew into the house.

"Doesn't she ever sweat?" Erin muttered beneath her breath.

"Stone doesn't sweat. Sit down. I'll get breakfast. The coffee you make is strong enough to etch stainless steel."

"So is yours."

"Yeah. We make a great team, don't we?"

Giving Cole a wary look, Erin sat down at the table. He stacked her camera gear close at hand and went into the kitchen. She knew without turning around that he could see her from inside the house, which was why he had put her in that particular chair. Cursing wearily, she flapped the cloth of her tank top, trying to create breeze. It was futile.

She dropped the cloth and began rummaging in one of her camera bags for the old photos she kept there along with Abe's poetry. The envelope was becoming soft and rather fuzzy from humidity and frequent handling. The photos were not. Erin held them carefully by the edges, looking at each image intently before going on to the next.

"Do you think the secret of the diamond mine is in those photographs?" Lai asked softly.

Erin's breath came in with a startled sound. She wondered whether Lai tiptoed around deliberately or if she simply didn't have enough weight to make sounds when she walked.

"No," Erin said. "But they might tell me the secret of Crazy Abe—why he lived and why he hated and why he died."

"He died of sunstroke," Lai said as she looked over Erin's shoulder at a photograph.

It was Erin's favorite, the one of her grandmother standing on a steep rise with dark, odd-looking rocks and stunted acacias all around, and a tall man standing off to the right watching with hungry eyes. With Cole's help, Erin had discovered that many of the photos were taken in the same area as Bridget's Hill, but from different angles and distances. One of the shots showed only the white slash of a woman's skirt poised on the top of a ridge like a star rising over the vast land. Erin wondered if her grandmother had amused herself climbing the rise while the photographer was otherwise occupied.

"Who is that?" Lai asked.

"My grandmother."

"And the man is your grandfather?"

Erin shrugged. "I don't know."

"Are they still alive?"

"No."

Clear black eyes looked unflinchingly at the photo, then at Erin, then at the photo again. After the space of four breaths Lai turned away.

"Human secrets have little value unless they lead to control," Lai said as she turned and headed back into the house. "Knowing the secrets of the dead is useless. The dead cannot be controlled."

Erin turned to give Lai a startled look, but the woman had withdrawn as silently as she had come. Relieved, Erin went back to staring at the haunting picture that had been taken when people now dead were young, vivid, vital, poised on the threshold of decisions that would shape their lives and the lives of those who came after them. She turned the photo over and read again the faded lines: *Some love for silver, some love for gold,/We love for the heat that never runs cold.*

On an impulse Erin bent down and sorted by touch through a camera bag, not looking away from the lines of poetry. After a moment she found the folded sheets of "Chunder." She pulled them up to the table, shook them out, and laid them next to the photograph. An odd sensation prickled over her skin.

When Cole came out to the table, Erin was motionless, her eyes fixed on the lines of "Chunder."

"Feeling masochistic?" he asked, setting the coffee down.

Erin looked up. In the sourceless light beneath the awning her eyes were a luminous green so pure Cole couldn't help staring. He had seen nothing quite so beautiful, even the green diamond itself.

"How much does a man's handwriting change over the course of his life?" she asked.

"A lot more before he's twenty-five than after, unless he's sick, drunk, or injured. Why?"

"I think Abe wrote the lines on the back of this photo."

Cole stood close behind Erin, looking over her shoulder at the photo and the poetry. The longer he compared them, the more he agreed. There was a similarity about many of the letters that went beyond the careful Victorian handwriting style.

"Could be," he agreed. "Does it matter?"

"I don't know. It just seems odd that Grandfather would end up with this picture if it had been written on by Abe."

Cole grunted. "Not if they were both sleeping with the same woman."

"What?"

"Don't sound so shocked. They might have been your grandparents, but they were human. She wouldn't have been the first woman in creation to be engaged to one man and engaged *with* another."

" 'Mistress of lies . . .' "

"Exactly."

"Well, that would explain why the two of them left for America."

"Yeah. Especially if she was carrying the wrong man's child."

Erin made a sound of protest. "That's not likely."

"Why not? Birth control and abortion were hit-and-miss in those days, and lust hasn't changed much since Eve seduced Adam into eating from her hand."

"You have a rather jaundiced view of women."

"I could say the same about your view of men."

Ignoring Cole, Erin turned the photo over and looked at the glossy, faded image again.

"Is that limestone?" she asked, pointing to the oddly shaped rocks that stood knee and waist high to Bridget McQueen Windsor.

"Probably."

"And underneath the rise?"

"More of the same."

" 'A dead sea's bones.' "

Cole grunted. "When those pictures were taken, Abe was looking for water for his cattle, not diamonds."

"Still, I wonder where this was taken."

"Why?"

"It's as close to a real big hill as I've found here," Erin said dryly. "I'd like to see what the world looks like from the top of it."

For an instant Cole's crystalline gray eyes focused completely on the photos in front of Erin, measuring the steepness of the rise against his abnormally precise memories of the land he had seen at various times on Windsor Station. After a few moments Cole decided that Erin was right. No location came to mind on the station. The other mineral claims weren't too likely, either. Most of them were on land that was even flatter than the station itself.

"Odd," Cole muttered, staring at the series of photos again. "It can't be that far away from camp or from a settlement, because her dress is wrinkled but not dirty."

He picked up the photo that had been taken from a distance, pulled a loupe from one of the many pockets in his bush shorts, and looked closely at the image.

"I'll be damned. That handsome jackaroo is Abe."

"Are you sure?"

"I can see a scar on his left wrist. Abe had one in the same spot, reminder of the day when he was young and foolish enough to rope a brush bull. It nearly did for him. He was lucky he didn't lose the hand."

"He's looking at Bridget with such longing."

"Poor son of a bitch. He doesn't know yet."

"What?" asked Erin.

"It's as clear as the sly, sexy little smile on her face. She wants the man behind the camera, not Abe."

"That must be Grandfather. It was a good match. She stayed with him the rest of her life."

Cole grunted, unimpressed. He moved the loupe slowly, examining the rest of the photo. "I don't see anything that looks like a seep, much less a billabong.

But it was the dry, which means they were going from waterhole to waterhole."

"Walking?"

"In those shoes? Abe used to ride everywhere before he turned the horses loose to live or die with whatever was left of his cattle. He and his brother and Bridget were probably on horseback, camping out and taking pictures and looking over the best place for the happy couple to build a home."

The savage irony beneath the surface of Cole's words made Erin uneasy. She sensed he was lumping her with her grandmother and Lai and Eve, women who had betrayed the men who loved them.

But then, Cole doesn't love me, Erin told herself, so the comparison doesn't apply. Besides, I wasn't the one who was stirring through old ashes looking for sparks.

Cole made a sound of surprise, slanted the photo to catch the light better, and peered at a corner through the loupe.

"Find something?" Erin asked.

"They were camping. There's a pack saddle and dry goods in the shade of one of the distant trees. Can't see a waterhole or anything like the kind of plants a waterhole would support."

"Maybe they carried their own water."

"Doubt it. Water is heavy and horses need a lot. You reach the point of diminishing returns very fast."

Erin watched Cole study the photo with an intensity that was almost tangible. She was tempted to grab her camera and take a portrait of him. Instead, she reached for the coffee and scones he had brought from the kitchen. As she ate, she thumbed idly through the pages of "Chunder from Down Under." When she re-

membered what the title meant, she grimaced: Vomit
from Australia. Then she recalled how diamonds were
brought to the surface in a violent rush of magma
from the depths of the earth.

"Did Abe have a sense of humor?" Erin asked.

"After a fashion. Why?"

"Would it have amused him to think of diamonds
as kind of cosmic vomit?"

Black eyebrows went up. Cole turned the full
force of his attention on Erin, making her feel as
though she had just been pinned by a searchlight.

"Yes," Cole said. "Any other thoughts?"

She hesitated. "You're going to think I'm crazy,
but those rocks look kind of like black swans to me."

Erin pointed to the photo where Bridget Mc-
Queen stood on the windy rise. For an instant Cole
was motionless. Then he picked up the photo and his
loupe.

"No," she said. "Not that way. Put down the
loupe and let your eyes kind of go unfocused."

"Like I was drunk?" he asked dryly.

"Why not? Abe seemed to spend most of his time
soused to his widow's peak."

After a few moments Cole said, "It's possible
those are swans, but the same probably could be said
of any ridge capped by lumps of eroded limestone that
had turned dark."

"But this isn't just any ridge. This is the ridge
where Bridget McQueen stood and smiled at the man
who was to become her husband, while Abe stood to
one side, thinking she was his."

"McQueen . . . Queen of Lies." Cole frowned.
"It fits, but Abe didn't know diamonds from quartz in
those days."

"Would you say he was obsessed with my grand-mother?"

"Probably. For revenge, if nothing else. A man who has been used like that wants his pound of flesh and then some."

Erin looked at the picture but it was Lai she saw, Lai of the flawless features and feline body. Revenge could easily be an extension of betrayed love. Erin glanced up quickly, wanting to ask if it was revenge and hatred that bound Cole to Lai rather than love. But that would have been the kind of personal question Erin had declared off limits.

"Isn't it possible," she said carefully, looking only at the photos, "that Abe went back to this place many times, as a kind of perverse shrine?"

"It's more than possible. It would have been just like him to go there, drink, remember, and rage away the days until he was too spent to care about anything."

Erin barely refrained from asking Cole if he had his own private shrine of betrayal and rage.

"How many brothers and sisters does your father have?" Cole asked absently.

She blinked. "None. He's an only child."

"If we're right about Bridget and Abe, you realize what it means, don't you?" Before Erin could speak, Cole quoted from the verses that had accompanied the diamonds. " 'Then come to my land/Grandchild of deceit/Blood of my blood/Bone of my bone. . . .' You're Abe's granddaughter, not his grandniece. You're the 'Descendant of deceit.' "

"Charming," she said, but her tone said the opposite. "Just what I always wanted, an ancestor who was crazy."

Cole smiled crookedly. "Don't worry. If there were any bad genes, they gave your father a pass. He's as hardheaded and tightly wrapped as they come."

Erin began searching through the poem once more. " 'Find it if you can,/If you dare to go/Where the dark swan floats/Over a dead sea's bones. . . .' Well, that's clear enough. But the next part is beyond me."

"Want me to explain it again?" he offered.

"Pass," she said quickly. "I learned enough yesterday about Aussie sexual slang to last a lifetime."

"You asked."

"And you answered." Erin grimaced. "Talk about reducing something to its logical absurdity. . . . On the other hand, I have to admit that the man had a knack for double and triple meanings. Look at the title. It can be read as a comment on the poetry, as a comment on how diamonds formed, and as a comment on diamonds themselves. Not bad. Not pretty, but not stupid."

Cole waited, watching Erin. Her long, slender fingers were tracing over the poetry, but her eyes were unfocused. He sensed the same intense concentration in her that she normally reserved for photography—or making love.

"Are you sure there aren't any caves on the station or the mineral claims?" she asked finally.

"None that I know of."

Erin sighed. "Well, it was a nice idea."

"What was?"

"If there were caves or passages through the dead sea's bones, and if you had Abe's warped view of life, you might see a man's penetration of a cave in sexual terms. As for seeing the cave in feminine terms, Mother Earth is a common metaphor."

Cole shot her a surprised look.

"I was an English major in college," Erin said. "Words were my passion. Then I discovered photography. Anyway, Abe was supposed to be some kind of literary scholar, wasn't he?"

"A good one, when he was sober. He used to recite Milton and Pope to me while we drank."

"Poor baby."

"Would you believe I liked it? He had an amazing voice."

Erin looked at Cole and realized that she did believe it. He was a man of unpredictable interests.

"But there's a problem with your interpretation of the poetry," Cole continued. "Several, actually."

"What?"

"No caves."

"We just have to find one."

"Right," he said dryly. "That leaves Abe."

"I don't understand."

" 'Crazy bloke/Drank holy' pretty well describes him."

"Wasn't he ever sober?" Erin asked.

"Yes. That's what I'm worried about. Remember the last lines of the poetry in the will?"

Erin shook her head and started searching through the papers in front of her.

"Don't bother," Cole said. " 'Goodbye, my Queen of Lies./And I am the King.' This whole thing could be Abe's gigantic joke on the world."

"But the diamonds are real."

"As real as death," Cole said grimly. " 'Secrets blacker than death/And truth it's death to speak./ But

I will speak to you . . . child of rue.' It's you he's speaking to, Erin. 'Child of deceit/Cleave unto me./ My grave, my bones,/Hear them moan.' It's you he's offering death."

"You should have been an English major. You're reading more into the lines than I am." She looked at the watch on Cole's wrist. "How much time before we go prospecting again?"

There was an electric silence before Cole accepted the change of subject. "I'll go run up the chopper."

He turned and went toward the helicopter without another word about death and poetry. Erin let out her breath in a long sigh, picked up her coffee, and drank. The steamy liquid was barely hotter than the day itself.

The helicopter ripped into life, then settled down to running steadily. It missed a beat, picked up again for a minute, then hesitated very slightly before running smoothly once more. Several minutes passed before the engine was shut off. Cole leaped to the ground, opened a panel, and began probing the chopper's innards.

Erin was just finishing her second cup of coffee when Cole walked into the awning's shade. She could tell by his stride and the line of his mouth that he was angry. He was holding a round metal cylinder in his hand.

"This shoots one day all to hell, and probably two," Cole said, holding up the cylinder. He looked at the sky, which was hazed by heat. There were a few areas where clouds were already forming. It was early for the wet to settle in, but the signs were there. Rain could come at any time, shutting down the possibility of finding Crazy Abe's mine until the dry returned. "Lai!"

She appeared in response to Cole's summons with a speed that said she had been standing just inside the door, waiting or listening or both. And Cole had known it.

"Yes?" she asked, looking only at Cole.

"Tell Wing to send down a complete set of fuel filters for the helicopter. Make that three complete sets. I'll keep the spares with me at all times."

Lai nodded and added a phrase in Chinese.

"Speak English," Cole said flatly.

"But you understand Chinese very well," she murmured.

"Erin doesn't."

"Why don't you teach her as I taught you?"

The question was simple, but Lai's voice evoked an image of two lovers endlessly intertwined, teaching and learning things that had nothing to do with language. The same vivid sexuality ran through Lai's graceful hand, the fingers slightly curled as though to plead or to hold a man in its palm. She made the implied intimacy of the gesture so great that Erin looked away.

"Call your brother," Cole said in a clipped voice.

Expressionless, Lai nodded and withdrew into the house.

"What happened?" Erin said.

"Dirty fuel."

"What?"

Cole unscrewed one end of the filter assembly and pulled out a paper cone. "Feel it."

Erin ran her fingertip over the cone, then rubbed her fingers together. At first she felt nothing but the fuel. Gradually she became aware of a vague, almost gritty texture. She looked into Cole's eyes, silently questioning.

"You expect some dirt," he said. "That's why you have filters. But it looks like half the grit in the Oscar Range ran through the system."

"How did the fuel get that dirty?"

"I could have left the cap off," Cole said neutrally.

"Not likely."

"Thank you."

Erin shrugged. "It's the truth. You've watched that helicopter like a mother hen with one chick."

"It was our best chance of finding the mine before the wet. Somebody else knew it and buggered the fuel."

"Sabotage?"

"It's what I'd do, if I was trying to slow somebody down."

"Or kill him?"

"Yes."

Erin looked up and shivered at the certainty she saw in Cole's eyes.

"They'll try again," he said flatly. "Walk away from it, Erin. From the mine, from the station, from Australia. Nothing is worth dying for, not even God's own diamond strike."

"The arctic taught me that walking away is another way of dying. I came here to find a new way of being alive. I'm staying."

Cole heard no doubt in Erin's voice and saw none in her eyes. Arguing would be worse than futile—it would further divide them, making her even more vulnerable to an assassin.

"Who did it?" Erin asked with a calmness she didn't feel.

"It could have happened before the fuel was delivered to the station. More likely, somebody did it right here."

Without thinking, Erin turned and looked at the door where Lai had retreated.

"Possible, but I doubt it," Cole said. "Not that Lai wouldn't kill for her family. She would. Hell, she did. But we're the Chen family's best hope of getting a piece of the diamond tiger, and she'll do whatever her family tells her to do."

"Lai killed someone?" Erin asked, appalled.

"She was seven months pregnant when Uncle Li ordered her to abort my child and marry another man, a Chinese man who would solidify the Chen family's position in Kowloon. She did it and never looked back."

Erin opened her mouth, but no words came. "I'm sorry," she whispered.

"Why? It wasn't your doing."

She simply shook her head, unable to explain why Cole's past pain was hurting her now. Before she could find words, Lai appeared in the doorway.

"Wing wishes to speak with you."

Cole looked at Erin. "Come with me. I can't see you from the radio room."

Although Erin's eyes widened, she said nothing as she stood and followed Cole into the stifling rooms of the station house.

"What else has gone wrong?" Cole asked Wing.

"Jason Street is on his way to the station."

Cole raked his fingers through his black hair and made a sound of disgust. "What happened?"

"We suspect the Americans threw the Australians a bone."

"Not good, Wing. Street was a lucky prospector before he took up running a mine security business."

"There is one welcome factor. Satellite photos don't show any break in the weather. The monsoons have not materialized yet."

"Damn good thing. Prospecting by Rover is a hell of a lot slower than by chopper. Anything else?"

"No," Wing said.

"Think hard, because I won't be checking in with you tonight," Cole said. "In fact, I won't be checking in at all until we find Abe's mine or until the wet begins, whichever comes first. Erin had an idea I want to follow."

"The diamond mine?" Wing said instantly. "Are you close?"

"Not as close as we were before the fuel was buggered. Go over the files on your men, Wing. I'm betting that at least one of them is cashing two paychecks."

"I will look, but it is doubtful. The men were vetted with exquisite care before they were sent. Is it wise for you to be out of contact so long?"

"Erin won't abandon the hunt, so I have no choice. We're going to ground. Don't send anyone after us, Wing. Attending your relatives' funerals puts you in a bad mood."

29

◆

SUNLIGHT AND HUMIDITY TURNED THE ROVER into a four-wheel-drive sauna. The previous night Erin and Cole had camped on a nameless patch of land beneath an acacia tree. They had awakened to silence and heat, for they were too far from water for any birds to be about. The silence had been consumed by the Rover's noisy progress. Now the Rover was being consumed by the searing day. On the flats some speed was possible, for Dog Four had been the most productive of the mines; as a result, there was a road of sorts. Other than slamming on the brakes shortly after dawn to avoid a handful of cows, the ride had been uneventful.

"After Dog Four, where are we going?" Erin asked.

Cole flicked a sideways glance at her before he returned to watching the road, which had a tendency to vanish among termite mounds and spinifex.

"Twenty miles beyond Dog Four there's a place where the station land is joined by a mosaic of Abe's mineral claims. I've never been there. From the looks of the map, nobody else has been either. But the satellite photo showed a highlands and what could be a karst drainage pattern. Maybe Bridget's Hill is there."

"What's a karst drainage pattern?"

"Water flows underground rather than aboveground. It's common in heavily eroded limestone areas."

"Does that mean caves?"

"Sometimes."

While Cole spoke, his eyes checked the gauges on the dusty dashboard of the Rover. The electrical system showed a steady charge. The oversized fuel tank was above three quarters. He wasn't worried about petrol. With the extra cans he had lashed on the Rover, he had ample fuel to check out the most likely spots for a steep limestone outcropping, with enough gas left over to reach a neighboring station before the wet made the country impassable.

At the moment Cole was more worried about keeping Erin alive until the wet than about finding a diamond mine. Jason Street's arrival meant the Americans were divided about how to handle her legacy, or the rest of the cartel had ganged up and forced Street down Faulkner's throat, or both. No matter what the reason, it left Erin exposed in a way she was too inexperienced to understand. It had been her American government connections that had prevented an outright assassination.

United we stand, divided we fall.

They were falling.

"It's running a little hot, isn't it?" Erin asked, seeing Cole's frown.

"Not surprising. It's about a hundred and ten in

the sun. Close to the ground, where the engine is, the temperature is even hotter." He looked at Erin. "Don't worry. The Rover was built to take worse in Africa."

"But I wasn't." Erin plucked at her cotton tank top in a gesture that had become as automatic as brushing away the outback's importunate hordes of flies.

"I like the way you're built. Sleek, soft, and sweet. How much longer are you going to punish me for something that happened years before I met you?"

For a moment Erin didn't believe what she had heard. Then she did. The flush on her cheeks deepened even as her heartbeat increased. She was aware of Cole with an intensity that had only increased since she had refused to share his bed.

"If you had been the one to walk in on a tender little scene between me and a former lover," Erin said finally, "what would you have thought?"

There was a long silence followed by a savage word. "Try trusting me," Cole said.

"If I didn't trust you, I wouldn't be alone with you in this rolling oven."

Cole thought it over and realized Erin meant what she was saying. "Then why the cold shoulder?"

"Cold? In this godforsaken climate?"

"You know what I mean," he said tightly.

"Call it a period of adjustment."

"Meaning?"

"Meaning I haven't had as much experience as most women my age," Erin said simply. "When it comes to what I should and shouldn't expect from a lover, I'm still nineteen years old with stars in my eyes. I assumed any man who was my lover would be as exclusively interested in me as I was in him. Childish of me, but there it is."

It was the first time in days Erin had been willing to talk about anything personal. Cole glanced quickly at her, silently encouraging her to keep going. She made an odd gesture that ended up with her fingers plucking at her damp top.

"When I catch up with my generation," Erin said, "I'll be able to hand my body over to an attractive man and keep my mind on hold. Until then, it's a complete package, and my mind looks at you and sees an emotional attachment to Lai I can't compete with."

"You're crazy," he said flatly. "I don't love her."

"I didn't say you did. Hate binds every bit as closely as love. Either way, hate or love, Lai has a hold on you."

"Shit!" Cole lifted his bush hat, wiped sweat that had been dripping into his eyes, and put the hat back in place with a yank. "Don't you realize how easily you're letting the Chen family manipulate you? You're a lamb among some very experienced wolves, and I'm damned if I'll let them cut you up for a snack. If I wanted Lai, I'd be screwing her right now. I don't want her. I want you. And I know I can make you want me."

Erin's breath came in and filled her throat until she ached. "We've been around this track before. You won't rape me and we both know it."

"That leaves ninety-nine point nine percent of the sexual field wide open. Think about it, Erin. I sure as hell have."

They drove in silence through increasing heat and humidity while hot air rose in columns from the land, creating an updraft that sucked in moisture from the

Indian Ocean in an endless river of clouds that would expand through the day until it slowly consumed the sky. That was when the climate went from ugly to unbearable. That was when the anticipation of rain hung in the air and lightning winked across distant horizons and veils of rein hung down, only to evaporate before touching the steamy land. That was when friendships and marriages broke apart. That was when men went troppo and killed their mates.

Divided we fall.

And there was nothing Cole could do about it except what he had done—grab Erin and vanish into the sultry, insufferable outback.

Just before the track twisted away from the flats and territoriums whitewashed by bird lime, Cole braked. The pedal responded sluggishly, which didn't surprise him. There had been a slow leak in the system since the Rover had crashed through the brush to avoid the road train. Cole pumped twice and the brake pedal firmed.

The Rover stopped close to a termite mound that was as tall as Cole. He jumped out, took a rock hammer from the Rover, and began chipping away at the top of the mound. Beneath the white bird lime the mound was a faded rusty shade. Erin picked up her camera, got out, and grimaced as the sunlight hammered down on her. She walked out among the mounds with a determined stride. Within minutes she had forgotten the brutal heat as she worked out angles and exposures, trying to capture the alien, sun-beaten world where billions of insects built a towering mud metropolis.

When Cole finished hacking at various mounds,

he looked around for Erin. She wasn't anywhere in sight.

"Erin," he called. "Where the hell are you?"

A languid, muggy breeze stirred nearby spinifex. The narrow, rasp-edged blades of grass made a secretive sound.

"Erin!"

"In a minute!" she yelled back.

From her voice, she was several hundred feet away, hidden among the towering, broad-based mounds. Cole looked at his watch. He had spent half an hour grubbing around in the termitorium. He hoped she had more to show for the time than he did. Lifting his hat, he wiped his face on his short-sleeved khaki shirt. The cloth was already dark with sweat from collar to hem. Cole unbuttoned the shirt, mopped his chest with it, and tossed the damp khaki in the Rover.

"Time's up," he called.

There was no answer.

"Erin!"

"I'm coming! Just give me a minute!"

Ten minutes later Cole searched through the mounds until he found Erin crouched over her camera. Her hat was on the ground beside her. She was staring through the viewfinder, oblivious to her surroundings. Cole picked up her hat and stood nearby, waiting until she finished the roll of film. Then he stepped in front of the lens and stuffed her hat down on her head.

Startled, Erin looked up, realizing for the first time that she wasn't alone.

"Wear the damned hat," he said in a clipped voice. "When you're taking pictures you don't think about anything else. If I hadn't been here, you would have been wonky from sunstroke before you had the faintest idea something was wrong. Get it through your stubborn head. This isn't Alaska. Out here, the sun is your enemy. Hear me?"

"Yes." Erin hesitated, then asked, "How long were you standing there?"

He looked at his watch. "Seven minutes."

"But you didn't interrupt me. Why?"

"You weren't in any immediate danger. I'd rather wait than take a chance on ruining another 'Uncertain Spring.' "

For an instant Erin thought Cole was joking. When she realized he wasn't, pleasure rippled through her, disarming her. "I doubt if there's another 'Uncertain Spring' in that lot, but thank you."

"Can you always tell in advance what you'll have?"

Erin shook her head. "That's why I protect the film so carefully. Each shot is unique and unrepeatable. I could have spent the rest of my life in the arctic and never taken another shot like 'Uncertain Spring.' Just as I could spend the rest of my life in the Kimberley and never have the same reaction to it that I'm having now, take the same photos I'm taking now."

"That's what I figured." Cole gave Erin a look that was half amused and half irritated. "All the same, the next time I find you in the sun without your hat, I won't wait until you run out of film." Without warning he pressed his thumb against her upper arm and watched to see how long the pale circle remained. "When was the last time you put on sunscreen?"

"When you stood over me after dawn," she said dryly.

"Then you're overdue. Even inside the Rover—"

"—reflected sunlight will burn my Scots-Irish skin to toast," Erin finished. When the line of Cole's mouth flattened, she said, "I know it's not a joke. I won't forget again."

Cole let out his breath in a rush of sound and said tightly, "Sorry. I'm not usually so irritable, even during buildup. You have a way of shortening my fuse. Come on. Let's get out of the damned sun."

"Pity we can't prospect in the dark," Erin said as she walked beside Cole to the Rover.

"For all the good I'm doing, we might as well."

"What were you doing, anyway? A vendetta against small segmented beasties?"

Cole swiped at a nearby mound with the pick end of his rock hammer and caught the crumbling bits of earth. He smeared them across his palm and held it out to Erin.

"Dirt," she confirmed.

"Every bit of it," he agreed, leading her toward the Rover.

"So?"

"So I know that the first forty to one hundred feet of earth around here is a fairly homogeneous layer of finely packed soil. Nothing interesting, although I'll look at it through the microscope eventually to be certain."

Erin blinked. "Those bugs go one hundred feet deep?"

"It's the only way to beat the climate."

"I'll keep it in mind. What were you looking for?"

"Indicator minerals that would reveal a diamond

pipe, or rounded grains of silica that would hint at old beaches or riverbanks.''

She eyed the shapeless, ugly termitorium. "Is picking at mounds a reliable way of prospecting?''

"It's how Lamont found the Orapa diamond mine in Botswana.''

"You sure he didn't just consult the guts of a chicken in the dark of the moon?''

Smiling crookedly, Cole wiped his palm on the seat of his shorts and climbed into the Rover. "This is science, not voodoo.''

She gave him a sideways glance and smiled in return. "Science, huh?'' she said, opening the Rover's passenger door. "And I'm the tooth fairy.''

"You can slip things under my pillow any time you're in the mood.''

Erin tried not to respond to Cole's retort but couldn't help it. Shaking her head, she snickered, then gasped when her bare thighs met the Rover's sun-baked seat.

"Lift up,'' Cole said.

When she did, he spread his discarded shirt on the seat. As he withdrew, she felt a breath of a caress over the back of her thighs.

"Try that,'' he said.

She sat down cautiously.

"Better?''

"Yes. Thanks.'' Erin looked at Cole. His legs were as bare as hers except for the dark patterns of hair. "How can you stand it?''

"Same way you took the cold in Alaska. I'm used to it. That doesn't mean I like it. I'd trade buildup for a dog and shoot the dog.''

Erin looked startled, then laughed aloud. "That bad, huh?"

The track veered away from the flats, heading toward an invisible destination. Only when Erin looked back did she realize that the land was slowly rising. Just as slowly, it was becoming more rumpled.

With no warning they crested a rise and found themselves driving between low, roughly parallel ridges that poked sluggishly from the ground. Stunted gum and acacia reappeared, along with an occasional grotesque boab tree. Spinifex grew more thickly, though never attaining a state that could be described as lush. Even so, Erin straightened in her seat and looked longingly at the lacy skirts of shade beneath the trees.

"We'll stop a few miles ahead," Cole said. "The government map doesn't show much, but the land rises about five hundred feet. There's a gorge I want to check out. It's on the boundary between a sandstone district and a limestone district."

"Is it in the what's-it drainage?"

Cole smiled at Erin's eagerness. "Karst. No. That's farther in."

"No caves, huh?"

"Not that I know of, but I've never explored the area. The last time I went to Dog Four, I came in another way."

Erin looked at him curiously. "When were you last in the Kimberley?"

"A while back."

"Why?"

"I'm a prospector."

"Did you ever find anything?"

"I've found my share," he said, dividing his atten-

tion between the increasingly rough track and a part
of the Kimberley he had never seen before.

"Any diamonds?" Erin asked.

"Some."

"Gold?"

"Here and there."

Erin's mouth flattened. "You know, each time the
subject of you and the Kimberley comes up, you either
change the subject or clam up."

"Look. I've got my hands full driving and at the
same time trying to guess what kind of strata are beneath the surface. Is there something you really want
to know about me and the Kimberley," Cole asked
bluntly, "or are you just feeling chatty?"

Erin slipped the khaki shirt from beneath her and
used the hem to mop her face. "How did you get
Abe's diamonds and the will?"

"A little late to be suspicious of me, isn't it?"

"Better late than—"

"—never," Cole interrupted sardonically. He
flexed his hands on the wheel and thought of Uncle
Li's thin neck. "Everybody who ever pegged out a
lease in Western Australia spent some time on Abe's
station. He was as close as the Kimberley came to a
Renaissance man. Miner, scholar, stockman, spy. You
name it, he's done it."

"Spy?" she asked in disbelief.

"Must run in the family."

Erin refused to be deflected. "If you knew that
about him, you must have known him very well."

"Is that an accusation or a question?"

"Take your pick."

There was an electric silence before Cole spoke.
"We sat out an early wet together one year."

"Why didn't you tell me before now?"

"You didn't ask." Cole gave Erin a swift, intense look. "Abe's dead. What we did or didn't do doesn't affect what I'm doing now. Nothing I did in the past affects us now. So instead of being suspicious of the one man in the Kimberley who's on your side, worry about the diamond cartel's latest entry into the sweepstakes—Jason Street."

"Are you worried about him?"

"I'd be a fool if I wasn't."

"Is that why we left the station?"

"One of the reasons." Cole shrugged. "But it will only buy us a day or two. Street knows the Kimberley better than any other white man alive. The Aborigines all but worship him the same way they did Abe. Fear, not love."

Erin looked out over the empty land. "Well, we've got a lot of country to get lost in."

"There are only so many waterholes. Street knows every one of them. What he doesn't know, the Aborigines will tell him. Sooner or later he'll find us. Sooner, most likely."

"Then why are we out in this bloody oven?"

"Out here, everyone we meet is an enemy. At the station I couldn't be sure. Hesitation can be fatal." He turned and looked at Erin. "I could have you on an airplane out of here in fourteen hours. Still want to go diamond hunting?"

"What do you think?"

"I think the ice chest full of film is in the sun."

Erin made a startled sound and turned in the seat. The reflective cloth she had put over the ice chest had slipped. She pulled the silvery cloth back in place.

"The ice will melt sooner or later," Cole said finally. "What happens to the film then?"

"Nothing, if I'm careful. The emulsion is stable even in this heat. It's just direct sun that can be a problem. The bag I carry film in when I'm shooting is insulated."

"How many rolls have you gone through since we left?"

"Not many."

He smiled slightly. "How many is not many?"

"Less than I wanted to. When I'm working, I can go through a roll of film every five minutes."

"No wonder you packed that cooler to the gills," he said. "Must be twenty pounds of film."

"Must be twenty pounds of shotgun shells, too."

"If I run out, I'll use your film."

"Wish I could say the same about your shells. How long are we going to be out here?"

"Until the wet."

"How long is that?"

"Until it rains."

"Thanks. I try to conserve film, but when I'm shooting I forget. Every image I see is so new. I'm afraid if I don't capture it now I'll never see it again."

Cole touched Erin lightly on the cheek. "I'm the same way when I'm prospecting. Every place is a treasure waiting to be found."

Before Erin could react to the brief caress, Cole returned his hand and his attention to the increasingly difficult terrain. Biting her lip, trying to ignore the leap in her pulse at such a simple thing as the brush of his fingertips over her cheek, Erin concentrated on the countryside.

"Look—kangaroos!" she said suddenly.

Cole glanced over to the right. "No such thing."

"What? Of course they are. Nothing else hops like that."

"Nope," he said. "Ask any Aussie. They're kangas or they're roos. Personally, I think they're roos. Kangas tend to hang out farther east."

Erin snickered and felt herself drifting more deeply beneath the spell of companionship that grew between Cole and her whenever she let down her guard and responded to him without calculation. He seemed to respond to her in the same way, without calculation.

You're a fool, Erin Shane Windsor, she told herself.

There was no argument.

Ten minutes later the Rover slowed to a stop in a patch of shade beneath an outcropping of rock. Cole got out, checked the brake fluid reservoir, and recapped it.

"Problems?" she asked.

"We're losing a little fluid, but not enough to worry about. There's a gallon of the stuff in the tool cabinet."

Cole wiped his forehead on the back of his arm, resettled his hat, and looked at the sky. Heat and moisture made it shimmer in a shade of incandescent silver-gray peculiar to the tropics. He turned his attention to the dry watercourse that had bitten through the earth near the road, eroding a channel for the overflow of the wet. There was no hint of water now. He hadn't expected any.

"I'm going to take a look at the gully walls. If you promise not to start taking pictures, you can stay in the Rover's shade. Otherwise you're coming with me."

"Why?"

"I don't want to spend half an hour tracking you down," he said dryly. "This would be easy country to get lost in."

"I'm coming with you. So is my camera."

While Cole studied the cutbanks of the gully, Erin absorbed the angles, shadows, and densities of the landscape. Gradually a subtle excitement permeated her, something she had felt only once before in her life, when she had accepted the arctic for what it was rather than what it wasn't.

As soon as Erin stopped looking for familiar lines and colors, the stark, enigmatic, completely inhuman beauty of the Kimberley began seeping into her. The savage heat of the day was balanced by the night, stretching undiminished by cities from horizon to horizon. The scarcity of vegetation was balanced by the vivid elegance of ghost gums and the fluid whisper of spinifex. The scarcity of animals was balanced by their startling shapes and unlikely means of locomotion.

And the stillness was complete, a silence more beautiful than music, a seduction greater than any easy beauty of water or grass or forest. The profound silence called to Erin's soul.

Slowly she became aware of Cole standing next to her, watching her.

"It's getting to you, isn't it?" he asked.

"What?"

"The land."

"It's extraordinary," she said simply. "Even with its hellish climate."

"Like the arctic in winter."

She nodded slowly.

"Be careful," he said in a soft voice. "If you fall in love with this land, there's no substitute, no second best. There's a whole Arctic Circle, but there's only one Kimberley Plateau. There's nothing like it anywhere else. The Kimberley will haunt you no matter where else on earth you go."

Erin focused entirely on Cole. "You love this place."

"Except during buildup, yes. And sometimes even then."

"Why did you leave?"

"I was searching for diamonds the color of your eyes. Until a few weeks ago, I thought Brazil was the best place on earth to find them."

"Are the diamonds here?" she asked.

He smiled ruefully. "There's nothing in that gully but dirt. If there are strata made by paleo-riverbeds or beaches, they're not showing."

When Cole reached the Rover, he turned to Erin.

"Would you mind driving? I want to spend some time with the binoculars."

"I don't care if you want to sleep. I love driving."

"Have at it. The brake pedal is a bit soft, so leave enough time to pump once or twice."

The station road ascended in a leisurely fashion, using a long, gently sloping ridge that allowed Erin to take the Rover out of low range and all the way into third gear. The balky gear box gave her problems, but nothing she couldn't manage. She shifted up through the gears, bringing her speed up gradually, enjoying the temporary breeze through the window.

"Too fast for you?" she asked.

"Go as fast as you want. I'm not seeing anything but sandstone."

The track continued to climb gradually until the Rover crested yet another small ridge and abruptly began to descend into a gorge that looked more than a thousand feet deep.

"My God," Erin said, downshifting quickly into second gear. "We climbed to the top of a mountain."

"Actually, we've just climbed the leading edge of a very minor range. In Alaska, it wouldn't even qualify as foothills."

"No problem. I've finally figured out I'm not in Alaska." She looked at the track snaking down in a series of long, steep switchbacks. "Time for low range."

Erin touched the brake pedal with her right foot. It went straight to the fire wall. She tried to pump, but there wasn't enough pressure to respond.

"No brakes," she said tightly. "I'll try for first gear."

She was going too fast for first gear and they both knew it. They also knew it was their best chance of slowing the Rover's descent. She threw in the clutch and tried to grab first gear. The Rover, freewheeling, picked up speed like a runaway train. There was a rending metal sound from the gearbox. Erin double-clutched quickly. Metal clashed against metal. She double-clutched again, and again metal screamed.

"Go back to second," Cole said.

Erin had reached the same conclusion at the same instant Cole had. Before the words were out of his mouth, she had slammed the gearshift back into second and dumped the clutch. The engine roared, the

Rover lurched, then steadied. But it was still going too fast for the steeply dropping track.

A quarter mile ahead, the road turned back upon itself in a tight hairpin curve. At the same instant Erin and Cole realized that the Rover would overrun the curve and go flying off into the gorge.

Even as Cole reached for the wheel, Erin yanked it to the right, where ghost gums grew in elegant array among the sandstone boulders. The Rover broke off one gum at the base and sent it flying over the bull bar. The second gum raked along Erin's side of the Rover with a high scream. The third gum was bigger. The Rover hit the tree and was deflected into a boulder. Erin wrenched the wheel again and sent the battered vehicle careening between two more gums. By then she had scrubbed off enough speed to grab first gear, slowing even more.

The last gum they hit shuddered and held. Dust, twigs, and leaves exploded around the Rover as the engine died. Erin slammed the shifter into reverse, holding the vehicle on the gears alone while Cole put the emergency brake on.

It became very quiet. As grit swirled through the interior, Erin looked at Cole.

"What, no cracks about women drivers?" she asked shakily.

"You can drive me anytime, anywhere," he said. "You want to get us to a level spot, or do you want me to do it?"

"It's all yours."

By the time they switched places, put the Rover in low range, and crept to the bottom of the gorge, the adrenaline had stopped running wildly through Erin's blood. She began to feel as flat as dust. When Cole found a level place and parked, she sighed with relief. He got out, rummaged in the Rover's battered tool-box, and vanished beneath the vehicle, taking a small flashlight, a crescent wrench, a screwdriver, and several feet of small black tubing with him.

"Don't you dare wander off and start taking pictures," Cole said.

Erin jumped, for his voice had come from beneath her feet. Guiltily she returned her camera to its bag. After a moment she grabbed the binoculars, stepped on the front fender of the Rover, and from there to the platform on top. Between one of the spare tires and a cluster of fuel cans, she found a reasonably comfortable seat. Much more comfortable than the ground was, if Cole's language was any indication. She pulled her hat firmly into place and began scanning the countryside.

Nothing moved but heat spiraling up from the land. The breeze was desultory, as sullen as the color of the sky. The gorge and the plateau on the other side were empty. No cattle, no kangaroos, no birds. Nothing but rocks and trees whose tenacity had to be seen to be believed.

When Erin lowered the binoculars, a subdued ripple of movement caught her eye. She focused the binoculars on a spot thirty yards away.

"Cole?"

A grunt was his only answer.

"What do Australia's poisonous snakes look like?"

Cole's head emerged from beneath the Rover, followed by his greasy, dirt-smeared torso. His shorts were the same color as the rusty earth. So were the backs of his legs. A narrow piece of tubing dangled from his right hand. He glanced up at Erin where she sat cross-legged on the spare tire, staring through the glasses. He followed her pointing finger and saw a snake curling across the dirt. The reptile was light brown with a faint blue blush along its belly. Glistening as though every inch of its five-foot length had been recently polished, the snake moved with the languid, muscular ease of an animal supremely at home in its environment.

"Some of them look like that," Cole said.

"It's dangerous?"

"As hell."

"Damn. I wanted to get close enough to photograph it."

"Why?"

"The contrast between the shiny scales and dust, the perfect curves against the angular land, life where there's nothing but rock and dust. . . ." She shrugged. "It's beautiful."

"It's a king mulga, and it's one of the most lethal snakes on earth. Stay away from it," he said flatly. " 'Beautiful.' Christ. I suppose I should have expected it. Anyone who believes in the tooth fairy is bound to be a little weird in other ways."

Erin looked at the tubing Cole had in his hand. "Now that's ugly. No doubt about it."

"Could have been deadly, too," Cole said, stretching. "There's been a slow leak since we tried to climb a termite mound on the other side of Fitzroy Crossing. The clip that was holding the tube cut into the rubber. When it got weak enough, the tubing gave way and the fluid dripped out."

"Now what?" she said. "More driving slow and praying fast?"

"No problem. The Kimberley is hell on vehicles. That's why extra tubing and brake fluid are standard equipment. I replaced the bad tubing and didn't find any other spots where fluid had bled through. Once I fill the reservoir again, we'll be back in business."

"Thank God. I wasn't looking forward to walking out of here."

"During buildup? Not likely, honey. You'd be lucky to get two miles before you keeled over."

Cole went to the rear of the Rover, opened the supply cupboard, removed a gallon can of brake fluid, and shook it. The can was almost full. He went to the front of the vehicle, opened the hood and took off the cover of brake-fluid reservoir. Remembering the helicopter's dirty fuel, he tipped a little of the liquid onto his index finger and rubbed. There was no gritty feel.

But after a few moments his finger burned. He sniffed the opening of the can. Beneath the heavy petroleum odor was something else.

"Son of a bitch," Cole said.

He scrubbed the fluid off his fingers with dry soil, then poured the contents of the can into a shallow runoff channel at the side of the road.

"What's wrong?"

"Someone added a corrosive to the brake fluid. If I'd used this to replace what we lost, there wouldn't have been enough tubing in the Kimberley to fix up the mess."

Erin looked at the empty can. "How far will we get without brakes?"

"Not as far as we will with them."

He began searching through the cartons of camping supplies. He pulled out several bottles, put them back, and then lifted out a big bottle of liquid soap.

Erin watched in disbelief as he poured it into the empty reservoir. When he was finished he capped the reservoir and smiled at her.

"Fluid is fluid. This is a little heavier than the regular stuff but it'll do." Cole smiled crookedly. "Look at it this way. We'll have the cleanest brake lines in the Kimberley."

"How long will it last?"

He shrugged. "We'll be the first to know."

30

◆

    THE FOLLOWING DAY THEY HEADED INTO THE area beyond Dog Four that had given promise of having a karst drainage pattern. As the day progressed toward stultifying afternoon, clouds towered and billowed, climbing toward a storm that never came. Erin looked at the sky hungrily, hoping to see in its shimmering turbulence the dark storm that would bring an end to the buildup's stunning heat and humidity.

"Rain, damn it," she muttered.

"Not today," Cole said. "Probably not for a week."

She sighed. "I wish it would rain and rain and rain."

"Tell me that in January. I've seen it start raining on one afternoon and not stop again for four months."

"Promises, promises." Erin flapped the cloth of her tank top, sending air circulating over her breasts. "No wonder people go crazy. The buildup is just one endless striptease. Like Abe's blasted mines, each one

a little better than the last, but none of them really
worth a damn."

Cole forced himself to look away as the cloth flut-
tered back down to conform faithfully to Erin's
breasts. Wanting her and not having her was making
him far more irritable than the climate.

"At least we're in limestone country again," he
said.

"Any luck with the dry panning?" she asked.

"Enough that I want to look farther upstream."

"What stream? The only water within miles is my
sweat. And yours," she added, looking at the shiny
trails that glistened through the dark hair on Cole's
naked chest. As she watched, a drop slid down the
median line of his body and vanished behind his cotton shorts. She looked away quickly.

"Don't forget the canteens we're wearing," Cole
said. "There's water in them."

"How could I forget? Mine weighs more than my
camera bag."

"Doubt it. You must be carrying five pounds of
film alone."

"And I've shot all but three rolls. I'd go back to
the Rover for more," she said, sighing, "but I don't
feel like walking that far."

"Is that a hint?"

Erin smiled wryly and shook her head as she
fanned her top again. "Thanks, but it's not necessary.
The sun is getting too high. It flattens out the shadows. By the time the light slants again, the clouds will
have moved in. Maybe there will be a break at sunset.
If not, there's always tomorrow."

Flapping her shirt again, Erin thought longingly
of taking off her canteen, but she didn't suggest it.

Cole had told her to wear the canteen every time she got out of the Rover to take pictures. He was no easier on himself. Not only did he carry an even bigger canteen for his prospecting expeditions, he also carried a large rucksack of prospecting gear.

She had been startled to see that a shotgun and several boxes of shells were as much a part of his gear as compass, binoculars, shovel, specimen bags, labels, sheath knife, survival blanket, and large swaths of plastic sheeting whose purpose eluded her.

"Drink," Cole said. "Water weighs less in your stomach than hanging on your hip."

Dutifully Erin unscrewed the top of the canteen and drank. The water was stale and warmer than her mouth. She sighed and thought of glaciers calving into an ice-blue sea.

"Are you going to take more pictures?" Cole asked.

"Am I breathing?"

He glanced sideways at her and smiled slightly. "Dumb question, huh?"

The contrast between Cole's amused smile and his powerful, nearly naked body made Erin's breath stop. A shaft of longing went through her, making her painfully aware of her own body. Memories poured through her, hotter and more vivid than the sun, images of a sensual time before she had seen the perfect Chen Lai in Cole's embrace.

"Just keep going upstream," Cole said. "That way you won't get lost. Okay?"

Erin nodded. "Where are you going to be?"

"Right behind you, dry-panning as I go."

The quality of Cole's voice caught Erin. "Did you really find something?"

"There must be some old streambed or beach deposits up there," he said, hooking his thumb toward the two low hills that flanked either side of the dry stream course. "I'm getting stuff that's much more rounded and of a different type of rock than the rest of the recent streambed deposits. The old stuff could have been washed from strata of river or beach conglomerate."

"Diamonds?" she asked eagerly.

"Nope. But that ridge is limestone, so watch for openings where the intermittent stream has cut into the underlying rock. There could be caves."

"Really?"

"Wherever there's limestone and water, there's a chance of caves," Cole said dryly. "Not a certainty. Just a chance. Most caves are discovered when a stream cuts down through the rock like a knife through Swiss cheese, showing all the little interior holes."

Erin's eyes lit up. She started to speak but ended by waving flies away impatiently.

"Time for more goo," Cole said, reaching into his big rucksack. "They sure love you, honey."

Grimacing, Erin squeezed out a puddle of white medicinal-scented lotion and began applying it. She worked swiftly, from the forehead down, covering every bit of skin that was exposed and a lot that wasn't.

"Watch for snakes," Cole said, picking up the gold pan again. "They'll be in the shadows and crevices. If you see any birds or bats, let me know. Could mean water nearby."

"Do we need it?" she asked.

"With what we've got in the Rover, we're all right for a few days, but if we can find a source of water that isn't on the maps, we can make Street's job harder."

Erin capped the squeeze bottle and handed it back to Cole. "Maybe Street is just what he's supposed to be, a man inspecting the Dog Mines for the Australian government."

"Maybe. Want to bet your life on it?"

When Erin would have said something, an abrupt gesture of Cole's hand cut her off. He stood motionless, head cocked to one side in the attitude of a man listening intently.

"What—" she began.

Another sharp gesture cut her off. Wordlessly Cole pointed toward the sky in the east. Erin shifted her position and listened intently. After a moment she heard the far-off drone of a helicopter engine.

Cole touched her arm and pointed again. She squinted into the shimmering sky. Finally she saw a dark dot skimming above the land. The helicopter was perhaps a thousand feet high and several miles away. If he continued in the same direction he was going, he would miss them by a wide margin.

"Somebody looking for Dog Four?" Erin asked.

"If he is, he just flew over it."

Abruptly the helicopter's direction changed. Cole cursed, grabbed Erin's arm, and sprinted toward a clump of gums that were growing along the outer curve of the streambed.

"Get down and stay there!" he said.

Erin didn't have any choice about obeying. He dragged her to the ground and pinned her with a forearm across her waist. Just as she opened her mouth to demand an explanation, she heard the sound of the helicopter. It was close enough to distinguish the

rhythm of the rotors whipping through the air. After a
minute the sound began to fade.

"No," Cole said when Erin would have gotten up.
"Not until we haven't heard him for five minutes."

She lay rigid, barely feeling the textures of grit
and stone and tree root beneath her, aware only of the
claustrophobic stillness of the day and the coiled tension of the man stretched out beside her. The sound of
a shell being jacked into the shotgun's firing chamber
was like thunder to her taut nerves.

"You're certain Dog Four is off in that direction?" she asked finally.

"Yes."

"Maybe he's lost."

The drone of the engine began to strengthen once
more, consuming the stillness.

"And maybe we're lying in a pool of cold water,"
Cole said grimly. "He's doing legs of a search pattern.
When I tell you to look down and be still, do it."

A chill moved over Erin's skin at the certainty in
Cole's voice. "What if he spots the Rover?"

Cole said nothing as he looked at the angle of the
sun. Darkness wouldn't come in time to do any good.
All he could do was hope that the trees he had parked
the Rover beneath provided enough cover. Having
flown over the Kimberley himself, he knew how tenu-
ous a shield the trees provided. Like everything else
that survived in the torrid land, the foliage of the gum
and acacia trees was thin and grew in such a way as to
minimize the amount of sunlight reaching the surface
of the leaves. In the outback, leaves were narrow and
hung straight down rather than broad and spread at a
right angle to catch every bit of light.

The engine noise came closer, echoing off the

limestone hills and between the steep walls of the ravine. Erin didn't need Cole's terse order to hug the ground. She already was. She pressed her cheek into the hot soil and wondered how the land could seem so empty one instant and be so full of human danger the next.

The sound reached a peak, then gradually fell away once more as the helicopter turned onto a different heading.

"He'll fly right over the Rover if he stays on that tack," Cole said. "If the chopper lands, I'm going to head for the Rover. If I don't come back and someone else starts calling for you, get up and walk into the open."

"But—"

"But nothing," he interrupted savagely. "Your chances of surviving alone out here in the dry are the same as mine of surviving an arctic blizzard buck naked. Street might have a reason to keep you alive. The land doesn't give a damn whether you live or die."

Cole took off his hat and mopped sweat from his forehead with the back of his hand as he studied the terrain. The bed of the dry ravine was narrow and twisting. It led up a gradual slope toward a notch between two low hills half a mile away. The heat was fierce. The thickening lid of clouds only made it worse, but the heavy air conducted sound very well. Both of them heard the instant the helicopter changed its heading.

"Why is he concentrating here?" she muttered.

"Because it's one of the few places around where the growth is thick enough and the land rough enough that a Rover could be hidden. He might even have equipment sensitive enough to pick up the Rover's metal frame."

"Or a signal hidden somewhere in the Rover?" Erin asked unhappily.

"Doubt it. I checked. Anyway, he's looking, not homing in."

The noise of the chopper surged suddenly. It had changed headings, approaching them once more. It was much too close. The sound of the rotors ricocheted around them. Erin tried to drag air into her aching lungs. It was like trying to breathe through wet wool. She closed her eyes and willed the chopper to disappear.

The noise slowly abated. Erin let out a sigh. Before she could speak, the sound changed, increasing steeply, then dropping abruptly to nothing as the helicopter landed.

"He spotted the Rover," Cole said.

He came to his feet in a rush, shucked off all burdens but the shotgun and a pocket full of shells, and ran down the streambed. The savage heat and bogs of sand slowed him, dragging at his feet, turning his lungs to fire and his muscles to lead. The Rover was a mile away, a distance he normally would have covered in eight minutes. Under these conditions, he would be lucky to make it in twelve.

Cole was still four hundred yards from the Rover when the helicopter revved and lifted into the air once more. The chopper held at one hundred feet and began spiraling out from the Rover in a clear search pattern. Dust lifted in thin billows. Abruptly the chopper veered and began heading straight toward Cole.

He turned and sprinted toward the thin cover of the stream-side gums. Just beyond, at the foot on a

steep rise, was a tumble of limestone boulders, legacy
of a landslide during the wet. He reached the rocks
while the helicopter was still a hundred yards away.
With the sound of the approaching chopper filling his
ears, he searched for cover. The best he could find was
an undercut where an old flood had eaten away the
dirt beneath some boulders, leaving them half suspended over air.

Cole dove toward the little cave as the helicopter
tipped and charged like an angry bull. The engine
sound was loud, but not loud enough to cover the
staccato burst of an automatic weapon. Bullets
thumped in the sand and whined off the rocks. Cole
pressed his back against stone and lifted the shotgun.
The sound of its blast was deafening in the enclosed
space. He pumped in another shell and fired, pumped
and fired, working as fast as he could, not bothering to
aim because the helicopter was too close to miss.

The helicopter pulled up and leaped away like a
startled hawk. Cole dug shells from his pocket and fed
them into the magazine one after another until it was
full once more. He threw the gun to his shoulder and
took slack off the trigger.

"Come closer, you son of a bitch," Cole said.
"Just a little closer. That's it . . . that's it. Come and
get it."

The helicopter hovered nervously just out of
range, feinting from side to side in sudden darts, trying to draw fire. Cole waited with the patience of a
predator at a waterhole, leading his cautious adversary
as the chopper swept across the front of the rock slide
once more.

The pilot either became overconfident or misjudged the distance. The instant he was within range,

the shotgun erupted, spewing round after round of
lead shot in a pattern that must have been too close
for the pilot's nerve, for the helicopter jumped upward
and kept climbing until it vanished.

Automatically Cole reloaded until his pocket was
empty of shells. The sound of the helicopter thinned
until nothing remained but the ringing in Cole's ears.
Cautiously he rolled out of the shelter and looked
around. Nothing moved between him and the Rover.
He would have preferred to wait for twenty minutes
just in case an assassin had been dropped off, but Cole
doubted Erin's patience would hold out that long.

Using the trees for the small shade and cover they
offered, Cole worked his way back up toward Erin. He
found her precisely where he had left her. When she
saw him, she jumped up and ran into his arms. For a
moment she clung to him fiercely; then she took a
ragged breath and stepped back.

"Are you all right?" she asked, watching him
with luminous green eyes. "I thought I heard shots."

"Nobody connected."

"Who was it?"

"I didn't get close enough to see. But it was the
station helicopter."

Erin didn't ask any more questions as she followed Cole down the baking dry wash to the place
where they had left the Rover. She was relieved to see
the vehicle. Its stultifying interior was preferable to
the unshielded rays of the sun.

Cole was the first to understand the significance
of the dark stains spreading out from the Rover. Even
though he had been expecting sabotage, the reality of
seeing it was no less stark.

"Cole?"

"It's just what it looks like," he said roughly. "Radiator fluid."

Silently Erin watched while Cole checked the Rover's engine compartment, dashboard, and equipment cupboards.

"The son of a bitch was thorough," Cole said, slamming the Rover's door. "Not one bit of hose left, and no water to use in any case."

"He took our water?"

"No. He took the food. The water he poured on the ground."

Erin took a swift breath. "The radio?"

"Gone. So are the maps."

Her breath came out in a rush. She looked away, not wanting to show Cole how frightened she was. "I see. Now what?"

He looked at the blazing sky and then at the woman whose skin was pale beneath the flush of tropic heat.

"Drink your fill from the canteen, honey."

"Shouldn't I save it?"

"You'd be surprised how many people have been found dead with water in their canteens. Dehydration is like hypothermia. It saps your judgment before it kills you. Drink while you can. Thirst will come soon enough."

31

ERIN LOOKED AT THE CONTENTS OF THE RUCKSACK
Cole had spread out on top of the thin survival blanket. He took the rock hammer off his belt and without hesitation set the hammer beside the steel pan, sample bags, and rock samples he had collected. The thermal bag she carried film in lay nearby. The compass was beside the canteen he had carried. So were matches, shovel, three boxes of shotgun shells, the shotgun itself, the knife in its wrist sheath, and several large, folded sheets of plastic. As she watched, he continued pulling things from the rucksack and sorting them according to their usefulness as basic survival gear.

"How much ice is left in the chest?" he asked without looking up.

"None. It all had melted even before he ripped off the lid. He must have looked in, seen only the rack holding the film, and gone on to more important things."

Cole grunted. "Is the film all right?"

"It should be fine. The canisters are tight."

Quickly Erin sorted unexposed from exposed film. When she was finished, she began stuffing rolls of exposed film into a military-surplus hip belt. From the belt hung a variety of pouches made of camouflage cloth.

"Don't bother with the belt," Cole said. "It will just be excess weight. We can't afford an ounce more than is absolutely necessary."

"How long will it take us to get back here?" she asked, looking at the mound of exposed film.

"We can't count on getting back at all," Cole said evenly. "It's seventy miles to the Gibb Road. That's if we fly. On the ground it will be farther."

"How far away is Windsor station?"

"Fifty miles, give or take, if we follow the road. Less if we don't. But there's nothing between here and the station except two limestone ridges and cracking clay flats that won't see water between now and the wet." He began packing the rucksack. "Even if we did make it to the station, the bastard in the chopper would be waiting and we'd be in no shape to out-smart, outshoot, or outrun him. There's a better chance of finding water between here and the Gibb Road, and a hell of a lot better chance of finding help once we're there."

What Cole didn't say was that their chance of survival was minimal at best. No food, little water, and mile after rugged mile of empty country, the kind of land that would demand everything from them and give back nothing in return but more demands on their failing strength.

Erin looked at Cole's bleak expression. Without a word she turned her back on the pile of film recording her first, irreplaceable perceptions of the alien landscape that was the Kimberley Plateau.

"Any water left in the ice chest?" Cole asked.

"Yes."

"Pour it into the empty canteen that's under the front seat. If that's too hard to do without spilling, I'll help."

Before Erin finished transferring the ice chest's water to the canteen, Cole came up to the Rover with the heavy rucksack in one hand and the shotgun in the other. He pulled on a khaki bush shirt and stuffed another into the rucksack. Then he watched as Erin carefully drained the last drops into the big canteen's mouth. When she capped the canteen and handed it to him, he hefted its weight with surprise.

"Almost a half gallon," he said. "Good."

He didn't mention how little of their daily requirement that amount of water was. He simply clipped the canteen to his webbing belt opposite the other large canteen he carried. It, too, carried about half a gallon of water.

"Take off your canteen and belt," Cole said, holding out his hand.

"I can carry it."

"Take it off."

"Cole—"

"No," he interrupted flatly. "I have three times your strength. Hand it over."

Erin looked into hard gray eyes and knew arguing would be futile. Worse, it would waste energy. She gave Cole the canteen and dropped the belt in the dirt. Automatically she turned to the Rover and pulled out her camera bag. The instant she realized what she was doing, she replaced the bag and let the strap slide from her fingers. When she turned back to Cole, she was empty handed.

"I'm sorry," Cole said, touching Erin's cheek briefly.

"It was just force of habit. Since we can't eat it, drink it, or kill with it, we don't need it, do we?"

"No. Wing will replace everything you lose."

She nodded. But even if she survived to have Wing replace her camera equipment, nothing could replace the exposed film. Erin put the thought out of her mind, because thinking about it would do no good.

Cole took a reading on his compass and headed up the dry streambed with an easy, long-legged stride that was neither fast nor slow. Erin followed, trying to ignore the sweat sliding down her body and the heat rising in sheets from the parched land. They walked up the wash for less than two miles before Cole turned aside and headed for a black velvet shadow that lay partway up one of the limestone hills. More alcove than cave, the overhang gave shelter and a good view back down the wash. Faded pictographs showed against the rough limestone. Tongues of soot rose where campfires had burned.

"Aborigines," Cole said, glancing around. "A band must have camped here during the wet."

Erin forgot about the heat as she looked at the pictographs and thought of how she would have photographed them if her camera was available.

"We can't be spotted from the air here. We'll be safe until dark," Cole said. As he turned away from the drawings he saw the expression of longing on Erin's face. "If it makes you feel better, there are thousands of places like this scattered around the outback.

This won't be your only chance to photograph an old Aborigine camp."

She nodded, wondering if Cole believed the implication of his own words—survival, not death. But she didn't ask. Their odds of living wouldn't improve by talking about it.

"Looking at those hand designs is rather eerie," she said.

"Holy ground."

"Really?" Erin examined the pictographs with new interest.

"Every piece of landscape that's the least bit different is sacred to the Aborigines. Every seep, every oddly shaped rock, everything that isn't flat and spinifex or rumpled and covered with sparse gum." Cole shrugged out of the rucksack and flexed his shoulders. "But we don't need to worry about guests dropping in. This place hasn't been used since white men came down under."

"How can you tell?"

"No broken bottles or beer cans." Cole pointed to the rucksack. "Use that for a pillow. Sleep if you can. We've got a long night of walking ahead."

"All night? Are you really that afraid of being spotted?"

"We'll need less water walking at night and sleeping by day."

Erin hesitated, then asked the question she had told herself she wasn't going to ask because the answers really wouldn't change the outcome.

"How long will it take to reach Gibb Road?" she asked.

"Four days, if we're lucky. Six days, more likely.

The country gets rougher than hell in the last half, and we'll be a lot weaker by then."

"How much time do we have?"

"With only the water in the canteens, we'd be dry by this time tomorrow. By the day after, we'd be staggering." Cole sat, leaned against the wall of the overhang, and pulled his hat down to cover his eyes. "If we get lucky, we'll find an unmarked seep. If not, there are other ways."

Before Erin could ask what he meant, he was asleep. She didn't think she would be able to sleep, but even the few miles she had walked that day had drained her. Her last thought before she dropped off was relief that she wouldn't have to face another hike through the brutal sunlight.

She didn't awaken until she felt Cole stirring beside her. The quality of the light told her it was late afternoon. Pale, almost invisible lightning stitched through the dark gray sky. The river of clouds had become a seamless, seething lid over the land, holding in heat without bringing the cool sweetness of rain.

"You're sure it rains here?" Erin said, swallowing to relieve the dryness in her mouth.

"Eventually. But not today. The clouds will be gone in a few hours. That's just heat lightning." He came to his feet and held out his hand to her, pulling her to her feet. "We'll make much better time while it's still light."

When Cole shouldered his rucksack, Erin followed him out of the rock shelter into the naked land. Even after the sun vanished with an abruptness that Erin found startling after Alaska's long twilights, heat still came up from the Kimberley's ground in tangible waves. The humidity was high enough to be stifling, but not high enough to preserve the moisture in her own body or to prevent the sweat that rolled down her skin from evaporating.

Cole walked steadily, reading his compass by flashlight until the clouds thinned and broke to reveal the glittering massed stars of the southern sky. The Milky Way was a tidal wave of distant light washing across a third of the sky. From unexpected quarters of the horizon, lightning stabbed upward, looking hardly brighter than the stars. The moon added its silver glow.

Erin walked in Cole's wake through spinifex and rocky scrubland. Their only rest came when he checked the compass against the stars or the black, uneven silhouette of the night horizon. More often than not, he chose to walk in dry watercourses despite the soft footing. In the dark, places where water had flowed were a lighter shade of black than the rest of the land and usually had less obstacles.

They drank the last of their water in the small, almost cool hours of night.

By the time dawn exploded across the sky, Erin was stumbling from weariness. The land around them had changed somewhat during the night. The hills tended to be steeper and separate rather than in long, low ridges.

Cole took advantage of the light to walk more quickly. He kept to a hard pace through the increasing heat until he found a place where thin-leafed trees shaded a ravine at the base of a hill. He stretched the survival blanket between two tree trunks and lashed it in place, creating a canopy to shade them as they slept.

"Lie down in the shade," Cole said. "Don't move any more than absolutely necessary."

He dumped the rucksack on the ground for a pillow, grabbed the shovel, and walked out until he was in a place without shade. There he dug a hole three feet wide by two feet deep and lined it with leaves he stripped from the acacias and gums. He put his large tin mess cup in the center of the hole, spread one of the plastic sheets over it, and anchored the sheet with rocks. A final rock was put in the center of the plastic, making it sag to a point over the cup.

Without pausing Cole came back to the shelter, grabbed several more plastic sheets and went to work again. These sheets he wrapped around the ends of living tree branches, then carefully gathered the edges of each sheet until it made a bag with green, living leaves inside. He tied off the neck of each bag tightly and went back to the shelter's welcome shade.

Erin looked up as Cole sank to the ground beside her. "What are they?" she asked, gesturing toward the shiny, clear bags.

"Stills. There's a lot of moisture in leaves. We'll let the sun work for us rather than against us for a change. Sleep."

She licked her lips, wondering how she could feel so dry when the air was so muggy. It was only a brief moment of curiosity. Sleep slammed down over her like a tropical sunset. Just as consciousness spun away, she felt Cole rubbing sunscreen into her skin. She tried to thank him, but the effort was too great.

The next thing Erin knew, she was being shaken awake.

"Erin. Wake up, honey. Breakfast is on the way."

The thought of food made her salivary glands contract painfully. She sat up and rubbed eyes that were gritty with dust and sleep.

"Breakfast?" she asked.

"You'll have to work for it."

"How?"

Cole pulled Erin to her feet. "See that?" he asked, pointing to a spot about fifteen feet away.

"What?"

A snake moved, curling sinuously through the dry debris beneath a gum tree, hunting prey or simply a cooler place to rest.

Erin made an odd sound. "Breakfast, huh?"

"If we're lucky." Cole handed her a leafy branch as long as her arm. "Take this and keep him occupied while I circle around behind. Don't stir him up, just hold his attention. He'll be a lot harder to catch if he makes it to the rocks."

"Is the snake dangerous?" Erin asked as Cole started out from the shelter.

"Only until I kill it. Then it's breakfast."

Erin shook off the last of her lethargy and walked out from the shelter to head off the snake. Though it was late afternoon, the sun beat down through the clouds with savage force. She rattled the leaves at the tip of the branch against the dusty ground. The snake turned toward the motion with a muscular twist of its body.

"I've got its attention," Erin said.

The reptile watched her with eyes like flakes of obsidian. The snake showed no nervousness at her presence. Mulgas were the undisputed rulers of the outback. For them a human being was a novelty rather than a threat.

"Don't get too close," Cole cautioned.

"Look who's talking."

Cole said nothing. He eased nearer the tail of the

snake while Erin made small movements that kept the mulga's attention fixed on her.

Suddenly Cole's hand shot out and fastened on the snake's tail. He jerked his arm, snapping the mulga like a bullwhip, breaking its spine and killing it instantly. He gave the snake a final snap to be certain, then waited. Four feet of breakfast hung limply from his hand.

Swallowing dryly, Erin reminded herself that protein was protein was protein. Her mind might know the difference between snake and sushi, but her stomach wouldn't. Certainly snake couldn't taste any worse than seal.

"There's a lot of water in snake meat," Cole said as he drew his knife from its sheath on his wrist. "If you don't believe me, watch me skin it out."

"No, thanks."

"Don't worry. After you cook it, the meat is white and tastes just like—"

"Chicken," she interrupted, grimacing.

He glanced up at her, surprised. "Did you eat snake in Alaska?"

"No, but I've been told the same thing about frog legs and grubs and every other so-called delicacy I've ever eaten. It's a lie. Chicken is the only thing that tastes like chicken."

"Snake is better than goanna."

"As long as it's better than seal, I won't complain. Much."

The corner of Cole's mouth kicked up. "Have I told you that you're good company?"

Without waiting for an answer he began dressing out the snake with quick, skilled motions. Erin watched through narrowed eyes and decided it was about as bloody as cleaning a fish and far less messy than seal.

"Get a fire going," Cole said as he worked. "You can roast the meat while I empty the stills. If you can't eat your share now, I'll save it for you. After we've walked all night and your stomach is gnawing on your backbone, mulga will taste better than smoked salmon."

She didn't believe Cole but she didn't argue. When the time came to eat, she would eat, because it was the only way to keep up her strength.

By the time Erin was finished roasting chunks of protein over the eucalyptus fire, Cole had emptied the four solar stills. The result netted just under a gallon of water. While she watched, he divided the water evenly between two canteens.

"This one is yours," he said, handing it over to her. "Drink."

The water tasted as exotic as the snake meat had, for both had been flavored by ecalyptus and acacia. Despite Erin's thirst, she drank less than a third of the water in the canteen before she reached out, took the tin cup from Cole's belt, and poured in half the water remaining in her canteen.

"This is yours," she said. "Drink up."

"Don't be ridiculous."

"You're twice as big as I am. That means you need twice the water I do."

"Erin—"

"No," she said, cutting him off. "If you can carry everything because you're bigger than I am, you can damn well take your real share of the water and food."

For a long moment Cole looked into Erin's clear,

beautiful green eyes. "I'd rather you drank it," he said finally.

"I'd rather carry my own gear, but I'm being sensible about it. If both of us are going to survive, we both have to be sensible, right?"

He hesitated, then drank the eucalyptus-flavored water to soothe the thirst that had been tormenting him. When he was finished, he bent and brushed the last drops over Erin's lips in a gentle kiss.

"You're quite a woman, Erin Shane Windsor."

"And you're quite a man," she whispered. "If I have to die, at least I'll have had a chance to live. Thank you for that, Cole. I wouldn't have made it alone."

His fingers caressed her cheek before he turned away and methodically began packing the rucksack. When he was finished, he consulted the compass and his memory of the map. Then he held out his hand to Erin.

"Ready?" he asked.

She smiled almost sadly. "As in 'Ready or not, here I come'?"

"Something like that. I know you're tired, but we do make much better progress with some daylight to help us."

Erin took Cole's hand and they set off into the staggering heat and emptiness of the Kimberley Plateau. He led her carefully around the area where he had spotted fresh human tracks that morning. There was no point in letting her know their meager progress was being watched. If she knew, she would begin wondering why they were being played with instead of being finished off in a single merciful stroke.

It was something Cole wondered about himself.

32

◆

BY THE FOURTH NIGHT OF WALKING, THIRST HAD become a savage companion. It was more pervasive than the darkness, more stifling than the heat, as vast as the star-strewn sky. Erin tried not to think about water. Instead she concentrated on the need to walk steadily. Cole walked in front of her, seemingly impervious to the grim rations and desperate thirst.

But she knew he wasn't. She had seen the fine trembling of his hands when he dressed out the goanna he had shot. Despite the endless humidity and daily cups of exotically flavored water, their bodies were drying out hour by hour, breath by breath.

Between black shapes of clouds, cold white points of starlight gleamed. Occasional strokes of heat lightning lanced through clouds that hadn't thinned as much as usual as the night wore on. Despite the scattered stars, moon, and lightning, the night seemed darker than any night Erin had ever endured and longer than the longest winter above the Arctic Circle.

A sheet of lightning ran from top to bottom of the

towering cloud formations along the horizon. In the sudden, stark flash of light, Erin caught a glimpse of Cole. He had turned and was holding out his hand to her. His expression was almost as dark as the clouds and the night. When she took his hand, he drew her close. He knew if they sat down they would sleep, wasting vital hours. So they stood quietly together, holding one another, resting in the only way they trusted themselves to.

Distant lightning flickered and flashed. The fitful rumble of thunder that followed was more felt than heard.

"With a little luck," he said in a raspy voice, "it will rain in a day or two."

Erin nodded, because it was too much effort to talk.

After a moment Cole pressed his cheek against Erin's and released her. He checked the compass, scanned the surroundings in the dubious illumination of lightning, and headed toward a ridge that was either near and low or distant and steep. Whichever, it lay across their path to the Gibb Road.

The ridge seemed no closer when the sky in the east began to slide from black toward gray. Cole stood and waited for Erin to come up beside him. He pulled the canteen from his belt, took two swallows, and handed it to Erin.

"Last one is for you," he said.

"No. Yours."

Cole took the water himself, then pulled her close for the kind of kiss he hadn't given her since Windsor station. When Erin's lips parted, he gently gave her the water she had refused to take from his canteen. Startled, she had no choice but to swallow. He laughed softly and kissed her until they both forgot their thirst for a few sweet moments. Then he held her as though it were the last time.

Just as Cole released Erin, dawn came up in a silent, seething violence of light. The sun exploded through half-formed clouds. Within seconds the earth was transformed into a place of startling distances, rich colors, and vivid textures.

"To hell with diamonds," Erin whispered slowly, looking at the glorious, timeless metamorphosis of night into day. "I'd trade everything for a camera and some unexposed film."

Cole smiled slightly. "I believe you would." He ran his palms over her tangled mahogany hair, pushing it away from her heat-flushed face. "Diamonds are to me what film is to you: the key to another world. But if I had Abe's diamond mine right now, I'd trade it for film and give it to you."

He saw the shock in her expression, felt it in the movement of her body as she pulled away to look at him.

"You mean that, don't you?" she whispered.

"I always say what I mean." Cole pulled Erin closer, shielding her brilliant green eyes from the sun. "Discovering *Arctic Odyssey* made me feel like I had just found a diamond mine—full of adrenaline and awe, alive all the way to the soles of my feet."

For a moment more he held her. Finally he stepped back. "Keep your eyes open for birds or a clump of lush vegetation. This is karst country. Water must have collected in cracks or deep limestone potholes or even in a cave or two. All we have to do is find where—and pray that nothing found it before us."

Erin and Cole drank the last of their water two hours after dawn. They lay in the shade of the thin blanket stretched between two spindly trees, watching waves of heat rise off the land. The water in the canteen was almost hot. It tasted strongly of the gum leaves that had given it up. Yet the liquid felt wonderful sliding down Erin's parched throat. As she drank, Cole studied the dark clouds that were streaming in from the Indian Ocean, thunderheads clawing toward the sun while the slate-colored bottoms of the massive clouds dragged ever nearer to earth.

"So close and yet so damned far away," Cole said hoarsely, measuring the wild, thick river of clouds that was already fanning across the sky, breaking into separate storm cells as air currents tore it apart.

After a few minutes he looked away from the distant chimera of rain and concentrated on the land ahead. Ghostly gum trees were scattered haphazardly across flat red earth. Waves of heat shimmered above the dirt. Clumps of hard spinifex competed for space with weathered blocks of limestone. The flats were surrounded by broken hills. In the distance a long flat-topped hill or ridge rose steeply, marking one edge of the basin where runoff water must inevitably collect during the wet, for there was no notch or ravine or canyon where the water could break free of the depression.

Yet no matter how carefully Cole looked, there was no sign that the flats became a temporary lake in the rainy season. As he realized that, a vague tendril of excitement uncurled in his gut, taking his mind off the hunger and thirst that had steadily eroded his strength.

"What are you looking for?" Erin asked, studying the landscape.

"Some sign of where water runs off during the wet."

She looked around in silence for several minutes. Then she frowned and looked more closely. "Didn't we come through here yesterday?"

Cole gave Erin a sideways look, wondering if heat, hunger, and dehydration were blurring her mind. "No."

"It looks . . . familiar."

"The landscape looks pretty much the same from here to the Admiralty Gulf."

"Are you sure?" Erin squinted through the shimmering heat, feeling more certain with each moment that she had been here before.

"Don't worry. I'm not wonky enough from thirst to be walking us in circles. Go to sleep," he added, standing up. "It will be time to walk soon enough."

"Where are you going?"

"Up there." He jerked his thumb at the small hill they had just climbed down.

"Why?"

"I want to take a look from the top. I might be able to see a splash of green or birds flying."

When Cole left the rucksack but picked up the shotgun and stuffed extra shells in his pocket, Erin looked at him sharply.

"Is there something you aren't telling me?" she asked.

"Sleep if you can. I won't be long."

"Cole?"

"It's all right. I'll be able to see you from the top of the hill."

He was gone before she could press her question.

With a sigh, Erin lay back in a kind of stupor while the clouds thickened, diminishing the hammering force of sunlight and dropping the temperature a few degrees. The air thickened too, becoming a weight that was too heavy to breathe and too thin to drink. The density of various cloud cells increased as the indigo promise of rain climbed from the base of the clouds to halfway up the towering clusters of thunderheads. One of the cells was directly overhead. Thunder echoed through it restlessly, pursuing hidden lightning.

Random drops rattled loudly on the canopy Cole had rigged. Erin came to her feet and shot out into the open, tipping her head back and extending her hands as though to catch any rain. After a moment she felt a drop fall just above her upper lip. Her tongue flicked out. The raindrop tasted sweet and clean, even though it was mixed with her own sweat and the fine dust that pervaded everything in the Kimberley.

A dozen raindrops fell. Lightning winked and flirted while thunder cracked with startling loudness. More rain reached the sere earth. The drops were fat and heavy, pregnant with the possibility of life. Each drop made a dark splash pattern on the dusty ground and vanished.

"Come on," Erin said hoarsely, trying to coax a steady rain from the threatening cloud overhead. "Come on!"

As quickly as the rain had started, it stopped. The storm cell moved on, driven by the sun's savage heat. Erin went to her knees with the exhaustion that the promise of rain had held at bay for a few moments.

She looked up at the steamy silver sky where clouds had been a moment before.

Erin didn't realize that Cole had returned until he pulled her to her feet.

"Get back in the shade," he said. "It's too hot for real rain. Almost all the drops are evaporating before they hit the ground."

Numbly Erin nodded and walked toward the canopy that protected them from the savage sun. She sank to the ground, no longer noticing its pebbles or gritty texture.

"Find anything?" she asked hoarsely as Cole stretched out next to her.

"Any water here is underground."

"How far?"

"That's the million-dollar question. I don't have an answer."

The harshness of Cole's voice was equaled by the grimness of his expression. With a hand that trembled she touched his mouth, stilling the bitter words.

"Not your fault," she whispered.

His hand closed around hers, holding it close. They fell into a sleep that was restless, disturbed by thirst, hunger, and the dry groan of distant thunder.

When Erin awoke, she was alone. Where Cole had been there was only the shotgun and a handful of shells resting on a sheet of plastic that still held a few drops of water from its recent use as a solar still. Heat poured down through the broken, seething lid of clouds, telling her that sunset was hours away. She sat up and waited for the dizziness to pass.

In the dirt just beyond the shotgun Cole had written two words: *Gone hunting.*

The other solar stills were untouched, taking ad-

vantage of every bit of sun to draw water vapor from
the leaves. Erin picked up the shotgun, checked that it
was loaded, and put it down within easy reach. Then
she stretched out once more and wondered what was
so urgent that Cole had drunk the contents of one still
and gone out into the vicious afternoon in order to
hunt.

The answer didn't come until just before sunset.
Erin heard a rustling from the dry scrub to the left of
the shelter. She grabbed the shotgun, snapped off the
safety, and waited.

"It's just me, honey."

The voice came from her right, not her left. She
spun around and saw Cole standing no more than ten
feet away. With a shiver, Erin realized anew what a
lethal adversary a man like Cole would make. She
snapped the safety back into place and stood up
slowly.

"You're lucky I didn't shoot you," she said.

"That's why I threw a rock into the scrub. If you
were the trigger-happy type, you'd shoot the rock instead of me."

She looked at his empty hands and the sheath
knife strapped to his wrist. "Find what you were hunting for?"

Absently Cole brushed dry leaves and powdery
grit from his hands. "Yes."

"What?"

"An Aborigine. He's about four hundred yards in
back of us."

"Right now?"

Cole nodded. "This isn't some tough young black
boy who's gone walkabout for the hell of it. We've

been followed since we left the Rover. I tried to catch him once before, while you slept, but he's too good."

She shook her head, trying to understand. "Why are we being followed. Is he going to kill us?"

"No. He's a Kimberley kite hanging back and waiting until we die. Then he'll call in the helicopter and our bodies will be 'found' the same way Abe's was," Cole said flatly. "Too bad, how sad, the two Yanks died in the outback when their Rover packed it in. No bullets. No signs of violence on the bodies. Nothing but dehydration, starvation, heat prostration, and death. No unhappy questions, no international inquiries, no nasty little investigations by your father and the CIA."

"No one will believe we just wandered off and died. That Rover was sabotaged!"

Cole's smile was as bleak as his eyes. "Was it? Or did we just run out of drinking water, drain and purify what was in the radiator, and set off on foot?"

He nodded as he saw comprehension draw Erin's face into harsh lines.

"They'll replace hoses, put the radio back in with a few loose connections to explain our silence, and then they'll wring their hands for the press," Cole continued. "Everything is going as they planned except for one minor detail. They didn't know that when I'm in dry country, I always carry the means to make a solar still in my rucksack. We've lasted twice as long as they expected. That cat-footed little Aborigine they sicced on us has finally run out of water. The bastard has to hunt for it just like we do. That's what he's doing now: hunting water."

"What are we going to do?"

"Pray to God he finds it."

33

♦

It wasn't possible to track the Aborigine in darkness. After sunset Cole pulled down the canopy and spread it for a groundcloth. As had become her habit despite the heat, Erin curled up against him and slipped into a state that was neither sleeping nor waking. The night passed in a torment of thirst that was barely touched by the aromatic water they had drunk from the solar stills.

Unlike past nights, the clouds showed no thinning as the darkness wore on. Huge sheets of lightning arced across the sky, transforming half the blackness into a blinding blue-white light. Thunder exploded. The last echoes hadn't faded before a different kind of fire came from the sky, small snake tongues of lightning licking at the edges of darkness, flaring in patterns that evoked ancient pictographs drawn on coarse rock walls.

Besieged by thirst and tantalizing hopes of rain, Erin and Cole slept fitfully. When the first light separated sky from earth, Cole slipped away to see if their guard had returned during the night. There was nothing but broad, barefoot prints in the dust where the man had circled their camp before heading off into the bush.

A sprinkle of water fell just after dawn. The raindrops were heavy and wet and teasing. But the promise of real water wasn't kept. Reality was the incandescent savagery of the rising sun.

"Hurry," Cole said. "Sign-cutting light doesn't last long in the tropics."

The first slanting light of day made tracks jump out of the landscape like neon paint. Cole pointed to the footprints.

"That's one end of our lifeline," he said, drawing a line in the dust in front of the prints. "The other end is somewhere out there at a waterhole."

Where the prints were clear, Cole walked quickly along the trail, marking tracks by drawing a circle around them in the dirt, then looking for the next track. When he lost the trail he returned to the last marked track and began again. The tracking itself was enough of a novelty at first that Erin could push aside her thirst while she watched Cole read the land in a way that was almost eerie.

But as the sun rose higher, beating down on them again like a hammer, Erin could feel her strength ebbing. Cole forged ahead without pause, cursing the changing angle of the light that smeared and smudged signs that had formerly leaped out of the ground to his eye.

All sign of tracks vanished on a stretch of windswept, sun-baked rock.

"Stand here," Cole said, pointing to the last tracks he could find.

Erin stood beneath the brutal sun while Cole checked the entire perimeter of the slab before he found the tracks again.

"Got it. Let's go."

She walked across the rock, wondering if the stone was truly hot enough to cook eggs. It felt like it, even through the thick soles of her walking shoes.

At a spot where the terrain presented several choices for a man walking over the land, Cole knelt and sighted along the hot ground, searching for the shadow traces of the trail the Aborigine had left.

"How far would he go for water?" Erin finally asked.

"As far as he had to. But he's moving at a good pace. He's not doubling back or casting around, and he's not climbing hills to get a look at the country-side."

"Is that good?"

"It means he knows where he's going. All we have to do is hang on to his trail."

Cole's eyes narrowed as he spotted a slight, regular disturbance in the surface of the earth. When he shifted to hands and knees, the pattern disappeared. He sat on his heels and sighted along the direction of the trail. A vague notch showed in the landscape ahead. Beyond it rose the flat-topped, steep rise that seemed little closer for the hours of walking.

When Cole stood up once more, he had two pebbles in his hand. He brushed them off on his shorts and offered one to Erin. The other he put in his own mouth.

"Think of it as a lemon drop," he suggested.

Erin's salivary glands responded instantly to the

idea. For the first time in two days, her mouth was moist again.

"It only works the first time," he said, almost smiling at her startled look when saliva ran once more. "But even when it doesn't work, the pebble gives your tongue something to do besides feel dry."

"A trick, huh?"

"That's all life is," Cole said thickly. "A trick played on death."

Erin followed Cole through increasing heat and humidity while monsoon clouds thickened and billowed toward the instant of rain she no longer believed would come. The trail proved elusive, forcing Cole to cast around again beneath the brutal sun while Erin waited and watched. Without warning the world began to dim and revolve slowly about an unknown center. She sank to her hands and knees, head hanging, until reality shifted back again into the dusty sunhammered pastels of Western Australia.

Slowly Erin realized that Cole was standing over her, shading her with his body and the khaki shirt he held between his hands in a makeshift canopy. When she tried to stand once more, he put his hand on her shoulder.

"Rest. The dizziness will pass."

This time.

But Cole didn't say it aloud. He had expected Erin to reach the end of her resources yesterday or the day before. Her continued endurance in the face of a climate her body was ill prepared for both amazed him and made him more determined than ever that she should survive.

"Better?" he asked finally, his voice gentle despite its dry rasp.

She nodded.

"Ready to try standing?"

"Yes," she whispered.

With Cole's help, Erin pulled herself to her feet. He led her to the thin shade of an acacia and went to work making true shade with the survival blanket.

"No," she said hoarsely. "We've got to keep going."

"Not yet. Give yourself a chance to recover."

Cole put his shirt back on and studied the land from the artificial shade he had created. The surrounding ground was still largely flat, still the floor of a basin that had no visible outlet. The only prominent landmark among the broken hills that surrounded the basin was the flat-topped hill that had been receding before them like a mirage. The hill didn't look flat any more. Nor did it look like a hill. It was rather more like a rough-surfaced mesa. Wind- and water-sculpted stone formations poked above the sparse vegetation.

"Cole?"

He looked away from the tortured rock shapes to the woman whose determination to survive was as great as his own.

"Are you sure we haven't been here before?" she asked.

"Yes."

Erin shaded her eyes and squinted, trying to see through the odd gloaming beneath the restless, opaque sky. Her breath came in with a tearing sound.

"Where are we?" she asked.

"In the Kimberley," Cole said gently.

"Yes, but where? Are we close to any of Abe's claims?"

Cole thought for a moment, reviewing his memo-

ries of the maps he had spent hundreds of hours
studying. He checked the compass, glanced at his
watch, did a few rough calculations, and looked back
at Erin.

"We could be on the edge of one. Why?"

For a moment Erin didn't answer. She felt as
though she had been sleepwalking and had just awakened to find herself in a new world.

"Were you ever here before?" she asked.

"No. It's a small claim. Gold hunters worked it
over real thoroughly forty years ago. They found just
enough dust to keep them trying for years before they
gave up. Just too dry."

"Did you ever hear Abe mention this claim?"

"Only when he was drunk, but he mentioned a
thousand places when he was drunk. He never at-
tached any particular importance to it. Why?"

"I think that's Bridget's Hill," Erin said simply.
"I can't be sure because the angle is different. If that's
the hill, the photographs were taken from somewhere •
off to the left and looking more north."

Cole narrowed his eyes and compared his memory of the photographs with the worn, eroded land.

"Be damned," he breathed. "You might just be
right. If you are, there should be water there during
the dry. That would explain how Abe camped there.
And that's where the tracks were headed before I lost
them."

Erin struggled to her feet.

"Easy," Cole said, bracing her. "There's no rush.
That pile of limestone has been there a long, long
time. It will be there for a few more hours."

"But will I?" she whispered as the world dimmed

and brightened in uncertain cycles that matched her erratic pulse.

Cole tightened his hold on Erin. "You're stronger than you know."

The sound of thunder rippled in the distance. A breeze came from the direction of the blackening clouds. Cole looked up and realized that the clouds had thickened perceptibly, dimming the sun's brutal strength. A dense, sultry wind gusted, bending spinifex and spindly gum trees alike. He sniffed the air as intently as any wild animal, and his nostrils flared at the unmistakable scent of rain.

"Cole?" Erin whispered, looking at the sky.

"It's coming, honey."

"When?"

Lightning arced invisibly, burning pathways through the clouds. Thunder came again. It was closer, louder.

"I don't know. I've seen it go on like this for days. And I've seen it rain an ocean within hours." Cole looked down at Erin's pinched face and the green eyes whose beauty even exhaustion couldn't dull. "We'll be able to find both shade and shelter at the base of Bridget's Hill."

"And water?"

Cole didn't answer. He had never lied to her. He didn't plan to start now.

Erin stared at the rugged thrust of land that was their destination. It looked very far away. She forced herself to walk forward.

For the first few steps Cole stayed beside her, ready to catch her if she fell. Watching her ragged progress tore at him, but he knew it would be stupid to carry her one step farther than he must, because his own stride was uneven, his own vision uncertain, his own body succumbing to dehydration and savage heat.

The teasing swirls of rain-scented wind lured Erin forward. Slowly she pressed on toward the hill she had first seen in photographs that had been taken when Abelard Windsor was still young enough to believe in a woman's love. Bridget's Hill seemed to be retreating a step for every one Erin walked.

"Are they moving it?" she asked finally, her voice raw. "We aren't getting any closer."

"Halfway," Cole said. "We're halfway there. The flat ground and the heat waves fool you."

They walked on another half mile, then another. Gradually the ground fell away beneath their feet in a long decline. The hill loomed even larger above the depressed earth, crouching over the land like a demon wrapped in shimmering waves of hot air.

Erin stumbled over a bit of spinifex. Cole caught her and supported her, drawing one of her arms across his shoulders and anchoring it with one hand while his other arm locked around her waist.

"Leave me—here," she said.

Cole didn't bother answering.

"Damn it—leave me—"

"Don't talk. Walk."

Half carrying Erin, half dragging her, Cole moved toward the dark, ragged limestone formation that crouched above the steamy flats. Thunder rumbled directly overhead. Neither he nor she noticed, for their whole being was fixed on the darker shadow of land rising above the shimmering flats. The closer they came, the more certain Cole was that Erin had been right.

It was Bridget's Hill that loomed over them.

Erin staggered and would have fallen if Cole hadn't already been supporting her. He waited, breathing hard. After a minute she straightened and resumed walking, or trying to.

They stumbled across the remains of a bonfire two hundred yards from base of Bridget's Hill. The charred ends of branches were partially buried in red sand. The fire had been huge, telling Cole that this was the gathering spot of several groups. Broken beer bottles and crumpled cans of Black Swann ringed the fire. There was no way to know the age of the tracks scattered everywhere, only that the Aborigines had visited this site since the last rain.

A shaft of lightning arced down to the top of Bridget's Hill, dimming for an instant even the savage light of the sun. Thunder followed instantly, waking Erin from her exhausted daze. Air twisted and rushed past them as though disturbed by a spectral force. She shuddered and swallowed dryly.

"It's sacred—ground," she said.

"Everything is, to them."

"Them?"

Erin blinked and looked around. She realized she was standing in the midst of a huge circle of burned wood. There was a ring of packed dirt, then another ring of broken glass and discarded beer cans.

Slowly Cole and Erin walked away from the bonfire to the blocks of limestone rubble that had collected at the base of Bridget's Hill. The steeply sloping land form was more mesa than hill, more reef than either, a massive network of compressed, interlocking, water-soluble stone that had been buried in the outwash of a higher, younger Kimberley Plateau. Now the dead sea's limestone bones were slowly being resurrected by erosion.

Cole looked at the steep, eroded limestone and knew that only a fey, wild white girl would think of climbing it, and only an equally wild white man would follow her up to take her picture. The limestone was old and eroded in unpredictable ways. The top of the formation would be a network of deep cracks and crevices, potholes and solution channels, a tortured landscape where nothing could live but lizards or birds. There was no way of knowing whether Bridget's Hill was the last remains of a once-huge limestone mass or the tip of a stone iceberg that spread out beneath the dusty lid of soil.

No matter how carefully Cole looked, he saw nowhere along the ruined face of the limestone where the lush green exclamation point of foliage marked a seep or a spring.

Lightning stabbed down repeatedly, dancing across the top of the hill. Thunder followed instantly in a drumroll of sound that shook the earth. Wind sighed down the steep, ruined face of the limestone and lifted veils of grit from the dry land.

"Water?" Erin asked, her voice hoarse.

Without answering, Cole headed for a notch cut in the base of the steepest part of the hill. It was the only place where a spring or a seep might be hidden.

The approach to the notch was strewn with limestone boulders whose faces had been eroded into hollows and cups and bowls that in the wet would hold rain. But that water had long since evaporated, leaving behind an eerie black sculpture garden surrounded by sterile drifts of soil as fine as powder. An empty watercourse snaked among stones like a dry, many-forked tongue joined to the notch at the bottom of the hill.

Across the top of the limestone hill, lightning danced with lethal grace. Thunder followed.

Erin followed Cole to the base of the stone ravine, where the ground would be shaded much of the time. Someone had been there before them. Small mounds of dirt were scattered at random, connected by the same broad, flat footprints that Cole had been following across the empty land. Cole went to first one hole and then another, and in each he found the same thing —dry dirt for a few feet and then equally dry limestone bedrock.

"So far the little bastard isn't having any better luck than we are," Cole said grimly.

The footprints went from the dry watercourse to the hill itself, then vanished on the stony surface. It was apparent that the Aborigine had ignored the danger from lightning and climbed up to the top of the limestone formation to look for sinks or deep potholes that might hold water from one wet to the next.

Cole knew he had no choice but to follow. Without a word he shucked out of the rucksack and began looking for the easiest way up the stone maze.

"No," Erin rasped. "Lightning."

Even as she spoke, a sheet of lightning went from horizon to horizon in an explosion of incandescent violence that left the air smelling burned. Thunder cracked, shaking sky and ground alike. The barrage of lightning continued until the hair on their bodies rippled and stood away from their flesh in response to the electrically charged air.

Between one minute and the next, the day darkened as though the sun had been ripped from the sky.

The world convulsed, exchanging air for water. Then rain hammered down as abruptly as lightning, as violently as thunder, an ocean turned inside out to inundate land and sky alike.

Holding each other, Erin and Cole laughed and turned their faces up to the life-giving water.

34

◆

AN HOUR AFTER DAWN ERIN WATCHED THE CAMP-
fire flicker beneath a sky that trembled with misty
light. By the time the downpour had finally stopped,
the sky had been black with night as well as clouds.
Just before dawn a rain-scented breeze had begun
blowing, bringing with it the sound of water running
from every crack and crevice on Bridget's Hill. The
sky was so thick it fairly breathed water.

Despite the shelter Cole had rigged from clear
plastic sheets, and wearing the spare shirt he had
brought for just such an eventuality, Erin was almost
chilly. The novelty of it was amusing, as was the fact
that she was actually looking forward to the rest of the
mulga Cole had killed when the first onslaught of water had driven it from a limestone crevice. She laughed
softly as she reached for a full canteen and drank as
much water as she wanted.

Cole looked up from the fire he was coaxing into
life and smiled. "Feeling better?"

"Ridiculously good," she admitted, putting the

canteen aside after only a few swallows of water. "We could die tomorrow or the day after, but I'm sitting here glad to be chilly and licking my lips over the idea of snake for breakfast."

His laughter was as rich and lively as the firelight reflected in his clear eyes. "Better than seal, huh?"

"No comparison." She stretched, shivered lightly, and sat up. "What a difference water makes! Although I have to admit, for a time there I was worried about drowning."

Cole smiled slightly. "So was I. I still can't believe a wall of water didn't come down through that notch and wash us all the way to the Admiralty Gulf." He looked at Erin, who was rubbing her palms over her arms. "Come sit by the fire while you eat," he said, stepping back from it. "In an hour you won't believe you ever wanted to."

"Eat?"

"No. Sit by a fire. It will be as hot today as it was yesterday, but it will feel even hotter. The humidity will be higher after the rain."

Erin shook her head. "What a climate. It's a wonder the Aborigines survived."

"A lot of them didn't," Cole said, handing her a chunk of fire-blackened meat.

"Do you think he did?"

"The one who followed us?"

She nodded, for her mouth was full of food.

Cole shrugged and bit off a chunk of mulga. "I didn't find any new tracks after the rain. If he came down off the hill, he didn't come down this side."

Before they were finished eating, the ground began to steam as the sun drew moisture from the earth.

Cole got up and began studying Bridget's Hill with the aid of the strengthening light.

"Cole?"

He made an inquiring sound.

"What are you looking for? The Aborigine?"

He shook his head slowly, his whole attention on the base of the hill.

Erin came to her feet and went to stand by him. She stared in the direction he was looking, but saw nothing except a small, transient cascade coursing down rugged rock.

"I'll be damned," Cole said finally.

"What?"

"See that cascade?"

She nodded.

"See where it leaps down between those clumps of hard spinifex and then between those stunted bloodwood trees and then into that rubble pile at the base of the hill?"

"Yes," Erin said, leaning forward.

"See where the water comes out?"

She leaned forward, frowned, and looked more closely. "No."

"Neither do I."

Cole bent, snagged the rucksack and shotgun, and began walking toward the cascade. Erin went alongside, stretching her legs to keep up.

The answer to the small mystery was no more obvious when they stood at the edge of the rubble pile. The cascade clearly washed down amid the tangle of boulders and scrubby trees. Just as clearly, the water didn't come back out.

"What—" began Erin, only to be cut off by an abrupt gesture from Cole.

"Hear anything?" he asked.

Erin listened. "All I hear is the cascade," she said after a minute.

He shrugged off the rucksack and handed her the shotgun. "I'm going to take a closer look. See if you can find any other nearby places where water runs off the hill but doesn't show up on the flats."

The longer Erin looked at Bridget's Hill, the more puzzled she became. Despite the fierce downpour, very little water was running off the huge, long rise of limestone. Even if she assumed that the pygmy trees, hard spinifex, and broken surface of the limestone concealed most rills and rivulets, she was left with the fact that only a few narrow tongues of water extended from the base of the hill to the depression beyond the big circle of charcoal left by the Aborigines. The depression itself held only a thin puddle after the heavy storm.

Cole scrambled down off the rubble pile and walked quickly to Erin.

"There's something odd about this place," she said.

"Damn little runoff," he said succinctly.

"Is that what you meant by limestone being a sponge?"

He laughed, but there was excitement burning in his eyes. "Not quite, honey. It takes time and pressure to force water into the tiny spaces between particles of limestone."

"Then where did all that water go? That's not a small hill, Cole. There must be at least four square miles of surface up top."

"Closer to ten. And we had at least an inch of rain, probably more like two."

"Did it all run off during the night?"

"If it had, we'd have been ass deep in a flash flood. I'll bet that only a fraction of the water that falls on Bridget's Hill ever sees sunlight again. Most of it runs down into joints and seams in the limestone and vanishes, working its way down through solution channels in the rock until it reaches the water table."

"Is that what happened to the cascade?"

He nodded. "Every drop of water that fell on top is trying to work its way to the bottom. I'll bet that limestone is rotten with solution channels."

"Caves?" Erin asked, her voice rising with excitement.

" 'God's own jewel box/Kept beneath stone locks.' " Cole's teeth flashed startlingly white against the black growth of his beard stubble as he laughed. "Come on, honey. Let's go find the keyhole."

Erin's first flush of excitement had plenty of time to wear off while she and Cole searched the base of Bridget's Hill for an opening that might lead to a cave. There were cracks in the stone where water went and didn't return. There were crevices where more water went in than came out. But there was no opening big enough for a hand, much less a man, to penetrate.

It was raining again, a slow, steady, warm rain that was rather like being trapped in somebody's throttled-down shower.

After two hours Erin took off her floppy cabbage-leaf hat, mopped her face with it, and sat on the steeply sloping, stony earth beneath the indifferent shade of bloodwood trees. The temperature was well over one hundred degrees. Between rainstorms, the humidity was total.

"At least you have enough surplus water to sweat," Cole said.

"I wasn't complaining."

He smiled and touched her cheek. "I know. You haven't complained about anything."

"Except the goanna."

"You said it was better than seal."

"So is starvation," Erin retorted. "Well, almost." She sighed again, stretched her arms over her head, and made a startled sound. "A miracle."

"What?"

"The cool breeze."

"You've finally gone troppo," Cole said, wiping sweat from his face. "There isn't a cool breeze between here and the Snowy River."

"Sure there is." She took his hand and held it over her head. "Right here."

The instant Cole felt the cool current of air, a wave of adrenaline went through him. He scrambled past Erin, forced his way through a tangle of hard spinifex and scrubby trees, and stopped short. There, all but hidden by vegetation and rubble, was a dark, narrow opening in the limestone.

"Cole? Is that what I think it is?" Erin stared past him. "It's so small. How big was Abe?"

"Smaller than me."

"Most men are," she said dryly.

With a supple movement, Cole unslung the shotgun and set it aside. The rucksack thumped to the ground.

"I'm going inside. Stay here."

"Not a chance."

"Caves are dangerous," he said flatly.

"The most interesting things in life usually are."

He slanted Erin a look, then smiled crookedly. "At least let me make sure there aren't any traps around the entrance, natural or otherwise."

"Good old Abe, the King of Lies," she muttered.

"Something like that. Although there's no guarantee this is Abe's cave. Like I said, the entire hill could be riddled with holes."

"But this particular opening," Erin said, deadpan, "rather resembles a woman's 'map of Tasmania.' "

After a startled instant, Cole gave a crack of laughter, grabbed Erin, and kissed her hard.

"For luck," he said, releasing her as abruptly as he had taken her.

Before Erin could tell him to be careful, he vanished as completely as the cascade had.

The opening wasn't as narrow as it appeared, for it was offset slightly from right to left. In a few instants Cole pushed from tropical sun into seamless darkness. He stopped to strike a match and shield it within the circle of his hand. The first thing the flickering light picked out was a mound of thick, creamy candles. The second was a row of miner's carbide helmet lamps and fuel.

The third was a rusted candy tin.

Cole picked it up with hands that trembled. Something rattled inside the tin. He stared at the tin while the match burned down to flesh. Swearing, he reached for another match.

"Cole?" Erin called. "Are you all right?"

He let out a long, ragged sigh, remembering to breathe. "I'm fine. Can you drag the rucksack and shotgun as far as the entrance?"

Erin retrieved the shotgun and rucksack. Its

weight surprised her. The thought of Cole carrying it through the killing heat while she walked unburdened made her mouth flatten. She scrambled over rock and brush until she could look inside the slit in the limestone hill.

Cole was lighting one candle from the flame of another. He held out a candle to her with hands that had a fine tremor of excitement rippling just beneath his control.

At first Erin didn't notice anything but the passageway itself, a cool darkness that absorbed light and gave it back from unexpected quarters where wet stone reflected flame. The sound of falling water came distantly. Nearby was a steady dripping, sliding, gliding rush of rivulets that was like a tremulous sigh expanding through the cave's endless night.

The limestone was alive with water.

"What's that?" Erin asked, noticing the candy tin for the first time.

"Something Abe left."

"Is it empty?"

"No."

"Is it diamonds?" she asked eagerly.

Cole pried the lid from the candy tin. "No. But in a cave, it's more valuable than diamonds. Matches."

There was a folded piece of paper inside, riding atop a nest of loose wooden matches and waterproof containers holding more matches. Gently Erin removed the paper and opened it. The faded, elegant lines of Abe's handwriting took shape in the flickering candle flames.

> *Granddaughter:*
> *If you got this far, you're more my blood than*

*Bridget's. She hated the Kimberley. Said it was fit only
for felons and black boys.*

*But it was me she loved, not my brother. It was my
child she bore.*

Mistress of lies.

Damn her.

Drink holy, child of my dreams.
Know where the black swan goes.
Touch God's own jewel box.
Feel the cold stone locks.

*Goodbye, grandchild of deceit, blood of my blood,
bone of my bone. Don't stay too long. You'll swallow
black and drown.*

"Looks like you were right," Erin said. "Bridget
was carrying Abe's child when she married my grandfather."

Cole grunted. "Queen of Lies." Working in darkness, Cole bent and started sorting through the rucksack, removing everything but the small flashlight.

" 'Damn their hot cries,' " Erin said quietly. She
folded the paper and put it back in the tin. "He wasn't
a forgiving sort, was he?"

"Would you have been?"

"So far, so good," Erin said with a shrug. She
removed a waterproof container of matches, checked
its contents, and stuck the container in the pocket of
her shorts.

"Does that mean you've forgiven Hans?" Cole
asked as he took the shotgun and propped it against a
rock near the entrance.

"It means I've forgiven myself for being stupid
and trusting the wrong person." She closed the tin

and set it on the floor. "I don't think old Abe got that far. I think he drank a river of beer rather than face himself."

Cole's pale eyes flashed in the candlelight as he turned toward her. "What about me? Have you forgiven me for not closing my hand and crushing Lai's throat?"

"You're asking the wrong person." Erin scooped up several fat candles and stuffed them in her other pocket.

"What does that mean?"

"You should be asking yourself, not me."

For the space of several breaths there was no sound in the cave but that of water seeping through cracks in ungiving stone.

Then Cole shrugged the rucksack into place and turned away. The sound of his footsteps grating over stone blended with the distant murmurings of water. He worked over the familiar carbide lamps, then tried lighting one. To his surprise, it worked. A clean flame burned steadily, multiplied many times by the mirrored dish. He closed the tempered glass shield, protecting the flame.

Cole snuffed out his candle and tried another lamp. It didn't work. Neither did the third. The fourth one did. He took off his bush hat, strapped one of the miner's helmet lamps on, and walked over to Erin with the other helmet light burning in his hand. She quickly learned not to look directly at the light he wore.

"Take off your hat," he said.

The helmet was too big. Cole adjusted the webbing of straps and tried again. This time the helmet stayed in place.

"Stay at least ten feet behind me," he said. "No point in both of us falling through the same hole."

Erin's eyes narrowed. She hesitated before blowing out her candle. "Are you trying to frighten me into staying here?"

"No. I'm simply telling you the truth. We could be walking on limestone that's as thick as a mountain or as thin as autumn ice," Cole said bluntly. "There's no way of knowing until the floor either gives way or it doesn't."

Uneasily, she looked down at the ground beneath her feet. It was uneven and felt as solid as the stone it was.

"Maybe we should hold off exploring until we can come back with ropes and things," she said.

All Cole said was, "Wait for me at the entrance. You'll be safe there."

"No."

"Then follow me and walk where I walk. If the floor holds me, it should hold you."

Erin blew out her candle and started after Cole, leaving ten feet between. The passageway quickly closed down until they were forced to duck-walk. To keep her mind off the darkness and the massive weight of limestone that was between herself and the sun, she thought about Crazy Abe Windsor.

"How old did you say Abe was?" Erin asked, breathing heavily from the strain of the unnatural walk.

"Old enough to be your grandfather, why?" Cole retorted.

"Maybe there's more to beer and raw croc liver than I thought."

He laughed, then swore when the ceiling came

down even more, forcing him onto his hands and knees. Water seeped from every surface, making the stone clammy and slick. Long horizontal stains ran the length of the smooth walls. As the floor slowly dropped, the stains rose.

"There's something wrong with this cave," Erin said after a minute. "It's little and narrow and ugly. Caves are big and grand and gorgeous."

"Only the ones you hear about. Most caves are small muddy wormholes that never get decorated."

"Why?"

A knob of limestone stabbed Cole's kneecap. He swore again and muttered, "Conditions aren't right."

"Why?"

"Because I said so," he retorted.

Erin took the hint and shut up. As she crawled, she turned her head slowly, playing the lamplight over the narrow passage, trying to reason with the cold fear that was whispering to her, telling her that Bridget's Hill was going to settle on her shoulders and crush her flat. She saw several shadows in rapid succession off to her right. When she turned her head, the light couldn't penetrate their depths. The openings were big enough to admit a man. From somewhere in their darkness came the sound of falling water.

Shivering, Erin pressed forward. Water dripped and gathered and twisted into thin streams, pulled by gravity through cracks in the limestone. The water was cool and almost secretive, sliding away into black crevices and vanishing or running in thin channels along the edges of the tunnel. The stain marks on the wall had disappeared. Puddles collected in small, shallow depressions in the uneven surface. The floor looked as if it had been scalloped by flowing water.

The passageway pitched down at an increasing angle. Erin thought about the alternate openings that had been revealed in the glare of their helmet lights.

"How do we know we're in the right wormhole?" she asked.

"Arrows."

The floor pitched downward more steeply. A limestone ripple gnawed on Erin's kneecap, sending pain lancing through her leg.

"How far have we come?" she asked.

"Fifty feet, max."

She hissed a word beneath her breath.

"That's not shit, honey. That's cave mud. Takes a hell of a long time to collect. In fact—don't move!"

Erin froze. "What's wrong?"

"No floor," Cole said succinctly.

He moved his head slowly, playing the light around the roughly circular shadow that had appeared in the floor a few feet ahead. Narrow streamers of water glittered and twisted from an invisible opening in the ceiling and disappeared through a hole in the stone floor of the passage. Stretching out on his stomach, he inched forward over the slippery, scalloped surface until he could point his light straight down the narrow vertical tunnel.

Water danced and spun away into blackness. About twenty feet below, the disturbed surface of a pool returned the light in random flashes. A more orderly pattern of light came back from a pile of what looked like tangle of flexible chain. Cole picked up one end of a heavy aluminum ladder and lowered it into the hole. Water splashed and slid over the thick metal surfaces. The top end was bolted into stone a foot from the lip of the hole.

Cole spent a long time shining his light on the huge bolts that anchored the top of the ladder to the mouth of the shaft. There was some sign of wear, but not much.

"Is it safe up ahead?" Erin called.

"I'm thinking about it."

Just when she was certain Cole wasn't going to say anything more, he began talking again.

"Abe was a good miner. The shoring in all the Dog mines is still sound."

"So?"

"So he probably bolted that ladder into place well enough to take my weight, not just his. Besides, those bolts could hold up the Brooklyn Bridge."

"There's a ladder?"

"After a fashion."

Cole grunted as he jackknifed his big body around and lowered his legs into the hole, supporting himself on his braced forearms. To Erin it looked as though he were trapped in stone up to his broad chest.

"Shine that light somewhere else than in my eyes," he said.

"Sorry," Erin said, hastily tilting her head down.

He found one of the aluminum rungs with his right foot. Slowly he shifted more and more of his weight from his arms to his foot, ignoring the water falling on his face and shoulders. His foot slipped, forcing him to catch himself on his forearms.

"Cole!"

"It's all right. The rungs are just wet."

This time he jammed his foot all the way to the rock wall. The metal took his weight without complaining or giving way. The bolts didn't even quiver. Deliberately he shifted his weight repeatedly, bouncing up and down, testing the bolts that held the ladder. Nothing moved.

"That old bastard wasn't entirely crazy," Cole muttered. He looked up at Erin. His light made the water falling over him sparkle and shimmer. "I'd just as soon you didn't try this, honey."

"Into each life a little rain must fall."

"I'd settle for a little, but it's the wrong damn season." Cole tilted his head and looked up at the black opening that was drooling thin streams of water over him. As he watched, he became certain that the volume of water falling had increased just in the few minutes he had been there. "This could be bad news."

Erin followed the direction of his lamp, adding her own light. Despite the fugitive glitter of reflected light, the thicker streams of water appeared more black than silver or transparent.

"Right now it's running enough to be annoying," Cole said. "In a few hours it could be a gusher. Depends on how much of the surface water it's a collection channel for, and how long it takes for the rain to get through the limestone above us into that channel."

"When Abe talked about swallowing black and drowning," Erin said, "I thought he meant claustrophobia."

"Doubt it. The deeper the mine, the better he liked it. Besides, he was a literal sort for all his metaphors. If he said drown, he meant drown. In water."

"Black water."

"No other kind in a cave." Cole eased his left foot onto the ladder. "We're under a high-water mark right now."

"What?"

"The horizontal stains on the wall on the way in. High-water mark."

"Very comforting."

"If you want comfort, go back to the entrance."

Erin took a slow breath and said nothing.

"The scallop marks we've been crawling over are proof that water ran through the tunnel at some time in the past and could run again in the future," Cole said.

"Could or will?"

"Once the limestone below gets saturated, the water level will rise and rise and rise until it overflows through places like the crevice we came through. If the level rises slowly, we'll be able to get out. Or if there are enough outlets lower down, we'll be safe."

"And if there aren't?"

"Then we'll find out how much black water we can drink before we drown."

35

◆

SLOWLY COLE SHIFTED HIS RIGHT HAND TO ONE of the flexible ladder's rungs. The stone was uneven enough to keep some of the rungs a few inches away from the wall of the shaft. Where the stone didn't slope, Abe had chipped out room for hands and toes.

"Cole? Are you sure we shouldn't wait?"

"I'm sure it's going to get a lot wetter down there before the dry begins. I'm damn sure the chances of my surviving the ladder are a hell of a lot better than our chances of surviving ConMin's attention for the next six months with only the *possibility* of a diamond mine as a weapon."

"Be careful," she whispered.

Cole grunted and shifted his left hand onto the ladder. For an instant the handle of his knife gleamed beneath the flap of the muddy leather sheath.

The ladder held. Cole let out a long, silent breath and began feeling for the next rung below. The ladder flexed and twisted slightly until it was brought up against rock. He found another rung and dropped more deeply into the hole. The rucksack scraped against rock and hung up in the narrow opening.

Cole cursed and went up a rung. He wriggled out of the rucksack and slung one of the straps over his right arm. Carefully he descended again. It was still a very tight fit. If he had put one more item in the rucksack it would have hung up.

"You're too big," Erin said. "Let me take it down."

"I was hoping you weren't coming down at all," Cole muttered, but he climbed back up again and handed the rucksack to her. "Put my extra shirt back on before you get any colder."

"How long will it take for the limestone to fill up?" she asked as she pulled out the shirt and put it on.

"I don't know. Maybe it hasn't filled this far for ten thousand years. Maybe it won't fill up at all." He glanced up and caught a flash of intense green from Erin's eyes. "But I'll tell you this, honey. I wouldn't plan on making more than one trip before the next dry."

Erin bit her lower lip as Cole went back down the ladder once more. She heard the scrape of stone against cloth and flesh, followed by Cole cursing the size of the very body whose strength had gotten them this far.

"Can you make it?" she asked.

"Barely." He grunted and swore again. "Abe was built more narrow in the shoulders than I am."

Cole vanished by inches into the hole. Water hissed when it hit the glass shielding the flame in his helmet.

"Have you ever used a flexible ladder before?" he

asked just before he disappeared completely below the stone lip.

"Every time I went from a cargo ship to a Zodiac. Usually in a force-five gale."

"After that, this will be a piece of cake. The wall slopes away enough so that you don't bang your hands much, but not enough to let you twist in the breeze."

When Cole called up from the bottom, Erin put on the rucksack, took a deep breath, and reminded herself that she had done the same thing before under worse circumstances.

But not in the dark.

Silently Cole watched Erin descend the ladder while water dripped and slid and splashed all around. The rivulets had become trickles as thick as his finger. They fell with increasing force. At the bottom of the ladder, the water was an ankle-deep pool. There was just enough space for two people to stand close to one another. A nearly circular passageway led off at an angle. The tunnel was smooth-sided and narrow.

"Watch it," Cole said, catching Erin when her foot searched for and didn't find a final rung. "The shaft is two feet longer than the ladder."

Her breath came in as cool water lapped above her ankles. "I hope we aren't going much lower."

"So do I."

Cole looked down and ran his helmet light over every bit of floor that was revealed. In a spot that would have been the base of a waterfall during the wet, the limestone floor had been eaten away, making an irregular bowl. Small hunks of water-rounded stone lined the bowl.

"Can you go back up the ladder a few feet?" Cole asked.

Erin climbed back up several rungs. "Is this far
enough?"

"One more."

Ignoring the cool shower of water, Cole sat on his
heels in the space Erin had vacated and began scooping out handfuls of stones, seeking the bottom of the
basin. Something in the eighth handful winked and
shimmered in the light with a life of its own.

"Bingo," Cole breathed.

"What?"

Without answering he stood up and held out his
hand so that it caught the full flood of his helmet light.
Between his thumb and forefinger was a rounded crystal the size of a small marble.

"Diamond?" Erin asked, hardly able to believe.

"As ever was. Hang onto it. I'll see if Abe missed
any more."

"Missed?"

"This is the first pothole I've seen. Abe must have
worked it over more than once on the way into the
cave."

The diamond felt cool on Erin's palm. Her heart
beat in double time as adrenaline raced through her
body. She closed her hand around the crystal until her
fingers ached. Below her came the sound of rocks rolling together as Cole searched through debris down to
the stony bottom of the basin itself. There was a long
crack in the bottom where water flowed out. He
probed the crack but found it too narrow for his fingers.

"Oh, well. If any diamonds are in that crack,
they're not all that big."

"How can you be so calm?" she demanded.

He laughed. "Calm? Honey, my hands are shaking almost as much as the first time I made love to you."

Erin looked startled, then hid a smile.

Cole stood and absently wiped his hands on his soaked khaki shorts. "Let's not waste any more time here."

"Waste? Cole, we just found a diamond!"

His only answer was, "Watch that last step."

He dropped to his hands and knees and crawled into the opening that began at a right angle to the bottom of the shaft they had just descended. The floor of the tube hadn't been pummeled by falling water, so it wasn't as deeply eroded as the plunge pool had been. The surrounding limestone was damp but not under water. The floor was scalloped.

Cole probed the scallops at random and found one small diamond. He tucked it beneath his tongue and continued on, not bothering to probe any more of the shallow scallops. Grimacing at the discomfort, he crawled deeper and deeper into the limestone formation.

Gradually Cole realized that the tube was descending. Water seeped from ceilings and walls and collected into steady trickles. The trickles gathered in shallow channels on either side of the tunnel floor or found small crevices and disappeared deeper into the limestone. He wondered how high the water table was in this area of the Kimberley, and how long it would take to saturate the ancient, partially dissolved reef until the tunnel they were crawling through became full of water.

"The ceiling looks scalloped, too" Erin said. "Does that mean this tunnel spends a lot of time full of water?"

Cole grunted.

From ahead came the sound of rushing water. Cole slowed down and began searching the flickering shadows ahead very carefully, seeking any openings in the floor.

Overhead, the ceiling shed water like a sieve from a handful of uneven holes. The tunnel widened from side to side. The floor became very uneven, potholed from the constant, forceful pummeling of waterfalls during the height of the wet. Some of the potholes were as big as bathtubs. Others were no bigger than a fist. Small mounds of stony debris had been dug out of potholes and shoved out of the way against the sides of the tunnel.

Water showered down on Cole and Erin, drenching them as they crawled forward. The temperature of the water had gone from cool to chilly. Erin began shivering as soon as she stopped to probe a small pothole, but she persisted. Even her cold hands could tell the difference in texture between fragments of limestone and the sleek texture of a water-rounded diamond.

"I found one!" she called out.

"Good for you. Put it under your tongue and keep crawling."

"But I found—"

"Abe's tailings," Cole interrupted. "See the debris shoved aside? He's already been over these potholes."

"Then why did I find a diamond?"

"Offhand, I'd guess he found something up ahead that made these potholes look like a waste of time."

While Cole talked, he kept crawling toward the

throaty, increasing sound of thunder that came from up ahead. Excitement sleeted through him, taking away the pain of cuts and bruises gained from crawling over stone. The ceiling rose until he could duck-walk and then walk almost normally. Water lapped around his feet. He ignored it as he flexed muscles that had cramped. When Erin's lamp appeared a few feet behind him, he turned and pulled her to her feet. She groaned with relief.

"This is more my idea of a cave," Erin said, shining her light around. "A little cramped from top to bottom, but lots of space otherwise. Lots of puddles, too."

Cole spat out his diamond and put it into one of the pockets of the rucksack she carried. Erin handed over her own diamond and watched it disappear. To her surprise, Cole made no move to press farther into the cave's wide horizontal opening. He simply stood and ran his lamp over everything within reach of the cone of light, memorizing his location within the larger opening. Then he turned and scanned the tunnel they had just emerged from.

A large, rough #1 had been gouged into the limestone above the tunnel. As Cole turned away, a #2 appeared just at the limits of his helmet light.

"See any more marked openings?" he asked.

Erin turned in the opposite direction and looked. All she noticed was a distinct clammy breeze.

"No more numbers, but there's a lot of air moving."

"Probably because there's a lot of water coming in and pushing the air out of the way."

"What?"

"Listen," Cole said. "That's not thunder. Somewhere up ahead there's at least one cascade or waterfall pouring from the ceiling down to whatever passes for the floor around here."

Shivering, Erin stood and listened.

"You're cold," he said.

"I've been a lot colder and survived just fine."

He hesitated, then shrugged. "We'd better get going. I don't know how much longer we have down here."

"Which way?"

Cole pointed to the wall. "See that arrow? We go in the opposite direction."

"Why?"

"In a cave or a mine, all arrows point to the way *out*."

Erin walked closer to the arrow and made a sound of surprise. "It looks like it was just made."

"A decade or two isn't much time when it comes to rocks."

Cole turned and began walking against the arrow. After thirty feet it became obvious that somewhere ahead water was pouring in faster than it could drain out. A thin puddle appeared on the floor. Within twenty feet, the water was over Cole's shoes.

"Don't trust the footing," he said. "There could be potholes underneath this puddle deep enough to drown in." He stopped and turned toward Erin. "You can swim, can't you?"

"Yes, but I'd rather not. This water isn't getting any warmer."

"Do you want—"

"No," she said, cutting across his words. "I don't want to go back. I want to see Abe's jewel box."

"We may be walking over it right now."

Instantly Erin's light flashed down to the water lapping over her feet. "Do you really think so?"

"Maybe, but not likely. I don't see any piles of rubble. Mining, even placer mining, is a messy process."

Accompanied by the steadily increasing thunder of distant water, Erin and Cole splashed through the broad, shallow puddle. He was careful to stay within sight of the wall and its arrows until the #2 opening appeared. The prospect of crawling through it wasn't inviting. The opening was small. The water was at least six inches deep and flowing with a pronounced current.

"Well?" she asked as she came to stand beside Cole.

"It's flowing away from us."

"So?"

He shrugged. "So I expected it to be flowing toward the sound of falling water, which is behind us."

With that he dropped on his hands and knees and began to crawl, cursing steadily. Erin followed. A few minutes later she understood why Cole was swearing so savagely. The ceiling came to within a foot of the floor and the sides of the tube closed in until his shoulders scraped both sides.

"Can you make it through?" she called.

His only answer was a grunt, followed by splashing and another round of curses as the tunnel took a hard bend to the left. He jackknifed through it and found himself in easier going. The ceiling lifted again. Soon he was standing upright, but sideways, for the solution channel was so narrow that his shoulders wouldn't fit any other way.

The sound of falling water filled the narrow

space, but only a few trickles showed in the lantern light. Twelve feet farther down the channel, another ladder appeared. It led up through another long narrow shaft that had been widened at one point by rushing water. The ladder was wet with runoff.

"Wait until I'm up top before you start climbing," Cole said.

Without hesitation he stepped onto the first gleaming metal rung. The opening of the crack was so narrow there was no worry about the ladder twisting and banging him against stone. Water poured over an unseen lip above, drenching the ladder with an insistent shower.

Fourteen rungs later, Cole's helmet light picked up another opening in the slowly dissolving limestone. He rolled out of the hole and called down to Erin.

"Come on up."

Erin's helmet light went out halfway up. Instantly Cole shone his own light over the rim. When her shoulders and the rucksack poked above the hole, he lifted her free, removed her helmet, and relighted the flame. She gave a broken sigh of relief.

"I was afraid it wasn't going to work again," Erin admitted in a shaky voice.

"That might happen, honey. Too damn much water." Cole hesitated. "We should go back."

"We have plenty of matches and candles, if it comes to that."

For a long moment Cole looked at Erin. Her face was drawn into taut lines. She was a woman who loved light, who had made it the core of her professional life. Being in the cave's total absence of light, even for a few seconds, had shaken her.

"You don't like it down here, do you?" he asked.

"I liked finding that diamond. The rest of it I can put up with for a while longer."

His grin flashed in the sidelight from her lamp. "Fifteen more minutes. If we don't find anything by then, we'll head back. It's too damn dangerous for you."

"But not for you?"

"I know the risks. You don't."

"So how risky is it?"

"If we live, I'll dream about this and wake up sweating," he said bluntly. "We're damn fools for being down here."

"Abe survived."

"God watches over fools and drunks."

"So we're half safe," she retorted.

Cole laughed. "Close your eyes, honey."

"Why?" she asked even as she closed them.

"So my light won't blind you."

Erin felt the smooth warmth of Cole's lips, the rough brush of beard stubble, and the heat of his tongue as the kiss deepened suddenly, fiercely. She felt the rucksack being stripped away as she was pulled off her feet and held hard and close. Almost as soon as it began, the kiss ended, leaving her shivering with more than the chill of limestone and water. A moment later he was gently stuffing her into his khaki shirt and buttoning it up, ignoring her protests at the third layer of clothing.

"I'll just rip it to pieces in the next narrow passage," Cole said calmly.

"You'll freeze without it." But she picked up the rucksack.

"I have twice your mass. I retain heat much better than you do. Ask any biologist."

Before Erin could argue, Cole turned and began making his way along another passage. This one was tall and so narrow that a crabwise progression was all that was possible. This channel, too, showed signs of having been filled with water at some time in the past. It also had arrows gouged in its sides at every point where new openings occurred.

The sound of running water came from everywhere around, making Erin feel as though she were pushing an air bubble through a maze of waterfalls and cascades. She was curious about how far down they had come into the limestone mass but decided against asking. She really didn't want to know the exact dimensions of the massive weight of limestone pressing down overhead. It was difficult enough to visualize their three-dimensional progress as they twisted and turned, crawling up and down and sideways to the sound of running water. If it hadn't been for the arrows, she quickly would have been disoriented and lost.

As Cole pushed around a corner, he felt the pressure of limestone walls fall away. He walked three steps and turned slowly in his tracks, discovering everything within reach of his helmet light.

It was the biggest space they had yet discovered. From all around him came the sound of water rushing and falling and cascading through unseen solution channels in the limestone. The ceiling was beyond the reach of his light. So was every wall but the one behind him. Air moved faintly, stirred by countless currents of water pouring into the space that had been dissolved by a thousand, thousand seasons of rain.

"Four minutes. No more," Cole said, looking at his watch.

Erin was too enthralled to argue. The unmistakable sensation of space around her was both welcome and eerie, for the opening was alive with the myriad voices of water, whispering, murmuring, rushing, pouring, pounding, tumbling, seeping, dripping, sliding: water everywhere she looked, a world seething with silver drops and dense blackness. A huge, shallow pool expanded into the dark as far as her helmet light could reach. Hidden currents caused streaks of light to twist over the water's surface like a silver aurora.

For the first time since Erin had entered the limestone maze she wished for her camera. Since her first brush with the long arctic night, she had encountered nothing quite so alien yet so beautiful as this lake.

The roving cone of her light fell on mounds of water-rounded chunks of limestone. The rubble piles poked up through the sheet of water that stretched away into the darkness. She grabbed Cole's forearm.

"Look!"

His helmet light cut a swath through the darkness until he saw more mounds rising from the dark lake. He walked to the edge of the lake. It quivered at his feet as though alive, responding to unseen currents of air and water. The lake was absolutely clear, having rid itself of surface grit on the long trip down through the limestone reef. If the lake hadn't caught the light with each disturbance of air or water, it would have been nearly invisible.

Slowly Cole turned, scanning the wall behind him, memorizing the location of the passage. Abe hadn't numbered the tunnel. Nor were any of the other cracks and holes he could see numbered.

"I don't see any arrows," Erin said.

Cole didn't answer. He walked to the edge of the trembling water, then began wading along the shoreline, searching for some sign that Abe had been there before them.

"Here. Underneath the water," Cole said after a minute.

He had to repeat the words more loudly, because the throaty roar of water had consumed the silence. Erin waded toward him until she saw the arrow mark gouged out of the limestone floor.

"Does that mean it was dry when Abe was here?"

"Probably," Cole said. "He wasn't much on water. Hated it, as a matter of fact. Couldn't swim."

"It must have been awful for him to explore the cave."

"Not in the dry. The water that's coming down now is new."

Erin's breath came in and stayed until she forced herself to breathe out. She thought of the torrential rains of the wet and ten square miles of surface limestone covered one inch deep, and all those drops gathering together into rivulets and tiny streams, which flowed into crevices that also joined together, creating runoff channels that ate down and down into stone, dissolving tunnels and shafts and small rooms, water lured by gravity farther and farther down; and each solution channel was the narrow end of a funnel whose mouth could be half a mile square, or a mile, or more.

Tons upon tons of water sliding down and down and down. When runoff filled up all the holes, there would be nothing left but darkness and water and stone.

Don't stay too long. You'll drink black water and drown.

With an effort Erin wrenched her thoughts away from the massive weight of stone and water balanced over her head. Deliberately she waded after Cole, keeping her head down and watching the silver patterns of water glittering around her feet. Overhead, long ribbons of water gushed out of darkness into the artificial light, creating random showers as though hidden faucets had been turned on.

"There are potholes among the rubble mounds," Cole said. "Channels, too. At one time this whole chamber had powerful currents of water moving through it."

"During the last wet?"

Cole didn't answer.

Grimly she concentrated on the water that was now halfway up her ankles. There was a definite sluggish current leading into the darkness they hadn't yet explored. While Cole knelt in the water and probed a small pothole, she looked for something to distract her from the ominous weight of darkness and the increasing thunder of water.

The cone of her light probed in the water for a pothole. A circular shadow caught her attention. At first she thought it was simply another water-rounded stone. Then she realized that it was too perfectly circular, and there were others like it, all circular, all perfect. She waded farther, then made a startled sound as she stumbled into a pothole whose depth had been concealed by the clarity of the water. She put her hands out to break her fall. Her fingers closed over a candy tin.

The pothole was full of them.

"Erin?" Cole asked, looking up from a handful of rubble he had gathered. "Are you all right?"

She tried to answer but couldn't speak. She grabbed a tin in each hand and held them up to meet the cone of light sweeping toward her as Cole turned. Water showered down her arms, reflecting light in countless glittering points of white and green and yellow.

Then Erin realized that it was stones, not water, cascading from the rusted tins. She was standing knee deep in God's own jewel box, and diamonds were pouring from her hands.

36

◆

"I'LL TIE IT TO MY ANKLE AND DRAG IT UP AFTER me," Cole said loudly.

The ladder closest to the surface was now buried in a cascade of water that was twice as heavy as it had been when they first descended its slippery rungs.

"Don't be silly," Erin said, shifting her shoulders beneath the rucksack's nylon webbing straps. "That ladder is going to be tough enough to keep your balance on without having the rucksack pull a foot out from under you. Besides, I've carried packs that weighed at least twice as much as this one. It can't be more than twenty pounds."

Cole gave her a worried look. She was shaking from the cold and from the knowledge that the lowest crawl space they had negotiated was more than half full of water and rising quickly. If they had spent another half hour in the jewel box, they wouldn't have gotten out until the water level dropped again. If ever.

"I'll go first," Cole said. "If your lamp goes out again, I'll be able to light the way for you. But don't wait long. You could drown climbing up that narrow shaft. If you get hung up, shrug your shoulders. If that doesn't work, breathe out and shrug again. If that doesn't work, back up, leave the rucksack at the bottom, and I'll bring it up. Understand me?"

Erin nodded, sending her light bobbing.

Turning his face to the side so that he could breathe beneath the pouring water, Cole went up the first rungs of the ladder. The runoff this close to the surface was cloudy and felt almost warm by comparison to the water down below. Ignoring the scrape of stone over bare skin, he went up the ladder on a single breath and lifted himself out onto the limestone floor. He jackknifed around and looked back into the hole.

"Up!" he called.

Taking a deep breath, Erin turned her head aside and fought up the ladder as water pounded over her, trying to drive her back down into the cave. Her cold hands locked around metal rungs, holding her against the water. The ladder shivered and rattled from the force of the runoff. She climbed two more rungs, driving herself upward into the narrowest part of the shaft. When she tried to go up one more rung, she found herself caught. She reached behind her back, shoving candy tins away from whatever obstruction had caught the rucksack.

Beneath Erin's fist, a rusted tin crumpled. Diamonds poured down into the bottom of the rucksack. She lunged upward, only to be brought up short once more. She tried to struggle out of the straps, but couldn't. Water beat down on her, making it almost impossible to breathe.

Fear welled up in Erin like black water from the cave below. Around her the shaft was filling with water, for her body and the pack were acting like a cork, preventing most of the runoff from draining. If she didn't move, she would drown.

She bucked against the sack, using the strength of her legs to drive her body back against the hard stone. More tins gave way, their rusted seams no match for her frightened struggles. It wasn't enough to free her.

Shrug.

Cole's advice came back to Erin as if he stood at her side. She drew her shoulders forward and arched her body, trying to slip past the obstruction. When that didn't work she forced herself to relax and let all the air out of her lungs. Another tin shifted, but it wasn't enough to free her. She rolled to one side. Nothing. She rolled the other way.

The contents of the pack shifted. Aching for air yet afraid to breathe, she rolled farther and felt herself suddenly freed. She went up several rungs in a tumbling rush before Cole's hands slipped beneath her arms and pulled her up and over the lip. For a few moments she lay half in, half out of the hole, gasping for air.

"Are you all right?" Cole asked.

She nodded. No light moved at the gesture, for her lamp had gone out again. He tried to light it, couldn't, and took off his own.

"Here," he said, switching helmets with her. "It's just a short way to the entrance."

The passage was too small for Erin to squeeze past Cole. He jackknifed again, turned around, and crawled until he could duck-walk, using the light cast from Erin's helmet to pick his way through the narrow cleft. His shadow loomed hugely ahead of him as it slid over and around the rough limestone, flickering with every motion he made.

It was his sliding, uncertain shadow that saved his life, confusing Jason Street. The blow that landed on the back of Cole's skull hit with stunning rather than crushing force. He had just enough consciousness remaining to fall bonelessly, sprawling with his left hand underneath his body, concealing the wrist sheath he wore.

"Cole?" Erin called, scrambling forward as she saw him fall. "What's wrong?"

"No worries, Miss Windsor. You're safe now. Did you find Abe's mine?"

The sudden white arc of an electric lantern blinded Erin just as a man's hand closed around her arm.

"Let go of me! Cole's hurt!"

"Don't worry about that bastard. He was hired to kill you."

"You're crazy!"

"Am I? Read this, luv. It's from your father."

Erin glanced at the bright yellow plastic being held out to her. She was shaking so much from cold and fear she could barely breathe.

"I won't look at anything until I help Cole."

Street smiled reassuringly despite his urgent need to know about Abe's mine. If the mine hadn't been found, he would need Erin's cooperation to find it. She had proved that she was better at unraveling Abe's secrets than anyone else.

"Check on Blackburn if you have to," Street said, letting go of Erin, "but you'll feel like a bloody fool after you read your father's letter."

Without looking at the man who was no more

than a dark presence looming behind blinding light, Erin hurried forward and knelt at Cole's side. A quick check told her that he was breathing regularly. Blood was welling slowly from a bruise at the base of his skull.

Relief raced through Erin, making her almost weak. She stroked Cole's forehead lightly, pushing wet hair away from his face. A motion just behind her made her look around. She saw the metal gleam of a pistol. The muzzle was trained on Cole.

"Well, Miss Windsor. How is he?"

"Out cold. Who the hell are you?"

"Jason Street. Didn't your father mention me to you?"

"No."

"Read this, luv. I'm on your side."

Erin stood and looked at the packet Street was holding out. From the corner of her eye she noticed that the pistol muzzle stayed pointed at Cole rather than following her movements. She shrugged out of the rucksack and sat down on it, ignoring the crunch and grind of ruined candy tins.

Reluctantly she looked at the packet Street was holding out to her. She really didn't want to face whatever was inside. She didn't want to know that once more she had been just another pawn in another international game played out in bed as well as in smoke-filled rooms.

At least this time no one was cutting her up with a knife. Yet.

Saying nothing, Erin held out her hand. Street smiled encouragement and dropped the packet on her palm.

"That's it, luv. Read it. You're safe now."

She undid the string and folded back the bright yellow plastic to reveal a thin pouch. It contained an envelope with the Central Intelligence Agency logo on it and her name scrawled across the front in her father's bold, masculine handwriting. Futilely she wiped her muddy hands on her shorts before she opened the sealed envelope. It took several tries for her to extract the heavy folded sheet of ivory paper. The stationery was familiar, for it had come from her father's desk in Washington. The letter was handwritten and brief:

> *Erin—*
> *I'm sorry, baby. I was a fool to let you go with Cole Blackburn. I've discovered that Blackburn is owned by the Chen family, the most powerful, ruthless, and ambitious tong in Southeast Asia.*
> *The man who brings this to you, Jason Street, can be trusted. He works for the Australian counterpart of the agency. Do what he says. Above all, do not trust Blackburn. He is your assassin, not your bodyguard.*
> *Be careful. I love you.*

The letter was signed as her father always did in his letters to her, with an aggressive, oversized *D* for *Dad*.

Erin closed her eyes and felt cold all the way to the center of her bones. When she looked at Street, he was watching her, but the muzzle of the gun was still aimed at Cole. Cole hadn't moved. He still lay on his stomach with one arm folded underneath his chest. His face was turned away from her.

She turned to Jason Street. "How did you find me?"

"It wasn't easy. The Chinamen Blackburn works

for had you covered like a bleeding blanket. If the black boy following you hadn't been broadcasting in the clear, I'd still be looking. As it was, I just homed in on the RDF."

"Chinamen?"

"The Chen family, luv. Blackburn has been in partnership with Chen Wing for years."

"Are you the one who gave that information to my father?"

"Is that what the letter said?" Street countered.

"How did you get the letter?" Erin asked.

"I work for the Australian government, although you won't find me on any civil service payroll form," Street said with growing impatience. "Sort of like your father in that. He and I do the same kind of work. That's why I'm here."

"Mistakes are made in your kind of work, Mr. Street. I believe my father made one. Cole Blackburn isn't my assassin."

"Like bloody hell," Street said coldly. "Just because Blackburn has been in your pants doesn't mean he won't kill you. Chen Lai is his number-one woman. He's been making jig-a-jig with Lai since you were in pigtails. He's just using you until you give him the clues to Abe's mine. Then you'll be deader than tinned fish and the mine will belong to the Chen family. But I'm here to see that doesn't happen. Now, did you find that bleeding mine?"

"I'm—I'm not sure."

"What do you mean?" Street demanded.

Erin stood up quickly, bringing the rucksack with her. Street's eyes flashed reflected light as he followed her movements, but the muzzle of his gun remained

trained on the man who lay less than two feet away.
Erin forced herself to go closer.

"I'm no geologist," she said as she jerked at the
buckles and ties on the rucksack, opening it up.
"Here. See for yourself."

With that, Erin stepped past Street and turned
the rucksack on end, spilling a sparkling cascade of
rough stones into the hard white light of the electric
lantern.

"Sweet Jesus and all the saints in heaven!"

For an instant the gun muzzle moved aside from
its target as Street gave the shiny stones his complete
attention. In that instant Cole came off the ground in a
lunge that ended only when he rammed the knife
blade up underneath Street's ribcage and into his
heart.

Cole caught Street's pistol before it could drop,
jerked the knife out, and let Street slump face first
across the dancing, rolling diamonds. Automatically
Cole sheathed the bloody blade and put the safety on
the pistol before he reached for the electric lantern.

Swallowing against the bile rising in her throat,
Erin said hoarsely, "Is he dead?"

"Pick up the diamonds."

The words were thick, almost slurred. Cole
grunted as he dragged Street aside and left him face
down in dense shadow. Moving with uncharacteristic
hesitation, as though he didn't completely trust his
own body, Cole went back to Erin. He held out the
pistol butt first.

"Can you use this?"

"Dad made sure I could shoot anything I could
get my hands on," Erin said numbly, taking the gun.

"Smart man."

Cole's words sounded to Erin as though they came from a distance. Vaguely she realized she was gripped by a combination of shock and cold, hunger and exhaustion. She was at the end of her strength and all she had to trust was someone who had just killed Jason Street in front of her eyes.

Street, who had been sent by her father to protect her from Cole Blackburn.

"So you believed him after all," Cole said harshly. "You're a fool, Erin Shane Windsor. I've killed men, but I'm not a hired assassin."

At first she didn't understand. Then she saw that the pistol in her hands was pointed directly at Cole . . . and she had taken the safety off. She let out a broken breath and lowered the gun.

"You're right," she said bleakly. "If you had been hired to kill me after the mine was found, I'd be face down in a black lake right now."

Cole's eyes glittered with fury. "Such carefully measured trust—from the head, not the heart."

"That's the way *you* trust," Erin said in a harsh voice. "It's the way my father trusts. It's the way the whole world trusts. I'm a slow learner, but I do learn eventually. And I'm damned tired of being screwed by men on their way to more important things!"

Cole turned his back on Erin. "If you want the bloody diamonds, pick them up and come to the entrance. I'm going to see if there are any more surprises waiting outside."

Without a word Erin put on the safety and shoved the pistol into the rucksack. Then she knelt and began scooping handfuls of diamonds from the clammy limestone floor. The stones made secret, almost musical sounds as they clicked over one another and the cold steel of the pistol.

Erin ignored the diamonds that had rolled into the darkness where Street's body lay. There wasn't enough money in all of Abe's mines to make her retrieve those diamonds. Street was welcome to them. He certainly had paid enough for them.

Before Erin was finished, Cole came back, carrying the shotgun. "Leave the rest. We're getting out of here before anyone else comes."

"I don't think I can walk very far," Erin said matter-of-factly.

"Neither can I. Street was flying the station helicopter." As Cole turned away he stumbled slightly, caught himself, and kept walking. "Move it, Erin. I've already loaded everything that matters into the chopper."

"Where are we going?"

"Windsor station. Now that Street's dead, it should be safe. In any case, it's the last place anyone will expect to find us."

Drawing together what was left of her strength, Erin picked up the rucksack and followed Cole out of the cave. For the first few minutes the steamy heat felt like a foretaste of heaven. By the time she had walked to the helicopter, she was back in hell, sweating. Cole wasn't. When he handed her into the chopper, his skin felt distinctly cool.

They had been in the air less than ten minutes before Erin realized that Cole was fighting not to lose consciousness.

37

◆

Rain fell in sheets and torrents, pouring over the bubble canopy of the helicopter, cutting visibility to a few hundred yards. Erin read the instruments for Cole as he pointed to them. Her voice was flat, as numb as her mind. She should have been terrified but she was simply too worn out to care.

She knew it must be much worse for Cole. She sensed a great weariness in him. His coordination and his vision were erratic. He was sweating but his skin was cold. Time after time the helicopter sagged to one side or the other in gusts of wind and each time Cole reacted more slowly to correct their course. Concussion had sapped Cole's strength. He was operating on nerve and reflex alone, and all around them a storm's dying fury gripped the world.

"We should set down," Erin said.

"Too far to walk. We wouldn't make it."

She didn't argue. It was the truth. She had barely had the strength to drag herself and the rucksack to the chopper.

"You have a concussion," she said.

"No shit. Read the compass."

Numbly Erin focused on the compass.

A lightning bolt sizzled from cloud to earth, making the earphones Erin and Cole wore crackle painfully. He flinched at the sound and turned the volume down on the radio.

They flew out of the squall as suddenly as they had flown into it. Within minutes wind had torn holes in the black line of clouds. Sun hammered through the rents with stunning force, pulling great sheets of steam from the drenched land. Off to the left a tin roof gleamed in watery brilliance beneath the gloom of a storm cell that still had enough power to trail thick sheets of rain from its wild clouds.

"Look," Erin said, touching Cole's arm and pointing to the left. "Isn't that the station?"

"Hallelujah."

The word was slurred. Cole's face was drawn in harsh lines of effort as he corrected the helicopter's course. They flew into the trailing edge of the squall. The helicopter bucked and quivered like an unruly horse. He swore at the controls and at the reflexes that simply wouldn't respond as quickly as they should. The chopper slewed through the rain and wind until the lights of Windsor station were a few hundred feet below them.

"Look for strange vehicles," Cole ordered.

He banked the helicopter and flew in a wide, ragged circle around the perimeter of the station buildings. Erin looked through veils of rain at the ground. Several lanterns glowed inside the large tent that had been erected as a bunkhouse for the Chinese men, but no one was out in the yard. Obviously the men had settled in to wait out the storm.

A pale flash caught her attention. "There's a white four-wheel-drive vehicle parked in back of the house."

"Street's. Any others?"

"No."

Cole let out a sigh that was almost a groan. "Good."

As he circled to the front of station house, the door opened and a small figure stepped out.

"It's Lai," Erin said.

"Alone?"

"As far as I can see, yes."

Lai stepped out of the shelter of the awning and looked up into the sky, shielding her eyes against the falling rain.

Cole shook his head sharply, then winced. "Shotgun. Get it."

Erin leaned over and pulled the shotgun from behind his seat.

"Is it ready to fire?" he asked.

She checked the gun, took off the safety, and said, "Yes."

"Put it across my lap. And keep the pistol in that rucksack handy. If there's a trap down there, no one will be expecting you to be armed."

Without a word Erin lifted the rucksack onto her lap, dug the pistol from beneath diamonds, and slipped off the safety. All she would have to do is reach in the rucksack and grab.

Cole wheeled the helicopter and dropped into the muddy yard in front of the station. The landing was hard. One of the skids dug four inches into the red

muck. The other slapped down a second later and vanished beneath mud. Cole shut down the engine, let the
rotor free-wheel, and slumped forward. Erin scrambled out while the blades were still slicing overhead
and went around to the other door to help Cole.

"Get out," she said, tugging at his arm. "You
can't stay here."

He didn't move.

"Get out!" Erin said urgently. "I can't carry you
to the house. Come on, Cole. Help me!"

Slowly Cole's head came up. He dragged himself
out of the helicopter, shotgun in hand. Clutching the
rucksack, Erin steered him through the mud to the
station house where Lai waited.

"I'm so glad Mr. Street found you," Lai said huskily, watching Cole with luminous black eyes. "We
were very worried. Wing has been beside himself."
She looked beyond Erin and Cole. "Where is Mr.
Street?"

"Dead," Erin said bluntly.

"Dead? I don't understand."

"Street tried to kill Cole. He missed. Cole
didn't."

Lai's breath came in with a soft, ripping sound.

Erin pushed past Lai and guided Cole into the
house. "Cole's hurt. Get some blankets, a first-aid kit,
and ice for the swelling." She looked at Lai, who was
standing as though bolted to the floor. "Move!"

"But first," Cole said thickly, "call Uncle Li and
tell him to send in reinforcements. We found the
mine."

For a moment longer Lai stared at Cole. He was
swaying slightly on his feet, but his eyes were focused
and his finger was on the trigger of the shotgun he

carried. When Erin steered him toward the couch he moved with a kind of ruined grace that spoke of willpower and muscle slowly losing control over injury and fatigue.

Lai turned and ran toward the back of the station house as Erin eased Cole down on the center of the couch. With a muttered curse, he slumped back and fought against closing his eyes. After a moment he pulled the shotgun across his lap. Erin set the rucksack at one end of the couch. As she knelt next to Cole to check his injury, her knee knocked against the butt of the shotgun.

"You've got a bruise half the size of my fist," Erin said.

He grunted.

"No more bleeding," she continued. "The swelling isn't any worse. Good thing you have such strong muscles in your neck. Otherwise, I've got a feeling we'd still be in the cave."

"Stone dead."

"How do you feel?" she asked.

"It comes and goes."

"It?"

"Nausea, double vision, dizziness."

Erin shifted again. Her knee hit the shotgun. "I'll take that," she said, reaching for the shotgun. "We're safe."

"Not quite, Miss Windsor," Lai said. "But you soon will be. Move away from Cole."

Startled, Erin looked up and saw an automatic pistol held in Lai's left hand. The muzzle was pointed directly at Cole's heart. Nothing about Lai suggested that she wasn't willing to pull the trigger. In her right hand was a small battery-operated tape player.

"Move beyond his reach," Lai said softly. "Even wounded, he is still very dangerous."

Erin retreated down the couch toward the rucksack.

"Put the shotgun on the floor and shove it away with your foot," Lai said to Cole. "Move slowly or you will force me to kill you."

In slow motion Cole bent over, set the shotgun on the floor, and shoved it away with his foot. Black eyes and the muzzle of the gun followed him every inch of the way. Lai's attention was so fixed on Cole that she didn't notice Erin's hand coming out of the rucksack.

"Put down the gun, Lai," Erin said. "I'm too tired to care if I kill you."

From the corner of her eye, Lai saw the gun in Erin's hands.

"Don't be foolish," Lai said quickly. "It is your life I'm trying to save!"

"I'm damn tired of being called a fool—and being taken for one. If Cole wanted me dead, he could have killed me a hundred times over by now."

"You don't understand what is at stake." Lai spoke in a calm, low voice, and her attention never wavered from the man on the couch. She knew very well his strength, coordination, and intelligence. Obviously Street had underestimated Cole. Lai never would.

"Street was playing the Chen family against Con-Min," Lai continued, "hoping to gain control of the mine for Australia. The Australian government wouldn't have ordered your death, Miss Windsor, but if you and Cole died in the bush and Street came to his superiors with the coordinates of the mine, the government would have registered the mine, declared you

dead of accident—or by Cole's hand—and ridden out
the storm of protest from the CIA."

"I'm alive," Erin said, "and planning to stay that
way. Put down the gun, Lai."

"If I do, Cole will kill you. Listen to me, Erin.
Your life depends on it. Cole has a forged gambling
note from Abelard Windsor giving him half of the
Sleeping Dog Mines."

"How do you know?"

"I oversaw the forgery," Lai said simply. "Now
Cole controls half of the mine outright, plus half of
your half. Don't you, Cole?"

"Whatever you say," he said. "You're the one
with the gun."

Erin looked quickly at Cole. He was watching Lai
with predatory attention, waiting for the least flicker
of distraction on her part.

"Fascinating," Erin said, "but Cole never said
one word to me about any gambling note."

Lai's mouth tightened. "He didn't have to use the
note. He had a much better lever against you: his
body. He is a skilled, powerful lover and you are a
woman of little experience. A very easy conquest. He
has probably asked you to marry him already. If not,
he soon would. And when you died a few months later
—and you would die—Cole would have control of the
mine in a way no man or government could question.
You don't want to believe me," Lai said quickly, "but
you will. Listen carefully, Erin Windsor. Your life depends on it."

"Cole?" Erin asked.

"Do as she says. You'll hear it all sooner or later.
Divide and conquer. The oldest game of all. But what-

ever you do, Erin, keep pointing that gun at Lai. The second you flinch, you're as dead as diamonds."

Lai pressed a button on the small machine. The tape started moving.

"The first speaker is my brother, Wing," Lai said. "You will recognize the second man. Cole Blackburn. The conversation took place the day before Cole came to you in Los Angeles."

After a brief silence, a voice came from the speaker.

The Chen family didn't hire you merely because you're a brilliant prospector, although you are. We brought you into this because you have a verbal promise from Abelard Windsor of a fifty-percent interest in Sleeping Dog Mines Ltd. as a full repayment of gambling debts incurred by him during a night of playing Two Up. Do you have an IOU?

Old Abe wasn't that crazy.

This was found at the station.

"Wing is referring to the IOU," Lai said in the silence that came when the men stopped speaking. "The IOU said, 'I owe Cole Blackburn half of Sleeping Dog Mines/Because I lost at 2-up one too many times!' "

After a few more moments of silence, Wing resumed speaking. *The Chen family has taken the liberty of having two handwriting experts certify this document, so you need not fear embarrassment on that score. Even without the note, it is a legitimate gambling debt. With the note, the debt will be promptly recognized by the Australian government when you press your claim.*

The tape went silent.

"There is more," Lai cautioned.

She watched Cole with unblinking attention. He watched her in the same way. After a few seconds of silence Wing's voice came again.

If a woman was all that stood between you and "God's own jewel box," what then?

I learned long ago that diamonds are more enduring than women.

And more alluring? There was a brief pause before Wing continued. *Whether you seduce her or not is your choice. Your job will be to keep her from getting killed while she unravels Crazy Abe's secret or until you find the mine yourself. After that, Miss Windsor no longer matters. Only the mine itself is important. That must be protected at all costs.*

Even at the cost of Erin Windsor's life?

Next to that mine, nothing else is important. Nothing.

A pause, then, *All right, Wing. Tell Uncle Li he has his man.*

The silence hissed with unused tape.

Lai waited, never looking away from Cole.

"I would like," Erin said hoarsely, "to hear that tape again."

Lai groped one-handed for the rewind button, then glanced aside to find it. Cole's foot lashed out and connected with her wrist. The gun went flying. As Cole's hand wrapped around Lai's delicate throat, she went utterly still. In a gesture that could have been a caress or a warning, Cole ran his thumb over the pulse beating visibly in Lai's neck.

"You're just one surprise after another," Cole said to Lai. "How long have you spied for Street against your own family?"

A shudder went through Erin as she heard Cole's

voice. There was no hatred, no passion, no anger, no emotion of any sort, simply a ruthless patience that owed nothing to civilization or humanity. It was the same for his eyes, icy in their clarity and lack of mercy.

"I began planning my revenge the moment I was forced to abort your child and marry a man three times my age," Lai said. Her voice was low, soft, husky, the voice of a woman talking to her lover. "I was the one who approached Jason Street. I was the one who sabotaged the helicopter and the Rover. I was the one who told Jason to have one of Abe's Aborigines follow you and report the instant that you died. Then Jason and I would fly in and fix the Rover, discover the tragic deaths, and take out new leases in our own names."

Slowly Erin's hand tightened on the heavy gun. Lai didn't even notice. Her attention was fixed on the ice-pale eyes of her former lover. She kept speaking, her voice sweetly musical, as though talking of love rather than vengeance and death.

"On the day I owned the mine, the family of Chen would count the cost of using me as a pawn," Lai said. "I am queen, not pawn. And the man by my side would be king."

Cole's strong fingers ran caressingly over Lai's neck. "Queen of lies." He looked over at Erin. Her face was pale, her eyes so dark they looked more black than green. "I don't suppose it would do any good to say I fell in love with your photos before I ever met you."

"Love? You?" Erin made an odd sound that could have been a laugh or a sob. "Sweet God, Cole, credit me with enough sense to come in out of the rain."

"Yeah, I figured that's how you'd look at it. Congratulations, honey. You've finally learned to be a survivor. Now you'll have the same problem I had—finding something worth surviving for."

Erin closed her eyes, unable to meet the bleakness of Cole's.

"I'm going to call Chen Wing and tell him to come and get his ever-loving sister," Cole said. "If you don't like that idea, you've got a gun. Use it."

Swaying, Erin fought the slow trembling that was taking her body.

"You saved my life out there," she said raggedly, lowering the gun. "I kept Lai from killing you. We're even."

Cole's smile made ice slide down Erin's spine. "Lai wasn't going to kill me. She was going to have me sign a marriage certificate—right after she killed you."

Lai's head dipped gracefully as she brushed her chin caressingly across the powerful hand that was still holding her prisoner.

"If the baby had been male," Lai said huskily, "I would never have aborted it. But the child was only female and you were in Brazil. It's not too late, beloved. She won't shoot you. Take the gun from her. Together we could rule the diamond tiger."

In the stretching silence, the sound of Erin's broken breathing was far too loud. Cole watched as the gun muzzle shifted to Lai's head and Erin's finger tightened on the trigger. He made no move to interfere, simply waited with inhuman patience for whatever Erin decided.

"You're better at handling snakes than I am,"

Erin said hoarsely, lowering the gun. "Kill her or keep her for a pet, it makes no difference to me."

Erin walked out of the room without looking back.

38

◆

"IT WAS GOOD OF YOU TO COME HERE," CHEN Wing said.

He closed the door of BlackWing's Los Angeles office behind Erin and Matthew Windsor. Wing's dark glance came back to Erin and stayed. She looked different from her photo. Older. More reserved. More controlled. Her hair was pulled back in a sleek chignon. Her clothes were expensive and casual.

But it was her eyes that had changed the most. There was a cool assessment in them that had been lacking before.

"Please. Sit down," Wing said.

He smiled slightly and gestured for Erin and her father to sit at the long conference table. A closed carton of computer paper sat in the center of the table. Erin eyed the carton, dismissed it, and concentrated on Chen Wing. In his own way, Wing was as striking as his sister. The same perfection of physical form. The same intelligence. The same shrewd black eyes.

"How is your sister?" Windsor asked blandly as he sat down.

"The psychiatrist offers great hope for her eventual recovery," Wing said. "Until then, of course, she will have to remain medicated and under constant psychiatric observation."

"Why?" Erin asked bluntly. "Cole broke her wrist, not her skull."

"I'm afraid Lai's mind was never very strong. We have had to—ah, oversee her daily life before."

"Really?" Erin said dryly. "Be sure her overseers have stout chairs and steel-tipped whips."

Windsor looked at his watch. "We're on a rather tight schedule, Wing."

"Of course." He looked directly at Erin. "Cole insists that he owns only half of Black Dog Mines, the half you gave him as a finder's fee."

"I gave him half of what I inherited. Whether I inherited all or half of Black Dog Mines depends on how well you like the signature on the IOU Lai mentioned. Unless you really subscribe to the notion that your sister is crazy."

"Cole refuses to press recognition of Abelard Windsor's gambling debt, although there is no doubt the debt exists," Wing said carefully. "Cole also refuses to make a deal with DSD for more than the half of Black Dog's output that BlackWing owns. The members of the diamond cartel are understandably . . . restless. Half a resource does not constitute a monopoly."

Erin shrugged. "So they'll make a little less money. So what?"

Wing looked at Windsor. "Haven't you told her?"

"My father doesn't own one carat of Black Dog's rough," Erin said distinctly. "Talk to me, not him."

"If the cartel is broken, industrial diamonds will be priced beyond the reach of emerging Third World countries such as China," Wing said.

"That doesn't make sense. If the diamond monopoly is broken, the price should fall."

"The price of gem diamonds, yes. But not the price of bort."

"Why?"

"The cost of cleaning out a diamond pipe is staggering," Wing explained. "Bort alone doesn't repay the cost of its own mining. For a diamond mine to make any profit, the gem diamonds must be sold at reliable, inflated prices."

"Then make industrial diamonds in your labs," Erin suggested indifferently.

Wing looked in silent appeal at Windsor, who sighed and began speaking.

"It's not that easy, baby. Lab synthesis is coming along, but it still isn't nearly as cheap as the cartel's bort. Besides, even if lab diamonds got the job done at a low price, Japan has the best process. No one wants the Japanese to have any more international economic clout than they already have."

For a moment Erin said nothing, weighing what had been said. And what had not. "What you're telling me is that it would be tough for Third World countries to industrialize without low-priced industrial diamonds."

A shuttered look came over Wing's face. "It would be nearly impossible. Diamonds are far more important in manufacturing than most people realize, especially in the type of manufacturing that is within reasonable reach of emerging economies." Wing spread his hands in silent appeal. "Isn't it better to let the luxury diamond trade in First World countries subsidize the cost of mining industrial diamonds for the Second and Third Worlds?"

"An industrialization the Chen family is in a position to control in China," Erin said evenly, "a country that has more than a fifth of the world population and a tradition of being central to all Asian power. Whoever controls China will soon control all the Pacific Rim economies except the U.S.A. and Japan. You could, of course, ally yourself with Japan. In that case the U.S. would be driven into even stronger economic alliances with Europe. Even with Japan's help, you can't expect to succeed."

Wing waited, understanding finally that Erin was as bright as Cole had warned him she would be. And as hostile.

"I won't even discuss the Chen family's persistent interest in strategic minerals, which are handled through one of ConMin's many companies," she continued. "Nor will I dwell on the fact that if the cartel goes under, Black Dog Mines' value goes through the floor and, with it, BlackWing's half interest in a hugely lucrative chunk of real estate."

Wing shot Windsor a look. Erin's father didn't notice. He was watching his daughter with amused respect.

"You've done your homework, baby."

"As in opening my eyes?" Erin smiled coolly. "As I said to Cole, I'm a slow learner, but I do learn."

"The Chen family is already quite wealthy," Wing said neutrally. "We don't depend upon ConMin for that wealth, or on Black Dog Mines."

Erin looked at her father.

"He's telling the truth," Windsor said. "The Chens aren't bucking Hugo van Luik and DSD just for money. They want power."

"How does Nan Faulkner feel about that?" Erin asked.

"She'd rather give the Chen family power than sink the diamond cartel. The Soviets need it too much. Besides, the cartel is the devil we know, and we've spent forty years learning how to get a handle on it. We've turned it into a game of checks and balances. At this point no single country's interests rules. Not even ours."

Erin waited. Her father said no more. "No advice for me?" she asked. "That's new."

"You're too busy looking for blood to listen." Windsor smiled slightly. "Besides, you don't need my advice. You've changed, baby."

"Being hunted like an animal does that."

"Don't get me wrong," he said quickly, smiling. "I'm not complaining about the changes. You can't own half of Black Dog and be a trusting soul. And you're not planning on giving up control of your half of the mine, are you?"

"I haven't decided."

"Three choices," Windsor said, yawning. "Hand over control of your half of the mine to someone and walk away. Keep control and grab a piece of the diamond tiger. Or kill the tiger by talking Cole into withholding his half of the rough from DSD."

Erin nodded. "As I said, I haven't decided."

With a small sound, Wing cleared his throat. "The third choice isn't a realistic option."

"What you're saying is that dear old Uncle Li

won't let Cole break the cartel," Erin said, a statement rather than a question.

The smile Wing gave Erin was as thin as the cutting edge of a razor. "Unfortunately, no one controls Cole Blackburn, not even my very clever uncle. But Cole is far from stupid. He knows it wouldn't take much of a bomb to close off the cave or even to destroy the commercial value of the diamonds with radiation and pass it off as a mining accident."

Mahogany eyebrows lifted. "Sounds rather drastic."

"Quit baiting the man," Windsor said, yawning again. "One way or another, nearly every country in the world has a stake in the cartel. No one would help you cut its throat. All of them would rather have Black Dog destroyed, and you with it, than have the cartel broken."

"Cole knows the danger," Wing said to Erin. "He doesn't want you hurt. He has made unpleasantly clear to Uncle Li exactly what would happen to the family of Chen if any—ah, accident were to overtake you."

Windsor's eyes narrowed. "Cole isn't the only one who would come down on the Chen family like seven years of bad luck if Erin had an 'accident.' "

Wing nodded. "Granted, but it is Cole Blackburn we fear."

With an effort Erin kept her face impassive, revealing nothing of her inner turmoil. "You're jumping at shadows, Mr. Chen. Cole Blackburn would trade me for a bucket of diamonds. In fact, he already did."

"Bullshit, baby," Windsor said instantly.

She kept silent.

"I've talked to Cole," her father continued, "which is more than you can say."

"When?" Erin asked before she could stop herself. "Is he all right?"

"His skull wasn't fractured. His brain is working just fine. As soon as he was back on his feet, he called to ask me two questions. The first was where Hans Schmidt is."

Erin couldn't hide her shock. "Why in God's name would Cole want to find Hans?"

"To kill him," Windsor said impatiently. "Why else?"

"I . . . that's . . ." Erin shook her head, too shocked to speak.

"So I told Cole where Hans was. Name, rank, serial number, and exact address of the hospital where Hans lives in unholy matrimony with a respirator and a feeding tube sewn into his gut."

Erin's mouth opened but no sound came out.

"Seems the sorry son of a bitch had an accident about seven years ago," Windsor said with icy satisfaction. "One of those nasty little tricks of fate. A car wreck. Glass everywhere, including in every inch of Hans."

"An accident," Erin repeated hollowly.

"He's completely paralyzed," Windsor continued in a soft voice. "Well, not completely. He could still blink his eyes, if he had any eyelids. He could see, if he had any eyes. He could talk, if he had a tongue. He could come, if he had a pecker and balls. But he doesn't have any of those things. His brain waves are normal, however, so his mind is intact. Lucky Hans."

Wing's breath went out in a stream of rapid Cantonese.

"Cole thought it over," Windsor continued calmly, "and decided that good old Hans would look on death as a favor, and Cole wasn't feeling particularly generous. He wishes Hans a long, long life. So do I, baby. So do I."

"An accident," Wing said in English. "How . . . convenient."

Windsor looked at him. "Nothing personal. A message had to be sent to the opposition about civilian dependents being mauled by professionals for no better reason than sadistic pleasure. I got to choose the message. It was received. Not one dependent has been touched in seven years." He looked back at Erin. "The second thing Cole wanted to know was if the letter Jason Street had with my signature on it was a forgery."

"Why?" Erin asked, her voice thin.

"Probably the same reason he wanted to know where Hans was," Windsor said dryly. "You may have walked away from Cole, but he hasn't walked away from you. I'll tell you the truth, baby. I'm damned glad the note was a forgery. That's one tough man you have."

"He's not my man. All he wanted was the mine."

"I don't believe that and neither do you."

"You would if you'd heard the tape."

"I heard several versions of it," Windsor shot back. "All of them were true as far as they went. They just didn't go far enough. People keep forgetting that Cole Blackburn is as independent as an avalanche. He didn't just wag his tail and line up for the Chen family's diamond-studded collar and leash."

"How do you know?"

"Simple. I went up to his office to have an off-the-record chat with him before I 'met' him with Nan Faulkner. I asked Cole why he was doing it. He told me that a woman who could take photographs like you was worth more than her weight in fancy diamonds.''

Erin made a small, startled sound.

"So I'll bet he took the IOU from Wing," Windsor said, "and went along with the game to prevent the Chen family from forging another IOU and cutting a deal with someone who wouldn't care if you lived or died. It's what I would have done if I'd been Cole and cared about your survival."

Wing smiled wryly. "Uncle Li recently arrived at the same conclusion. You and Cole are a lot alike, aren't you?"

"In some ways," Windsor agreed. "But not in one. I'd rather die than be down in that damned black hole right now, racing the monsoon rains for a bucketful of diamonds, watching the water level around me rise and rise and rise until there's no way out but death."

Erin's hand shot out and grabbed her father's wrist. *What are you talking about?*

"You heard me."

"But Cole knows how dangerous it is! He wouldn't risk his life for more diamonds, no matter how many!"

"Why not? What else does he have going for him? The woman he would have died for—and damn near did—walked away from him. That leaves him with second prize, the richest diamond strike ever made and the most expensive slice of hell ever owned by man."

"You're wrong," Erin whispered, forcing the

words past the aching constriction of her throat as she remembered the cold, relentless rise of the black water. "I meant very little to Cole. I was a small affair on the way to a big strike."

"For God's sake, Erin—"

"Is that all, Mr. Chen?" Erin asked, cutting across her father's words.

"Except for the matter of turning your property over to you, yes."

"What property? You've already replaced the camera equipment that was destroyed when the Rover was buried in a flash flood. I took everything else I owned out of the station when I left."

"Not quite."

With quick gestures, Wing reached for and opened the carton that had sat in the center of the table. He tipped over the box, sending a cascade of eight-by-ten color photos across the surface of the polished wood.

"The negatives have been duplicated. One set is in a vault in the government casino in Darwin," Wing said. "The other set is in the safe here. Cole didn't want to take a chance on losing any of your work."

Pieces of the outback flashed and gleamed like glass in a kaleidoscope: termite mounds creating an alien city beneath a steamy silver sky; fragile, dusty, incredibly tenacious acacia trees growing out of stone; lightning arcing across an empty sky; land stretching away to all horizons, relentlessly desolate, absolutely flat, the quintessence of loneliness; and over all, the sun, always the sun, the blazing eye of an omnipotent god.

Every single image had been taken from the rolls of film Erin had left behind in the sabotaged Rover.

"These are really good," Windsor said, sifting through the photos intently. "Hell, they're incredible. It's the best work I've seen you do, and that includes *Arctic Odyssey*. What do you think, baby?"

"I think—" Erin's voice broke. "Why did you lie about the Rover, Mr. Wing? It wasn't destroyed. These photos are taken from all the rolls of film I had to leave behind."

"The Rover and everything in it was destroyed," Wing said flatly. "Cole carried the exposed film in his rucksack until you went down into the cave."

"But why?" she whispered, going through the photos as though the answer was in one of those images. "We were desperate after the Rover was sabotaged. Every ounce he carried was for our immediate survival. There were *pounds* of film. He can't have wasted his strength carrying it. That's crazy, and Cole wasn't crazy."

"I pointed that out to him," Wing said dryly. "He said you had taught him there was more to life than just survival, but all he had taught you was the opposite."

Numbly Erin sifted through photo after photo. There were hundreds of them, but the one she kept looking back at was the photo she had taken of Cole in the dry watercourse just before the helicopter had come and sent them on a desperate odyssey across the Kimberley. Cole had been examining a handful of dry-panned grit when he had noticed her stalking him. He had looked up the instant before she triggered the camera. Even shadowed by the brim of his hat, his eyes shone like clear crystal. The intensity in him was almost tangible, as was the hunger for her he had never bothered to hide.

If I had Abe's diamond mine right now, I'd trade it for film and give it to you.

Erin closed her eyes, unable to look at the photo any longer and know that Cole had carried her film through a hell of thirst and pain and danger and had never given up so much as an ounce of his burden.

"You really didn't know, did you?" Wing asked, watching the slow, silent fall of Erin's tears.

"He never said anything about saving my film," she whispered.

"Not the film. Cole. He loves you."

A shudder went visibly through Erin's body. In the silence that followed Wing's words she heard echoes of other words, her own accusation and Cole's matter-of-fact response.

You and Abe were a lot alike. Once burned, forever shy.

You should know, honey. You're backing away from the fire as fast as you can.

Closing her eyes against the tears that would not stop falling, Erin asked herself if it was true.

"Forgive me, Miss Windsor, but I must ask again. What are you going to do with your half of Black Dog Mines?"

Without a word Erin stood up and walked out of the room.

39

◆

LIKE THE MULTICOLORED FOAM OF A BREAKING wave, a sinuous line of extraordinary rough stones ran the length of the DSD's conference table. Like water itself, the predominant impression was of transparency flushed with blue, yet there were rainbows trapped within. Rising like bubbles amid the clear foam were flashes of chrome yellow and vivid pink, and exclamation points of a green so pure it had to been seen and touched and held to be believed.

Cole shook the last stone from the battered rucksack and walked the length of the long polished table where crystal ashtrays, sparkling water, and ballpoint or fountain pens awaited the pleasure of the members of the diamond cartel. He nodded slightly to Chen Wing, who was pulling BlackWing's "prayer" from a sleek leather folder.

Saying nothing to the other people who were staring in shock at the centerpiece he had poured down the table, Cole went to the chair that had been placed at his request along the wall rather than among the other members. A rising hum of excitement ran around the table. Mr. Feinberg picked up a pink stone the size of his thumb, pulled a loupe from his pocket, and began muttering in reverent Dutch.

Nan Faulkner gave Cole a shuttered glance, poured a glass of ice water, drank it, and walked over to him.

"I didn't know Street was compromised," she said without preamble.

Faulkner spoke in a voice that carried no farther than his ears. Not that she needed to worry about being overheard. The cartel members were transfixed by Cole's casual display of incredible roughs.

For a long moment Cole looked at Faulkner with eyes that were as hard and emotionless as the clear stones he had dragged from beneath the relentlessly rising black water.

"That's what Matt told me," Cole said finally. "If he believes you after the stunt you pulled with that forged letter and house arrest, I guess I can."

"Does that mean you'll extend your agreement with DSD?" Faulkner asked quickly. "Three years ain't shit in the diamond trade and you know it."

"That's up to my partner."

"Mother of God," muttered Faulkner. "Erin locked herself in a hotel room. She refuses to see me or any representative of DSD."

"Do you blame her? You nearly got her killed."

With a narrow black look, Faulkner turned away.

"Faulkner."

Warily she turned back and faced Cole, warned by the quality of his voice.

"Don't get in Erin's way again."

"I hear you, babe." Faulkner grimaced. "I heard

Matt, too. But both of you would make life a hell of a lot safer for everyone—especially Erin—if you'd get her off the goddam dime!''

With ill-concealed frustration, Faulkner stalked to the head of the conference table, lit a cigarillo, and opened a beautifully worked Moroccan leather folder. Instantly the room became still but for the soft rustle of prayers being passed up to her and the muted crystal music of stones being returned to the center of the table. Faulkner blew out a stream of smoke, set the cigarillo in a crystal ashtray, and began gathering up the prayers.

"Before I proceed to the business of the day," Faulkner said, stacking the prayers neatly in front of her, "Mrs. van Luik asked me to express her thanks for your sympathy at the death of her husband. It's times like this when you find out who your friends are."

Cole didn't see the black sideways glance Faulkner threw in his direction, because he was staring at the green diamond Erin had given him to seal their bargain. The stone had been extraordinary in the rough. Shaped, polished, and set in a small brushed-platinum band, the marquis-cut diamond was a brilliant green flame burning with every dream, every secret, every hope of man.

Slowly his hand clenched around the ring until the stone's unfeeling edges bit into his flesh.

"You will be pleased to know that a scholarship has been set up in Mr. van Luik's name," Faulkner continued. "The money will be used to train promising young geology students who wish to specialize in the discovery and utilization of diamond mines. Bringing such mines into production in an orderly, rational manner is crucial to maintaining stable prices in the diamond market," Faulkner said calmly. "At a time when economic regimes are collapsing more quickly than we could have imagined a few years ago, maintaining DSD's stability is pivotal to the economic hopes of many nations."

She flicked her cigarillo against the crystal ashtray, opened a folder, and withdrew DSD's answers to the various prayers. After she stacked the papers next to the prayers, she poured a glass of ice water, drank it, and set it aside. The room was silent except for the muted murmurs of men who still couldn't believe what had been set before their eyes.

"ConMin isn't bulletproof," Faulkner said bluntly. "We're at a crossroads. The reason is spread down the table in front of you. I've talked privately with every member of the advisory committee. Does anyone have anything to add?"

This time the silence was complete.

"Then I would like officially to welcome the newest member of the advisory committee, Mr. Chen Wing. Mr. Chen represents the interests of BlackWing Inc., the source of the diamonds you've been admiring. Thanks to Mr. Chen's strenuous arguments with his partner, we will be handling fifty percent rather than twenty-five percent of the output of Black Dog Mines."

"For how long?" Yarakov demanded.

"Three years," Faulkner said flatly.

An unhappy muttering in several languages ran around the table.

"That is not enough time for short-term economic planning," Yarakov said.

The intercom began chiming with sweet insistence. With a sharp curse, Faulkner slapped the switch.

"This better be good," she snarled.

"A Miss Windsor is here."

"That's real good, babe. Send her in."

The big door opened and Erin walked through. She didn't notice the approving masculine appraisal from the various cartel members as she walked the length of the table. She looked only at the big man who sat removed from the conference, his eyes hooded as he watched her. He was dressed as he had been when she first saw him: black silk sport coat, gray slacks, white shirt, no tie. She also was dressed the same as she had been then: black shirt and slacks still rumpled from the suitcase.

"Well?" Faulkner demanded when Erin would have walked by without a word.

"What did Cole say?" Erin asked without stopping.

"A trial run. Three years, fifty percent of the output."

"One year, one hundred percent."

"Two years, one hundred percent," Cole suggested as Erin stopped in front of him.

"Two years, one hundred percent," she agreed.

"*Mazel und broche,*" Faulkner said quickly, sealing the bargain.

A chorus of *mazels* went around the table, echoed by Erin and Cole.

With a look of shuttered hope, Cole watched the woman whose eyes were more beautiful than the diamond clenched within his fist.

"Two years, huh?" Cole asked, his voice deep, almost rough.

"Not for you." Lifting her left hand, Erin traced Cole's mouth with fingertips that trembled. "You don't get off that easily. No trial run. All the years of your life. One hundred percent."

Silently Cole opened his hand, revealing the green flame of the diamond ring. "What about you?"

"The same. One hundred percent. All the years of my life."

Cole put the ring on Erin's finger and pulled her onto his lap. Just before he kissed her, he whispered against her mouth.

"Welcome aboard the diamond tiger."

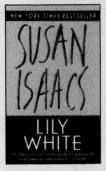